Also by Vicki Covington

The Last Hotel for Women

A NOVEL

Vicki Covington

Simon & Schuster

New York   London   Toronto

Sydney   Tokyo   Singapore

SIMON & SCHUSTER
Rockefeller Center
1230 Avenue of the Americas
New York, NY 10020

Simon & Schuster and colophon are registered trademarks
of Simon & Schuster Inc.

Designed by Jeanette Olender
Manufactured in the United States of America

10 9 8 7 6 5 4 3 2 1

Library of Congress Cataloging-in-Publication Data is available.

ISBN 0-684-81111-1

ACKNOWLEDGMENTS

My deepest gratitude to Becky Saletan, my editor; to Earnie Stanford, Jack Marsh, Joey Kennedy, Dennis Covington, Ashley Covington, Laura Covington, Katherine Marsh, Nancy Nicholas, Binky Urban, Bill Wolaver, David Smith, Katherine B. Smith, Dale Chambliss, Rickey Powell, Sheila Howard, Susan Binford, Randy Marsh, George Hodgman, and Jim Neel; to Charles Collins for his painting, *The Entry of Jesus into Birmingham*; to William Nunnelley's extraordinary book, *Bull Connor*; to the work of Taylor Branch and Leah Rawls Atkins; to the Birmingham Public Library's Archives and Tutwiler Collection of Southern History and Literature, the Birmingham Civil Rights Institute, the Birmingham Historical Society, *The Birmingham News*, Stockham Valves & Fittings; to Katherine Windham's story of the ghost in the blast furnace; to the people who saved Sloss Furnaces; to the memory of the old terminal and the original Tutwiler Hotel; and to all the people of Birmingham—living and dead, good and bad.

For my brother, Randy Marsh

PROLOGUE

Life doesn't begin at conception. It begins long before, in that moment when your mother's eyes and your father's eyes lock up in an understanding that they'll make love someday.

That's why you can remember what happened before you were born. That's why you can imagine your mother almost asleep when the truck creeps into the yard. Her legs are still under the cover. Her heart is racing just like it does during church when boys look at her. She's facing the window, and her name is Dinah. The men's cigarets are glowing in the dark. They've come for the chickens. They're in the broiler house, catching the girls for slaughter. They're stuffing them in crates. Sawdust is moving. Feathers are flying. She is paralyzed with desire. It's all mixed up—church, chickens, men in the dark. Jesus will come like a thief in the night, the scripture says. Even that, she thinks, is rather exciting.

Later, when it's light, she wakes to the teakettle. Throwing on a blue robe, she walks to her father in the kitchen. He's eating fried eggs and a ripe tomato. The curls of his sandy-colored hair are flecked with the gray of middle age. He's wearing overalls. Dinah turns on the faucet, lets water take her hands, looks out at the chicken house.

"The girls are gone," she says, her back to her father.

"That's right. The girls are gone."

It's nothing new. Chicken farmers go through this every nine weeks. But still it's strange—the way they pretend the men haven't come. In midmorning, they get in the pickup and ride to church.

The church is in the woods, set back from the road.

Dinah is wearing a gray dress. She can't wear makeup or rings because she's holiness, but in her heart is all the gold, onyx, bronze, and scarlet cloth used to build the tabernacle of Moses. Porpoise skins, acacia wood, spices for incense, oil for anointing, men to design, carve, engrave, and make her cry.

"The girls are gone," she says once more to Tyler.

"That's right, the girls are gone."

Tyler, her father, wears a starched shirt and blue jeans. Dinah begins to hum a song, but her father mistakes it for the rumblings of the baptism of the Spirit. He starts to pray. "Oh mother, keep us safe."

It's something they don't tell anyone—that they pray first to Dinah's dead mother. The Spirit always comes.

Tyler stops beside the church. Pale morning sun washes the pines and hardwoods. Dinah takes her hands from the dashboard. A man is walking from the road. He's short and dark complected, and he wears trousers and a sailor's cap. Dinah likes how he looks.

The Holy Ghost leaves the car like smoke in the wind.

The sailor speaks through the open window, reaching over Dinah to shake her father's hand. "Pete Fraley," the sailor says and takes off his cap.

"Tyler Ash," Dinah's father says.

"I'm here for worship," the sailor says and, nodding, acknowledges Dinah.

It's quick, but she sees that he's seen that she's beautiful.

Because she hasn't always been beautiful, it still stuns her the way boys—men—take her in. It makes her run her fingers down her arms. "Your skin is Mediterranean," her father says. "Not a thing like your mother's." She wonders what the word implies.

"Where did you serve?" Tyler asks the sailor boy. He is taking the wooden snake boxes from the backseat. It's almost spring. The snakes are beginning to come out of hibernation. That's good, because Tyler needs more. He's been down to two ever since one got loose over in Georgia. Dinah eyes the copperhead—its thick body and mustard gold bands. She's only received the sign of Pentecost. She's never been anointed to handle a serpent, but she knows she's close.

The sailor is looking at the snakes. He doesn't flinch; he's either a holiness man or a superb actor. "Where did you serve?" her father repeats.

Pete smiles. "Everywhere," he says. "Guadalcanal, New Hebrides, Manila." He looks at Dinah. "Tokyo."

Dinah helps her father with the snake boxes. She gives one to Pete, watching his hands. They are small and dark, like the rest of him. She wonders for a moment if he's a mulatto.

They walk through the maples carrying the snake boxes. In the distance the chapel stands.

Dinah's father unlocks the doors. Nobody is here yet. The pews are painted ivory. A tattered rug leads to the altar, where a *watercolor of Jesus kneeling by a rock hangs. His feet are buried in a tropical mire of turquoise and salmon, as if he were on a coral reef. Dinah loves and hates this picture. Jesus is looking right at her. She knows he wants her. It's her soul he wants.*

Dinah's father places the snake boxes beside the altar.

"Here," he says to the sailor. "Just set it here."

Pete bends down to get a closer look.

"You ever handled snakes?" Tyler asks him.

"Yes sir."

Dinah walks out to the steps and sits down. Before long, Pete joins her.

"What's your name again?" he asks and sits so close she hides her bitten nails.

"Dinah," she says.

"I'm Pete," he repeats.

She nods and looks up. The sky is blue, the tulip trees budding. "I love it when spring's busting loose," she says.

Pete looks at her.

"Where did you come from?" she asks, staring at him so directly he moves his head back.

"I'm from here," he says. "Henagar. You lived here long?"

"We moved here when I was twelve," she replies.

She waits, knowing he's going to ask where her mother is.

"Just you and your father?"

"Yes," she says.

A truck pulls up beside the graveyard, tooting its horn at her. She sees that it's the Lawlers. The girls are scared of the snakes. The mother lets them collect leaves, nuts, and berries outside during that part of the service.

"You lost your mother," he says, more of a statement than a question.

The Lawlers are spilling from the back of the pickup. The boys' red hair is wet, like strawberry jam. The girls have baskets for gathering.

"Everybody up here looks alike," Pete says. Dinah understands what he means. They're all from Scotland, England, and Ireland, according to her father.

"Everybody but us," she says and holds her olive arm to his butterscotch one. It's an intimate thing to do, but she can't help herself. It's natural as Jesus.

He doesn't ask her anything else about her mother. It's a good thing, because she feels like she might just spill the beans, tell him that she was born in a brothel in Birmingham, that her mother ran the best whorehouse in the world. She's been to the place over the Chinese laundry, where the girls are all Oriental, like the ones he probably slept with during the war. She knows he's not mulatto because she's seen mixed breeds—the girls over at the terminal station brothel, who were popular in a city like Birmingham. There was even a place where the madam was black, the girls white. Her father preached to them all. But she doesn't tell him any of this. She just watches the Lawler kids tumbling from the back of the pickup truck.

When the service begins, she sits next to Pete. He's wearing sneakers with his navy blues. She keeps staring at the size of his shoes. He's like a boy.

They're on the last pew. The congregation is tiny. Besides the Lawlers, there's big June Cargo, who wears her apron to service like she's in the middle of fixing dinner. There's Buddy Simms, who plays the guitar. Reggie, skinny as a scarecrow. Marla, who keeps the anointing oil until it's time. Some peanut farmers, a waitress at the L&K in Henagar, a widow who wears makeup.

"Jesus," Dinah's father begins, shaking his head, smiling at the floor, as though Jesus is a kid who's acting up. "Jesus," he repeats, looking up at Dinah. She feels Jesus coming in the door. She can almost hear the door creaking.

June Cargo's hands are moving in her apron pockets.

When Tyler calls for prayer, the people kneel in front of the pews. Everyone is praying different things. The room is like a beehive, or a nursery of hungry babies.

This is Dinah's favorite part of the service. It's when the Spirit starts moving. It's like drop-the-handkerchief. It's the not knowing. It's what might happen. It's whose shoulder might be tapped. It could be her. She's ready.

Beside her, Pete is praying for somebody in Japan. A girl, Dinah thinks. She's going to ask him if he ever killed an enemy pilot. Words like kamikaze, periscope, ensign, Hitler *enter her brain. The war is only an exotic idea to her.*

Pete's hands are folded like a girl's.

After the prayer, June Cargo takes her apron from her hips and walks to the snake boxes. Undoing the latch, she takes a canebrake rattlesnake up, surveying its coiled body like you might a ripe, dark eggplant. "Oh, Jesus," she says.

"Bless her," Tyler says, hovering nearby like a gardener watching a new set of hands working the earth. In time, the snake opens up, its grand body moving. The Lawler girls are easing from the pew in order to escape. It's beyond Dinah that

16

*they can leave at this moment. She takes Pete's hand. A brother
in Christ. Later, when she desires him, it'll feel like incest. This
will drive her crazy—the idea of making love to a brother in
Christ. But Dinah likes things ajar. She likes an angle. Pete
inches from her. He's going to take the snake from June Cargo.
It's not his first time. He's anointed. She can tell.*

"It'll wash over you," June Cargo has told her.

Tyler is taking the copperhead from its box.

Pete is speaking to the canebrake like it's a mere grasshopper.

*Dinah's hair is closing like curtains over her face. She's felt
the rush of water. "The new wine," June Cargo says. It's in-
toxicating. She holds her hands up near Pete. She wants the
snake. Her throat vibrates. Years later, in a passionate argu-
ment, Pete will tell her this is where she learned to act. When
they're almost forty and in Birmingham during the summer of
freedom rides, he will stand with his baseball cap in hand,
home from the foundry—hot and handsome—and she will tell
him the truth about who she is. But all their marriage they'll
return to this place, to this hour, for arguments, accusations,
assurance, comfort, and love. She will always think of this moment as the nucleus of her life, and time will spread backward,
forward, and around it. Pete hands the canebrake to Tyler. And
in this way, it's her father—not Pete—who first lets her take up
serpents. He places it in her hands, and she holds it there, in
midair, for one solid moment, certain of everything she's ever
been or ever will be—forgiven, clean, on the brink of love, at
war's end, virginal and innocent, in 1945.*

This is where desire begins.

If your name is Grace, this is where your life begins.

1

In the starlight, Gracie wonders when her life will begin. Because it hasn't yet, there's nothing to do but stare at her reflection, superimposed over her big brother's, in the glass. Benny is on his bed listening to "Telstar."

"It's named after a satellite," he tells Gracie.

She turns, closes the French doors.

"What is?"

"The song," he says.

Gracie looks at his clock radio. They're listening to WSGN. She hangs on every word he says. Since he's turned seventeen, he's let her back in his life. He wants to educate her. "The album cover has a flying saucer," he tells her.

She nods. She has no idea what he's talking about.

Benny is short and muscular like Pete, his father. He has his mother's skin.

The family runs a hotel in Birmingham. The hotel's eight rooms are full this evening. Gracie knows something is going to happen because of all the journalists from up North. Mr. Connor has been eating lunch in the café every day, bent over in conversation with their father.

Gracie sits on the edge of Benny's bed.

From his window, she can see the minarets of the terminal and a half-moon. Benny gets up on an elbow. "Telstar," he says once more, glancing over at Gracie. She watches him blow a smoke ring.

There are some things she'd like to tell Benny, like how she can't play tackle football anymore because when the boys tackle her, they straddle her, put their weight on her chest, and it makes her want to do something she can't even name. She knows he has the answers. But Benny's getting up, shooing her on. It's time for him to cruise the underside of the viaduct—blast furnaces, train yards, Negroes.

"What's going to happen?" she asks him.

He lights another cigaret. He is a mechanic at the Sinclair station. His work shirt bears the green dinosaur logo. A shark's tooth hangs from a lanyard around his neck.

"Who knows," he says.

"I mean with Mr. Connor."

"Nothing."

Gracie jingles her charm bracelet. It's new. Tiny silver items dangle from it—ballet slipper, snowflake, typewriter—that have nothing to do with Gracie's life.

"Bye, now," he says, slapping her butt with a magazine.

It is a tradition that Benny and Gracie rise at dawn's light to fix Mother's Day breakfast. The hotel café is a fine place: black-and-white tile floor, ceiling fan, drugstore soda fountain stools, yet with the ambience of a rural kitchen. A big black pot of black-eyed peas that's soaked overnight, a dusty icebox. They are at the grill, cracking eggs into a blue bowl. "Get the toast," he tells her, a cigaret dangling from his lips.

Gracie reaches for the bread near the soda fountains.

"Here," he says, handing her the butter.

She pops a few slices into the toaster and hears water running in a few rooms overhead. "Shit," Benny says. The journalists are up. Dinah's Mother's Day breakfast will be a public event. She waits for Benny's cue. "Let's take it to her in bed," he says.

"What about the guests?"

"Make some coffee," he tells her.

"What'll we feed the reporters?"

"Donuts. They won't be hungry." Benny wipes a hand on his madras shirt. The colors *bleed* when you wash it, he says. Gracie has watched Dinah toss it into the washing machine, pull it out thirty minutes later, and toss her head back, laughing at the lack of color change. "There's no magic in this world, baby," she tells Gracie.

They never get close to serving Dinah breakfast in bed.

At seven sharp, Mr. Connor drives up in front of the hotel, parking on the yellow line. He jumps from the city car, tossing his cigar into a sewer. He draws in his pudgy self and peers in at Gracie.

"Open?" he mouths.

Benny goes to the door and lets him in.

Connor has been eating meals with them for years. He has a glass eye. It's from a playtime accident. As a kid, he'd been peering into a fence hole when a friend shot an air rifle through the other side. Gracie has never laid eyes on his wife, and there is a big rumor that his daughter is in Washington and may go to work for John F. Kennedy.

Benny shakes his hand, and Mr. Connor asks him what's up. "They're upstairs," Benny says, meaning the journalists. Mr. Connor is always searching for Northerners, like an exterminator on the lookout for pests.

Gracie keeps spreading butter for toast.

"Morning, Gracie," he says to her.

She smiles.

"Making breakfast for Mother?" he asks. He always knows everything. Gracie watches his glass eye, the color of a robin's egg.

As if summoned, her parents come down the spiral stairs into the café. Dinah wanders in like a dark Gypsy, wearing anklets. Pete's got on a work shirt and baseball cap. "Sit down," Benny instructs, and leads Dinah to a table.

They keep on cooking until they've set a feast of eggs, grits, bacon, toast, and jelly in front of Pete, Dinah, and Mr. Connor, who's taken it upon himself to join them. In time, the journalists arrive from upstairs, smelling like Jade East and wearing dog chains of credentials. They swarm Mr. Connor, flipping tiny spiral notebooks and asking questions like what he is going to do to prevent violence and whether or not he's heard the news from Anniston and if he wants to make any statements to the press concerning his lack of response.

Dinah smiles warmly at the yolks of her eggs. "How sweet of my children," she says, glancing up at the journalists. "It's Mother's Day," she reminds them. Her legs are crossed under the table. Beside her is the New English translation of the Bible. Gracie knows she's going to read scripture because she always does on Sundays. Opening to Genesis, she reads how God called the light day and the darkness night; the dry land, earth; the wet, sea. She reads of all the fruit, seasons, gardens, how God broke it to the woman that she'd have sorrow and pain in childbirth, but Adam called her Eve anyhow, because she was the mother of all living. The hushed reporters grow more uneasy by the minute. Pete adjusts his baseball cap, straddles his chair for a good view of the impending theater.

Mr. Connor walks behind the counter for a glass of ice water.

"How many of you got mamas living?" he asks the room. He's tossed his herringbone hat aside; his fat chest bulges over red suspenders.

They just stare at him.

"Well?" he presses, taking a long drink of water.

22

"How many police on duty today, sir?" a reporter asks.

"That woman's handled snakes," Connor replies, gesturing to Dinah. The journalists look over at her. Dinah smiles, shrugs, puts grape jelly on her toast.

Gracie thinks they are trying to avoid staring at Dinah. But they'll carry this image with them all day, this Slavic-style Southern woman holding a serpent, her palms sweating against its skin. Connor knows this, too, and isn't going to let the idea die quickly. "Ain't that right, Pete?" he asks. "Didn't she pick up a canebrake rattlesnake the day you met her? In *church,* boy," Mr. Connor goes on, sticking an accusatory finger in the reporter's face.

Pete's legs vibrate under the table.

Dinah's colorful bracelets dangle, barely missing her grits. Over the years, she's developed a kind of tic in her right eye that causes her to have a perpetually raised eyebrow.

"We forgot to pray, Gracie," she whispers. "Oh, what the hell," she concludes brightly and stares at the reporter beside Connor.

"You all got your little rosebuds?" Connor asks the reporters. He's still behind the soda fountain. He sets saucers and cups on the countertop, as if he is running the café. "Yeah," he chuckles, "got to wear your little rosebuds to church, red if your mama's living, white if she's passed. We all do this here. You do it there?" he asks the reporter nearest him.

The reporter—he is gangly, arms like a marionette—just grins.

"Where do you go to church?" he asks Connor.

"You ever played sports?" Connor counters.

"Baseball," the journalist tells him.

"Could have guessed. Pete over there plays for his company team. Down here where people work for a living, we have what you call a company family. Men play ball, wives play bridge. I used to call the Barons' games. You know," he points his cigar at the reporter, "who the Birmingham Barons are. Guess the base-ball matinees were before your time, though. We'd call the games from a studio, using telegraph wires."

"You used to work as a telegrapher," the reporter affirms.

"Boy's done his homework," Connor says to Benny, who's moved to the jukebox. He's selected Patsy Cline, "I Fall to Pieces."

Gracie likes the song. It makes her know that love's got a side to it.

"Yeah," Connor says, spitting cigar smoke in three quick gusts. "I'd get it all from ticker tape, then just make up the rest. That's why they call me Bull. I'm a real good bullshitter, can you tell?" he asks and gets a pitcher of fresh cream from the icebox.

He's really on today, Gracie thinks.

Dinah rises. Gracie watches the men watch her.

She goes to the window. The hotel is near the train station, which is made of light buff brick, with terra-cotta roof tiles, its dome flanked by minarets. A sign over the west portal of the underpass reads BIRMINGHAM THE MAGIC CITY. She stares at the yellow apron of steam heralding the arrival of the Crescent, en route from New Orleans to Atlanta.

"So why don't you people ever write anything true?" Connor concludes.

"You intend to keep the riders safe, then?" The reporter is leaning over the counter. Connor is toying with Dinah's trivet, hot pads, biscuit cutter. "What's your story for today, son?" he asks.

The reporter doesn't look up.

"You people write what's going to happen before it happens, don't you? Then you fiddle with facts after the fact, to make it look right." Connor keeps up a running monologue. Gracie learns what she already knows, for the most part: that students are coming in on a bus, that Mr. Connor "feels sorry for their mamas on Mother's Day," that he wants these journalists to understand that all this started with the steel industry, too many industrialists and loan sharks, that this is a blue-collar city built on fire, nails, and guts, that the workingman has suffered at the hands of Northern opportunists.

"This siege mentality is precisely what is destroying the city's reputation in the press," one of the reporters says. Connor walks from behind the counter and puts his cigar in the guy's face. "That's cute," he says. The reporters hardly get a chance to smoke. They flip page after notebook page, aghast with the wonder of it all, having Mr. Connor come to their hotel in this way, having him come to *them*. The truth of the matter, Gracie knows, is that he hates the media, yet he can't resist them.

"You got people at Greyhound and Trailways, sir?"

"This Birmingham of ours is a lovely place. It is a city where fear does not abide. Did you see Mr. Salisbury's article? What he reported, we all should know, is in substance untrue," Connor says and stares at his chubby fingers, white as bread dough.

"I don't work for that newspaper," the reporter says.

"Which newspaper do you work for?"

The reporter doesn't reply.

"You from New York?"

"Are your officers in place to protect the citizens?"

"Is your mama alive?"

"How big is the PD here, anyhow?"

"Mine died when I was a little boy."

"Have you been to City Hall this morning?"

"I've been up all night, boy," Connor says. His double chin is trembling. Gracie loves this part of an interview, and she's seen plenty at the café. This is the part where Mr. Connor is going to split open—either in fire or surrender.

"What's the story?" the marionettelike reporter asks him. "What's the story here, Mr. Connor?" The others draw in, hounds at the neck of trapped prey.

"That's not my job."

"I think you understand what we're asking," the reporter presses.

"No, son, I don't."

"Klan active in Birmingham?" the mustache guy asks.

"Sure is," Connor replies, drawing on his cigar.

"You know men in Klavern 13?"

"Go on now, boys," Mr. Connor urges, waving them toward the door. "Get your little Brownie cameras and walk on over to the bus station so you can see your comrades pull in," he says, his face darkening like a bruise.

"What time are they coming?" the marionette asks.

"My mother's name was Molly," Connor spits. "She died when I was eight. She caught pneumonia right after my baby brother was born. I hardly remember her, but I tell you, my mother was a saint."

"They all are," Dinah chimes in. She's gotten a broom from the pantry and is sweeping the black-and-white tile floor. The reporters' heads turn in unison, like puppets. "Mine was a prostitute," she says with a sigh. Pete, wearing his baseball cap backwards and washing plates at the sink, glances at Gracie in the mirror.

Benny, bent over the jukebox, grins.

"Is it true that you were once arrested for violating a city ordinance concerning sexual conduct?" the reporter with a mustache asks Connor.

Mr. Connor picks up his cigar. For a fleeting instant he glances

26

over to Gracie, to see if the word *sexual* has registered. It has. She tucks it away, to check out later with Benny.

"Is this your story, son?" Mr. Connor asks the reporter.

"He was making it with a woman in the hotel," Benny tells her later. They are taking a walk in the park. The city is dark from steel-mill smoke. They walk by the war memorial obelisk and the bronze soldier running with a bayonet.

Making it. She's not heard it put this way, but she likes it. It contains a clue. It puts it in the realm of pottery, finger painting, or baking—sex is something you shape with hands.

"What hotel?" she asks.

Imbecile, Benny's face says. "*Our* hotel, Gracie. You know, the place where we live, sweetheart?"

She is wearing coral pedal pushers that have gotten short on her. They rub her kneecaps. She is growing tall. Boys like long legs, Benny has told her as part of her education.

Benny explains that Mr. Connor had been caught in a room with his secretary and forced out of office ten years ago. Gracie asks him how he knows this, and he says that everybody knows it. He tells her there is a city ordinance that makes it against the law for a man to be in a hotel room with somebody other than whom they are married to. "Especially this hotel," he goes on, kicking leaves with his penny loafers.

She looks up at him.

"You know," he says and tosses a cigaret butt into a dogwood tree.

She shakes her head.

"*Grandmother's* hotel."

She can't grasp it all yet—that the hotel was once a whorehouse—but it holds a certain charm. Gracie knows that her mother has known Mr. Connor all her life, that he'd been a regular at the hotel during the 1930s—before Dinah's mother was killed and Dinah moved up to the chicken farm to live with the preacher. She knows her mother can't kick Connor out of their lives. He talks to her about the old days, her mother, how men hungry for a girl sat smoking into newspapers.

"How do you know if you're in love?" she asks Benny.

"It gets in your hair, Gracie," he tells her, running a finger in her bangs. "In your eyes." He looks at his watch. "Almost time," he says, speaking of the arrival of the students. They leave the park shortly after three. The last thing Pete said to them was to stay away from the bus station. Benny leads Gracie to the bus station's back side. It is dark, with the stench of garbage, liquor, exhaust. They sit on a ledge, and Gracie rests her chin on a rusty old retainer rail. Her legs are dangling, the coral pedal pushers coming up over her bony kneecaps. She looks at her reflection in the bus terminal window. Her bangs are brown, cut straight. She likes to think of herself as Scout in *To Kill a Mockingbird*. It makes her think she's a boy.

Benny holds a Marlboro like an old ranch hand, telling her this and that. "No police, Gracie. You see, there is not a soul. Right? This is calculated. Mr. Connor is the big director. Cops and robbers. We're the bad guys, hon, but don't let that bother you. Mom and Dad are mere spectators. We just run a business." He stops occasionally for a drag of his cigaret, puffing it like those fake five-and-dime cigarets made of sugar that disperse clouds of baking powder if you blow. "We're in the audience," he goes on. "Birmingham is under a microscope. This is Golgotha. All of life is a stage."

Benny likes drama.

In the distance, a drove of reporters are coming up the street, carrying cameras. Gracie's heart starts going. She looks right in Benny's emerald eyes.

"What's going to happen?" she asks him.

Mosquitoes and gnats are starting to bite. It's hot. Gracie feels that she has spent the past few years on the edge, waiting for something to happen. It took a lifetime for Alan Shepard's rocket to go up. All those T-minus-so-many minutes and counting. It took an eternity for Kennedy to be elected. And now she is sitting here, on Mother's Day, waiting for a bus to arrive.

It's coming down Fourth Avenue. It stops for a traffic light, and Benny tosses his cigaret into a cylinder barrel. "Get up," he says.

There is an S&H Green Stamp logo on the side of the bus.

It says TRAILWAYS in big red letters.

It squeals and lumbers into its stall. Benny crawls over the rail. The bus door swings open. Several white men step down to the landing, where they stand in a cluster, hands jammed into trouser pockets, as if surveying the place for a way to escape. They look, to Gracie, the way people look when they wake up confused, at midnight, to the sound of a dog barking or a phone ringing. "They're normal people," Benny tells her. She looks at him. "*What?*" she whispers. "They're innocent," he goes on, leaning over the railing. Gracie stares at them. She can't get a handle on any of this. They disappear down the dark corridor that branches into white and colored waiting rooms. The hall is crowded with men who wear T-shirts and have an unshaven look as if they've just left a ratty old sofa bed and a case of beer. "The Klan," Benny whispers. Gracie's heard the word, but it means nothing to her. The riders make their way along the corridor. Others emerge from the bus door. One of them has blood caked on his face. Gracie feels sick. "Let's go home," she says to Benny.

A few colored men step off to the landing. A white man and a colored man walk side by side, the colored man reaching over to hand the white man—who's got a bloody nose—a handkerchief. "He hit him!" somebody shouts from the corridor. The white man says, "Don't hurt him. He didn't do anything." Gracie peers down the corridor. Somebody shoves the colored man into the colored waiting room. Gracie thinks of Loveman's, where she shops with her mother. She thinks of the signs over the water fountains. She thinks of bathrooms, cafés, hospital nurseries, white churches, where everybody sits still, colored churches, where they sway. The colored man who's been tossed into the colored waiting room is nowhere to be seen. "Let's go home, Benny," she says. But Benny is running to the other side of the station. The streets are empty except for a vehicle marked WAPI NEWS. A man with a club is chasing a broadcast journalist. The man rips the newsman's microphone apart, and Gracie starts to cry. The newsman flees. Gracie keeps thinking a policeman is going to break it all up, but there isn't one in sight.

Benny is inside the terminal. She follows him. Suddenly, it is as if somebody has blown a whistle, unleashing a drove of ballplayers or a stampede of bison. Papers fly in all directions. In the colored waiting room, the bus rider is being thrown up against a concrete wall again and again, like he's a dummy, like he's a sack of potatoes. "Benny!" she shouts, even though she's right beside him. She backs up to a peanut machine. The glass has been broken, and peanuts are all over the floor. She pulls Benny's jacket. "I'm going," she tells him, but she's afraid to leave his side. Now there's a white man helping the colored man up from the floor, but it's only to situate him at the right angle for another pelting. The colored man and the white man who had the bloody nose are side by side once more. "They're friends!" she shouts to Benny, and she doesn't know why she's said it, what it matters. She's light-headed now, like she is in her dreams when she's able to fly. The room is bright. It's like looking into the lights at a football stadium during a winning score. She can't understand why they're beating the white man. She's never witnessed a real fight, never heard the cracking of fists on a rib cage. Skin on skin is the only noise—like a scrimmage practice—and that's what makes it so frightening. When the screams finally begin, it is a relief.

"It started on the bus!" a woman shouts.

"Kill the Negro," somebody behind her calls. Gracie turns. Benny grabs her arm, jerking her up against a Coke machine. "Get on the floor," he whispers, then sits on her. She can see the corridor where the rest of the bus riders have come in. Gracie spots a man holding a newspaper up to his face. She can see where he's punched a hole in it, so he can witness what's happening without getting noticed and beaten up. If you're not a witness, you're not dangerous. She closes her eyes for a moment, hoping nobody will see her watching, but she can't stand the darkness. She squints, the way you do when you're trying to trick your mother into believing you're asleep. The colored man is crawling like a worm, slithering in between the legs of the people who're beating him, struggling for a door. A man comes out of the bathroom. He is instantly slugged. Gracie sees him on the floor, still, like he's dead. A white man is being beaten with what looks like a giant ring of keys. A photographer snaps a shot and is instantly tackled and pummeled. He wrestles to get the film from his camera before the men start to jerk the case, strangling him. Some men are knocked into a stack of boxes, and they all domino-fall over the cigaret-ridden floor of the terminal. Gracie will never ride a bus as long as she lives. She'll never come here again. She's starting to pray now. It's a typical prayer that makes her feel like trash, a please-get-me-out-of-here-and-I'll-never-do-anything-wrong-again kind of prayer. An I'll-be-a-missionary-and-marry-a-preacher-and-take-care-of-orphans kind of prayer. Benny's heavy, but she's glad he's on her. They'll have to shoot all the way through his body to get to hers. There is no gunfire, but Gracie thinks there is. She thinks there are guns and knives and ice picks. Out the window, she sees that the WAPI News car has been bricked. The sight of broken glass makes her think she might vomit. She hates broken glass. Broken glass is worse than anything she can imagine. It makes her think of broken skin, blood, trails of it. She keeps a steady watch on Benny's face. He looks like he's watching something interesting but distant. It keeps her going, how calm he is.

When the police finally arrive, carrying clubs, it is too late. The attack has lasted only a matter of minutes, but it has been instant, brutal, decisive. People are on the floor, on benches, huddled in corners, crying and bleeding. Benny helps Gracie up, and they tiptoe to the door.

That's when they see the girl, standing by the restroom door. One of the reporters from the hotel is interviewing her, reassuring her, holding a handkerchief to her bloody lip. Gracie remembers having seen her with the other riders—the tiny frame, dark pants, and boots.

"Take her to your mother," he tells Benny.

They jump in a taxi.

"Crescent Hotel," Benny instructs.

The cab driver's face is alert, on edge. The three of them—Benny, Gracie, the girl—ride cramped in the backseat. The rider's hands go to her face. "Where are we?" she asks Benny.

"Birmingham," he tells her.

Gracie stares at the floorboard—her own Keds, Benny's loafers, the rider's boots. The cab driver pulls up in front of the hotel. Before Benny can pay, the rider has reached into her back pocket—like a boy—for her wallet. She hands the driver a five.

Inside, Dinah is listening to a transistor radio at her big cherry desk in the foyer. News has traveled fast. She scolds Benny for being at the bus station, grabs Gracie like she is a stray dog who's been hit by a car.

32

Then she stares at the girl. She just says, "Get the Merthiolate and an ice pack, Benny," once she notices the bloody lip.

"What's your name, baby?" she asks. Gracie studies the girl. She almost looks colored. It's the kind of look you can't stop looking at, like, is she or isn't she? Her blond curls are like Shirley Temple's, yet she is dark.

"Your name, baby?" Dinah repeats.

"Angel."

Dinah glances up, takes that in.

"Come on in here," she says, leading Angel to the parlor. Dinah draws the velvet curtains and sits on the hearth, surveying the cut lip. When Benny brings the Merthiolate, Dinah paints her lip with the red stick. The ceiling fan makes havoc of Angel's hair. Dinah holds a dishcloth of ice to Angel's lip. She tells Benny to call his grandfather on Brindley Mountain, to have him start praying for "this madhouse city." She lectures Angel about everything from chicken farming to local theater. She asks, "Do you hurt anywhere?"

Gracie doesn't know, at the time, what a complicated question this is.

Gracie is in Benny's room watching him stand at the antique mirror over his chest of drawers, combing his sand-colored hair. He's getting ready to go out. Dinah has put the freedom rider in Gracie's room for the night.

"Where's my leather jacket?" he asks. Gracie dissects the bedside pile of dirty laundry.

"Here," she tells him, retrieving it, but she doesn't give it to him.

"What's wrong?" he asks, taking the jacket from her hands.

"Is she colored, Benny?"

"What the hell, Gracie. What does it matter?"

"She has that half-breed kind of look," Gracie says.

Benny zips the jacket halfway up. "Don't talk like that," he says to her. "You sound like Connor." He gets his cigarets and opens the door.

The hall is quiet. The reporters aren't back yet from gathering the city's trash. This is the family suite, a cranny of balconied rooms. A broken, old-fashioned cuckoo clock stands up against the wall beside Gracie's door.

Gracie knocks but doesn't wait for an answer. Angel is holding a blanket to her bare chest. "Oh, hi. There was blood on my shirt."

Her legs are crossed. She jerks a T-shirt from her backpack and pulls it over. Her chest is like a boy's, flat. Benny is in the hall, lighting a cigaret. "You can come in, too," Angel calls to him.

"You all right now?" Gracie asks her.

She shrugs, crams her bloody shirt into her knapsack.

"We can wash that," Gracie reminds her.

Gracie looks back at Benny in the hall. She gestures to him and he comes in. He sits at Gracie's desk. Angel's hands fly to her light curls. "I must look awful," she says.

"What're you doing here?" Benny asks, studying her with a journalist's cryptic eye.

"I'm a part of the CORE riders."

Benny looks at her. He doesn't know what that means.

"I'm sorry to intrude," Angel says, tosses her knapsack aside, then begins unfastening her boots. Her arms are compact. *Horsewoman* is Gracie's idea of her.

Gracie is taken with her—the way she stares right at her with ravaging hazel eyes and plum lips. "My father is Mexican," she says, as if reading Gracie's mind.

"Mine's from north Alabama," Gracie tells her.

Gracie wants to ask her a hundred questions. Who is she, why did she ride the bus, where is home? "Maybe you better phone home," she suggests, staring at Angel's cut lip.

"Birmingham," Angel says. "I mean, I can't believe this is happening to me. It's like the end of the world; it's like Cape Town or New Guinea or the Yucatan." Gracie looks at Angel's hands. They're dark, tiny. Her socks have a jungle print. Gracie stares at Angel's legs, snug in jeans, wanting to ask, what do you want to be when you grow up?

"Have you been to the Yucatan?" Benny asks her.

"No. My mother is an anthropologist," she says and shakes loose a cigaret from her pack of Kools. "She wanted me to do this, to come here. Well, not necessarily here, but she did want me to do it."

"Do what?" Gracie asks and watches Angel blow the match.

"Ride the bus."

The train from Atlanta pulls into the terminal, throwing an exhausted noise all over the place, a flash of light. Gracie has never felt this way about a stranger. She is scared, scared of all that she's seen, scared of staying in the hotel, of what might happen next, scared of the city on the other side of her windowpane. Most of all she's scared of Angel.

"They told us we'd never make it through Birmingham. They were right," she says. She's got a raspy twang in her words. Benny gazes at her. Gracie tries to get behind his eyes to see her flat chest, tiny hands, and big eyes as he does. "They burned a bus in Anniston, before the one I was on."

Benny doesn't say anything.

"You want to call home?" Gracie asks again.

"No."

"I wonder where the others are," Benny says.

"The only reason I'm here is because I'm a girl," Angel says. "They would have never asked you to bring me here if I was a boy.

They would have taken me to jail with the others. Why's Bull Connor's car here?"

Gracie glances to the window. The viaduct's underside is orange. The blast furnaces are in operation.

"Who was the man who asked you guys to bring me here?" Angel asks.

"Journalist," Benny tells her.

"He's staying here?"

"They all stay here."

"Where am I?" Angel asks, touching her cut lip.

"Birmingham," Benny reminds her.

"But what is this place?" she insists, speaking of the hotel. "All this furniture. It's like it's from another era. It's cool. Do you live here?"

"It's a hotel. Our mother owns it," Benny tells her. "We're between houses. We sold our old one and we're building a new one. So we're going to live here for the summer."

Angel gets up and walks to the window, jamming her hands in her back pockets. She stands there, staring at sunset's last colors. "Red sky at morning, sailor take warning," she says.

It's night, Gracie thinks.

"Sailor's delight, then," Angel says and turns, as if she's heard Gracie's thought.

Gracie wants to ask how she chipped her tooth.

"I'm sorry to be in your bedroom like this. I hate to get in somebody else's space. This isn't what I'd planned," she says, dabbing her cut lip with the ice pack.

Gracie stares at her.

"Guess you've seen a lot, living in a hotel."

"We've just lived here a few weeks."

"Still, though," Angel says. "You've hung around here, haven't you?"

36

Gracie has never questioned anything. She figures everybody's grandmother was a prostitute, all mothers have picked up a rattlesnake, all fathers wear baseball caps and work in a foundry and wash breakfast dishes in a café with a jukebox blaring. All the world is moving to a subdivision with green manicured lawns, staying in the family hotel in the meantime.

"Your mother is nice," Angel says to Benny. Gracie wants her to smile, so as to give them a piece of that broken tooth.

"She grew up here, in the hotel," Gracie tells her. Gracie's back is to the window. Behind her is the city, where police cars feign a patrol of neighborhoods, where men in basement laboratories are storing dynamite and making homemade bombs.

"Our grandmother was a hooker," Gracie says and glances at her rabbit's foot keychain on the bedpost.

"Tragic," Angel replies.

On Gracie's desk are photographs of classmates, a fake megaphone, a row of Nancy Drews. She feels this wholesome motif makes her appear a liar. "Mr. Connor was my grandmother's friend."

Angel's eyebrow is up. "Birmingham," she sighs.

Gracie has been raised on public approval. She doesn't know why she said what she said about her grandmother. She knows Benny is going to get on her for saying it. She stares at Angel's body silhouetted against the first moonlight. The train is leaving the terminal. Gracie doesn't know where it's going on Mother's Day. Trains are part of her existence, their lights playing on her bedroom walls for these few months. They make animal figures in the shadows they create. All her life she will dream of trains.

"See you," Benny says and turns to go.

Angel smiles at him. He stands perfectly still in his jacket, a cigaret between his lips, holding her gaze. Gracie feels something moving between them. It excites her.

They hear voices from the sidewalk. Reporters are coming up the steps, to the blue awning. Soon they'll be in the parlor, where the banquet lights reign over mantel scarves, summer fire screen, and onyx stand. Tasseled draperies hint of a Victorian drawing room. They'll pass the Imari vase, candelabra, umbrella stand glowing in the dark. They'll come to Dinah's cherry desk, wondering where on earth they are. The hotel is a misfit, they'll think. It's got class, charm. It's not for this city. But they'll be wrong, as they make their way up the staircase, holding the banister. The hotel *is* the city.

2

The foundry where Pete works was once a ramshackle car barn where steam-powered machines turned out streetcar wheels. Now they make valves and pipe fittings.

This morning, smoke rises from the cupola and blows over the warehouse, pattern storage, bronze, and malleable units. Pete walks through the gate, where the guard nods at his ID card, then into the grey iron building. His eyes adjust to the world of fire. The screams of the tumbling mills sear his eardrums. The castings are being cleaned of sand—a raucous noise that nobody understands but foundry men.

Pete's unit is a crew of twelve. There are core makers, molding machine operators, sand mill guys, arbor maker, cleanup, but most important is the iron pourer, the man who hauls the bull ladle. Pete stops briefly at his desk, which is an ugly, dank green metal contraption. On it he finds the day's lineup, delivered at daybreak by the dispatcher. It says this: make sixty six-inch flanged Ls, make fifty eight-inch Ts, make one hundred six-inch valve bodies. Pete scratches his head and glances at his face in the mirror that allows supervisors a view of the entire unit. He's getting crow's-feet. He goes over to the bin to check the scrap from the day before to see how many castings have defects. He was brought to this unit because scrap mistake was high, morale low.

His men begin to arrive. A few play on the colored baseball team. They go by names like Isiah, Mosis, Elija—biblical names spelled wrong. He signs their paychecks on Fridays. The illiteracy rate in Alabama is awful, according to the freedom rider Dinah's taken in. Pete thinks of the freedom rider's plum lips and murky eyes. She's got a strange kind of beauty. She's like a native, like Tarzan's wife. Pete's men are working now. The molten metal can burn a man in two. That's why the pourer is so important. That's why he has steady hands, an iron will, and a set of eyes that won't travel.

Pete's pourer is named Nathan. He's never spoken a word to Pete. Pete wonders if he's deaf. He is big. He wears blue overalls flanked by protective leggings so the fire won't splash in his boots.

"Nathan," Pete says to him this morning, nodding.

Nathan is wearing safety goggles. He acknowledges Pete with a blank look. Pete stands there, hands on hips, and watches Nathan get the first bull ladle of metal from the cupola—eight hundred pounds of it. He pushes it along the monorail and pours three molds. Pete always feels like an ant next to Nathan and the cupola.

"We need a hundred valve bodies," he screams over the tumbling mill.

Nathan nods.

"Scrap was low yesterday. That's good," he yells.

Nathan pours the last mold and moves the bull ladle along the monorail, back to the cupola. His hands are big as baseball gloves. The same color, too.

"Get a good night's sleep?" he yells.

Nathan nods.

"Wife all right?"

40

Pete hates this feeling—the way he thinks he's somehow responsible for whatever it is that makes colored men mute. "I see you're playing ball this season," Pete calls to him. "Catcher," he adds. The superintendent of foundries has given all the foremen a roster of the colored team with a note that says *For your information.*

Nathan pours the molten iron from the ladle. A few drops break loose and hit the concrete floor—bright orange droplets of fire. Occasionally the tiny globs hop in Pete's shoes, and it stings like wasp bites.

Pete paces up and down the unit, watching the core makers, molding machines, arbor makers, the shaking out of castings from flasks. He checks his watch. By midmorning they ought to have a fourth of the day's lineup done. At break, his men sit on the floor and pitch washers. They've got brown paper bags from home. Pete wonders what they talk about when they talk about things. He looks over the Ts and Ls to see what's making up right.

He stands over his dark green metal desk, calculating. After a while, he walks over to Nathan, who is eating an apple near the big brew of hot metal. Pete bends a knee. "My life's insane," he says. "We've taken in a freedom rider," he goes on, watching how Nathan's lips kiss the apple as he bites a big chunk.

"I think it might cause us trouble."

Nathan looks at his apple's core.

Pete runs a hand through his hair. He's close enough to smell the mixture of perspiration, metal, and Dentyne on Nathan's breath.

"Bull Connor has practically moved in with us. You hearing me, Nathan?" Pete asks, getting under the man's dark, wet face. The whites of his eyes are yellow. His nostrils flare like a horse's. He can see straight up the guy's nose—a tunnel of darkness.

"The city is at his mercy. So is my wife," Pete says. "The man sits for hours, spinning tale upon tale for her. He was a friend of her mother. Her mother was a prostitute."

Nathan watches the carousel of castings turn where the others are getting back up to work. Pete wonders if colored men discuss prostitution. "We aren't a political family," Pete tells Nathan as he gets up. "It's our job to take people in. We do it for a living," he insists.

Nathan gets his safety goggles and helmet, gazing at Pete. His eyes are hazel, the kind you can't miss in a black man. It dawns on Pete that Nathan might hate him.

"My son and daughter were at that bus station," Pete says weakly.

Break is over.

All afternoon, Pete keeps his eyes on Nathan—the biceps flexing as he maneuvers the bull ladle down the monorail to the cupola. Occasionally, Pete saunters over Nathan's way and says a few words, hoping for a reply. But Nathan is mute, like a quarrelsome wife who pouts and withholds and manipulates, causing a man to lose his bearings. Right before day's end, Pete walks over to the machining shop. He talks a while with Bo Harper, who plays third base on the company team. They talk about the season. They talk about where they ache—Bo's got a bad knee and he rubs wintergreen on it.

Pete's arm isn't what it used to be. Bo Harper sky dives. He's in the Green Beret reserves—he says. Once he jumped into the Okefenokee Swamp, and he claims he's eaten armadillos. Pete likes Bo Harper's philosophy of life. Bo believes a story is meant to make your skin crawl. His wife is so beautiful it hurts Pete to look at her. She's got eyes the color of steel.

"You know that colored fellow of mine, the pourer?" Pete asks Bo.

Bo nods, lights a Camel.

They're standing beside a team who are putting holes in flanges and valve seats on bodies. Bo's free hand is in his work pants pocket. He tells Pete they've put five new colored women in the core room.

"The pourer," he says after a while. "Nathan?"

"Right."

"He was under me in the bronze unit five years back. Lost a baby that year," Bo says and jiggles the loose change in his pocket. He tosses a nickel in the air. "Baby boy."

When the afternoon whistle blows, Nathan has accomplished the day's work. He waits for Pete to walk over with his lineup that says make sixty six-inch flanged Ls, make fifty eight-inch Ts, make one hundred six-inch valve bodies. He'd like Pete to say, "Good job, Nate." But instead, Pete will just stand there with his white man's guilt, like some forlorn and jilted lover trying to make conversation. This is precisely what he does. "Got ball practice this evening, Nathan?" he asks. Pete's got a thin, snaking grin, like a boy's. Nathan feels like gathering him up and tossing him in the pond beside the baseball diamond just to bring him to his senses, make him see that the city's problems weren't caused by him and don't need to be rectified by him.

But sometimes it's best to just let a white man talk. Sometimes it does him a world of good to just ramble on. This isn't the only reason Nathan won't answer him. He's waiting for the right moment. When that moment comes, he'll speak. Nathan watches Pete checking the scrap, mulling over the castings, talking to the core makers, machine operators, arbor makers, and sand mill operators. But he knows this is just Pete's job. He knows that Pete's *vocation* is his preoccupation with him, Nathan. Pete should've been

43

a preacher, not a foundry man. The white preachers who're sympathetic with the movement are the only men in Birmingham who sleep at night. Sure, they live with the threat of burned crosses and bomb threats, but that's better—Nathan thinks—than the kind of impotence Pete feels, working for a racist company.

Nathan takes the corridor to the colored shower room and lets the water hit the palms of his hands. It's like rain, fresh as the mint in Lydia's garden. Standing under the water, he thinks of making love to her, and this bleeds into what the baseball lights are going to be like at dusk. They're all nice thoughts. He wraps his blue towel over his waist, rubs wax in his dark curls, and throws on his slacks.

The parking lot is emptying. All of management is spinning off in their turquoise Chevys, whose hoods are rusty from the cupola's sediment. Nathan waits at the bus that will take him to the projects on Graymont. He's proud to have left the old gray shotgun for the new government apartments, where folks plant rose gardens rather than gawky sunflowers, where the eaves of the units are crisp white, where spring rain runs down the long drain and into the street.

A family place, he thinks as he enters the apartment, smelling the aroma of oxtails and turnip greens from Lydia's big black pot. Lydia keeps the pine floors waxed so hard they glisten. Red begonias are growing beside the window. The furniture is used, from the home where Lydia does domestic. She is wearing the starched white dress she always wears to her employer's. She smells like that home. It's a smell Nathan can't describe, but he associates it with baby powder, coconut, and sweet milk—white things.

He hugs her. His hands run along her bony spine till they reach her rear. "Let's go drink some beer," he says to her, and she says it sounds good to her.

44

Nathan walks to the bedroom, which is dark from the drawn curtains. He checks to make sure his catcher's mitt is lubricated and ready. He puts a fist in it. He parts the drapes. The street is a mess of bus fumes, litter, and stray dogs. He thinks of his boss, of the foundry, of all that's fixing to happen, all that nobody in this city is ready for. He feels sorry for Pete. He feels sorry for all white folks like Pete who don't understand that water will boil over if you let it get hot enough. He's still thinking these things as he and Lydia walk over to the Silver Moon for a beer. It's a neighborhood bar, with a concrete floor painted burgundy, a *Playboy* foldout of a white girl on the lime green wall, a leaky faucet. But all the same, it's a quiet place where industry workers drink a beer and go home. The wooden bar is L-shaped. Nathan takes a stool, orders a Colt 45 for Lydia and himself. He speaks to Mr. Hoots, the old black man who runs the place, who cooks pig ears and spareribs and neck bones for lunch. Hoots is a hundred years old if he's a day. His scalp is a series of red-blue veins, a road map for the lazy traveler. Hoots takes Nathan's quarters, drops them in a cigar box, and spits snuff into a baby food jar that has a cute white baby on it.

"Nice day," Nathan says to Hoots.

Hoots says, "Sho nuff," and wipes the counter with a rag. He wipes the counter incessantly, like it'll never be as clean as he wants it. Nathan thinks Hoots ought to take down the dingy yellow curtains and let some light into the bar, but this won't happen. Old black men like the dark, Nathan thinks.

Lydia's hands are folded on the bar top. They're a nice shade. She paints her nails. The white folks over the mountain fight over whose she is. She works for a Mrs. Light, who loans her to neighbors who're having a big party, a new baby, or a death in the family.

The bar is hushed. It's the kind of quiet where you keep thinking you're going to be jarred by a sudden noise, a clanging like the way dimes hit the bottom of a beggar's cup. When the baby died, Nathan felt like he was a coin that'd been thrown from a skyscraper. He's heard if you toss a penny from way up high, it'll growing heavier and heavier, so heavy it'll crack sidewalk. He's felt like this for years now, like he's made of copper and floating in midair, anticipating the sudden jolt, bang, the sidewalk. He's never hit, though. He's suspended in space, screaming. The baby died five years ago. Lydia hasn't gotten pregnant since. She says her monthly time is like a funeral, a tiny private funeral. He wants a baby for her more than he wants anything in life. Church-women tell her it's because she's so wispy; she ought to eat more pork or drink more milk, get her skinny ass fatter. It makes her want to spit nails. Nathan watches her big dark eyes when they tell her things like that. He watches them now in the bar. He watches how they fix on an object—her silver can of Colt, the mole on her wrist, the naked white girl under the lightbulb. It's like she's concentrating on something he can't see, like she sees the insides of things.

"What's in your head?" he asks her.

Lydia turns. "Nasty things," she says.

"Nasty how?"

She studies her nails. "We were talking on the bus today." Nathan takes a sip of beer and wipes the suds from the mustache he's letting grow. He looks over at Hoots, who's eavesdropping, holding a broom. "You know, like what if I decided to be one of those riders?"

He waves it away. "Get out of here," he says.

"I've a mind," she says. She unbuttons the top buttons of her maid's dress. "Whew," she says and lifts her dark curls up. "It's hot in here, Hoots."

46

Hoots nods. He starts sweeping the concrete floor, but he's sweeping it aimlessly like you do a sidewalk, back and forth, just stirring up dirt. He drives Nathan crazy in the way an old sour uncle might—that kind of affection mixed with impatience. Nathan looks down Lydia's dress. He pulls the side of her collar for a better view.

They drink another can of Colt. They don't say anything. Nathan's thinking of baseball; he's thinking of catching curves and of fastballs with backspins. He's thinking of the women in the stands going berserk, of the boys under the bleachers and of how someday one of them is going to be his. He's thinking of a merciful God. He's thinking these things when the door creaks open, allowing a brief view of the fading afternoon sunset. A white man walks in and sits at a table beside a box of Dixie cups. Nathan turns back to Lydia. Hoots walks over to the man, carrying a menu that says, *Dinner: BarBQ ribs, bread, sandwich, onions, greens, beer, Nehi, colas.* Lydia glances over, then eyes Nathan. It's a look that lets him know she's taken note of a white man being here. She starts humming a familiar tune, like something his daddy used to whistle when he'd get off the train. He was a car inspector for Frisco rail. But she stops whistling it before he can remember if he's remembering correctly.

His heart is racing. He could swear it was his boss who walked in the door. He's scared. It's not uncommon for the bosses to check on colored men who lay off work drunk. They come to visit sick families, too. They come to funerals. But it's always on the wings of bad news. For a long while, Nathan can't make himself look back. When he finally does, he sees that it is, indeed, Pete. He's never seen him out of his work clothes. He's got on his baseball cap, a T-shirt. Pete stands there, his thin lips pale. "Nathan," he says.

Nathan looks up at Hoots, who is wiping the bar.

Lydia turns on her stool and smiles at Pete. "You're Nate's boss man? Mr. Pete?" she asks. Her eyes draw him in. It's part of her job—being charming to white people.

Nathan takes a sip of beer.

He hates the idea of breaking his silence. He's hoping Lydia will carry the ball. "I'm Lydia," she says. "I'm Nathan's wife. Nothing's wrong, is it?" she asks, and Nathan watches Hoots toying with his hearing aid, trying to get the drift of the conversation.

"No," Pete says. "I just went by your place, and the neighbors said you were over here." Nathan glances up so as to get a view of him in the bar mirror. Pete's holding his baseball cap. Nathan knows now he's here for no good reason. Nathan knows he's eaten alive with something bad—that thing that makes some white men take responsibility for the whole human race getting kicked out of the Garden.

"So, you've just dropped by," Lydia pursues sweetly. "Would you like a beer?"

"No," Pete says.

Nathan loves her for her acting. He's getting the feeling he's not going to have to say anything to Pete, and it makes him want to get drunk, it's such a nice thought. "Just wanted to let you all know—" Pete stops in midsentence. Lydia's feeling sorry for him—Nathan knows it. She's catching on to him.

Lydia looks him in the eye. "We'll let you know," she says, "if there's ever anything we need."

Pete holds his cap. Nathan watches in the mirror. "I'm sorry about your baby," Pete says finally, and Lydia says it's OK, it's been a long time, we're fine. When he finally turns to leave, after a few more seconds of awkward mumbling, Lydia sits back down on her stool. "Jesus," she says. "News travels slow in management."

"He's new on this unit," Nathan tells her, but he can't shake the fact Pete felt like he had to come say this to him, to her, in their neighborhood, at their bar. When they get home, he lies in bed with Lydia, listening to traffic from the busy street, watching the light change from red to yellow to green through the pale curtains Lydia made over on Mrs. Light's fancy sewing machine. He takes Lydia's hand under the cover but says nothing. He smells her—all mint and musk. He says it in his mind. He says, I can't speak to him, Lydia. But the words only run in his brain. The venetian blinds clink in the dusk breeze. He naps for a short time and dreams of Mr. Pete handing him a baby boy. They—Pete, the baby, Nathan—are going in and out of bus terminals, train stations, airports, saying nothing. Travelers, a voice says, right before he wakes up and gets ready to play ball.

Dinah sits in the bleachers, watching Pete's game wind down. The players are animals, she thinks. Gorgeous, sculpted, fruitful males, running forward into summer nights. It's a ballet—the fancy leaps, shortstop charging, Pete's left leg coming up as the inner thigh almost winces.

The game is almost over. Dinah likes how the players don't notice the spectators. Staring from the bleachers this evening, she'd like to have them all. There's nothing more desirable than your husband's teammates, who'd never lay a hand on you, she thinks.

Connor's black city car is parked under a canopy of trees.

She keeps an eye on his car, and at the top of the ninth, he gets out. He lumbers over to a bunch of white and colored boys who're under the bleachers. It makes Dinah's temperature rise, watching as he urges them to go their separate ways. As if there's something of danger in this kind of boys' play! Her cheeks burn.

Pete's team is at bat. Bo Harper is on deck. His wife is in the backseat of their Ford, nursing a baby girl. Dinah thinks of Bo's wife's milk letting down. Bo's antsy and dancing as the other team's pitcher stares at home plate like Bo's a dragon he wants to slay.

Connor is moving toward Dinah in the bleachers.

She can almost smell his Old Spice aftershave. She hates that he's here. It ruins her night. It makes her wish she'd never known him. "You can do it, Bo," she yells, partly to let Connor know she's too involved in the game to talk to him. Bo hits a pop fly to left field. It's caught, and he's trotting back to the dugout.

Connor is carrying a hot dog. He hoists himself up to her level, pulling on his pants leg the way fat men do.

"Hi," she tells him but avoids his eye.

"Think they'll hang in there?" he asks her.

She brushes dust from her shins. Leaning forward, she says, "Don't know if they'll hold it or not."

Connor's baggy pants are gray. They need pressing, she thinks. She's never met his wife. She's seen pictures of her in the newspaper, though, watering ferns and sprucing up her rose garden. She reminds Dinah of Aunt Bea on the *Andy Griffith Show,* jolly and apolitical.

The next batter strikes out.

Pete's team emerges from the dugout. Bottom of the ninth. They're up by two, and Dinah's worried. Connor eats his hot dog in three big bites. Then he clears his throat over and over as if there's a fish bone lodged. He always does this during tense moments of a game. "Stay in one place," he yells to Pete. "Keep her steady. That's right, big boy," he says as Pete tosses a few. "Keep her calm, baby."

Dinah looks at Connor's nubby hands.

Connor signals to nobody—holding three fingers downward. "Curve," he says. Pete winds up. "I knew a man whose arm popped, broke that bone right in half the minute he released. We heard it all the way up in the press box," Connor says and spits.

Pete throws wild. "This guy will sucker to an inside pitch," he says and fidgets. "Pete'd make a fine relief pitcher in the minors," he says. "I've told him that. He knows that. He likes to throw hard. Crazy man," Connor says and signals again. The batter hits a grounder to right field and is safe on first. Connor spits.

Dinah's back is hurting.

"These bleachers," she complains.

Connor calls, "You can do it, Pete." Dinah hates it when people yell things to Pete from the stands. "Pick him off," Connor whispers. "Just a tiny wrist flip inside the bag. Crisp, low," Connor says lightly. But Pete's coach is telling him to stay inside himself, forget who's at first. "Pete oughta be in the minors," Connor repeats.

Dinah's blood pressure is up. The batter's just hit a ground ball to the shortstop. It's an error, and everybody's safe, even on second. Dinah watches Pete going to pieces. It's nothing visible to the naked eye, but she knows what he's thinking; she knows how his right eye is twitching like it does when he's mad or frantic.

"This next fellow ought to sacrifice," Connor says.

The manager trots over to Pete. "He's going to take him out," Dinah says. "Don't do that, Gandy." She stands up. Connor stands, too.

Gandy just says a word or two to Pete. It's clear he's not taking him out, and Dinah sits back down. "I hate this," she says to Connor. "I hate this game."

"No you don't, baby. You love this game," Connor says and

takes a handkerchief from his pocket. He blows his nose.

"I hate it," she says.

"There's a colored woman," Connor says, nodding toward a dark lady wearing a starched maid's dress. She is climbing up toward Connor and Dinah.

"They've got a game after this one," Dinah says to Connor, before the lady sits down behind them. "They got a right to be here. It's their stadium, too," she says and feels her face on fire.

"They shouldn't be mingling in the stands with white folks."

"You're going to hell in a handbasket."

"You ought not talk like that. What would your mother say?"

"My mother was a hooker."

She knows this makes him want to come out of his skin. She knows Connor has a penchant for false propriety, that he likes to think of her, of himself, as ladies and gentlemen. It makes her want to rub it in, just to feel him squirm.

"This is private property. This isn't your domain," she tells him.

He yanks a new cigar from his shirt pocket. She looks him in the eye—his glass one. She likes to look into his fake eye. She thinks it's a curious blue. "It's my domain if it's trouble for the city," he tells her.

She smiles, turning back to the game. "You're in overdrive."

"I'm here to protect you," he replies. "Pete, too. All of them," he says and gestures to the playing field. "I'm here because I give a damn about these men."

"You ought to go home and sleep."

"I never sleep."

"I believe that," she says.

"You'll thank me someday. So will your kids. Where's Gracie?"

"At the hotel."

"Benny?"

"Chasing girls," Dinah tells him.

"Is he dating that half-Negro bus rider?"

"You shouldn't be here," she tells him. "It's bad for your health." He inches closer, his trouser leg brushing her knee. She can feel his anger, but it's nothing more than a boy's. She loves the power she has over him. It's exhilarating. She throws her head back. The moon is up. She smells the May night.

Nathan stands behind the fence.

It's almost painful for him to watch Pete pitch. He winds up fast and his release is a bullet so precise you wonder why the guy isn't playing pro ball. His problem, though, is distraction. He can't keep his mind on business. When there's a guy on first or second, Pete is a bundle of nerves. His manager, Orland Gandy, from over in the malleable unit, spends the entire night in the dugout consoling Pete like a mother. "Stay within yourself," he'll holler as Pete's eyes dart to the bases and back to the batter. "Not your problem, one-one," he'll say, referring to Pete's jersey number, which is eleven. "Don't worry, one-one, that should've been an out. Not your fault, one-one, not your fault." It's all Nathan can do, as he stands clutching the spaces in the chain-link fence, to keep from shouting. To Nathan, Pete is clearly a relief pitcher. He's wild and impulsive enough to get in and do danger. But they have him pitching three nights a week. By game's end, he's fit to be tied.

Pete's in the bottom of the ninth. His team is up by two. The colored team always plays after the white team. There's a brief moment when the colored family members are starting to arrive and the whites haven't finished playing. The colored children play under the bleachers with the white ones. They look for rats who've set up home under the seats—waiting for the remains of a hot dog, a discarded box of popcorn, stray M&M's. If the boys kill a rat and take its corpse to the concession stand, they get a free drink. The white boys pussyfoot around, taking a few stabs with pipe they've gotten from scrap piles. But they don't really make a kill until the colored boys come and take the rodent's head off in one quick decapitating strike.

This evening, the moon is up. Nathan sees that Lydia is maneuvering to find a seat behind Pete Fraley's wife. Nathan knows who Pete's wife is because she came to Family Day, when the wives and kids get to tour the foundry. Nathan remembers she was tall, dark, with a stormy kind of quality to her. The other wives stood back from the liquid metal like it was a dangerous cliff. Pete's wife got right up over the ladle of fire and smiled into it, like she was watching something interesting swim in the brew.

Nathan looks hard at the white man sitting beside Pete's wife. That's Bull Connor, he thinks. Son of a gun. He remembers what Pete said at the plant today, how Connor won't leave his family alone, how his wife is the daughter of a prostitute that Connor knew. The webs we weave, he thinks, as his eyes go back to the field. "Stay within yourself, one-one," Pete's manager insists.

Pete winds up. The ball is wild high. Pete released too soon.

The ump holds up two fingers. The next time, Pete is wild low. He held the ball too long. Nathan watches Pete move back up on the mound. There's a player on first and second. It's making Pete crazy. His eyes stray. The manager tips his cap, runs a finger along his cheekbone, holds his palm up. The batter is prancing, ready for Pete's arm. Nathan almost can't watch it.

The next ball is tipped, not caught.

Pete winds up. Wild high again. The batter walks to first. Pete winces, shakes his head, puts his hands on his knees as if he's going to throw up. He stays like this a long time, too long, so long the manager yells, "Within yourself, one-one, within yourself. Not your fault, one-one. Not your territory. Stay with yourself, one-one. Just you, honey, just you."

Honey, Nathan thinks. This manager ought to be hung up a tree. What Pete needs is a good catcher, like Nathan, to give him the right signal. If he were catching this game, he'd be up near the mound at this moment asking Pete, "Tired, Bud?" or, "Tell me what you need." He might even ask him what he's going to do with his wife later. That works with some pitchers. Sometimes they need to get loose and remember a game's a game and there are other things to look forward to later on. A wife is good to you if you lose. Or at least a wife like Pete's is. Nathan can tell by looking at her. He can tell she's the kind who's apt to see what a comfort love is. Nathan wants him to strike this new batter out so bad he can taste it. He's pulling for Pete. He says, "Jesus, help him," under his breath. He looks over at Lydia, behind Pete's wife. Lydia's bent forward so far she's almost in Pete's wife's long hair. Nathan suspects she's sniffing it, labeling the shampoo brand, all the while pretending to be in the heat of the game's final moments. She's always got something going with white folks.

He wonders if she's got any idea she's sitting behind Bull Connor. Nathan's heard Connor is an old baseball man. Nathan looks at the boys under the bleachers. They've filled a Dixie cup with sediment—the mixture of mud and scrap that lines the foundry grounds. They've made a ball from the loaded cup and they're batting it.

Nathan turns back to the field. Pete is on the mound. I'd call a sharp-breaking curve, Nathan thinks as his fingers grip the fence. A sharp breaker, he thinks. A sharp breaker that breaks down and away, catching the outside of the plate at knee height. Instead,

Pete throws a hanging curve. It breaks slow. The batter swings.

It's a strike.

Pete's chin is up. He's getting his shit back together, Nathan thinks. Pete steps to the mound. He winds up. It's a knuckleball, the kind Nathan hates to have thrown his way. Pete's knuckleball is perfect. No spin, no fast travel. It dances in midair all the way to the plate, where the batter stands confused and, way off cue, swings late, and it's strike two. Pete's coach is silent, and Nathan's happy for this. No more *one-one* or *honey,* and this game is history. Pete pauses, starts to wind, pauses again, ignores the bases, and releases.

Three.

The game is over.

Pete's hands go to his knees again and he bends his head almost to the dirt, like he is indeed going to throw up now that it's over, but he doesn't. He trots over to the dugout in his blue-and-white uniform and gets congratulations from his buddies. Nathan's team begins to drift to the field. A few of the colored team congratulate the white players. The family members give their seats to their darker counterparts, and that's that. A few white players linger as if to watch, but for the most part, this sport has no gray area.

Nathan looks back up to the stands and watches as Lydia takes a final breath of Pete's wife's long hair. Lydia says white women know all kinds of doctors. She's heard them on the phone, complaining of headaches and cramps and nerves. They've got wine-dark vials of paregoric all over the bathroom. If Mrs. Light or Mrs. Pete Fraley or one of them made a phone call on her behalf, maybe she'd get a drug to make her expect a baby. *I have this colored girl who works for me, and she's having trouble bearing. Is there a pill she could take?* Or *I'm calling for the wife of a colored man who works for my husband over at Harcort Foundries.*

Pete's wife turns to go, but Lydia stops her. Pete's wife breaks into a smile. *Well, I'm so happy to meet you,* he guesses she is saying. Lydia ducks her chin.

Pete's wife is wearing short pants the color of a canary. She's got legs. Her eyes take Lydia's. Lydia's hands are cupped in front of her. Pete's wife turns to Bull Connor and it appears she's introducing Lydia to him. Lydia tries to shake his hand. Connor stares at her fingers like they're a mess of snakes.

Pete's wife twirls her key with her pointer finger. Her smile is warm, and she's right in Lydia's face. Then she hops down the bleachers, light-footed like a runner or a dancer. Bull Connor lumbers his way down, too.

Lydia sits back down.

Pete's wife gives Pete a hug and her hand falls from his waist to his ass and lingers there. Nathan puts on his catcher's mask and pads. He is about to join his teammates on the field when Bull Connor suddenly raises his hands up to the stands as if he's a maestro conducting an orchestra. Dust flies up as boys scurry under the bleachers. "Ladies," he calls. A few colored women peer down at him. "Ladies, may I have your attention, ladies?" By now, all the players—the colored ones, warming up on the field, and the white ones, who're preparing to depart—are looking at Connor. The place is quiet. Connor's holding a cigar. "Ladies and gentlemen," he says looking back at the baseball diamond, "we just can't have this mingling." Nathan's pulse is going. He feels it in his wrists and neck and thighs, all the tender parts of his body.

"He don't work here," somebody whispers.

"Now, I'm not trying to meddle in company business," he says to the players who've wandered over. They're white men, concerned and dusty, hands on skinny hips.

"I'm just your commissioner of public safety, that's all."

Connor maneuvers his body among the players as if to be one of them. Their heads are bowed.

"And I don't think it's safe for us to mix." Connor studies his cigar. "It's not you good people," he says. "I know a company like Harcort would never stir up trouble. It's just we got these meddlers in Birmingham now, and they'll show up at your baseball games. They'll show up at your cafés, at your theaters, parks, *bus stations*," he adds with emphasis. "They'll show up at your home if you're not careful. They'll pretend to be one of you. They're liable to be right up there with you this very moment, ladies."

He tosses his cigar in the direction of the dugout.

Nathan wonders why he's addressing the ladies when there's men here, too.

"See, when there's a group of whites and coloreds gathered in one place, the agitators are like a bee to honey. When you've got coloreds and whites in one place, there's going to be the recipe for disaster, because you've got your whites and you've got your coloreds who like to fight. Now, I'm not this type who can't mix. You're not. But these outside agitators are here to start fires among us."

"Huh?" somebody says.

A white player nearby says, "He's a nut. Just let him be."

Connor looks at his hand as if he's wondering where his cigar went.

Nathan spots Pete and his wife. They're beside the concession stand staring at Connor. He wonders what's going through their minds.

"You've got your agitators staying in the homes of people you'd never dream. You've got your agitators attending churches here. You've got your Northern journalists on every street corner with their little notebooks writing their little lies for their big newspapers. You've got the entire nation poking fun at common people like you. I'm talking to you colored people, too. It's a war, honey," he says.

Nathan laughs. He's never seen Bull Connor in the flesh.

"It's a war like the war we once fought, right here in our own backyards. Nobody from Birmingham owned a slave. Did you know that, ladies? They used us then like they're using us now. They're using this city for their battleground. They'll come into your garden and kill your chickens and take your wife."

Connor wipes his brow with a handkerchief and sits down. Nathan knows what Lydia is thinking: if she worked for his wife, she'd iron his pants better. Connor's speech means nothing to her. Ignoring reality is something she learned to do when she lost the baby. Lydia keeps a calculation of where she is in her cycle. If she's on day twelve, she'll want him. If Nathan has her during those particular days in the middle, it might work. She says she can feel something like a balloon heaping up in her when she is ripe.

After the game, Pete and Dinah drive by the place where they're building the new home. They pass by other foundries, the airport, bars, and Negro quarters. They haven't said a word to one another. The aftereffects of Connor permeate the car like stale cigaret smoke. It's in his hair, the insides of his nostrils, in Dinah's blouse. It makes him want to die. It makes him want to run the car over the edge of the embankment to the driving range below, where tiny yellow golf balls are disappearing in the night sky. He crosses the railroad tracks and turns at the sign marking the new subdivision.

He takes a left, and they drive up the street of the neighborhood where they're going to build.

The homes are in various stages of construction. Generally, Pete loves coming here. The smell of wood, the piles of red brick, zoysia grass, a kind of hope he never felt living by the foundry. Mothers wearing tropical colors push babies in strollers. He wants this for Dinah. He hopes it's not too late. Pete is thirty-seven years old. He's putting all his eggs in this basket: a new home. There are no sidewalks here, the lots aren't big, your neighbor's driveway kisses your own, the ranch-style brick homes are carbon copies, everywhere are predictable forms for life to take, like a Monopoly game.

Pete stops at their lot.

He adjusts his baseball cap, turns off the Chevy, and steps in the mud. The lot is on an incline. He likes this. His place will be set a bit higher than the other homes. Pete wants a blue-tiled shower stall. In some ways, it's all he's ever wanted. He can feel the water spraying, a light mist on his eyes.

Dinah takes off her sandals. They stand under the stars. The crickets sing under nandina bushes, where red berries will come in winter. The place is like most new subdivisions—muddy, quiet, with the remnants of wildlife scurrying in the night. He thinks of coyotes, owls, skunks, possums, gray foxes, and blue herons, lost somewhere in his memories of growing up.

"Connor's lost his mind," Dinah says and bends to pick up a clump of dirt. She makes it a ball and tosses it underhand to the center of their lot.

"Yeah," Pete says. His blood pressure is up. He's going to die young. He can feel it, and when he's this mad he wants to do something awful, like take somebody else's wife. He looks at the new homes, at the curtains that hide the women inside. He thinks of Bo Harper's wife.

They stand here, quiet.

"I met a colored man's wife," Dinah says.

He turns to her. In the dark, her eyes have depth.

"Who?"

"Nathan. Wife's name is Lydia. She was sitting behind me. She introduced herself."

For a moment, Pete's afraid Lydia might have told Dinah how he showed up at their neighborhood bar like a fool. It's something he should tell her himself, but he can't. It's too embarrassing. He feels like he's off the deep end. He's got to forget Negroes and Connor and other people's wives.

"I think Nathan's deaf," he says to Dinah, digging his cleats into the mud, where they haven't yet started pouring a foundation for his home. He asks if he ought to learn sign language. Dinah laughs and says, "Not till you know he's deaf." He says Nathan might hate white men. She says he has a right to, if he does. They stand quiet after this. They look at the empty land they've purchased, a quarter acre.

"My daddy'd die," he says as he looks at the plot. He thinks of acres and acres of cruddy farmland, of dropping the seeds in and the seedlings that come up and thrive and grow even in bad soil. Food, survival, neighbors being five miles away. Neighbors now live so close to one another you can almost hear how they make love.

"It was a great game," Dinah says to him.

Pete wants a cigaret. He hasn't smoked since the war. He thinks of himself standing on deck, tossing a butt to sea. He thinks this was the happiest time of his life, when he was fearless.

"Look," he says to Dinah, facing her, "we've got to have Connor out of our life. It scares me."

"What does, Pete?"

"He's dangerous," Pete says.

Dinah kneels and taps the hard mud with her finger. Pete looks at her dark legs, her smooth skin. He wants to hurt her when she's like this. "He's a bygone," she says and smiles up at him.

"He's not a bygone. He holds public office. Did you hear him, Dinah?" Pete shouts. "Did you hear that speech he made? He was standing on private property. Harcort's going to call his office tomorrow and want to know what the hell is going on in this city. I wanted to kill him. Do you understand me? I wanted to kill him."

Dinah shakes her head, staring at the sky.

She gets up from the ground. "Where do you think the driveway should be?" she asks him and brushes bits of dirt from her kneecaps.

"Please," Pete says, and he hears the hoarseness he associates with the way he used to plead with her never to handle a rattlesnake again, or to tell him once and for all she never worked for her mother, or to swear she'll never leave him.

After a while, they get in the car. Dinah turns on the radio. It's Tammy Wynette singing "Stand by Your Man." Dinah belts it at the top of her lungs, and the wind whips her hair. She smiles like a movie star, as if things are wonderful, as if nothing matters. They drive in the dark. She puts a hand on his leg.

But when they get back to the hotel, Pete sees Connor's car parked on the yellow line. "Damn," Dinah sighs. He pulls into the alley behind the hotel and parks under the big oak tree. He walks into the dark hallway, where Connor's herringbone hat tops the umbrella stand, then into Dinah's kitchen behind the café.

Connor's cigar burns in the ashtray.

Gracie is having to entertain him. It makes Pete's skin crawl. Why is he here? Why was he at the ballpark? Why is he stalking the family like this?

Dinah hugs Gracie. Gracie, seeing that her hostess obligation is over, leaves the kitchen. Pete hears her footsteps running up the stairs. He wonders if the freedom rider is here. He wonders who all is here. For a moment, he panics. He left a twelve-year-old here at night, in a hotel, with strangers. He vows it won't happen again.

Connor rises.

"Pete, we're under siege," he says, lips pinching his cigar. His blue glass eye shines under the ceiling light.

Pete says nothing. He's going to try to keep from killing Connor.

"Good game," he adds, pointing his cigar. "Your company ought not let the coloreds get there when you're still playing, though. There'll be a riot one of these days."

"You made a total ass of yourself," Dinah snaps.

Connor smiles at her.

"The company has two teams; you know that," she spits. "The coloreds play after the whites. You can't make them wait for their game inside the foundry or in the parking lot," she goes on. She lays her hands on the table. Her nails are the color of tangerines.

Connor has the evening newspaper spread before him on the table. MOB TERROR HITS CITY ON MOTHER'S DAY, it says. Pete stares at the photograph of Anniston's burning bus. Underneath it is the mob scene at Birmingham's Trailways station. He can't look very closely because he feels that he knows every single man in the shot—the one in the T-shirt, all smiles; the bug-eyed, clean-cut bystander; the one who looks like Clint Eastwood, staring at the colored man who's getting beat up. Pete feels he knows them all, though he doesn't really. It might as well be a Sunday school class, his coworkers at the plant, a family reunion portrait. He feels that he's one of them. It is this fear that will drive him to the brink.

"Let's have blueberry cobbler," Dinah suggests.

Pete wants to take off his cleats and his uniform, but he can't leave his wife with Connor. He throws his cap on the table.

"Look at this," Connor says, scrunching his rotund body forward to the table's edge. "Look at this, Pete," he says, biting his cigar. He points to a line that says that Grand Dragon Robert Shelton of Tuscaloosa was there. Connor looks up at Pete for a reply. Pete isn't sure what Connor wants.

"Both sides were from out of town," Connor hollers.

Pete goes to the icebox, where they keep leftovers from Sunday dinner. He cuts three slices of chocolate pie. Blueberry cobbler has disappeared—the kids.

Connor directs Dinah's attention to the headline. CONNOR'S STATEMENT: TROUBLE BLAMED ON OUT-OF-TOWNERS. Pete gives Connor and Dinah a slice of pie. She glances at Connor. "That's nice, hon," she says to him. She takes a bite of chocolate pie, then dabs her lipstick. Pete points to a reference to Attorney General Robert Kennedy assisting the bus riders. Pete notes that Connor's hands shake as he tries to eat his pie. Connor hates Washington. Pete slides the newspaper over so he can see it. He reads that the FBI will conduct an investigation in Birmingham. He turns to the editorial, "People are asking: Where were the police?" It makes him understand the weight of Connor's presence in his family's private kitchen. It makes Pete feel like a celebrity, exposed and in danger.

Connor turns to Dinah. "I'm not going to stand for outsiders to force their ways on hardworking Southern boys. Like Pete," he yells, bumping a fist on the ivory tablecloth.

"Pete's not even involved, sugar."

"The hell he's not."

"He's a foundry man," she urges.

"He's going to be sharing a bathhouse with Negroes."

"Pete doesn't care who he takes a shower with. He's been in a war, for Christ's sake." Dinah sits erect, tossing her long hair to one side. Pete knows what's coming. "You're wrong," she announces. "You're just plain wrong. That's it. That's final. You're just wrong as sin," she concludes.

She does this a lot with Mr. Connor. She isn't a bit scared of him.

"What would your mama say?" he laments, snubbing out his cigar as if he were going to leave, when he has no intention of doing so. They've been in this conversation so many times it's a song.

"You know who killed her," he sings.

When Pete turns back to them, they are staring at the floor, heads to one side, like lovers considering important words.

Pete thinks of Bo Harper's wife. She's the only diversion he has these days.

"One final note," Connor says. "You're harboring a fugitive," he declares, pointing his cigar at Dinah. Dinah throws up her hands. "A fugitive? A fugitive from what, from where?"

Connor chews his cigar.

"I thought fugitives were people running from something, like the law. She's not running from the law. You are the law. You're standing right here. Take her if she's under arrest, for God's sake." Dinah draws her hair up, then drops it, letting it cascade. "Let's go to the café. It's hot in here," she says.

They all get up, carrying plates of pie.

In the café, Pete gets coffee. Connor likes his black. Dinah likes cream, no sugar. Pete likes his with a chunk of ice. Connor walks to the window, thumbs in suspenders.

"Monday night," he says, staring at the dark street. "How's the house coming, Pete?"

"Fine."

"Moving up in the world," Connor notes.

Pete eyes him.

Dinah gets up and walks behind the counter until she has Pete's ear. "I'm sorry," she says. All Pete wants is to get in bed with her, to put his face close to her. All he wants is peace and quiet. But the minute he thinks it, Gracie and Angel come into the café, and Connor's fat chin is up.

The girl's wearing an outfit of things Pete can't size up. A tan suede jacket with fringe. Boots.

Connor takes her in. There is something between them, a sniffing out. Pete feels it. He doesn't know who started the idea that her parents were a Mexican-German mix. Maybe it was Gracie's doing, maybe Benny's, or maybe the girl herself invented it; all he knows is that she's dark enough to make Connor question her ancestry.

Pete sees the questions making Connor's big chin quiver, but the man doesn't miss a beat. "Honey, this is no place for a girl," Connor says, hands on hips, his fat belly pushing hard against his suspenders.

"Where you from, Boston?" he asks, reaching to put his cigar in an ashtray. He dwarfs the girl. Connor is like an old elephant with his gray skin, his lumbering, tusky way of probing.

"Nashville," she says.

"My ass," Connor replies, moving in to her.

"Best way to make grits is with heavy cream, fresh butter, cooked on a warm eye for nigh an hour. A Yankee wouldn't know that, would she?" Angel asks, her eyes meeting his.

Connor grins.

"Corn bread?" he asks.

"In your grandmama's big black iron skillet—hot—cornmeal,

eggs, sugar, *lard,*" she emphasizes. "Put it in the oven, not on the eye, to make it crisp."

Pete knows the core of Connor's hate isn't race. It's class. A purely geographical war that never died, which the Kennedy Camelot reinforces. The enemy is blue-blood intellect. Southern blacks are the victims, as are Southern whites, of "meddlers." It's better if the girl's a blond Southern Negro than a rich white Easterner.

"You a reporter?" Connor asks her.

"No," she says.

Pete hears Connor's mind silently correcting her. No *sir!*

Connor picks up the saltshaker, fingers the cut glass. "Then what brings you to this fine city?" he asks her. It's not a rhetorical question, Pete knows. Connor wants to know the mind-set of this new movement. He's curious about foreigners—their habits, their ideas.

"I'm part of the CORE riders," she tells him.

"Uh huh," Connor says.

Pete takes Connor his coffee. "Want some?" he asks Angel.

Her eyes seize his. She couldn't be a day over seventeen, Pete thinks. "No," she says.

No *sir,* Pete thinks. He's been hanging around Connor so much, he's afraid his mind is beginning to work like Connor's. He's afraid he's got Connor in his blood, and it's a horrible thought. The thing about Connor is that it's not just his prejudice. There's the way he's using Gracie, at this moment, as a prop. His arm drapes Gracie's back. She's studying her charm bracelet. She's got enough of Dinah in her to ignore Connor's old elephant ways.

Gracie's eyes fall to the newspaper that Connor's placed on the table. She begins to turn the pages. Pete wishes she wouldn't. She

67

stops when she gets to the photo of the WAPI newsman whose car was clubbed. "I saw this!" she says to Pete. "I saw this."

Connor pats her back, chuckles. "No you didn't, sugar," he says.

"I did," Gracie says to Pete.

Dinah gets leftovers from the icebox. "Anybody hungry?" she asks. It's Monday. Wash day meal—kraut and wieners, mashed potatoes, corn bread. An old habit from the country, one that Southern women can't resist. Dinah loves to cook for people. Connor stirs his coffee, still waiting for the girl to tell him why she's in Birmingham. He looks at her haughtily, as though peering over half-rimmed glasses.

Her lip trembles. She covers her face as if to cry, and Pete sees what a tiny girl she is. Connor bolts from her chair, like there's been an accident. He fusses at Dinah. "Get her some water." He puts his cigar in his saucer. He stands over Angel, hands on hips, belly protruding. "For God's sake," he says.

That's when the first of the reporters comes in the front door. They're still in town, though the incident is over. They can't leave Birmingham. Pete understands this. It's a great place to work, if you like to scrub other folks' bathrooms. He realizes he dislikes the journalists more than he dislikes Connor. As they stand here staring at Connor's big body, the freedom rider's crying face, and Dinah behind the counter, he understands that this is a bad time in his life. He understands that if his family must accommodate guests, the journalists ought to be the first to go. He'd rather feed people like Connor and a mixed-up girl masquerading as a futurist.

When he tells Dinah this that night, she pulls him to her. It's almost midnight, and the train is coming. He can't hear it yet, but he knows it's time. The room will light up. Dinah is wearing a blue nightgown. Her legs are tangled up with his. He feels her strong calf muscles.

"Don't worry," she whispers.

"I mean, I'm starting to feel like I'm some kind of animal," he insists.

Dinah laughs.

"I'm serious," he says.

"What makes you think that?"

"I don't know," he says. "I think I'm going to die."

Dinah rises up in bed. Her profile in the pale light is angular. He wonders if the journalists are thinking of her at this moment. He can almost sense it—all over the hotel.

"Nothing's wrong with you," she says. "We're just between houses, that's all."

She reaches to the nightstand for a tissue. It's spring. Her sinuses are acting up. When this happens, her blue eyes become watery, but even this, Pete thinks, makes her sexy. "This place is a dust bowl," she tells him. "I should have thought of it before we moved in. I'm going to sneeze for weeks. We should have just rented an apartment. I didn't think ahead. I never think ahead," she tells him and maneuvers her body back under the sheet.

Pete reaches for her hand.

He can make out the fireplace, vanity, crown molding. He feels like they're sleeping in a castle. He can't think about the fact that this was once her mother's room. It's the days prior to knowing her that burn in him. By the time they married, she'd told him things that made him nuts. She grew up in a world of women with names like Ruby, Pansy, Candy—things to eat or wear or smell. Dinah watched them all.

She rolls over. "Talk to me," she says to him. "Tell me everything you're thinking." Once he starts, he can't stop. He tells her he's worried over Benny leaving for college. They don't have funds. He tells her he's worried over Gracie. He tells her he's worried over Connor, the city, the journalists. He tells her they probably all want to sleep with her. "Smart guys," she says. At midnight, the train comes roaring in. For a brief moment, light takes her face.

After he's fallen asleep, Dinah strokes his dark curls. She's sorry he's worried, but it's Pete's nature to be agitated. It drives him to play baseball, run the grey iron unit, and make love like a madman.

Pete's concise.

He even makes love concisely. She loves making love with Pete. She loved it the first time.

They are standing in her father's chicken house, only a few weeks after she'd met him. She is mixing castor oil and kerosene. His eyes are on her.

"What're you up to today?" she asks, wiping her hands on her slacks.

"Leaving," he says.

She stops, turns to him.

"It's a war," he says and shrugs. He looks past the chicken house into the field, where the wildflowers are growing. She backs up to the wall and takes off her gloves. A butterfly lights on the rafter.

"Are you Greek?" he asks.

"Don't know."

"Your mother? Was she beautiful, too?" His eyes are on her.

"Yes."

Pete moves closer. She is up against the wall of the chicken house. He takes her face and holds it. She hardly knows him. He is a sailor on furlough. His lips are on her—rough, chapped, but she's beyond this fact in a flash. After that, it's his hands. Fast, free, like a robber searching for contraband, they travel. She's his size, his equal. His body fits hers in all the right places. They wrestle each other to the sawdust. Their arms and legs tangle up, antlers, hard, bony. "You're strong," he whispers. It's his leaving that makes her want him. He crawls over on her, a boy scrambling for something—his hands going, legs moving.

This was how Benny was conceived. She remembers it now as she tiptoes to Benny's room. She scoops his Sinclair shirt from the doorknob and holds it to her face. It smells like gasoline. She stands over Benny in the dark.

She bends to kiss his sandy head.

His shark-tooth lanyard lies over his bronze chest, where dog chains once hung on his father's generation. "No war," she thinks. "No war for Benny."

It's good she can't see into the future.

Dinah can't sleep. She hasn't the heart to tell Pete she loves living at the hotel, that it's what she always wanted. No matter how sordid your past, it's still yours. It's all you've got. Your mama's always your mama.

She tiptoes to the door and into the hall. The Oriental rugs are soft to her soles. Peeking into Gracie's room, she sees that the freedom rider isn't anywhere in sight. She wonders if she has left for good or if she's just out somewhere in the city. She looks at Gracie. She remembers how they used to cross the viaduct—Gracie, Benny, and her, after Pete left for the foundry in the morning. It was so easy to make the children happy—a bluebird on the telephone wires, a ride in Dinah's giant hotel laundry basket, a grape sucker. Gracie and Benny knew every nook and cranny long before it was their home—the cellar, widow's walk, butler's pantry, guest rooms, the café, where their preacher granddaddy visited bearing squash, turnips, ripe tomato. At day's end, they'd drive back to their house over by the foundry, the city disappearing in the viaduct's arc.

As she turns to leave, Gracie whispers in the dark, "Mom!"

Dinah turns back to her. Gracie is sitting up.

"Are you all right?" Dinah asks and goes to sit on the edge of the bed. She cuddles Gracie's head. "These are hard times, baby," Dinah says. They lie together on the bed and stare up at the water stain on the ceiling. It's the shape of Africa.

Dinah props up on an elbow and bends over to study Gracie's face.

"What was the scariest part?" she asks.

Gracie stares at the ceiling.

"Do you understand what's going on, baby? Hell, I don't either. I ought to shoot Mr. Connor, don't you think, angel? Don't you think I ought to just go ahead and put him out of his misery?" she says and lets a smile rake her face.

Gracie grins.

"Not that it's his fault. Sure gives the hotel a lot of business, but damn!" Gracie smiles at her. Gracie has told her she ends too many sentences with *but damn!*

"It's not funny, is it, pumpkin? Not so funny at all," she says, tucking Gracie's brown hair behind an ear. "I'm sorry to put that girl in your room. Where did she go? Did you show her the bathroom?"

"She doesn't shave her legs," Gracie says.

Dinah turns to her. "Nobody does in Europe."

"This is America," Gracie reminds her.

"Maybe she doesn't think it's necessary."

"But everybody does it."

Dinah sits up, draws her legs in.

"The girl won't be here long," she tells Gracie.

"I think she's upset," Gracie says.

"Of course she is."

Gracie gets up, parts the sheer mint curtains. When this was Dinah's mother's room, the curtains were green velvet. Dinah has accepted the fact that most of her mother's old items in the hotel are broken or otherwise scarred. Beside each bed is a washstand with tiny towels, a pitcher and bowl—chipped. The chenille bedspreads, once bright colors like magenta, gold, turquoise, and a shade of watermelon, are now faded to pastel.

Dinah can see herself in the mirror on Gracie's vanity. You look like Judy Garland, people have told her. Now that she's nearing forty, she wants to believe it.

In the mirror, she watches Gracie get up and walk outside to the balcony. The final engine has sputtered in from the Atlantic seaboard. A half-moon hangs over the terminal's dome. Dinah walks out to the balcony and puts her hands on the banister next to her daughter's. She notices how their knuckles are from the same mold. "Her mother's German," Gracie says, speaking of the girl they've taken in. "Her father's Mexican, a nightclub singer. I think she's a hooker."

"Benny tell you that?"

In the distance, the Sloss furnaces burn beside the viaduct. The by-products plant tosses fire in the sky. The terminal is quiet. Gracie is holding a flashlight—the one she keeps beside the bed, in the event of a power outage. Gracie puts the yellow orb to her hand, studying it. "Corpuscles?" she asks.

How does she know concepts like hookers and corpuscles? Dinah wonders. Dinah's aware of how tall she's gotten—though she's only twelve, how classic is her beauty, despite the awkward gait and bony kneecaps; how much like Dinah she is becoming.

"They're riding buses to let us know we shouldn't keep Negroes from riding buses with us," Dinah tells her.

"Where are they coming from?"

"All over. That funny-looking reporter with the skinny arms is in the hospital. We're in for more of this type thing. Mr. Connor's wrong. He's our friend, but he's wrong."

"That's what grandmother did, isn't it?" Gracie says.

Dinah looks at her.

"Hooker," Gracie says.

Her mother's bedroom was situated so that, from the keyhole, Dinah only had a piece. Candy—her mother—did it precisely the same way every time. It has dawned on Dinah that Gracie is the age Dinah was when she was staring into keyholes, watching her mother's face come apart. That, among other things, haunts her.

"Wake me early," Gracie says to her and kisses her mother's cheek. Dinah turns to go. "Sleep good," she says and walks out into the hall. She hears water running. The journalists are stirring. They're having a hard time sleeping, here after the fact, after the incident. They'll be leaving Birmingham, but there'll be others. The Huntsville hotels can't accommodate all the NASA program people. They spill down into Birmingham. It's good for business.

Dinah takes the stairway to the hall below, where she finds that Mr. Connor has left his herringbone hat on the umbrella stand. In the dark, she takes it in hand, running her fingers over the shabby old pheasant's feather. The hat smells like mothballs. It smells like Connor. Connor won't budge, he won't leave the hotel, he won't give an inch on anything. Dinah walks into the parlor, pulls the drop cord to dim the light, making the walls the color of fresh peaches. She sits on the sofa, staring at the fireplace and mantel scarves. The old cuspidor is painted with gladiolas, just like her mother left it.

It's September 1934—a hot Indian summer. The girls are in the backyard, bathing in the wash pot under the oak tree, wearing underclothes, hidden by a fence of tangled honeysuckle vines. Jasmine, the cook, is at the clothesline in an apron, hanging black lingerie. Dinah is standing on the landing above, chewing a piece of pine straw. It's dusk. The city is astir. Stores are closing. Streetcars are moving. Men are smoking. She can hear the distant music, the drums of the Speckled Queen, the banjo, a lame old whore. She sees a cluster of ladies wearing pillbox hats and colorful suits cross Twenty-second Street. A man is with them. It's the preacher named Tyler—the man Dinah's mother says is her father. Dinah hasn't seen him in a while. The ladies dodge a paperboy, ignore a beggar. They are headed en masse straight for the brothel. Dinah leaves the landing and goes back inside. She stops at the bedroom mirror. She studies her legs. Her body is starting to shape up like her mother's.

*Leaving the bedroom, she makes her way down the spiral
stairs. She peeks through the banister to the parlor below. Her
mother stands beside her cherry desk wearing a rainbow
shawl, a tiny woman with a red ponytail.*

*"Child," one of the ladies says, "we've come to save your
soul."*

*Another says to her, "You're a good woman. Come to Jesus.
You can do so much good." Dinah's mother embraces them
fully. This is how she was: physical, warm. She kisses them one
by one, lingering to inhale perfume, massage hands, study
eyes. Dinah watches the ladies. They love coming here. They
want something her mother has—not sin, men, or jewelry.
Something else. Something Dinah wants—wants, remembers,
but can't name. It's the thing women want from other women.*

The first lady takes Candy's earrings from her ears.

"Give these to us for Jesus," the lady presses.

*"Take them," Candy urges. The lady holds the blue stones in
her palm. "Whatever it is y'all do with jewelry for Jesus, just
do it," she says. Tyler breaks in. He is blond. Orange slices of
sunset come in where the drapes are parted. It makes certain
objects in the room—the Imari vase, the candelabra, the umbrella stand—glow in the dark. A train whistle blows. In the
kitchen, Jasmine, the cook, stands in the doorway holding a
colander of beans. Tyler takes Candy's hands. "Pray with me,"
he says. Candy closes her eyes. "Jesus, wrap your arms around
her. Fill her up," Tyler instructs. Then he drops her hands and
takes a Bible from his coat pocket. Candy moves away, drawing up her rainbow shawl. Tyler's eyes take in the parlor table,
the tasseled draperies.*

"I like how you pray," Candy tells him softly.

"I'll pray for you more," he tells her.

"Now?" she asks. A few loose strands of red hair come loose from her ponytail. Her chin is tucked, making her look shy. Her makeup is beaded with perspiration. Tyler looks straight at her. "No, not now," he tells her.

"Sometime, then. Some other time."

"What do you want me to pray for?" he asks her.

Candy says, "For my soul."

Dinah watches the church ladies clustered up against the wall, clutching their pocketbooks, paralyzed by it all.

"Do you know your soul?" he asks her and puts his hands in his trouser pockets. Dinah eases down the staircase for a better view. She is marveling at the sound of his voice, the vernacular of the Appalachian foothills. But more than anything, she's amazed at the way he and her mother are staging this show for the church ladies. "No," Candy says, "I don't know my soul. Where is my soul?" she asks. "Is it here?" she asks, and she opens her rainbow shawl up and puts a hand on her chest. Dinah's heart is racing. She is at the bottom of the staircase. She's in awe of this production.

The ladies turn and go, but he lingers.

"Where did you get that shirt?" she whispers. It is faded blue, a farmer's shirt.

"Savannah," he replies.

"When have you been to Savannah?" she demands. And this is when Dinah knows her mother loves him. She starts pulling bobby pins from her hair. Tyler grabs her wrists, making her drop the bobby pins. They hit the hard pine floor. He pulls

77

Candy into the parlor and closes the doors, but Dinah knows where to spy.

The keyhole. She's done it a thousand times.

The minute the door is closed, Candy is up in Tyler's face. "Where have you been?" she demands. They are standing by the old cuspidor.

"I've been a farmer," he says.

"Why were you praying for me like that in front of all those church idiots and my daughter?"

Tyler looks away, toward the fireplace. He reaches for his Bible.

"Don't hide behind that. Why did you have to come calling with those ladies? You should have come like most men come, in the dark, with a wallet of bills," she says.

"Jesus loves you," he says.

"Does he?" she says and stretches her body to its limit to make herself tall. Gathering her up, he inhales it all—the perfume, the skin, the gold.

Dinah remembers how they looked standing there. She remembers studying him and wanting to memorize every detail of how he looked—the farmer's blue shirt, the tanned arms, and the eyes.

3

Connor remembers. He was there. He was in the back kitchen, talking to Jasmine, the cook, that September afternoon in 1934. He saw the preacher enter the brothel parlor and went in to investigate. He stood right behind Dinah. He's not sure if she remembers him being there. He's never asked her. There are things he knows are personal. He likes to think of himself as a man of principles. He doesn't want to do anything that will cause Dinah embarrassment. The reason he stalks the hotel, he tells himself, is that he wants to protect her dignity. He believes that people got a right to a new life.

Let bygones be bygones, he thinks, as he chews his cigar in the black city car.

It's Tuesday. Connor's sure the reporters will clear by nightfall.

He's riding over the viaduct, where the puppy food factory now greets you, its logo a winking beagle. It's a nice sight, Connor feels. It softens, for the occasional tourist, the blow of the pig iron furnaces. Connor is proud of Birmingham. He turns at Forty-first Street and backtracks in the direction of the foundry where Pete works. A better fellow never lived, Connor thinks, than Pete Fraley. It is Connor's heart's desire to stay in Pete's good graces. If Pete Fraley likes him, Connor is all right. They make valves and pipe fittings at Pete's foundry. Connor's been inside before. The Negroes work where it's hot. Whites supervise. Connor feels this is the natural order of things. Connor likes things to make sense.

The baseball diamond is crisp. Buttercups line the sidewalk. Connor rolls down his window and checks out the yard of the family who've moved into Pete and Dinah's old home. Connor knows their name is Craven. Byron and Arlie Craven. He's checked it on police records. There's no mention of Byron Craven. Fellow doesn't have a record; a few parking tickets, a speeding back in '54. But otherwise clean. That's good, Connor thinks. You want decent people moving into Pete Fraley's place. You don't want trouble at your heels, ghosts haunting your old home place.

Connor hangs an elbow from the window, staring at the baseball diamond. The sun's bright. It's a May like no other. He thinks of his daughter, who was once a May queen. Now that she's got a degree from college and a family of her own, she hardly needs her daddy anymore.

To make this idea go away, he thinks of baseball.

One year, Pete's company came home as national amateur champions. They got to the tournament by winning six straight games in the city play-off, with disaster kicking because they lost the opener. The semifinal was under the lights with thousands of fans—not theirs; they were playing up North—looking on. Pete pitched a shutout, matched by a series of hit-and-runs that left the other guys shaking their heads in confusion. Bunch of rednecks know how to play baseball, they were thinking. In the finals, a two-of-three with Dayton, Pete's team dropped the first game in the ninth inning, with two men on and two out and two strikes on the hitter. The Dayton first baseman blooped a single to center field that scored the winning runs. Pete was in the cooker. But in the final game the last afternoon, Tick Harkins unloaded a grand slam in the third, and Pete allowed only one in the last of the seventh.

That's when Pete broke his nose.

Bubba Crawley backed him up and kept the Dayton hitters tied in knots with a series of pitches from every angle he could throw. Bo Harper hit a home run in the ninth, and that was that. The team came home to a cheering company.

Connor has told this story to Gracie, Pete's kid. Connor thinks this kid hung the moon. She's not like her mother. She's quiet, the type you want to watch in the teen years. She'll be the kind who'll want to get educated. She's the kind to have a mess of ideas. But right now she's got a thin smile, brown bangs. Right now cute as a button, Connor thinks. What gets Connor is how different they all are, the grandmother, mother, and daughter. Different as night and day and night. Makes you wonder, Connor thinks.

He turns on the radio to listen for calls. A patrol car has been fetched to a grocery store in Woodlawn, where a woman has fainted. "She dropped a sack of fresh vegetables," they're saying.

Connor lights his cigar, thinking how he wishes the reporters could hear this, could hear what a truly quaint city this Birmingham is. If that's all the problem you got on a Tuesday morning, you've got a nice life as commissioner of public safety.

Let bygones by bygones, he thinks. It's the watchword of the day. It's the thing he has going in his mind. He gets something like this going in his mind and it won't quit. Connor reaches in his sack for a donut. He's spilt coffee on his starched white shirt. His wife will chuckle. Beara knows he can't keep clean. He's got a special knack for catsup on neckties. Connor crosses back over the viaduct, but rather than turning for City Hall, he takes the big hill up over the north side. He's going to the cemetery. Connor licks sugar from his fingers and enters the cemetery gate. He hasn't been up here since all the trouble started, since the students rode the bus in. The gate is made of iron, painted black but rusting, in spots, to the color of peanut husks. Connor parks beside the marker, gets out of the car, hikes his pants, and surveys the place.

The sky is blue as Connor's glass eye. The city's dark smoke can't mar it on certain days, like today. A few wildflowers Connor can't name dot the grass. Connor likes this view of Birmingham. Most folks see it from the other side, from atop Red Mountain, where the TV stations broadcast nasty news, where Vulcan draws tourists, where people dance at The Club. Nobody ever comes to the north side and views the city from this angle. Connor walks over the markers until he comes to the one that says Candy Gentry.

This is where Dinah's mother is buried. This is where she ended up. Connor can see the terminal station, but he can't see the hotel from here. He can see City Hall. He can see Loveman's, Empire Theatre, the library, park, and all the traffic lights on Twenty-second Street. He can't see much more. Connor has trouble seeing things. He has an eye for danger, intruders, and elections. But he can't see the forest for the trees. Just let things float to the surface, Dinah told him one day in the café. He has no idea what she meant. She told him he can't let things be, he can't let things evolve. It bothers him when people use words like this. It bothers him when people don't understand law and order.

Connor bends to brush his stubby fingers over Dinah's mother's marker. What was it? he asks himself every time he comes here, every time he lets himself think it. Maybe it was her skin. A ripe plum. Try to keep from breaking the skin with your fingernail, to see the juice run. There's a part of you that wants to bruise it. It was like Candy understood this part. She was making $100 a week in 1930 by simply letting her skin be broken. The other girls were shadows, traveling from parlor to bedroom, asking men the same questions night after night: what's your name, where you from, what do you do, what do you want to do now?

He'd arrived after it happened. It was the men from the klavern, he knows this. They'd said they were there to take the child, Dinah, off to the welfare. Candy told them, "You're taking my dead body with her." So one of them shot her in the head. They left a cross burning in the yard with a note that read:

> Every criminal, every gambler, every thug, every libertine, every girl ruiner, every home wrecker, every wife beater, every dope peddler, every moonshiner, every crooked politician, every pagan papist priest, every shyster lawyer, every K. of C., every white slaver, every brothel madam, every Rome-controlled newspaper, every black spider is fighting the Klan. Think it over. Whose side are you on?

Connor turns for his car. He'll never forgive them, though they think they own him. They think they got a right to kill whores, but they think wrong.

Lunch is a mess. The café is a swarm of madness, a new influx of reporters. Dinah's slinging plates of macaroni and cheese, green peas, and pork chops, which is the special for the day, according to the blackboard. Connor quickly notes that the freedom rider is wearing an apron. He understands this means trouble. Dinah has hired the girl, no doubt. She'll deny it, say she's merely taking care of running this damn business, thank you.

Connor waits for the reporters to take note of his presence. They do.

"Mr. Connor," one of them says, knocking over a glass of iced tea in his hurry to retrieve a notebook from his knapsack. "Anything you want to say about the editorial your newspaper ran yesterday?"

"Ain't *my* newspaper, son."

Connor takes a seat at the counter. Dinah half smiles at him. Her hair looks like it hasn't been brushed. It rains down her back, all the way to her waist. The student rider is making somebody a strawberry milk shake. "Working the fountain, huh," he says to her.

She turns. Under her apron is the cowgirl getup.

A reporter slips in beside Connor. Connor takes in his sideburns. "You from Nashville?" he asks.

The reporter takes a pencil in hand. "Where were the police Sunday?"

"Boy, this is old news."

Connor peruses a menu, though he knows it by heart. He glances down to see what kind of shoes the fellow is wearing. They're the color of muscadine berries.

"Nashville?" Connor presses, looking squarely in the reporter's eyes. He watches how the reporter tries to figure out which eye to look in. Connor feels his glass eye is, in the end, better than a firearm. It throws the stranger for a loop.

"No," the reporter says, looking at his pencil.

"Well, then?" Connor goes on.

"Anniston."

Connor puts a hand on his shoulder. "Well, you're a homeboy. For the love of Jesus, why are you here in Birmingham, boy? You got your own burned buses back home. You know Ohatchee?"

"I didn't grow up in Alabama," the reporter says.

"I got people in Ohatchee. How far's that from Anniston, now?"

"Not sure," the kid says.

Connor studies the kid's face. He sizes it up. Kid's father is a subsistence farmer—kid's grown up running through one too many lines of okra. Been to college a year, likes the big city, wants a big story. "See that girl," Connor says, gesturing to the student. "She rode in on the bus Sunday. I think she's got a story."

The reporter's eyes jab her.

"Yeah," Connor whispers, holding the menu to hide his words. "She got a bloody nose. They beat the stew out of her."

"Who did?"

"The Ku Klux Klan," Connor says, deliberately making each syllable distinct for the kid. The kid is smart, though, looks at Connor sideways, looking for the facetiousness he knows is there.

"I'm serious as a heart attack," Connor says. Dinah breezes by, and Connor takes in her perfume.

"You got your food, hon?" she says to the reporter.

"Yes ma'am," he replies.

"Don't you love it," Connor says to her, "when they say, 'Yes ma'am'? Don't you love the homeboys?"

Dinah waits for Connor to order, the whole time taking in the café. The tables are full. It's not all businessmen. There's a few regular people, mothers who've shopped at Loveman's and what-not. Connor orders a cheeseburger. Dinah whirls to the grill, slaps on a patty, and wipes her eye with her wrist.

"Here's what I've got to say," Connor says to the kid reporter. "This is all out-of-town meddlers. Both sides were from other places, the ones who got whipped and the ones who did the whipping. They staged it for Mother's Day, when we try to let off as many of our policemen as possible to spend Mother's Day at home with their families. We got to the station as quickly as we possibly could. As I've said before, we're not going to stand for this in Birmingham. We will fill the jail full, and we don't care whose toes we step on. I am saying now to these meddlers from out of town, the best thing for them to do is stay out if they don't want to get slapped in jail. Our people of Birmingham are a peaceful people, and we never have any trouble here unless some people come into our city looking for trouble. People look for trouble, they'll find it," Connor concludes and turns to see if the freedom-riding cowgirl making the strawberry milk shake is listening.

Fire is in her eyes. "You're insane," she says. Her blond hair looks like it's been in an electrical socket. She's had some kind of Toni, Connor thinks, remembering how the stuff smelled when Beara used it on their daughter.

He watches her hands holding the big milk shake tumbler under the blender. Her fingers are childlike, and as if reading his mind, she glances up at him seductively. Then her face falls quickly as if shamed. A grin, an apology—all mixed up in a recipe he knows well. Child hooker.

The idea ignites him. It makes him hungry for the cheeseburger that Dinah's flipping with a spatula. It makes him light a new cigar. Now it all makes sense why she's staying on here, why she wants to hang around Dinah and why Dinah wants to hire her to make milk shakes. They got things to *explore,* to talk over. He loves it when his mind works like this, when he's on target. The kid reporter has returned to his table by the window. He's jotting something in his notebook. Somebody has chosen a song on the jukebox, the one that begins, "In the jungle, the mighty jungle, the lion sleeps tonight." Connor wonders what this song means. It makes no sense, just like most people make no sense these days.

"Here you go, hon," Dinah says, throwing a mess of dill pickles beside the cheeseburger. "Just let us know if you need anything else, hon." She smiles, but it's her businesswoman smile. She hardly knows who he is. She is at work. Connor thinks that there's nothing on the face of the earth any more alluring and powerful than a woman running a business.

It makes him, in a way, admire the student rider—especially, he thinks, if she's a whore or, better yet, if she was one when she was younger. If it's all an act—her politics, fringe, boots, and suede jacket—if she's just a woman who's good at what she does, then he bows to her; she wins. It's what he loved about Candy. It wasn't her submission that thrilled him, it was knowing that she was faking it; it was the power of the theater, the way she carried herself into, over, and beyond a man's hands.

Connor walks to the reporter's table. "Do me a favor, boy," he says to the kid. "Find out that girl's last name."

The kid reporter swallows his macaroni, takes a gulp of iced tea, and gives him a questioning look.

Connor hates having to ask a favor of his subordinates—the journalists. "It's important for the story," Connor tells him.

"I'm not onto her story," he replies.

Connor backs up, hands on hips. He juts his belly forward so that his suspenders give. The reporter lights a cigaret. "Give me one of those," Connor says.

"See," he says, sitting down. "You need to do one of those human interest stories on her. You know, where you say she's got blue eyes, et cetera." Connor pauses, letting the nicotine run its vertigo. "You go into her story, get the reader's sympathy."

"I don't do that kind of journalism."

Connor leans forward. "You know the truth when you see it, don't you, bud?" Connor bends over and whispers the question: "So is she colored or not, what do you think?"

The reporter half smiles.

"I'm serious," Connor says, trying to figure out how old this kid reporter is.

The reporter looks back over at the freedom rider, who's behind the counter squirting fake whipped cream on top of a hot fudge sundae. "Can't say," he replies. "Can't say if she's a Negro or not."

"How old are you?" Connor asks.

"Thirty-three."

Connor is surprised. "Thought you were a kid," he says in all seriousness.

The reporter shrugs. "Good genes," he says and puts more sugar in his tea. "Why do you need her last name?" he asks. Knowing his age, Connor is feeling less amicable, but there may be a way for this to work for both of them. "I think she works for the government," Connor says. Sometimes it's better to not shoot straight with a man. He doesn't want to tell anybody what he really thinks about her.

"You want to run a check on her, then."

"What's your name?" Connor asks.

"Sleigh."

"From Anniston," Connor confirms.

"I'm not from Anniston; that's just where I worked last."

The guy looks like Sugarfoot on TV—that kind of fake-rawhide kid, a pansy under the war-correspondent air. He's the type a certain kind of woman will fall for, Connor thinks. "Never mind," Connor says, crushing the cigaret into a spoon.

Sugarfoot struggles to make it register—just which eye is glass. Connor watches his eyes scramble, decipher, coagulate. Yes! He's figured out which eye is real. He peers into Connor's natural, left iris. "You're a good journalist," Connor tells him. Sugarfoot stares at him. Connor stays at the table, and when Dinah comes by, the reporter orders a slice of lemon icebox pie.

"Nice hotel," he says to her.

She looks around. "This is my favorite part," she tells him, bringing her arms up to sweep over the room. "The café," she clarifies. "Like the antiques in your room?"

"Don't he look like Sugarfoot on TV?" Connor asks her.

Dinah surveys his face. She doesn't really take note, though. She's still busy, still running a café, still incapable of seeing anybody other than a paying customer. "Well, he sure does," she sings and waltzes off to get him a piece of pie.

"Her daddy used to handle snakes in church. You met her husband?"

"No," Sugarfoot says.

"Best man you'll ever know."

Connor watches him eat his pie. He takes bird-size bites. "Make it last a long time, right?" Connor asks. He can't understand why the reporter isn't asking him questions anymore. It makes him antsy. It makes him want to ask him a thing or two. "You up there in Anniston when the bus burned?"

"'Fraid so," he says.

"Who burned it?" Connor asks.

Sugarfoot shrugs.

Connor sees that the crowd has thinned. The student rider has vanished. Connor gets up to see where she's gone. He walks over to Dinah, who's washing dishes behind the counter. "Put on some music, hon," she says to Connor.

He looks at his watch. "Got to work," he says.

Dinah lets her hands rest in the suds. She stares out the window. The May sun takes her eyes, makes them sparkle. Connor wonders what kind of housewife she'd have made if she'd been a regular kind of woman. He wonders if this is what Pete has in mind, building her a new place over where it's nice with green grass. He wonders if Pete wants her at a kitchen sink—the kind that's got a sprayer where she can spray her dishes and plant roses and think the kinds of things most women think, whatever those things are. He wonders what women think. He wonders what he's going to do when he gets back to City Hall, where even his own men are starting to ask questions.

"What's her name?" Connor asks Dinah.

She glances up at him, lips zipped.

"Where's she from?" he asks.

"She's a boarder."

"She's not paying."

"That's my business," Dinah tells him.

"She may be working for somebody you don't want to have dealings with," he warns. Dinah gives him a funny look. He turns. Sugarfoot has walked up. His pencil is traveling. Connor doesn't care what he hears. He hopes Mr. Movie Star can get to the bottom of this story. "She may be working for the FBI," Connor tells her.

Dinah throws her head back, causing her long hair to fall even below her waist in the back. "For crying out loud," she laughs. "She's just a girl. She's just trying to do what's right."

Connor feels his heart going. "You think she's right?" he presses.

Dinah glares at him. "Of course I do."

He tries to get deep into her eyes. He tries to make her understand what he suspects about Angel. He wonders if she suspects it, too. But she won't give him any signals. She never acknowledges anything the two of them share.

The journalist is taking copious notes. This isn't the human interest story Connor had in mind. He turns on him. "What do you do, the social page?" he spits.

All the way back to City Hall, Connor fumes. He can't get that damn song off his mind. In the jungle, the mighty jungle. He can't figure out the word they're saying. It sounds like *a-wing-a-wet, a-wing-a-wet*. Connor wonders what it means. He's starting to worry there's a meaning to everything. Nobody understands the meaning, but the young people think they do, and there's nothing more dangerous than that. He chews on his cigar. The cheeseburger isn't digesting right. The May sun dances off the chrome of his car. He thinks of how you can actually see heat, how it makes a mirage on the highway. He thinks of how Beara has started talking to their preacher, trying to make their preacher convince him to resign from public office, no less. If it wasn't for the café and people like Pete and Dinah Fraley, he'd do it. But he owes it to the public, to the good people of Birmingham, to fulfill his duty to this city. He tries to forget the freedom-riding whore and all that he admires in working women. Yet he knows he's at their mercy. He wants the women to keep the hotel open. If they closed the hotel, he wouldn't have anywhere to go. The women run the hotel. It's not just Dinah, it's all of them, every last ghost. It's the last hotel for women, and if it closes, he won't have anything left to remember.

4

The high school Benny attends is old, built at the turn of the century. Its Gothic architecture is confusing to Benny. It's like a fort and a prison—archways, pinnacles, and gargoyles that fan over to rows of identical windows that cage restless spirits.

In the auditorium is a mural. A boy and girl are coming into the world through a blue globe. They're awestruck with violent scenes of a woman chained to a gear where a muscled man is saving or killing her, Benny can't tell. A Nazi-looking boy holds a sword over a nymphet. Deformed faces in trees witness coal miners, factory workers, and train yards. Telephone poles bend in the wind. A woman stands in a cornfield, a nude is reading a book, a sprite throws magic dust into a dying African's face. Social realism. The Industrial Revolution is hurting people, Benny thinks as he leans against Nick's Sundries, staring at the school. He likes to ponder things like this when he stands across the street smoking. In two weeks he'll graduate. He's learned the art of escaping yourself. He likes dramatics. He had the lead in this year's production of *The Music Man*.

Carpe diem—seize the opportunity—is his school's motto. Benny was voted best Latin student. It's one of the things he tucks away, an arrow to be used later when he thinks of the future. He has to smoke, wear a jacket, stand under the awning at Nick's, but he knows there's more, much more, up the road. He straddles the fence, walks both sides of the aisle, mixes with the ins and the outs, both breeds of students. He likes the song "Walk on the Wild Side," but he also cries at his grandfather's holiness church. He's got a deck of genetic cards that won't quit. Benny's high school annual has all kinds of quotes, like "Character is the keystone in the arch of destiny"; and "Wisdom is the principal thing. Get wisdom and with all thy getting get understanding"; and, his favorite, "In this theatre of man's life it is reserved only for God and angels to be lookers on." This is the thing Benny says over and over to himself. He wants to show it to Angel. He's never met a girl like her. Benny falls in love with every girl he meets, but he's never met a girl from outside Birmingham. He can't get her off his mind. Last night, he took Ginger Fortenberry parking over by the new subdivision where his family's home is under construction. The whole time, he was thinking of Angel and what it'd be like to run his tongue over that chipped tooth of hers.

Today, a spring rain has left a river of water running alongside the street, carrying cigaret butts. Benny tosses his in, watches it speed toward the sewer. The sky overhead is crisp, blue. Benny takes off in the direction of the filling station where he works. This neighborhood is where he grew up. He knows it like his fingers: the hardware store, sundries, library, grocery, dry goods. He grins, remembering how his daddy will sometimes still say *warsh* and *rinch* for *wash* and *rinse*. His mother says *libr'y* for *library*, *okrie* for *okra*, *dinner* for the noon meal. Benny thinks how the generation that raised him still has one foot in the country, how his granddaddy's church is like a pep rally—all those hands flying up, *touchdown!* He jams his hands in his jeans pockets, walks fast, staring at the sky, trying to think loftier thoughts than making love to a freedom rider in his mother's hotel.

The Sinclair station is right below the railroad tracks that separate the old neighborhood from the new. Crestwood, the new subdivision, is over the tracks, up the hill, into the forest that's being demolished. Progress, Benny thinks. He stares up at the station's green dinosaur logo, lamenting anew the school mural's message, though he has no idea what it all means in the long haul. All he knows is that Birmingham is a city on fire. Dirty, mean, hateful. *I'm into the arts,* he hears himself telling Angel.

His boss, Mr. Kysor, is at his desk inside the station, playing with his coin collection. Mr. Kysor reminds Benny of a scarred-up Bob Hope. He's got a face marked with war but a big, friendly way. Pete's told Benny that Kysor was burned in combat. It makes Benny uneasy. It makes him think things he doesn't want to think, like how he'd refuse to fight in a war. It's inconceivable, throwing away your life like Pete had to do, all for the sake of patriotism.

Benny and a colored guy named Skipper run the place while Kysor studies copper pennies under a magnifying glass and reads the newspaper. "Benny," he says when Benny clocks in, so to speak. There's not a timepiece in sight, but Kysor calls it clocking in. Kysor likes to think of himself as an entrepreneur.

Today, his newspaper is spread over his coins. Kysor prides himself in getting a fresh-off-the-press copy of the nightly news.

"Look here," Kysor says to Benny.

Kysor's gnarled finger points to a series of photographs. "Do you know any of these men?" the paper asks. It's the men from the bus incident. Benny stares hard, but he can't recall the faces from Sunday. "I was there," he says to Kysor and lights a Marlboro.

"Say what?"

"I was there," Benny repeats and leans against the wall. The inside of Mr. Kysor's gas station is home to a desk, chair, and *Field & Stream* calendar. The walls are painted chartreuse.

Kysor is half deaf. He holds a hand to his ear. Benny gets close.

"I said I was there, at the Trailways station. On Sunday. I was there. I saw it," he shouts.

"So you recognize any of these men?" Kysor presses.

"No," Benny says.

Benny takes off his jacket. He's wearing his mechanic's shirt. He sees that Skipper's gone in the truck. A service call. Skipper, the colored guy, takes all the service calls. Skipper is a real mechanic. He's tried to teach Benny to be one, but there have been moments, like when Benny drained all the transmission fluid from a racked car when he was trying to change the oil. "Can't you see what color it is?" Skipper yelled. It was, Benny knew, a bit golden for dirty oil. Once Benny poured too much gas into the carburetor to prime it; it ignited and shot fire up, burning the hood. Skipper looked on incredulously. But the worst was when a metal radiator cap blew off, releasing a jet of hot antifreeze which ricocheted off the open hood and onto Benny's shoulder, burning it so badly they had to call a doctor. Benny wonders what Skipper does when he leaves the station at dark. He is a thin boy, all spidery in the way that certain coloreds are, Benny's noticed. A rubbery quality that makes for a fast sprinter, a God-bred athlete. It's a kind of sensuality that Benny broaches only on the grounds that he understands what made Greeks worship the male body.

The garage is empty. Benny sits on the ledge beside the pumps, studying the sky. Dusk is coming. The spring rain has washed the sidewalks clean. The service station, set up where the railroad tracks begin, gives Benny a view of the neighborhood of merchants as they close the hardware store, the drugstore, the post office.

Tornado season, Benny thinks.

They come funneling up from Tuscaloosa here in spring. You never know what's going to happen at five o'clock in May. Any moment, the radio might blast a warning. Angel. He can't shake her. He's never seen a girl with hair like hers. It's matty and thick and looks like she doesn't brush it. Skipper's black truck bounces over the railroad tracks. When it arrives beside the pump, Skipper hops from the cab. He's wearing baggy pants, a greasy T-shirt.

"Hey, man," he says to Benny.

Benny gets up.

"What's happening?" Skipper asks.

"Nothing."

Skipper wipes his brow with his forearm. Benny hands him a Marlboro. They like to smoke. They like to stand beside the pump island under the green dinosaur, growing hungry for dinner. It's the first job Benny's had, but he already understands the camaraderie of a work ethic. Benny is dying to mention Angel, but if he does he'll have to admit he was at the bus station, and he can't bring himself to do it. He wonders what terms like *freedom rider* and *integration* and *Bull Connor* mean to Skipper. They don't have conversations, in a way. It's all Marlboros under the stars, flat tires, Roy Orbison—Skipper's falsetto version of "Cryin." But Benny can't help it; he spills the beans the moment Skipper lights up, wrapping his mouth over the cigaret's tan.

"I met a girl," he tells Skipper.

Skipper smiles. In the mauve light, he's all teeth. Benny glances back at Kysor, who's turned on a gooseneck lamp. He wonders if Skipper reads the newspaper. It never dawns on him that Skipper can't read, that he is, in fact, fifteen years older than Benny, that he's the father of five kids, that he has a wife named Lucretia, that he knows every single thing happening in Birmingham, that he sings gospel at church, has experienced Pentecost, drinks Jack Daniel's, has a junkyard, loves his mother, and wishes Bull Connor would take a slow boat to China.

"She an outside agitator?" Skipper says, grinning.

Benny's heart races. Why did he know to say that?

Skipper picks up a wrench, turning it over and over. Benny looks at the hardware store owner closing for the night. He's bent up, a hunchback. It makes Benny uncomfortable in the same way that Kysor's burnt face does. It makes him want to go to college, forget home. He isn't sure what to say to Skipper. Finally, he looks him squarely in the eyes. It's one of Benny's better habits— cutting the mustard. "Yes," he says. "She's an outside agitator. She's a freedom rider. My mother took her in Sunday, at the hotel. You know I told you we're living at my mother's hotel."

"Sho nuff," Skipper says.

"She's got light hair but looks like she ought to be colored," Benny says, staring into the dark of Skipper's irises. Skipper taps his palm with the wrench.

"You want her bad," he says—a statement, not a question. "I mean bad," he says, and Benny feels himself drowning in this. When Skipper says it, it carries weight. A car pulls up to the island. It's a lady with a hat, a red hat. She says to Benny, "Ethyl. Fill it with ethyl, sugar," then fumbles in the purple folds of her pocketbook for a wad of bills. Benny pumps while Skipper lifts the hood of her Ford. His nappy scalp disappears under it.

Kysor emerges from the station, leaning on a cane.

"Helen," he greets the customer.

She's a regular. Her husband works at the foundry with Pete. She asks Benny how his daddy is doing. He says fine and washes her windshield with a dab of gasoline. It's the best way to clean glass, according to Skipper. When she leaves, Benny and Skipper drive the pickup over to Birmingham Manufacturing. It's a peculiar operation, a huge monster of a cinder-block plant up on a hill overlooking the railroad crossing. Benny's never been inside. His job is to pick up one hundred metal rims and valve stems in order to make tires over at the service station. They're always mysteriously stacked on a particular area by the plant entrance, as if a fairy left them there. They will return to the station, where a hundred tires have arrived on a Ross Neeley truck. Benny assumes he's part of a cycle, an absentee assembly line, and that the tires—once he and Skipper have put them together and returned them to the manufacturing plant—will then be used for trucks. But this is all guesswork. Benny doesn't understand production. When he visits Pete's foundry, he stands away from the dragon's fire, wondering how Pete can love to make valves and fittings.

Benny and Skipper return with the rims and valve stems, and stack pyramids. They work silently, using a ratchet to screw valve stems in, a tire mounting machine to put lubricant around the tire. Using a metal bar, they pop the tire in place. It grows darker and darker until there are stars, a moon, and a caravan of headlights in the distance, coming over the viaduct, where they make pig iron. Benny's knows it's what's made in Birmingham, but he's never asked what pig iron is. It's always conjured up burnt offerings and snake-handling practices he associates with his mother's coming of age. Pig iron is stored in the place where nightmares are made. *I'm more into the arts,* he says once again, inwardly, to Angel.

"You might have her," Skipper says.

Benny doesn't know what he'd do with her if he got her. It's hardly a physical thing. "It's cerebral," he says to Skipper, liking the way the word sounds.

They load the pickup with the completed tires and head back to the plant. In the dark, Benny studies Skipper's profile—a night predator, he thinks.

"You have a bad habit of lust?" Benny asks.

"Do *what?*" Skipper says.

"Lust," Benny repeats.

Skipper hangs an elbow from the window. "You mean women?" he asks.

"Yeah, women."

"I be a bad sort of man if I didn't," Skipper says.

"But I'm talking about even the ones who aren't pretty, even the ones you'd never really do it with, the ones who're older."

"Do I be wanting all of them?"

"Yeah."

"Don't every man?"

Benny shrugs. He feels his shark's tooth lanyard against his skin. He was in a play with a girl named Sinny, rumored to be Scandinavian. During library, he studied a globe. Running his fingers over the Kjølen Mountains, which separated a purple Norway from a yellow Sweden, he'd get crazy with desire for her. Benny wonders why you feel this way about people you're in a play with. He feels like he's in a play with Angel.

Skipper stops at a traffic light.

"You say she looks like she's colored?" Skipper says.

Benny thinks of her frizzy blond curls. "Well, they say her father's Mexican."

"Who says that?"

"She does," Benny tells him. Skipper puts the truck in gear, and it spits and resists. It's an old pickup. It isn't meant to travel more than a ten-mile radius.

"You believe her?" Skipper asks, and the truck finally lurches forward.

Benny turns to him. "Why shouldn't I?"

"You say she's a outside agitator."

Benny's confused. He doesn't understand racial politics. He can't tell if Skipper is on the side of the outside agitators or not. They go up the hill to the manufacturing plant, hoping that no tires will escape the truck's bed. "Women got passports these days," Skipper tells him.

"What?"

Skipper grins in the dark. "You know, they be in-cog-ni-to," he says. "Yeah, they be doing all kinds of things these days." Skipper chuckles. Benny isn't sure what he means. He sounds like Mr. Connor, talking this way.

Back at the service station, Benny helps gather up the day's charge slips, which are clothespinned in a metal box. Kysor makes the night deposit over at the bank, and they lock up. Skipper begins his trek along the railroad track to up where the colored people live.

Benny takes the bus to the hotel. It runs along where the old streetcar used to run. He gets off at the blue awning. In the café, his mother is serving pork chops, rice, and peas to Gracie and Pete. The other guests—only a sprinkling—are beside the window. At night, the café serves only to boarders.

Dinah leaps from her chair.

"Hi, hon," she says, surveying his dirty self. She always greets him like she does Pete, with an eye for laundry, injury, or hurt pride.

Benny sits at the table and grabs a handful of napkins from the silver dispenser. Dinah serves him a plate of food along with a basket of hot rolls. He jabs a pat of butter, thinking how he's the only guy in town who gets restaurant butter every day—perfect, tiny squares.

"How was school?" Dinah asks him.

"Fine," he says, cutting up the pork chop.

Gracie passes him the catsup. They can, between the two of them, eat an entire bottle of Heinz if Dinah's fixed something like hamburger steak or fried shrimp.

"She's upstairs," Gracie says to him, as if he asked.

He shrugs, sets his Marlboros on the table, and takes a huge bite of rice and peas. Pete turns on his transistor radio. A local newsman says, "Birmingham police arrested an Alton man early today on charges in connection with gang attacks on a group of CORE integrationists at the Trailways bus terminal Sunday." He reports that the man gave the police a statement in which he admitted he was in a group that beat up bystanders and riders, that he was being held on charges of assault, that he said the Ku Klux Klan had called him and asked him to be at the terminal on Sunday.

Pete shakes his head. Dinah cuts fat from her pork chops. Gracie pours a river of catsup on her peas. Dinah says to her, "That's enough catsup, sweetheart."

Pete turns his baseball cap backwards. "Got a game tonight?" Benny asks him. Pete says no, just practice, but there will be one Friday night. Benny wonders if they can afford to send him to a college up North, where they have girls with blond crinkly hair, no Negro problems, a good drama department. Time's running short.

"Jesus," Pete groans.

Benny looks up.

Pete's staring out the window. Benny turns to see Connor's car parked on the yellow line. He's talking into a car phone. "Car fifty-four, where are you?" Gracie sings.

Pete grimaces. "I wish it was just a TV show." He looks at Dinah. "You've just got to do something."

Benny runs his roll through the pork chop gravy. They love to argue over Connor. They've been doing it for as long as he can remember.

Dinah's bracelets clink against her iced tea. "I can't make him do anything, Pete," she says. "This is a public place."

"We own it," he argues.

"Gracie, see if those guests need more tea," Dinah says.

Gracie gets up.

Pete sighs long and hard. Benny knows his father. In a minute, Pete will take off his baseball cap, run his hand quickly over his hair, put it back on, then the table will start vibrating from the jiggling of his legs. Benny thinks Pete needs a vacation; he's been staring too long at valves, fittings, orange fire, and sweating Negroes. He needs a trip to Florida, where the turquoise ocean makes a high tide, where shells, starfish, bikinis, tropical colors are everywhere. He needs a trace of whatever it was that made him marry a nut like Dinah.

Dinah is opening the door for Mr. Connor.

His cigar smoke blows in the wind.

"Is she making him leave?" Benny whispers to Pete. Pete's legs are going ninety miles an hour under the table, making the plates shake. "Calm down," Benny tells him. He is sure he'll never get himself in this kind of pickle once he's grown. He's leaving this city. He gets up, puts a nickel in the jukebox, and selects "The Lion Sleeps Tonight." Connor gently nudges Dinah aside and heads straight for Benny. "What does that song mean?" he demands, his fat belly bulging dangerously close to Benny's plate. Gracie sings along with it, grinning at Connor: "In the jungle, the mighty jungle, the lion sleeps tonight." Connor tries her. "What does that mean?" he says, pulling up a chair next to Pete. Pete gets up, carries his empty plate to the sink behind the counter. "What lion, what jungle?" he beseeches Gracie. "What village, what quiet village?" Benny studies Connor's face. The man looks particularly concerned, almost in a state of panic, as if he's just heard an awful piece of news.

Gracie shrugs. Her brown bangs have grown over her eyes. Benny keeps forgetting how old she is. He thinks she's twelve, but maybe that's not right. She may be thirteen.

"Dinah," Connor calls, "what're they saying in that song? They're talking about a lion in a jungle. The lion's asleep. What does it mean?" he asks a journalist who's just come down from upstairs. "Sugarfoot," Connor says to him, "what's that song saying, Sugarfoot? Benny, you watch Sugarfoot on television? This fellow is his i-dentical twin. You know they say we all got a i-dentical somewhere in the world."

Connor has moved behind the counter, where Pete is washing the dishes, his baseball cap over his eyes. The journalist is studying a menu. Benny wishes he hadn't put on the song, but what's done is done. He finishes up his dinner and heads for the family suite. He takes the steps two at a time, catches his breath as he steps onto the Oriental rug in the hall. He knows this feeling. He's felt it in basketball games, or when he's getting caught, or right before an altar call at church. He can't stop breathing hard. He's going to hyperventilate. He knocks on Gracie's door. When Angel opens it, she is wearing a long T-shirt with, he thinks, only panties underneath. It dawns on him that she isn't his age. He studies her dancing eyes—the eyes of a sociopath, a liar. He hears Connor's voice saying, "She works for the FBI." Words like *undercover, espionage, sabotage,* and *danger* enter his mind. He thinks of James Bond, 007, private eyes, and things like this. But once her face bends to smile, it all evaporates. She is a runaway, Del Shannon's "little runaway." He thinks all she needs is for him to kiss her.

"Have you eaten?" she asks him.

"Yes."

He feels his heart going. She's smiling at him like she'd like to do something to him. She is taking him all in. For a brief second, they stand here like this. Angel inches to him as if narrowing the lens, exploring a tiny piece of his eye, growing microscopic in her probe of it, until she seizes the speck. Benny can't quit staring at her lips, all drawn up in a haughty petulance. Her mother is German, father Mexican. She's a government informant, a scared girl. A freedom rider, a runaway slave. A Yankee, a Southerner. A potpourri of mixed messages. "Come on in," she says. He quickly closes the door behind him. Her hair is unruly and for the first time he sees how honey-colored it is. She walks over to the vanity. She stands by the mirror and he looks at her legs. They're dark and sculpted, like a swimmer's or a gymnast's, one of those girls you see on the Olympics from somewhere on the other side of the world, like Romania.

"I think I'd better throw on some jeans," she says.

His back is to the door.

He can't think what to say.

She opens a drawer and gets her jeans. They're black, and he watches her tug them up her thighs and button them at the waist. She tucks her T-shirt in and says, "Let's sit on the floor."

"Are you in college?" he asks her. He knows it's a stupid question, but he can't think what else to say.

Her eyes dart to the ceiling. "Most of the time," she says and looks at his lips.

"Where?"

"In the East."

He knows he's supposed to know what this means. He thinks of Massachusetts and New York and places like Delaware and Maine that he knows are either too far up or too far down. He can't pin the tail to the right place on the map.

They are sitting on an intricately patterned Asian rug. Her legs are crossed, and he sees that she's wearing a band of leather on her wrist. He wonders if it means anything. "What does Bull Connor think of me being here?" she asks him. He doesn't know what to tell her. "Is he a close friend of your parents?"

"Yes, he is," Benny tells her.

He hears somebody coming up to the stairs. He tells her he better be going. He walks out into the hall, but there's no one in sight. He thinks of going back into the room with her, but he can't take but a little of her at a time.

He goes downstairs and back into the café, aware of his body, aware of what the sight of her standing there in that T-shirt did to him.

Connor is at the table drinking a cup of coffee and smoking his cigar. He studies Benny. And as if he knows everything that's going through Benny's mind, he says, "I think she's a Negro." It takes him by surprise. It's not that it's a different angle. It's just Connor saying it that makes it streetlike and dirty. He can't forget it. Gracie's put on that stupid song "Big Bad John." Sugarfoot is asking Connor if he's here at the hotel to protect the freedom rider. Connor says she isn't a freedom rider; she's working at the café, can't he see? Benny walks outside to smoke a cigaret. He wishes he'd gone with Pete to play ball. He'd like to sit in his old backyard, over by the foundry, where he can see the lights of the company field. The men run under the lights, abide by the rules of the game, in the natural order of play. They are friends, a company team, a family. Benny loves the blue-and-white uniforms, dust coming up like an apron when your daddy steals home.

5

Gracie hates current events the same way she hates having periods. It all makes her long for days gone by. She sits staring at a newspaper photograph of the WAPI News director, who was dragged from his car at the bus terminal. Gracie hates the sight of the picture. The reporter's face shows through a shattered windowpane that looks like spider web.

"Gracie," her teacher calls.

Gracie's teacher is old and wears gigantic black shoes that remind Gracie of *The Wizard of Oz*. Gracie is popular. Boys like her. All the girls think she's got a wonderful mother. They're dying to stay at the hotel. So what's wrong? she thinks as her eyes travel from the window to her teacher. "My current event is the fight at the Trailways station last Sunday," she says. This is, of course, everybody's current event. Birmingham is a current event. Living in this city is beginning to make Gracie feel like she needs a bath.

"I was there actually," she says and feels the eyes of her classmates take her in. "I saw this man get dragged from his car," she says. Her best friend, Melissa Carpenter, whirls to her. Gracie hasn't told her any of it. She hasn't told anyone until today. Gracie reads the newsman's statement from the paper: "I was a witness and a victim of violence yesterday in Birmingham. It happened in broad daylight. They dragged me out of the car. They tried to blackjack me. And to keep the public from knowing what was happening, they tore the microphone out of my two-way radio unit."

"Does anyone have a question for Grace?" her teacher asks. The class is quiet, the cloakroom door ajar.

"Did you see any coloreds get beat?" a boy asks Gracie.

"Yes," she replies.

Gracie doesn't elaborate. It's something she's learned at the café: smart people answer a journalist's question with only yes or no.

"Other questions?" her teacher presses. A plane roars overhead. Gracie's school is near the airport. They hear every single takeoff and landing. The children here are mostly foundry kids who've grown up watching their fathers wash up at dusk from a day's work then hit baseballs. Their mothers play bridge at the company hall on Friday nights.

"Did you get hit?" Melissa Carpenter asks. Melissa is wearing a boy's ID bracelet. She has taught Gracie how to close your eyes as you're being kissed.

"No," Gracie says.

"Did you think you were going to?" Melissa asks.

"Yes," Gracie lies.

"Wow," Melissa says, and the others echo it.

According to Melissa's dentist, thirteen-year-old girls are like ripe fruit. You can blow air on a prepubescent girl's gums and they'll bleed, the dentist told Melissa's mother. That's just how horrible the hormonal storm is. Gracie hates this kind of talk among grown-ups.

Gracie watches her teacher's crabby face drawing up like a raisin. "A scene of mob violence is no place for children," she says, and Gracie knows her current event has gone too far.

107

"We have a freedom rider at our hotel," she says.

The other kids are backwards, sideways, all over their desks in a struggle to hear every word.

"Her name is Angel," Gracie says. Her teacher has turned to the blackboard. She is writing a homework assignment. She wants Gracie to be quiet, yet she is hungry for gossip. Her name is Imogene Fields. She is only fifty-seven—though the kids think she's old. She's voted for Bull Connor every time he's run for public office, and she has a colored washwoman who chews Dentyne and has never—Imogene Fields brags—stolen a penny from her. Imogene Fields has taught seventh grade since 1931. Today, she writes this on the chalkboard: "Geography test Friday." She brushes yellow chalk dust from her charcoal-color skirt and looks at Gracie.

"Well, we're just full of news, aren't we?" she says.

"Yes ma'am."

Gracie gathers up her things. They're allowed to use cartridge pens. The desks' inkwells are empty.

When the bell rings, they all clamor for the hallway.

Melissa Carpenter takes Gracie's arm. Melissa has on raspberry lip gloss. "Why didn't you tell me?" she whispers. "What is a freedom rider, anyhow?" They walk past the lunchroom, lockers, and out the door into the May sun.

Gracie stands under the oak tree beside the playground and tells Melissa that Angel is part of a group, that she doesn't shave her legs, that Mr. Connor thinks she works for the government, and that Melissa needs to spend the night with her Friday. Melissa's boyfriend, Jake Harrison, is standing there. Gracie likes his dark eyes. He plays baseball, builds model airplanes, and wrestles with boys—but all the time he's wanting Melissa.

"Kiss her," Gracie says. The words are out of her mouth before she understands why she's said it. She just knows what Jake is standing there wanting to do, and she feels sorry for him. Gracie has kissed Melissa, practicing for boys. Melissa's like a juicy bite of watermelon.

Kiss her. The moment the words have been said, Melissa is laughing and turning pink in the face, "Gracie," she says, "please. This is a public place." Gracie knows this. She lives in a public place. It's the fact that this *is* a public place that makes her want trouble.

Jake Harrison is staring at Gracie, his army knapsack lopsided like his grin. All his hopes are pinned on Gracie's instructions to Melissa. Gracie takes in the playground, the rusty fence, home plate, and the blue dome of sky over it all. "Your skin is made for July," Melissa told her as they lay on big cheetah beach towels at the city pool last year.

Gracie takes Jake's arm. "Kiss her," she says.

Jake drops his knapsack.

Melissa wipes off her raspberry lip gloss with the back of her hand.

Jake's green eyes are wild in the afternoon sun. Gracie takes a stick of Wrigley's spearmint gum from her purse. When she gets home, she'll change into jeans. She's decided she's going to carry things in her back pocket like Angel. She's starting to get a mental picture of the kind of girl she wants to be, riding a horse under a Midwestern sky, maybe in the direction of the Sierra Nevadas. She thinks that she might marry a foreigner, a guy with a ticket to the Orient. She saw the movie *Around the World in Eighty Days.* In the song, it says, "No more will I go all around the world, for I have found my world in you." That's too romantic; that makes it like love is enough. Gracie thinks, as she stands here waiting for Jake Harrison to kiss Melissa Carpenter, that she's not going to settle for love. She's going to be a freedom rider.

A breeze makes the oak leaves flutter against the sky. Jake's lips are taking Melissa's. Gracie's knees buckle. "You must remember this, a kiss is just a kiss," she hears her mother singing as their Chevy speeds over the viaduct at sunset, but Gracie knows it's a lie. A kiss isn't just a kiss as time goes by. A kiss grows and blooms and sends its roots deep and lingers and makes you want more. When you're thirteen and have only a bouquet of kisses to remember, a kiss isn't just a kiss, a sigh a sigh, and the fundamental things don't apply as time goes by.

"There's your mother," Melissa whispers. Dinah has driven up in the Chevy and her holiness hair is blowing free. Jake picks up his knapsack. He's got a military grin—a general saluting her. "Thanks," he'll say when he calls Gracie this evening.

When they arrive back at the hotel, Gracie sits in the café and reads her geography homework. It's a chapter on "cultural islands"—beginning with a people called the Amish who live up in Pennsylvania, Ohio, and other parts of the Midwest. They drive buggies, plow land, and don't marry into the world. Gracie finds this—for geography—interesting. She bites her pencil eraser and stares at Dinah, who is behind the café counter, stirring a pot of vegetables with a wooden spoon. Dinah's wearing bluebird earrings that fly when she moves. She tastes a carrot.

Gracie is trying not to eavesdrop on a conversation Angel is having on the café's pay phone, but it's hard. Angel's got a husky, crisp way of carrying on a conversation.

Angel is leaning against the wall in dark pants, a T-shirt that's got *Kingston Trio* written on it. Gracie can't conceive of Angel in Bermuda or Jamaican shorts. She knows Angel has thrown away all her circle pins, if she ever had any, all her monograms, pedal pushers, Frankie Avalon records. The idea of Angel crooning over "Venus, if you will, please send a little girl for me to thrill" is simply out of the question.

Dinah comes from behind the counter. "I've moved her from your room," she whispers. "She's in seven, next to Sugarfoot." Neither Gracie nor Dinah can remember to call the journalist by his real name, Beau Sleigh. They've heard Connor call him Sugarfoot for three days now, and it's one of those things they can't shake. He is Sugarfoot, and whenever Gracie lays eyes on him, she thinks, *Cattle roping, easy loping Sugarfoot. Carefree as a tumbleweed, a-rolling along with a rifle and a song, just a fight for right and wrong with a Bible and a book about the law.* The real Sugarfoot on TV's got it made. A lawyer cowboy. It's an idea, all right—Gracie pictures herself on the horse, carrying her education smugly into the sunset.

"What is it, baby?" Dinah says to her.

She's lost in the Sugarfoot fantasy.

Dinah takes Gracie's hand. "You all right?"

"I'm fine," Gracie says.

"Tell me," Dinah urges. The ceiling fan is blowing, cooling the place. The black-and-white tile floor is scrubbed to perfection. The stew smells nice.

"Tell you what?"

"Whatever's on your rambling mind," Dinah says.

Gracie points to the photograph of the Amish family in her geography book. They're standing beside a log cabin with aqua-colored curtains. Gracie tells her mother that the color signifies purity. She says they don't have TV or radios or washing machines; they don't even know the world's news. Dinah says, "It sounds wonderful, doesn't it?" They talk over the pros and cons of cultural islands and what culture means, and in the middle of it Angel slams down the phone. She sits at the table between Gracie and Dinah, catching the drift of their conversation.

"Don't you think Birmingham is a cultural island?" she asks. "Or more like an archipelago. An archipelago unto itself?"

Gracie racks her brain for what an archipelago is.

"Well, if you'd lived here, you'd understand it more," Dinah says.

Angel's raises an eyebrow, as if to say, "Oh, yeah?"

"You have to be a native," Dinah says to her.

"My friends are in jail," Angel says. She looks at Gracie. "Your Mr. Connor's holding them there *for their protection*, as he says. Police took them into custody after *Southern* bus drivers refused to take them out of the Greyhound station. It makes me want to kill."

"This isn't the group you came in with, am I right? This is the new group that arrived today?" Dinah asks.

"Yes, that's right," Angel says, looking inquisitively at Dinah.

Dinah glances at her nails.

"Well?" Angel demands.

"Well what, hon?"

"Well, so what do you mean by that—that it isn't my group?"

Gracie knows what Dinah means. It's the question that's been forming in her mind. Why is Angel still here? Why didn't she leave when her group left? Is she afraid? Is she having fun? Is she in trouble? Is she—what? Is she, like Connor says, working for the government?

Dinah shakes her hair way back, making her bluebirds rise. "People here feel that the country uses us as a scapegoat. It's all got to do with the steel industry, the way Northern wealth swooped in to buy cheap industry labor years ago."

She is, Gracie knows, quoting Connor.

Angel's eyebrow is up. "Tell me," she says, "can't people change?" Dinah gets up to stir the vegetables. She seasons them with a rain of salt and a half stick of butter. She cuts an onion, which makes her eyes swim. She can slice, chop, mince faster than lightning. Gracie wonders if she'll be able to perform these culinary maneuvers like her mother, if she will learn to sort colors and wash and mend socks and make people happy.

"Yes," Dinah pronounces as if finally conjuring up a reply to Angel's question. "Yes, they can change, but they don't, they won't, if they feel like somebody's trying to make them change. You, of all people, ought to understand this, hon," Dinah says, gesturing to Angel with her wooden spoon.

Gracie hasn't heard Dinah challenge Angel like this. It isn't the pleasing-the-public attitude of a hotel operator, and it is in this moment that Gracie knows Angel isn't a guest anymore.

Sugarfoot comes in and Dinah greets him warmly.

He's wearing a backpack, like a Boy Scout.

"What do you know?" Angel asks him, straddling the stool beside Sugarfoot's. Her legs dangle, knocking up against the silver bar.

"Your buddies are in jail," he tells her, raking a hand through his blond curls.

"Right," she says.

"News travels fast," he says, sipping the mug of coffee Dinah's just set in front of him. "They just jailed them a few minutes ago." Sugarfoot didn't shave this morning. His face is dotted with dark gold stubble. Gracie watches Dinah kneading dough for yeast rolls. Her fingers work up and down, press, fold.

"Did you see a black guy named Jet?"

"Jet who?" Sugarfoot asks.

"That's his last name," Angel says.

"Who is he?" Sugarfoot wants to know, taking a pen from his pocket. Angel readjusts her belt buckle, stares at Sugarfoot. She's not going to answer this question.

Nobody says a word. There's the tapping of Angel's boots against the silver bar, Dinah's stew simmering, Sugarfoot sipping coffee. Otherwise the café is quiet.

Finally, Angel takes her wallet from her pants pocket and shows Sugarfoot a picture of Jet. It's like a school photo. Gracie's never seen a color photo of a colored boy.

"Never seen him," Sugarfoot says. "Who is he?" he presses her.

Angel jams her wallet in her back pocket. Sugarfoot watches her. Gracie wonders if he thinks Angel acts like a boy. She wonders if he thinks Angel is cute.

Sugarfoot says to Dinah, "Connor is checking with attorneys to see if Fred Shuttlesworth can be charged with inciting to a breach of peace."

"For what?" Dinah asks, pressing her hands against the dough ball.

"For telling the world that the new riders were coming today."

"Jesus," Dinah replies.

Sugarfoot smiles at her.

"Connor's a friend of the family's?" Sugarfoot queries.

Dinah gives Sugarfoot her eyes. "He was a friend of my mother's," Dinah tells him.

"When this was a brothel," Sugarfoot says.

Dinah puts her fingers in a bin of Crisco. "Uh huh," she says and prepares the baking sheet for rolls. Gracie is at the table. She wonders where Sugarfoot's going with all this.

"She was a redhead. Men cried when she died," Dinah says. Gracie is glad her daddy isn't here. It drives him crazy for Dinah to say things like this to boarders.

"When did she die?"

"Nineteen thirty-five."

"How old were you?"

"Twelve."

Sugarfoot stares at the Formica countertop. His legs are hugging the stool's base. The afternoon light is throwing a spirit of peace over the café. Gracie walks over to the jukebox and punches in the Platters' "Smoke Gets in Your Eyes." She stares out the window. She thinks of all Benny's told her, how love gets in your eyes.

She walks outside. The sky is starting to change colors. This time of day makes her homesick for something she can't name. She sits on the steps under the awning.

Connor's black car moves slowly up the street, the chrome work catching the final rays of sun left in the sky. She thinks of running away—into the café, up the stairway to her room. But Connor suddenly accelerates as if chasing a lawbreaker, and she is frozen. His car screeches to a halt, and he jumps from the driver's seat. Hiking his pants legs, he plops down beside her. "Good day at school?" he asks her, breathing hard.

She stares at his shiny shoes.

"Fine," she shrugs.

"Mama cooking a good dinner?"

She shrugs.

"Got a favor to ask you, Gracie," he says, and she glances up for a peek at his glass eye.

"Want you to find out Angel's real name for me, honey."

Gracie runs her hands in her bangs, pulling them to the left side. Connor puts a hand on her shoulder. "You're a big girl now, and you can be a big help to city government. These are important times we're living through, and history's happening right in this place," he tells her, pointing his cigar back to the hotel.

He gets back in his car and drives off, leaving a trail of smoke.

That night, when the moon's up, she sits in the café, holding the pay phone, talking to Jake Harrison. He tells her he's going to ask Melissa to go steady. Gracie says, "I thought you already had. She's wearing your ID." Jake tells her that was just a token, that he'll give her his YMCA football jersey for the summer. Jake says he can't do his homework for thinking of Melissa. Gracie tells him the geography chapter is interesting; it's on cultural islands. Jake says he hates things like that. "Like what?" Gracie laughs. "Whatever you just said," Jake says to her. Gracie draws her leg up and runs a finger along her ankle. "When are you going to call her?" she wants to know. Jake says he will as soon as they hang up. There is silence. Jake is fixing to ask her a big question, she can tell. "What does she say about me?" he asks her. "She says your eyes make her melt," Gracie lies. She can feel Jake absorbing this. She loves the telephone.

The café is semidark.

"What are the rooms like in your hotel?" Jake asks.

Gracie tells him they have old furniture, fireplaces, and bedspreads the color of fruit. She says the halls are like a museum with Oriental rugs, timepieces, and nudes.

Jake says, "Cool." Gracie runs her hands up her legs. They're smooth as stones. She never nicks her shins like some girls do. "Melissa tastes like watermelon, doesn't she?" Gracie asks him.

"How do you know that?"

"I've kissed her."

"Why?"

"So she could practice, getting ready for you," Gracie says, then listens to Jake's silence. Gracie knows this about herself, that whatever she lacks in beauty, she makes up for in words.

Gracie hears footsteps and when she turns, it's Angel. Gracie tells Jake she has to go, puts the phone back, and moves her chair away from the wall back to the table.

"Your boyfriend?" Angel asks.

"Yes," Gracie lies.

Angel takes a chair backwards, the way Pete does. Resting her chin on the back of the chair, she studies Gracie's face. Gracie feels bad about lying, so she tells Angel the truth, that she's been talking to her best friend's boyfriend.

"Ah," Angel says. "Other people's love."

Gracie lets her eyes wander to the sidewalk, the sky, stars.

"Psychologists call it projection when we feel this way about other people," Angel whispers. Gracie is frozen. She isn't sure what Angel means, but she feels like she's been caught in an act of theft.

"What's his name?" Angel asks.

Gracie whispers, "Jake."

Angel puts a hand on hers. "Do you love Jake for Melissa, or do you love Melissa for Jake, sweetheart?" Angel puts her legs up on the table. She's barefoot like Gracie. "I don't love either one of them," Gracie says.

Angel nods. A few blond tendrils have escaped the black band and they're in her eyes. Gracie resists the urge to ask if she's had a Toni.

"So, what do you want to be when you grow up?" Angel asks.

They hear footsteps overhead. A few aeronautical engineers from Huntsville arrived after supper, and they're washing up for a night in Birmingham. Gracie runs a hand over her bangs. "A lawyer," she says.

"That's nice," Angel replies.

117

Gracie stares at her. "How did you chip your tooth?"

"A boy broke it with roller skates."

Gracie tries to picture this.

"His feet flew out from under him. I was sitting on the side-walk. He kicked me in the mouth. Wrong place at the wrong time," Angel says and smiles so that Gracie gets a view of the damage.

"Why don't you shave your legs?"

Angel draws up her capri pants leg. "Well," she says, studying the tiny golden hairs. "Let's see. If I shave my legs, I might cut myself, right?" She raises an eyebrow to Gracie. Gracie shrugs. "And then I have to ask myself, why am I doing this in the first place? Am I doing it for a man's hands? Am I doing it so I will distinguish myself as a girl? Am I doing it because the *culture* says I must? Am I doing it because my mother does it?" Angel leaves her leg exposed—a piece of evidence for the jury.

Gracie meets her eyes, says nothing.

"The answer to all these questions would be yes. Now, if I happen to hate razors and believe that shaved legs don't make a woman a woman, and if I think the culture is a crock of shit and my mother is a victim of it, then why should I do it?" Angel asks.

"Who is Jet?"

"Why did you ask me that?" Angel says, uncertainty falling like a curtain over her eyes. "Oh, I know, I know," she says, getting back her dignity. "You're going to be a lawyer. You listen to things. I like that."

Gracie smiles.

"Jet's a boy."

"Your boyfriend?"

"No," Angel replies. "Just a friend."

"Can I see that picture of him again?" Gracie asks, recalling the way it looked when she showed it to Sugarfoot.

"Don't have my wallet," Angel says and drums her squared fingernails on the tabletop. The café floor is cool under Gracie's bare feet. Breakfast plates are stacked, ready for dawn's light. Everything is in order.

Angel gets up, unlocks the café door, and steps into the dark night. You can see the park, library, City Hall, where Bull Connor is working overtime, talking to lawyers in his office. At the newspaper, an editorial writer is blasting Shuttlesworth for shouting fire. People are scurrying from this side to that side, unsure of which side they're even on anymore. Pete's tossing baseballs under the company lights. Benny's drinking a chocolate soda with Ginger Fortenberry and trying to forget freedom riders. Dinah is in her bedroom sewing a summer dress for Gracie, putting in the bodice seams that mark the place where Gracie's body is changing. Sugarfoot is trying to file a story. Gracie and Angel are standing on the yellow line where the sidewalk meets the gutter. It's the kind of night that makes people want to ask questions. "What did you call it?" Gracie asks, and before she can complete the question, Angel says, "Projection."

"And what is it?" Gracie asks.

Angel considers her reply. "When you put yourself so far into another person's shoes that you forget your own. Or something like that." She grins, hands on her snug hips. "The Magic City," she says, reading the sign over the terminal overpass. "What a strange thing to call this place." Her eyes scan the city like a spotlight. Gracie and Angel are quiet for a while, then Angel says, "I think we always fall in love for somebody else the first time. It makes it bearable." She puts her finger in Gracie's bangs and says, "Don't cut them." Gracie waits for more, but Angel turns back to the street.

"I'm going for a walk," she says.

"You shouldn't. It's dangerous."

"Who's going to get me?" Angel asks and zips up her cowgirl jacket.

Negroes, Gracie thinks.

"More likely to be Klansmen," Angel rejoins, as if she's read Gracie's thoughts. "Sure you don't want to come along?"

"You're barefoot," Gracie reminds her. She stares at Angel's naked feet. She wants to say, "You might step on broken glass," but she fears Angel will laugh.

"Barefoot in the park," Angel says to her. "It's a New York play. A love story. You'd love it. You're the type."

"What type am I?"

"A romantic. How old are you now?"

"Almost thirteen."

"You're so tall," Angel marvels.

Gracie watches Angel head for the park, barefoot. The fact that she is tiny makes her all the more interesting, and Gracie wants more than anything in the world at that moment to be short.

"Boys love long legs," Angel calls back over her shoulder.

I've heard that before, Gracie thinks as she locks the café door. Inside, the jukebox lights make the place a bit yellow-blue. All the guests have keys to let themselves in the main hotel entrance, under the awning. The idea hits her like a jolt: the master key. Gracie leaves the café, enters the hotel foyer, and opens the secretary drawer. The key is gold and says *Mstr*. Gracie holds the banister, traveling up the spiral case to the second floor. Nobody is in the hall. She considers an alibi. If she's caught by her mother, she'll say that Angel must have accidentally taken her this or that and she's just looking for it.

She puts the key in Angel's door. She knows every room of the hotel by heart. All her life she has changed these beds with her mother, parted the dark drapes, and stared at other people's things. "Don't ever touch anything that doesn't belong to you," Dinah taught her. The bedspread in this particular room is a salmon color, the drapes forest green. The wall tapestry is of a passing regiment of military officers who're making a social call on ladies in a manor courtyard replete with rose arbor, gazebo, teacups, and linden trees. They make Gracie's skin crawl, things like this. They make her realize just how common her family is.

Get out of here, her conscience tells her.

But right before she turns to leave, her eyes are drawn to the desk. On it is a notebook. She can't help it; she loves what people write. Other people's words are like love; you can't just turn the other way. She opens the notebook—it's red like her Nifty spirals. But inside, the paper is parched and formal like it belongs to a fancy business operation. Angel's handwriting is backward, the way left-handed people write. Angel has written this: "May 16, 1961. I think if I keep running, I can forget. I think Dinah knows. I haven't asked her much about herself, but we talk. Jet is mad, he sounds mad. I'm not going on to Jackson."

Remembering what Connor asked her to do, she starts to pick through the things in Angel's knapsack. There is a pack of Kools, a brush, Life Savers, and a wallet. Gracie opens it. The driver's license is right there. *Maria Juarez.* It is a California license, and Gracie gets a pencil from the desk to jot down the license number.

Gracie eases back to the door. On the way, she runs her fingers over the plaster of paris dove on the mantel. She lets her hands splay flat on the ivory walls and chenille bedspread. This is all her mother's place, and it is sacred. She doesn't know what it means, the things that Angel has written. The fact that other people have intimate conversations with her mother bothers her. Her mother belongs to her. But this is a public place, the hotel. It's like a bathroom or a bus terminal—people come, people go. She hates the hotel. She wants to be back in her old house by the foundry or the new house that's not even built. It's a mere blueprint, white etching on charcoal paper. It's the future, Pete has told the family. The old is past, the new is coming. But right now they're stuck in the hotel. She wishes she'd gone to baseball practice with her daddy.

6

The point of baseball is to get home, Pete tells Sugarfoot Saturday morning. He says it's the perfect sport for a twentieth-century culture that still fancies itself a nineteenth-century Midwest town. Sugarfoot thinks this is an interesting observation for a Birmingham foundry man to make. Sugarfoot likes Pete Fraley.

Sugarfoot can hardly think of himself as Beau Sleigh anymore. The moment he sets foot in the hotel, it's as if he's left his horse tied up at the cedar post under the awning. He is Sugarfoot, Dinah is Miss Kitty, Connor is Matt Dillon, Pete is Cheyenne, and the hell-on-wheels FBI informant is Annie Oakley. He has no reason to believe, of course, that Angel works for the government. That's just Connor talking.

"Dates back to ancient Egypt," Pete says and stirs his coffee. They're at the table by the window. It is almost ten, a bright sunny Saturday. A spring rain has washed the city.

"Didn't know that," Sugarfoot says.

"Balls and bats, I mean. Not necessarily baseball as we know it. They found some tombs with drawings of women taking swings. Seasonal cycles, fertility ritual, that sort of thing."

Sugarfoot nods.

"You play?" Pete asks.

"No. I used to run."

"Distance?"

"Sprint. What's the name of your company?"

"Harcort. We make valves, pipe fittings."

"You work in the foundry?"

"I run the grey iron unit."

"Got black men working there?"

Sugarfoot watches Pete's eyes wander to the window, take in the sidewalk, sky. Pete shakes his head, takes off his blue baseball cap, and slaps it on the tabletop. "Can't escape it, can you?" Pete asks.

Sugarfoot waits.

Pete looks him square in the eye. "Race," he clarifies.

Sugarfoot resists the urge to reach for his pencil. It's like all he does these days is resist urges. He resists saying he understands Pete's dilemmas. He resists saying he understands this city. He resists staring long and hard at Pete's wife.

Pete pops his knuckles.

The café is quiet. They don't serve anything but breakfast on Saturdays.

"Like the new job?" Pete asks him. "Like the paper?"

"It's good," Sugarfoot replies.

"Now, where did you come from, originally?"

"Iowa."

Pete frowns, his dark eyes drawing up. "Let's see," he says, and Sugarfoot can almost see the map of America in Pete's mind, Pete searching the purple and yellow Midwestern states for a clue, but they're all tiny squares in Pete's brain. Sugarfoot knows this is not a United States. It is a cluster of peculiar tribes who don't know anything but their own borders. When he left for the South, he didn't even know that Alabama brushed the Gulf of Mexico. Georgia, Tennessee, Mississippi—all one big glob of bigotry.

"Corn?" Pete asks.

Sugarfoot smiles. "That's right."

"Flat?"

"Yes."

"Farmers, Hawkeyes, stubborn." Pete's mind is starting to work, Sugarfoot can tell. He's trying to get a grip. Now he's put his baseball cap back on, and he's studying Sugarfoot as if he's seeing him just for the first time. "And you?" Pete asks.

"Farm boy," Sugarfoot tells him. It's a good thing to tell somebody in Alabama; it's an in.

Pete gets up for the coffeepot. He pours Sugarfoot a cup, gets a couple of donuts more from under the glass dispenser. He doesn't ask him if he wants these things, he just assumes he does. Sugarfoot knows Pete's going to trust him now. "So I guess you saw a lot of baseball, didn't you? Bet they played it in the open fields."

"That's right," Sugarfoot says, though in reality, he can't remember much baseball. Just seeds, plows, hogs, and various copulation and birthing scenarios. "What's Connor's deal with this girl who's staying here?"

Pete moves his chair back from the table.

"He thinks she's working for the government. What do you think?"

Sugarfoot shrugs. "Everybody's working for somebody."

"What do you mean?"

Sugarfoot sighs, taps his spoon on the table, and stares at the minarets of the train station. It's the thing he hates about his job—nobody can see the big story. He turns back to Pete. "This is a bad time for all of you here."

Pete stares at him.

"Equivalent of war, in some respects, wouldn't you say?"

Pete nods. Sugarfoot sees it all over his face—the jagged lines of midlife, the way things are taking a bad turn for Pete, how much he hates all this for his children.

"So, in these circumstances, you never know who's working for who, but you can count on it that everybody—in the political arena, I mean—is talking to somebody. I mean, there are sides, you know, in a war."

Pete's face is glued to Sugarfoot's. He is, Sugarfoot recalls, a pitcher. The key to pitching is control. He wrote for the sports page up in Des Moines for a season; he hated it. But some things come to him in this moment. Put your hip pocket in the hitter's face. Velocity, rotation, change of speed, deception with control: these are the pitcher's tools. It's the spin that makes a curveball curve, a slider slide, a sinker sink, a screwball screw, a fastball rise.

"I hate this," Pete says.

"I bet you do."

"I have a family."

Sugarfoot thinks of Pete's daughter with the bangs, of the teenage son who wears a black jacket, the mother who's handled snakes. *Did your wife actually pick up a snake?* he thinks but doesn't say.

"I don't like Connor," Pete says, and Sugarfoot quickens. He needs a pencil. He thinks of how it would look in his hand—the yellow painted wood, the lead tip.

"I don't like how he parks illegally," Pete says, and Sugarfoot thinks, A pitcher can't show emotion, nor can a manager. Think of the ball as an egg, don't grip it tight.

"I don't like his car here, all hours of the day and night. He was in love with my wife's mother. He thinks of himself as Dinah's father. I've often wondered if he was ever with her mother."

126

Sugarfoot nods. It's amazing, never ceases to be amazing what people will say to a reporter, how they'll spill it all, like they've never in their lives had a person who truly gave a damn until now.

How they'll say incriminating things, personal things, things they'll regret so hard they'll call you at three in the morning and beg you to stop the presses.

"I don't think it's right—separating the races like this. I take my daughter by one of those whites-only water fountains and I think I'm going to cry, the way she looks up at me with the big question."

Sugarfoot pictures Pete's daughter doing this.

"I wonder what she thinks of her mother's relationship with a man like Connor. I wonder if she thinks we agree with him. What she tells her friends. How she's going to see all this years from now."

And your son? Sugarfoot thinks.

"A boy's different," Pete says.

He's going to tell me I'd understand if I had one, Sugarfoot thinks.

"It's just different. If you had one, you'd know what I mean."

Sugarfoot nods.

Pete's legs are vibrating under the table. A small man has a better chance at a perfect swing. A big man will hit the ball farther, but a small man might make history, Sugarfoot knows.

"Are we just all over the place?" Pete asks.

Sugarfoot says, "What's that?"

"I mean, does the whole world know what's happening in Birmingham?"

"Yes."

Pete's eyes go for the window. Sugarfoot knows that Pete is thinking, Thanks to people like you, buddy; thanks to Midwestern journalists and Eastern liberals. But Pete can't help but keep talking. "Connor had an affair with his secretary ten years ago. They got caught here, in this hotel, in eight. That's the room you're in," Pete says with something akin to a smile.

Sugarfoot smiles back. It's the thing with these Southerners. They love a scandal more than they love life. They talk. They're such easy targets it makes you want to go easy.

"Got a game tonight. You ought to come," Pete says and walks behind the counter. "But then, you're not a sportswriter, are you?"

"Did it once. Hated it."

Sugarfoot watches Pete squirt detergent into the sink. He lets the suds grow big as grapefruits. He's staring at milk shake glasses, hot fudge sundae bowls, and the limeade machine. Pete is—Sugarfoot reasons—thinking of Bull Connor, of his daughter, of black men in foundries who have their own children, who're answering the same questions at the same water fountains. Sugarfoot thinks he ought to take his picture. It'd break your heart, if you had one. But there's no story here, not the kind you'd print in the paper.

Sugarfoot hears Dinah coming before he sees her.

"Hey," Pete says to his wife.

Dinah is wearing a summer dress.

"You get a kiss," she tells Pete.

Sugarfoot wonders why. It makes him want to be married. It makes him sad he didn't marry the woman named Tara in Iowa who played the dulcimer, fixed fried clams, and worked the metro desk. She had eyes the color of Dinah's dress—a pale green.

Pete is lost in the conversation they just had—Sugarfoot can tell. In a minute, he's going to pick it back up; he wants to say more. There's so much left in Pete to say.

"We were talking," he says to Dinah, gesturing to Sugarfoot. "We were discussing the situation." Sugarfoot likes words like this: the situation, the predicament, the problem. *El problema* they'd call it in a war-torn banana republic. People caught up in something like this refer to it in the most abstract and delicate of terms as if it might—itself—overhear its real name and rear its ugly head.

"We were talking about Bull."

It's the first time Sugarfoot has heard Pete call him Bull.

Dinah flings her long curls back. "Well," she says and leans over the counter, staring at Sugarfoot, "I bet you love this city, don't you, Sugarfoot?" Sugarfoot avoids her eyes. They're like quicksand.

"He's from Iowa," Pete tells her.

Dinah's summer dress is the color of party mints. She's got a swan neck, long arms—but what Sugarfoot can't forget is rattlesnakes. He's got it in his head she's got a murky side.

He takes a dollar from his wallet, but Pete stops him. "This isn't breakfast," Pete says. "This is on us."

"I massage Pete's pitching arm with wintergreen and alcohol," she tells Sugarfoot, as if this is germane. "He's a kept man."

Sugarfoot picks up his satchel and starts for the door. He knows they're trying to be friendly, to make him feel a part of the family.

"Don't you think she ought to tell Bull to go to hell?" Pete calls.

Sugarfoot turns.

This is where they draw him in, like a priest or a marriage counselor. People always do it. This is where they're going to let him see the only thing they've ever disagreed on.

They follow him out the door. Dinah's barefoot. Pete's carrying his cap in hand. They bend Sugarfoot's ear. They give him a

blow-by-blow of their blueprint—how the new home will have a
bay window. Dinah likes bluebirds, ruby-throated somethings;
the state bird is the yellowhammer, did he know that? Pete's got
a story of galvanized fittings coming from a zinc bath at the
plant—how a colored man was burned. There's one who works
for Pete who's never uttered a single word. Name is Nathan;
Pete's sure he's deaf. "Pete thinks he's supposed to learn sign language," Dinah says and puts a forearm up—the sun's higher
now. Pete jiggles change in his pocket. They're all staring at the
sidewalk. Sugarfoot wants to go, to get over to the pressroom.
They want him to linger. Dinah says there was a Negro cook,
Jasmine was her name, worked for her mother. "Her mother
was a prostitute," Pete reminds him. Dinah's eye catches
Sugarfoot's. She says something like, "You have these friends
who're Negro. You don't know what to do. What do you do with
this kind of thing? Is it really friendship? Can it ever really be?
How is it," she wants to know, "if you're not Southern? If you
don't have these awful prejudices?" Sugarfoot wants to take her
hand, but he doesn't.

"It's not just you," he says. "Yankees are sorrier than you
think."

For a moment, he forgets he's younger than Pete and Dinah.
He wants to offer them something, but there's nothing to give.
Pete flips a penny. It falls, tails, in his palm. Sugarfoot says he's
got to be going. "See you this evening," Dinah says. She knows he
needs to go. She's sorry they've kept him, is what her eyes say. But
they'd keep him all day, if he'd stay. They'd stand under the
awning of this hotel all night, trying to say why they're caught
like this—between homes for a summer. We won't always live like
this, they'd say, as if he were one of their children. They'd try to
tell him who, exactly, Bull Connor is and why they can't boot him

from the place. He's all tangled up in the past, they'd say, and we can't just turn our backs like that.

Sugarfoot takes the elevator down, not up. He likes this old newspaper building—its arches, precipices, and stuffiness. He takes the elevator to the basement press deck. He loves it here. The big half-moon lead plates; the way they put the cylinders on the press and lock up with a bullhorn; the bins of newsprint that weigh more than an elephant; freight elevator, reel room, mail room; the men wearing overalls and smoking cigarets. They're coal miners, Sugarfoot thinks as he watches the ink mist darken their faces like smoke—or black damp, to be more precise. These are the real guys, he thinks and finds himself despicable in comparison—a wimp, a writer. He sits on the stained floor, back against the wall, and waits. The presses will run in less than fifteen minutes. It's like sex, how fast they go, going, going, and gone. You can feel the vibration all over the newsroom. You can be at your desk, finger in a glue pot or writing a head on a piece of copy, and you can know they're going down there. It crawls up your legs, groin, spine, and brain and back down again, like orgasm—only better because it keeps on going until there are thousands and thousands of copy, of story, of print. And you know the ink is in your blood; it makes you want more, and you get more, day after day. It kills you and you keep coming because it's better than coming—the story. It's not the writing of it, it's the living of it. It's parachuting into the eye of a storm.

Today, the pressroom is hot. The men have the back door open, letting a shaft of light fall over the press. Once, Sugarfoot was sent to a scab school in Oklahoma when the printer's union at his paper was threatening to strike, but by the time he got back to Iowa, things were all over. Nonetheless, he got an education in hop type, lead plate molds, and ink mist. Now he stares at men who've all been treated for ruptured lumbar disks, hernias, and hip socket mishaps. He's never picked up a plate but he knows they're heavy. "This will all be obsolete someday," a journeyman once told him. He thinks of this often, though he can't see the future. It would break his heart if he could—the men in OSHA soundproof glass rooms, "quiet rooms," wearing earplugs and lab coats, staring passionlessly at machines that have replaced labor. But on this morning in May 1961, Sugarfoot is sitting cross-legged against an ink-stained wall, waiting for the presses to roll.

When they do, he closes his eyes.

He doesn't think a thing. He just lets the roar take him up like music. He knows the pages are passing quickly by, a series of incidents and accidents and births, marriages, deaths, sales, cartoons, and catastrophes. He wonders what God thinks of man's need to do this, to live it, print it, and read it. Newspapers end up in trash cans, incinerators, dumps, and the floors of bird cages, yet they are—somewhere—stored, saved, given to posterity. He gets up, waves at the printers, and takes the elevator up to the newsroom. A few reporters are playing crackaloo on the tile floor, spinning quarters to see who can get closest to the line. He's been at the paper for only a few weeks; he hardly knows anyone.

He goes directly to the morgue. It's on a kind of mini mezzanine overlooking the newsroom. It has one desk, hundreds of tiny drawers, and a counter. The librarian isn't here because it's Saturday, so he has to poke around to find what he needs. He searches the clipping files until he finds Connor, Eugene Theophilus "Bull." There are clippings upon clippings of the 1952 trial of Connor and his stenographer clerk, who were accused of tending to break the peace, cohabitation with a person other than a lawful husband or wife, and jointly and privately occupying a hotel room with a person of the opposite sex. There are two photos: one of Connor standing beside the bedpost in the hotel room, wearing his hat while being confronted by a detective. The other is of his secretary standing by the bathroom door, wearing a fur coat and hat, high heels with thin ankle straps. Sugarfoot studies her. She looks like Lauren Bacall. He can't believe this is Dinah's hotel, that Connor would do something so utterly stupid. The newspaper accounts are wonderful, replete with testimony from the cleaning maid, who says that she can tell if a pillow has been used by the wrinkles, a telltale dent. The smoking gun in the story is a tiny bath towel that was, according to a detective, "reeking of semen." A physician discounts this, saying that semen doesn't reek. A group of churchwomen ask for Connor's resignation. It is a wild, sordid, fantastically Birmingham kind of story. Sugarfoot is savoring it when somebody from the newsroom calls his name.

He leaves the clippings on the desk and goes down. A sportswriter named Bluet hands him the phone. It's Connor.

"Sugarfoot," he says.

Sugarfoot says, "Speaking."

"It's Bull."

He says it with punch, as if it's an old buddy. Sugarfoot waits. Connor says he ought to come over. He says, "I've got a story for you, cowboy."

Sugarfoot gathers his things and takes the elevator to first. He runs along Fourth Avenue, not because there's a rush but because he feels great. He feels like he's ten years younger. He passes cafés, shoe stores, hot dog stands, and lawyer's offices. He cuts over to Sixth and runs past the library and into the park. The goldfish pond is mossy, dank. But it's a bright, crisp day. He's gotten used to what passes in Birmingham for a blue sky—as if it's been tossed a handful of pewter. At City Hall, he takes the back steps, passing security guards who nod at his dog chains and let him by. They know where he's going. They know how Connor uses the press. They know a lot, and Sugarfoot wonders just exactly what they know.

Connor's spent all morning answering mail. If only people knew how many letters he gets. Most are job inquiries, and Connor has singled out the ones that interest him for this Saturday morning. One is from a kid who is thirteen years old and wants to know the school subjects required for duties of a motorcycle officer. Kid says that he's always had high respect for policemen because there's a "large amount of people who's always doing wrong." Connor's going to send the kid a formal reply on City Hall stationery, because he believes kids ought to know the ways of the business world. He's going to say: "I am in receipt of your letter," and things like that. But he'll end it on a personal note, saying he hopes the kid'll realize his dream someday.

Connor's desk is walnut. He's got a new swivel chair. He's proud of this, along with the Underwood typewriter, sand urn for cigarets, and the Neiman sofa pushed to the wall. He's kept the table lamp given him by Chris, his secretary, who left town after the hotel scandal. Connor's cried more than once when turning the lamp on. The shade is bent, crooked, and contrary, like his heart. Connor can't understand love or anything anymore.

If only the world knew of all he's called to manage. If they could just see the papers that cross his desk, like the complaint about the Catfish King Restaurant, posted by the beauty parlor next door, regarding odors—fish, poultry, and certain vegetables—that fill the alley. Which vegetables are those? Connor'd like to know. Or the report of Alton L. McWhorter, city engineer, to Mr. J. T. "Jabo" Waggoner, commissioner of public improvements, in regard to the storm sewers of the city of Birmingham. There's the sanitary sewer bond fund, the highway improvement fund; there's the widening of highways, the widening of sewers, the widening of streets. Everything needs widening. Nobody cares for the straight and narrow anymore.

He takes out the Housing Authority report on urban renewal. It discusses Loveman's Village, Smithfield Court, South Town, and other Negro neighborhoods. He stops at Tuxedo Court, which is located in Ensley, the home of the Negro singer Erskine Hawkins, who made a mint with a song called "Tuxedo Junction." Connor ponders this as he waits for Sugarfoot to knock on the door. He stares at Tuxedo Junction. He thinks of how he's going to tell Sugarfoot about this man's success story, how it all works out in the long run if you let Negroes control their own destiny. He glances at a photograph of a colored man and wife sitting at home reading a newspaper. They've got a den, no less. A set of encyclopedias! He's going to show it to Sugarfoot. "I rest my case," is what he's going to say.

He reaches in his *in* box for a new batch of letters.

One says, "Please give my friend Vincent Banna a job with the ABC Board." Who the hell is Vincent Banna? Connor wants to know. It says, "In the future if I can help you in this integration mess just call me at VE5-7135."

Connor dictates this letter: "I'm afraid I can't help your friend Vincent Banna with an ABC job. I don't have one bit of pull with that crowd in Montgomery. [Signed] Bull Connor."

There are several letters from girls who want to be police officers. He answers all of them by saying they can be citation officers someday. He knows this reply would make Dinah furious.

Here's one from one who wants a job as policewoman. "I am

26 years old, single, 5'7" tall, weigh 190 pounds." It's from a Miss Jackie Hayenga at 137 South Washington Street in Rochelle, Illinois. Hayenga? What kind of name is that? Connor hates trying to figure out ethnic things.

And what have we here? he thinks. It's from a Felix LeGrand of North Carolina, who says he is a university professor with a Ph.D. in history who has a large private practice as a marriage counselor in the many large cities in which he has taught. Mr. LeGrand is finding it increasingly difficult to teach in universities because he believes in states' rights, separation of the races, and the old American and Southern way of life. The radicals and race mixers have taken over the universities, and Mr. LeGrand feels that Birmingham, Alabama, and Jackson, Mississippi, are the last places left in America where radicals don't live. He'd like Bull to find him a teaching job, and furthermore he feels he can help run off the freedom riders, who are going to think twice before they force their thinking and their ways on Southern people.

Connor saves this letter. He folds it in the center and puts in his drawer. He puts a paperweight on top of it. The paperweight is a quartz crystal or something like that, given to him by the secretary who followed after Chris and whom Connor didn't fall in love with. Connor thinks he has a character flaw because of women. He didn't fall for Chris at first. But one day she was taking dictation—it was, he remembers clearly, a memo about how the only way for sewage to get out of Birmingham was through Village and Valley Creeks. Chris was taking this on the Neiman sofa. Connor stopped in midsentence and told her he was an adulterer.

Squarely, she pierced his eyes with hers and replied, "That's because your mama died when you were a boy," and the moment the words were spoken, he fell in love with her, too.

After that, he was in a chronic state of suffering. It was like every morning he'd drive to work and he'd start shaking. Her ankles were the most devastating thing—ivory, defined. He was petrified of her. She was tall, classy, blue-blood. Why she was working at City Hall was a mystery.

I'll never be over her, he decided one summer day, in his ultimate surrender. Wearing sunglasses, he walked over to Saint Paul's Cathedral and asked if he could make a confession even though he was a Methodist. The priest said calmly, "All right." Connor knelt on the tile floor because he thought that was the Catholics' style and said he had committed infidelity. The priest, a man of integrity, prayed with and for him. Then he made the sign of the cross, and Connor, for months afterward, practiced genuflecting at home alone. He harbored a secret desire to convert, but he never did.

He thinks Chris might be in Little Rock.

He's heard all kinds of rumors. After the trial, folks sent tea cakes, casseroles, and note cards as if there'd been a death in the family. It made him feel sick. Beara just busied herself with the garden, planting gladiolas, daffodils, and tulips—anything that came in bulbs and made you force your fingers into the earth.

"It's therapy," his new secretary—who knew the story—told him.

He didn't even look to see what color her eyes were. He wasn't going to make a mistake twice. To this day, he won't allow himself a view of a woman's ankles, and he limits his social contacts to Dinah and her café, even though that, too, isn't altogether pure because of Dinah's mother and what he had with her.

He puts the last of the letters back in the *in* box. He can't answer them all today. He pulls out the latest stack of reports from the Negro church meetings. They read like unofficial, voyeuristic

137

minutes. They're from the police chief, who acts as Connor's spy, only it's all understood and in the open. The Negroes know who he is and why he's there. He reads the one that says:

> The meeting opened with prayer. Then they sang a Negro song. Then one Negro got up and said he saw something to-day he'd never seen; he saw a white man catch a Negro woman to keep her from falling. He also saw a Korean woman and her two white friends eating lunch in a café, and two police came in and looked around and left. Not an arrest was made. "Take that back to City Hall," he said. Then a colored holiness preacher got up and preached a sermon that was hard for us to understand in that he was chanting in tongues like they did in Paul's day. This lasted approximately 37 minutes, and twice he had to be restrained and held in the chair by the other preachers on the rostrum.

Connor tries to picture this. He stares at his calendar on the wall—it's got a fisherman catching a bass—and tries to think of a colored preacher going out of his mind.

He is still visualizing this when he hears the knock on his door. It's Sugarfoot.

Connor gets up, adjusts his suspenders, and tells Sugarfoot to come on in. Sugarfoot's carrying one of those steno pads journalists carry. He's wearing a jacket, looking smug as a Yankee at a race riot.

"Welcome to City Hall," Connor says.

Sugarfoot's got a tight grin. Connor glances down at Sugarfoot's Weejuns. He's not wearing socks, and Connor finds him disgusting. He didn't have a reason in the world to call Sugarfoot over this morning. It was a whim. Just to see the kid run. Just to remember how bad they want to play in the dirt. But as

Connor sits here, working his hands like he's holding a ball of clay, an idea takes hold. "I'm escorting the new batch of riders from Birmingham this evening." He pauses, thinks of drama. "At midnight," he adds.

Sugarfoot's all ears. His pencil is flying.

"Just wanted a reporter along to report the truth. You want it?"

Sugarfoot looks him in the eye. Sugarfoot's got eyes like the quartz crystal in Connor's drawer—transparent and threatening to crack in certain places.

"Bet you have a lot of women, don't you?" Connor asks him.

"Haven't been in love since 'fifty-nine," Sugarfoot replies.

Connor is interested. Connor's always interested in other men's love. He wants to know if they've been jilted. He's dying to know if they're as scared of women as he is.

He lights a cigar.

"Who was the lucky one?" Connor asks.

"Back in Iowa," Sugarfoot says. "She was in the business, too."

Connor nods and slides the sand urn over. He offers Sugarfoot a cigar, but Sugarfoot won't accept it. Connor takes a breath and proceeds with his new plan. He tells Sugarfoot he'll go over to the Birmingham jail at 11:30 P.M. and he'll take Sugarfoot, a few deputies, and they'll drive the riders to the Tennessee state line, where they'll be let go.

"Who'll take them from there?" Sugarfoot asks, pencil in hand.

Bull studies the fringe on Sugarfoot's jacket. He dresses like the freedom rider, only he's a boy. He's still wondering who this newspaperwoman was back up in Iowa. He wonders if she broke it off with Sugarfoot. He's never been to Iowa. "Was she nice?" Connor asks.

Sugarfoot frowns. "What?"

"That Iowa girl."

"Who'll take the students once they've crossed the state line?" Sugarfoot repeats. Connor hates reporters' minds. They're always wanting sequential events, even when they haven't yet occurred. "I'm not a soothsayer, I'm a public servant," Connor replies and drags his cigar through the urn's pile of sand.

"So you'll just leave them by the side of the road?"

Sugarfoot's growing angry, trying to be cool. Connor tells him, "We'll just have to see what happens. Dinah and Pete been treating you right over at the hotel?"

"It's fine. It's a nice place."

"They been giving you some down-home comfort?"

"They've been very pleasant."

"That Yankee girl still there?"

"You think she's working for somebody?" Sugarfoot asks.

"I most certainly do think she's working for the Federal Bureau of Investigation, don't you?" Connor asks, though he really doesn't think it himself.

"What makes you think so?" Sugarfoot asks, his pencil flying. He's one of those reporters, Connor sees, who's learned to write while he looks at you. He wonders if Sugarfoot likes tall women.

"Why else would she be staying here? Of course, it may just be there's a love angle."

"What do you mean?"

Connor loves to bullshit like this with journalists. They're like bad fishermen, who cast whichever way the wind blows.

"I mean, maybe she's in love with one of those Negroes over at our jail and she's waiting for him to get free," Connor says, thinking how the one named Jet is probably a pimp, her pimp. "Or maybe she's fallen for somebody at the hotel. Maybe it's you, Sugarfoot."

Sugarfoot says, "You like romance, don't you?"

Connor snubs his cigar into the sand. He leans back in his walnut swivel chair, studying Sugarfoot's face: the pinched lips, quartz crystal eyes, and sandy curls. It's disgusting—youth.

"What makes you think I like romance, Sugar?"

"Had an incident a few years back, didn't you?"

Connor's heart races. Boy's been digging in the morgue files over at the newspaper, read it all. Connor wants to throttle him.

"She was beautiful," Sugarfoot says.

Connor turns to the window. The spring sunlight makes a path of warmth over his hands. His fingers are gnarled, nubby. Everything about him is cut off. "Nipped at the bud," he says.

"What's that?" Sugarfoot asks.

Connor won't look at him. "Thinking aloud, son, just thinking aloud."

"Were you in love with her?"

Connor is dying to answer this question. He jerks a bottle of Hiram Walker from his walnut desk. "Want a drink? You like whiskey?" Connor asks him and takes a glass to the watercooler in the hall. The pea green walls are shiny. Connor wonders why they paint city government interiors this ugly color. Back in his office, he retrieves highball mugs from the file cabinet. He hopes this impresses Sugarfoot, who probably thinks Birmingham people don't know proper glassware. Connor fills the highballs with a half glass of water then pours whiskey, watching it swirl amber. He gives one to Sugarfoot. They sit and drink it, sip by sip, and they don't talk. Connor loves whiskey, the way it burns and makes rancor subside. It makes him like he wants to be, a man of leisure, the type who'd never be fat or make mistakes. "I lost an eye," he tells Sugarfoot. Sugarfoot's leaning forward, setting his empty highball glass on Connor's walnut desk. Connor mixes up another. He tells Sugarfoot how he used to lie to women, say he lost it in baseball or war or police work. He says he's embarrassed at what actually happened.

"Afraid somebody'll think you're a Peeping Tom?" Sugarfoot asks.

Connor glances up to see if this is a serious question. It's not. Sugarfoot's pale face is flushed with liquor glow. Sugarfoot is on the Neiman sofa, where all the secretaries have taken dictation, wearing pastel garters and carrying mint-colored hankies on spring days when the pollen makes their perky noses run. Connor hates it all—the fanciful way they hide lust, the way they say "tipsy" for drunk.

"That's where they sit," he says to Sugarfoot.

Sugarfoot's eyes are glazed.

"My secretaries."

Sugarfoot's not asking questions. His yellow pencil is secured behind his ear. All reporters are missing some brain glue, Connor thinks. It's evident in their pinball machine personality, how they just ding, ding, ding wherever you hit the ball.

"Ever go watch baseball?" Connor asks him.

"No."

"Ole Pete Fraley's got an arm."

"That's what I hear," Sugarfoot says. He is bent over, staring at his boots. Connor's got a bird's-eye view of the top of his head. It's like a mess of pale yellow yarn, like a Raggedy Ann doll who's been given a clip job. Maybe that's how Iowa farm boys are—all tow-headed and roughly hewn. Kid needs a haircut if he's going to re-side in Birmingham, Alabama. "I wrote sports copy," he adds.

"That so?" Connor says.

"You know, baseball wasn't played much in the South until af-ter the Civil War," Sugarfoot tells him. "Confederate soldiers watched Union soldiers play. I saw a photo once of a bunch of gray-clads watching a game up in a prison camp in Salisbury, North Carolina, in eighteen sixty-two."

"So you think we owe it all to Union soldiers, that we play down here?"

"No," Sugarfoot says, smiles crookedly, and shakes his head.

"What do you know about hitting?" Connor asks him and drains his whiskey glass. It is lunchtime. After Sugarfoot answers this question, he's going to say why don't they walk to the café.

"Balance is the key," Sugarfoot says. "You must be balanced before the swing, during the stride, and after contact with the ball. Weight should be on toes, waist slightly bent forward, hands comfortable—no tension. Stand away from the plate so you won't bail out or open up too soon. To tell you the truth, I've always been scared to death of the ball," he concludes.

Connor leans back, studies the boy. He likes this answer. It makes him think he likes Sugarfoot, and that makes him want to tell him something awful—some horrible, bad truth fit for the occasion. Connor leans back in his chair. From here he can see the park, the county courthouse, the pond, the terminal, and the hotel. The hotel is disproportionate in size. It's only a three-story building, and the blue awning has bird shit stains on it. You can't see them, but Connor knows they're there. He's stood on the balcony and gazed down at those ugly spots. He knows every room in the place. He made love to Dinah's mother in every spot—on the stairs, in the cellar, in her bedroom. He hates what he's about to do. People don't think he has a conscience, but he does. He doesn't know why he's going to do this, but he knows he's going to do it. He's not going to do it for malice; he's going to do it because he's got a sneaking suspicion that Sugarfoot's got a thing for Dinah, and he wants to ruin it. These are the times that try men's souls, he thinks. He can't remember who said that. He's drunk. He turns back in his swivel chair and stares squarely at Sugarfoot. Sugarfoot knows he's fixing to hear something. Connor sees the anticipation in his baby blue eyes. "You've got a nice beat with the newspaper, don't you, boy? City Hall during the race riots. Here's what I got to tell you, Sugarfoot. I'm her daddy."

Sugarfoot's eyes widen. Connor loves it when they get this look. He loves how the journalists try not to flinch, just like women who try to be ladylike during sex. Connor gets up and adjusts the venetian blinds so that Sugarfoot's face is striped with shadows. It gives him a sinister look, and Connor thinks this is becoming. "You're not going to want to repeat that, of course."

"That's right," Sugarfoot says too quickly. He's mad, Connor thinks. He sits back down in his swivel chair and analyzes Sugarfoot's anger. It might be some puritan ethic, some Midwestern breadbasket-of-the-world morality that makes him want to protect Dinah. It might be that he thinks Connor is lying. Connor picks up his jar of paper clips; they're making them now with a plastic coating—a waste.

"How do you know that?" Sugarfoot snaps. "Her mother was a whore. You may have had her, but everybody in town probably did. Don't ever tell anybody else that, Connor."

Sugarfoot's leaning forward, making his trousers rise up over his ankles.

"You really ought to wear socks," Connor tells him.

"You like to shovel up dirt," Sugarfoot says. "You think you own the city. You're the little emperor, the king of Siam, Father Abraham, the root of Jesse. You know what's best for the world."

"You're in love with her," Connor says.

"*You're* in love with her."

144

Connor looks at Sugarfoot's baby blues. Connor wonders what women like most about him. He studies Sugarfoot's hands and wants to flip them over to check his palms for calluses. Women like rough spots. "Her mother was my first love," Connor says. "Ever been with a prostitute?"

"No."

"What's your impression of Miss Freedom Rider?"

Sugarfoot's gathering his things up. He jerks his yellow pencil from behind his ear and jams it in the spiral of his notepad. He thanks Connor for the whiskey and says he'll see him at midnight at the city jail. Connor knows Sugarfoot won't let all this rest for long. The knowledge will drive him crazy. He'll hate himself for pursuing it, knowing it has nothing in the world to do with the City Hall beat. He'll try to think of other things; he'll try to think of riots and Negroes and freedom riders. But he'll start to see Dinah in a new light. His desire for her won't be the same now. He's going to feel protective of her, and that makes for the kind of soft kisses women hate. Women like to be scuffed up. They like it if you don't say a word when you're making love. Connor hates this about them. He hates it they can't take a nice guy.

When Sugarfoot gets back to the hotel the other guests are gone, and Dinah is washing dishes behind the counter. He takes the table near the window—the one that's got only two chairs and wobbles a bit. Dinah wipes her hands on her ass, then walks to him. She tells him she's got some beef tips and rice, carrot salad, and Jell-O.

"What color's the Jell-O?" he asks her and looks right in her eyes. They're a forest. He's got to file something, but there's nothing to file other than the story she is Connor's blood. The whiskey is dulling, and he feels heavy. He wishes Connor hadn't told him. People always tell you unnecessary things that're more interesting than the story at hand. They're always wanting you to know every sordid thing, like you're some kind of priest. He's going to call work and tell them he'll have something after midnight. They're going to say, "What in hell's name could possibly happen after midnight in Birmingham?" He'll say Connor's escorting this CORE group from town, and that'll be more than enough to satisfy the city editor. Dinah brings his food and sits down with him. He sprinkles salt and pepper on the meat and rice. "It's funny, isn't it," she says, "how rice is never salty enough. Same with a baked potato. You just have to keep adding more." She gazes out the window to the gathering dusk. She's going to start talking about the city. He can feel it brewing in her.

"Worried about your kids?" he asks her. He can't look at her. He knows if he does, he's going to start searching for signs of Connor in her. He's going to take her face apart, to size up her hands and her eyes and the way her knuckles work.

She looks into his eyes, then at his lips. It's a thing about Southern women he's noticed. They don't mean to be sultry, they just are. They'll just drip their eyes right down the middle of your face and linger where your lips part. It's like they don't care, like they're always miserable and hot and at the end of their rope, like they're drunk in a heavy kind of way, on grasshoppers or Kahlúa and cream. She stares at him and doesn't answer his question. He picks up his fork, looks at her, takes a bite of beef, and chews it. The place is quiet. He can hear the sound of himself chewing, and it makes him uncomfortable. She's staring at him like they've already made love, like she knows what he's like. "I didn't get your tea," she says.

"I'll get it," he says and walks behind the counter. She lets him, and he knows he's no longer an ordinary guest. He scoops up a glass of ice and pours tea. The lights of the jukebox cast a yellow glow over the darkening room. She's left the overheads off, and the place is beginning to assume the atmosphere of the dark bars he likes. In the streets, a few passing businessmen glance in the window, but it's only to see their reflections as they make their way to the train depot. They're on their way back to Atlanta. A few will travel on up the Eastern seaboard, but only a few. Most people in Birmingham don't travel past the Carolinas. Something won't let them; some force keeps them nailed to the home place.

"I've known him all my life," she says, for no reason. Sugarfoot tries to keep eating. Connor is everywhere, in every conversation, in every waking thought of his, hers. "He used to hang around the hotel when I was a kid." Sugarfoot can't eat anymore. He can't get another bite down. He lights a cigaret and runs it along the inside rim of an ashtray. This is her story. Connor is her story. "He adored my mother." Sugarfoot nods, says nothing, avoids her eyes so she'll keep talking. "He was here every night, playing cards and smoking and making my mother laugh. He'd bring her baseball stuff."

Sugarfoot looks up.

"He was handsome, if you can believe it." She throws her hands up, shaking down her colorful bracelets. Her arms are strong, dark.

"He was always in this place, at the table or in the parlor or standing on the sidewalk under the awning. I can't remember a time he wasn't in the picture. I thought he owned the train terminal. I thought he owned the trains. I thought he stood on the platform and pushed buttons allowing trains to come and go, just like a kid with a train set. Like he said who couldn't enter the city, and I thought he made that sign that says *Welcome to Birmingham, the Magic City*. I think he told me that. I think he told me he

147

made the sign. After my daddy came and got me—this was after Mother died—Connor kept trying to visit us up in north Alabama, but he was scared of the snakes."

Sugarfoot nods.

"Tyler, my daddy—the preacher—was in and out of our lives. He'd show up then disappear. My mother told me he was my daddy, and I wanted him to take us away from here, but he didn't. After my mother died, he convinced the local authorities I was his daughter and he could give me a good life. Connor didn't try hard to stop him. He'd of liked to have adopted me, but in order to do that, he'd of had to tell his wife he'd been hanging out at a brothel, and he couldn't very well do that."

Sugarfoot puts out his cigaret. He can't stand it, suddenly—the South.

Dinah runs her hands over her neck as if massaging. Her body is a piece of work. She can't be kin to Connor, he thinks. The place is smoky. The smoke is like fog, and it stays at a certain place like it's apt to do in a valley, hovering and wrapping itself up in nothing and everything. He's starting to want a drink. He's thinking of vermouth or triple sec or something like that, something not meant to be had alone but only in conjunction with a harder liquor. The room has grown dark. He hears a door open. It's Angel going out the side door. She stands under the hotel's blue awning in her boy's jacket. He's dying to ask somebody the ten-thousand-dollar question, which is, does this girl like girls? The traffic light changes red, yellow, green several times before she makes a move.

"Listen," she says and rolls up the sleeves of her gray sweatshirt. "You're a reporter. This is all a story for you, but this is my life. I've got kids," she says like he knew she would. If they've got kids, they got a monopoly on safety.

He looks at her chin. It's up.

"I didn't plan this," she says. "If I'd known all this was going to happen, I'd of never, never sold the house by the foundry and moved in here for the summer. Most mothers won't even come shopping downtown anymore. They won't even ride the bus over the viaduct with their children to buy an Easter dress at Loveman's, and I'm living here. It's a bad place, just like it was when I was growing up. You think you've made a decent life for yourself, you think you've overcome something, then you find it's the same old dirty place."

She stares out the window where Benny has just pulled off with the freedom rider.

Dinah takes Sugarfoot's wrist in her left hand, clasping it. "Do you hear me?" she asks. "It's the same old dirty place." He nods. "I hear you," he says. He wants to kiss her. She's leaning all the way over the table, and she's knocked over the silver napkin holder and the pepper shaker. Her gray sweatshirt sleeve is in the ashtray. "Tell me," she says and grips hard. "Does this girl work for the FBI?"

"Everybody's working for somebody these days; everybody is an informant."

"Are you?" she asks.

He laughs, and he's immediately sorry. She is on the verge of crying, and her dark, tropical eyes are living things. He pries her hand from his wrists and puts his hands over hers. He tells her this: "So what if she's talking to somebody at the FBI? That doesn't mean a thing."

"But that means Connor's right about her."

He says, "There are two wings to the FBI, you got to remember." He watches her absorb that. "There is Bobby Kennedy"—he waits, lets it sink—"and there's J. Edgar Hoover." She nods,

149

and he sees that she's getting it. "Now, we don't know who all is here in the office here, in Birmingham. We don't know where sympathies lie. Understand? She might be talking with somebody who's trying to get the goods on CORE, not on Connor." He sits back, and she looks at him, not blinking, understanding—he thinks—the situation.

"I like the South," he tells her. "People come here for a reason. They like to think they're here to save Negroes or to change history. They're here to save themselves. They're here because they like the sun. They're here because you all are willing to act out what they repress in themselves. Connor's just a player," he tells her. "The press loves it," he whispers. "He's doing all the work by being the fool he is. I feel for him. For you, for all of you. I'm sorry," he says, and when he says it, he knows just how much he means it. He is having an affair with all of them: her, Connor, Pete, the kids, City Hall.

They study each other's faces in the dark, watching how the traffic light makes their skin change color every minute or so. By midnight, the yellow caution will take over, and it will be the driver's discretion as to whether to stop, slow, or proceed. "I feel like I'm in some kind of movie with you," she says apologetically, and he knows she's game. Once people realize they're in the middle of a mess, they start looking for trouble, and they'll think all kinds of things they'd never think in ordinary situations. She's studying his eyes now, and he can feel every drop of her. The café is warm and dark and quiet, and they don't say anything. He hears Pete pulling up in the back. He thinks he ought to move, to turn on a light, but he doesn't.

Pete comes in the back door from baseball. He tosses his cap on the table, straddles a chair, and asks them if anything has happened, if there has been trouble, if Connor has been there, where are the kids, and did Sugarfoot get enough to eat. He fingers the blue-and-white baseball cap, turning it over in his hands. The traffic light changes. They stare at the silver napkin holder and the burgundy bar stools. Sugarfoot feels like he's married to them.

Pete has felt this way only once before. It was shortly after Gracie was born and Dinah had taken a part in a play. He had broken his nose in a baseball game, and it throbbed all the way home from Dayton, Ohio, where they'd won the national amateur championship. Dinah put ice on it. Straddling his chest, she gently dabbed his face with the cold handkerchief and told him she was going to have to kiss the leading man in act two of her play. The memory sweeps over Pete now as she bends over to kiss him in bed, wearing her jeans. Pete can smell Sugarfoot on her—a mixture of leather and pencil shavings.

It's not that he thinks Sugarfoot touched her; it's more the scent of what he knows is Sugarfoot's preoccupation with her. It makes him mad and happy and empty all at once.

Pete is stretched on the bed, staring at the stucco ceiling. It is growing hot in the hotel, and he's wondering how it will feel by July. Dinah stands by the chifforobe, then takes off her pants. Her legs are like sculpture.

"Come here," he tells her.

The French doors are open, allowing a view of the train station's minarets. For a moment, he's glad they're staying at the hotel. It makes him think of New Orleans, Savannah, Charleston, a Southern city that's got a pretense of charm. The night has a thousand eyes, he thinks and pulls her down, making her long curls rain on his chest. He smells her hair, earlobes, and shoulders for signs of Sugarfoot. The reporters and the aerospace engineers from Huntsville are always in love with her, but it's different with Sugarfoot. Pete thinks she might like him, that she might be harboring something she'd never admit. It's this idea—that she's withholding a bit of information—that makes him press hard against her and forget everything but how beautiful she is and how her throat quivers. She never closes her eyes when they make love but insists on putting his face under her scrutiny. "I like the way your eyes look," she's told him. "Don't you ever think of their faces, other women's faces—the way they look when they're making love and getting close to it?" *It.* He thinks of Bo Harper's wife, but he can't think it long because all he can think of is Dinah. Even when he's making love to her and he thinks he should think of somebody else like Bo Harper's wife, he's thinking of Dinah and who wants her and who she might want and the information she's withholding. Now, as he watches her watch him, as he sees her hands flat against the watermelon-colored bedspread, as a train rumbles into the depot, he thinks of the way she's capable of deceit. It's not that she's cunning, just that she's wise in a way that other women aren't because she grew up in a whorehouse and wants to be spiritual but can't quite get the kinks all out of her blood.

He wants her, and he has her.

7

Gracie watches the wind hit Angel's face. They're barreling down First Avenue in the family car. They pass by a neighborhood near the airport. Angel's driving fast like a cop might, like she has a reason to run all the lights. Gracie isn't sure where she's taking them, but she doesn't care. She's never felt this way in her life. She is sure that Angel and Benny will fall in love, and she can't think of anything else.

Angel shakes her head back, letting her unruly hair go berserk in the night air. She turns into an alley, and Gracie sees that they're near East Lake. Angel parks the car under the branches of a big oak tree, turns off the ignition, but keeps her hands on the steering wheel as if she's going to take them clear into the lake. The water shifts idly under the stars. Angel stays like this—hands fixed on the wheel—for several minutes, then finally rolls her window down. The sounds of bullfrogs and crickets fill the car. Gracie tastes salty perspiration on her lip and wonders if people taste this taste when they kiss on summer nights.

"Do you know Hudson Evert, who works for the FBI?" Angel asks and shakes a Kool loose from her pack in the semidark. Her face lights up when she holds the match's fire up to her cigaret.

Gracie says, "No."

"He's brought me here," Angel says. Gracie doesn't know Hudson Evert, but whoever he is, he deserves to die. Gracie feels that the night is ruined. Hudson Evert is a threat to everybody's happiness, including her own. But Angel leans over and puts her face right up under Gracie's. "Don't worry, we didn't do it," she says and grins.

Angel begins to unlace her boots, the Kool dangling from her lips. "I thought he was a journalist when he asked me to get coffee, but when he showed me his FBI badge I fell in love with him," she says, tossing her boots to the backseat. "I wish I didn't fall in love with people because of inanimate objects they carry. Uniforms charm me despite the fact I know I'm not supposed to like law and order," she says. "After all, I've been sent to the South to break the law." She slumps a bit in the driver's seat and smokes like a man smokes—distant and lost in ideas.

Gracie stares out into the lake. She's heard rumors that people's bodies are thrown in its depths, that it's haunted by a drowned girl.

Police lights flash on the other side of the lake. She tells Angel it's the east precinct.

Angel says, "My father was a cop."

Gracie waits for more.

"He'd like Bull Connor. They'd probably play Rook."

Angel draws lines in the dust on the car's dashboard. Her legs are drawn up. "My mother has always been so suffocating. She is a Marxist anthropologist."

Gracie watches the flashing blue lights on the other side of the lake and thinks of how she and Benny always end up hearing confessions. They're like a switchboard. People will sit for hours in the hotel café with all kinds of bad things to report, with love affairs gone wrong and business dealings that failed. But Gracie hangs on every word Angel says. It's something to chew on later; it's something to think about at night, in the dark.

"My dad liked to chase women and drink scotch."

The police cars have disappeared on the other side of the lake, following after the scent of whatever's brewing. Gracie wonders if it's an automobile accident or a burglary or a race riot.

"He used to take me to shooting galleries when I was little. When we went hunting or patrolling, he'd let me take swigs of whiskey from the canteen he kept in the glove compartment."

Gracie's barefoot. She looks down at the mud beside the car, thinking of how it'd be to let it ooze up into the places between her toes. She sees a duck, ivory against the dark night. It quacks and makes its way to the car, wanting a piece of bread. "I've never seen a friendly duck," Angel says. "It's so *Birmingham*."

Gracie can't believe she's sitting here at a neighborhood lake with a freedom rider. She thinks she'll remember this all her life. The breeze picks up, and a bad smell rides in from the lake—Village Creek's city sewage.

"Phew," Angel says and shudders. "The city's waste. All those racists and all their garbage."

"We're not all racists," Gracie tells her.

"I know that," she says.

Angel flicks ashes out the window and says, "My father loved murders and fingerprints and interrogation. He played the good cop in these situations. It made me want to grow up to be an actress or a psychiatrist." Angel can't find any music she likes on the radio, so she turns the ignition off.

"Want one?" Angel asks, holding a Kool up for her. Gracie says no, that she doesn't smoke because emphysema runs in her family. It's something she's heard Pete say.

Angel says this is unnecessarily cautious, and she chalks it up to Gracie's being from the South that she'd even collect family health facts in order to deny herself a simple pleasure like nicotine. She puts the Kools back into her jeans pocket. Cigarets make her want something else, she says. It's always this way, she says. She isn't sure if what she wants is coffee or fruit or a magazine. "I like the hotel," she says. "No doormen or safety precautions or adequate fire escapes, just good food and stories of whores. For a city so on the brink of war, it's got a kind of placid veneer," she says, "this aura of innocence that makes me feel so shitty, so sorry to play a part, to have to witness its demise. I think I'm going to leave here soon." She blows smoke rings. "It's hard to leave, though, with all you weird and wonderful people and your weird and wonderful stories. I think your mother's a mystic. What do you know about her childhood?" Angel asks.

"Not much," Gracie says.

"I mean, growing up in a place like that. Wonder if she ever saw anything?"

Gracie lets her head rest on the back of the seat. In winter she will be able to see the Ram, the Fish, the Cat, and the Hunter. They all have names like Aries and Taurus, Lynx, Lepus, and Orion. But tonight, she can't make out a thing other than the way her body feels—achy, spinning, and bright.

"Don't you wonder?" Angel presses.

Gracie doesn't know what to say.

"Sometimes little girls are forced to do things they don't want to do."

Gracie thinks of what she read in Angel's journal—about talking to Dinah. She doesn't understand where Angel's going with this conversation. She turns away.

"So what's going on with your friends?" Angel asks her, sitting up straight in the driver's seat, changing the subject. "Are you still in love with other people's love?"

Gracie feels her heart going. Angel has remembered Jake and Melissa. She's onto Gracie. She knows Gracie's mind.

"Well?" Angel pursues. "Are they still in love?"

Gracie says, "I think so."

"Oh, come on," Angel says and studies her like a mother. "Are

156

they or aren't they, and have you decided which one you're in love with?"

Gracie shrugs and looks down at her hands.

Angel brushes Gracie's bangs from her eyes. "You know," she says, pulling them straight up, "you'd look good without these things. You've got the forehead of a squaw. Let these bangs grow, and pull them back with a band. Do that for me, OK?"

"Are you in love with Benny?" Gracie asks her. It's out of her mouth before she can stop herself. Angel tosses her cigaret butt into a mess of wildflowers.

"He's so svelte, I can feel it in my legs," Angel says and raises an eyebrow.

Gracie looks at her. She thinks of the word *svelte*—how it's spelled, what it means. She thinks of Angel's legs, of her feeling something in her legs.

"He thinks I'm colored," Angel says to her.

Well, are you? Gracie wants to know but can't bring herself to ask. Angel pulls her knees up, crosses her legs Indian style. She holds her chin up. She smiles at the lake. "You know, when I was in high school, I thought I was in love with my best friend." Angel lights a cigaret, and Gracie watches the flame burning blue. "She was Catholic and wore kneesocks and had a hammock in her backyard. This was in Michigan," she says.

The lake is moving now, as if something from within has stirred it. Gracie wonders if there are turtles, water snakes, or catfish causing the ripples. The car is growing warm, and the spring night is evident in the cicadas.

Angel flicks ashes out the window. "Sometimes you can't help who you fall in love with. You just do."

"I've never been in love," Gracie says and looks up at the stars, searching for constellations. When she was little, Pete taught her to find Cygnus, the Swan, and Draco, the Dragon, and the

Herdsman, the Queen, the Sea Goat, the Scales, the Bear. They did this on summer nights. It makes her want to cry. But she keeps her eyes on the stars now because if she concentrates on patterns and animals and planets, she won't have to think of the lie she just told Angel; she won't have to let the truth float up to the surface of her heart, that she is in love with the thought of Benny and Angel being in love.

When they get back to the hotel, Angel parks by the curb on the yellow line where Connor always parks. The blue awning makes an arc over the entrance. A car pulls up, turns into the alley, and parks under the big tree. Gracie sees that it's Benny, home for the night. Benny's tan is dark, and he's wearing a Saint Christopher. Angel turns back to Gracie. "He's raw," she says.

"He's a lifeguard," Gracie tells her.

Benny opens the car door. He's tired looking and Angel asks him if he had a hot date. He says yes simply and without any trace of embarrassment. She says, "Why don't we sit here?"

They sit on the curb. Angel surveys Benny's legs. They're hairy and strong, and he's wearing shorts like nobody up North wears, according to Angel. "I like those Weejuns," she says mockingly.

"Thanks," he says.

"It's kind of a Southern thing, not to wear socks?"

"Sugarfoot doesn't wear them," he says to her. She takes in his eyes. Gracie sees that Angel thinks Benny is the exact specimen of what she thought Southern boys would be like—handsome, rough, and jocular.

Angel leans back, then drops her body back to the sidewalk for a view of the sky. It's hard to see the stars because of the industry smoke and city lights. Benny looks down at Angel. Gracie leans back in order to get a view of his green eyes. He gives her a please-get-lost look, but she doesn't budge. "I lied to you when I first got

here," Angel lies to Benny. "My father isn't Hispanic, he's colored."
Gracie can see Benny's eyes widen. Angel can't make the lie last,
though. She takes his wrist. "I'm kidding, Benny. My daddy's not
colored. I don't know why I look like I do, but you did think it,
didn't you?"

A band of sweat paints his forehead. "I don't care what you
are. It wouldn't have mattered if you were colored."

"Don't apologize. I know you're not a bigot," she says and
pulls him down to her. Benny gives Gracie one last get-lost nod.
She gets up and goes inside.

The café is dark. She puts "A Summer Place" on the jukebox
and watches Benny and Angel through the window. She sits at the
table in the dark, watching the record spin in the machine, letting
the music saturate her. She can feel summer creeping up like a
dark prowler. Summer is a bad sign. She's seen it in the movies,
how romances split up in August. Love is for winter. She walks
over and picks up the telephone. She's going to call Jake or
Melissa. She's afraid they're going to break up this summer, and
it's up to her, she thinks, to keep them together. If she works hard
enough, if she delivers enough messages, she can keep their love
alive. She dials Jake's number. He answers. "It's Gracie," she says.
She wraps the phone cord around her index finger and watches
Benny and Angel drive off. The night is dark, and the city is going
to sleep. The trains will come all night, though. In her bed, she
will feel the rumbling and the distant whistle; then the hotel will
shake and the bedposts will knock the wall and it won't be sad
because even when it's over, there'll be another one on the way.
The trains keep coming from everywhere, and as long as Birmingham
has the terminal station and her mother has the hotel,
Gracie can anticipate the trains and the strangers and the way it
makes her feel to know one is coming.

Right as she hangs up the phone and turns to go upstairs, the pay phone rings. It's Connor. "You been talking a while," he tells her. "I been trying to call. Where's Mama?" he asks her. In bed, she tells him. "Things all right there?" he asks her. She tells him things are fine. He doesn't say anything, and she can almost hear him breathing. She wraps the cord around her index finger and waits. Finally he says, "What's her name, honey? You don't want to endanger your family." Gracie doesn't even hesitate. He's a cop. "Maria Juarez," she says, "from California."

"Go find the number for me, honey."

She lets the phone dangle in midair and races up the stairs. She opens her own diary and gets it. She goes back to the café and calls the numbers to Connor, one by one.

Benny props himself up on his left elbow and looks down at Angel's face. She's all the way back, lying on the sidewalk, staring at the sky. It's making him nervous to be here on the sidewalk, at the very spot where Bull Connor parks his city car, right under his parents' window, but he can't let her know he's uneasy. "It's incredible up in the upper peninsula," she is saying. "Michigan snow. Bet it never snows in Alabama."

"Every now and then," he says and looks at her lips. He hates this feeling. He knows she can see how desperate he is for her.

"I've got a favor to ask," she says quickly and sits up. "Connor's taking the guys who're in jail to the state line tonight at midnight," she tells him. "I need to find out what that's about. I need to run over to the jail. Can you take me?" she asks him.

For a brief instant, Benny thinks of Ginger Fortenberry, who's wearing his senior ring. It's got a red stone and 1961 engraved on it. She's put wax inside it to make it fit her slim finger. He thinks of what his father might say about him going to the city jail, where there might be trouble. He doesn't even walk into the hotel. They go back over to the family's car—a pink champagne '57

Chevy. He doesn't want to take his own beat-up Ford. Instinctively he doesn't open her door, like he would for a normal girl. It's like they're on business, like she's a partner in crime. He thinks of 77 *Sunset Strip* and private eyes. He cranks the car, and they're past the train terminal and on the other side of the city before he even glances over at her.

They don't talk. He thinks she's lost in something, like maybe she's thinking of her friends being in danger. They pass all the movie theaters, the department stores, and the hot dog joints. He's trying to remember just where the city jail is. He knows it's somewhere on the outskirts near the west side before you reach the cemetery. He smokes and tries to get his bearings. It'd be embarrassing to get lost, to admit he can't remember where the jail is. "This isn't exactly a common route for me," he confesses and looks over at her. "It's on Sixth, I think," he says and begins to slow down. He goes under a railroad trestle and smells a familiar smell—a mixture of baking bread and cat food. "Smell that?" he asks her.

"What?" she asks and hangs her head out the window.

"I smell that every time I go past this place," he tells her.

"I don't smell anything," she says.

He shrugs. Maybe Yankees can't smell Southern things, he thinks. Every part of the city has a particular scent. Paper mills are distinctive—the pungent, bathroom kind of smell. There's a mothball kind of odor near Bessemer. Tarrant has a smoky, charred stench. Here, under this trestle, it's like buttery popcorn that's molding under a car seat. There's no way to tell Angel these things. There's no way he can ever explain the smells of Birmingham.

"Who was that man you were with the other day?" he asks her.

"His name is Hudson. He works for the FBI," she says.

Benny nods. He can't believe she knows people in the FBI. He feels like he's in a movie. He thinks of high school graduation, of how he's going to feel walking down the aisle. He's wondering if he will have made love to her by then. It's only a week away. He reaches for the radio knob, then thinks better of it. Music seems somehow superfluous, inane, something made for people who've never ridden in a car with somebody like her. He wants to ask her more about the FBI, but he thinks it wouldn't be cool. He wants to act right. He wants to make this night perfect. Right as he passes under the railroad trestle, he sees it on the left. The Birmingham City Jail. It is white brick, bigger than he remembered it being. He turns into the parking lot and the moment he does, he sees Connor's car—big, black, the sight of it familiar as a family member.

"There he is," Benny comments.

It's not him, of course. Just his car. But the vehicle might as well be Connor. It's a crow, a raven, a gigantic swoop of black color that controls the world. Benny parks as far away as he can, and they sit here.

"We'll just wait," she tells him.

"For what?" he asks.

"For everybody to come out."

He looks at his watch. It's almost midnight. He turns off the ignition. He looks at himself in the side mirror, at his night beard and his tan and his eyes. Then he looks over at her. She's pulled her legs up. "Bet you've thought about kissing me, haven't you?" she asks him.

His heart pounds.

She throws a Kool butt to the pavement. It lands close to Connor's car. He's not going to answer her question. They sit in the dark. If they were anywhere else, he'd shove her down in the seat and get on top of her. But they're in the parking lot of the city jail, where her buddies will soon exit the bars, escorted by the commissioner of public safety. He lights a new Marlboro and inhales so deeply his chest hurts badly, but he likes it. It makes the rest of his body feel not so fiery. She holds two fingers up, like she wants a drag of his cigaret. "Boys don't like menthol, do they?" she asks him and takes it to her lips.

He looks at her mouth.

"Your baby sister says she won't smoke because emphysema runs in the family."

He keeps his eyes on her lips.

"I think that's funny," she says. "I think if you want to do something, you ought to do it."

He thinks she's wearing dark lipstick, now that he knows she isn't colored. At first, he thought her lips were a natural plum color. He tries to remember what it felt like to think she was colored. He tries to remember the heightened pulse.

"Where did you say you're from?" he asks her.

"Michigan."

He sees it in his mind on the map. He knows it's got two parts to it, that it hangs into lakes. "You swim?" he asks her.

"Yes, how did you know that?" she asks and looks right into his eyes as if he's magical—a palm reader, a soothsayer. He shrugs. "We'll have to swim sometime, then," he tells her.

When he says it, she smiles.

She moves closer to him. She sits in the middle, where Ginger Fortenberry sits, and he can't bring himself to touch her. Connor's car is worse than the eye of God. He can't stand it any longer. He gets out of the car and paces the pavement. There are yellow numbers painted in the slots. Some say *City Car*. Others say *Visitors*. He looks up at the bars. He thinks of the men inside who've broken a law—not a big one, or they'd be over at the county jail. This is a place for rookies, like himself. He bends over to give his body a break from it all. He puts his hands on his kneecaps. He tries to go limp all over.

He looks up at the sky, the stars, the moon.

She's getting out of the car. She leans up against a chain-link fence. He tries to not look at her, the way she looks in those jeans and boots. She's tiny, clutching the fence like she's the prisoner. Her fingers curl over the metal. She presses her face into the diamond shapes and stares at the white brick jail with the black bars. She shoves a hand in her back pocket and leaves it there. He thinks of how it'd feel to be up against her.

He walks up behind her, and without looking she reaches back with her hands and draws him up to her backside. He hugs her from behind and puts his fingers in her belt loops. For the first time, he notices that her belt is studded with red and turquoise beads like Indian art. He puts his face in her hair, and it smells like life—not hair spray, but gasoline and cigarets and wind.

"I think this is the place to do it," she tells him.

He puts his hands all over her, on her breasts and her belly and her thighs, like he's a cop, doing a search from behind. She's made of brass. Again, he puts his nose in her curls and smells the many smells of a girl who's been on the road. It makes him almost seasick that she's making this so easy. It's like riding a wave, one that carries you all the way to shore. He looks around for a place. The parking lot is big. He isn't sure what lies behind the city jail. Maybe there's a field or a mess of low-lying bushes or a ditch. He takes her hand, and she obeys. They walk deftly, not behind the jail but across the street to a mill of some kind—a stark brick place with dark windows and an L-shaped turn in the building, where tall weeds have broken the pavement and sway in the night wind. The sky has turned to buttermilk, and the moonlight comes and goes as the clouds curdle and sail. Benny backs her up against the brick and puts his palms over hers. She isn't soft like Ginger Fortenberry. She is muscular and crisp. He is up against her body, kissing her and taking her buttons, one by one. Her shirt is a faded blue and wrinkled, like a work shirt. After he gets the third button, he steps back a bit to see her chest. Right above her left nipple is a tattoo of a red rose. "Jesus," he says and puts his mouth to it as if it has sustenance—nectar, juice, or sweet milk. He can't get past it. It's another surprise in a string of surprises. He touches the rose with his fingertips and looks into her eyes. They are daring and erotic, like she's a runner on alert for the go signal. "I like it," he says of the rose.

"I know."

He puts his hands into her shirt and feels how bony she is. He's aware of her shoulder blades and her rib cage as he watches her eyes give in to what he's doing. It's a relief. She's a girl after all, and no matter how hip she wants to be, she is at the mercy of nature. Benny pulls her up from where she's pinned to the brick building and holds her hard. He hates this feeling, like there's no way he can get close enough to her, that even when he's in her, he'll still be struggling to get within the woman within the woman. It's always like this, and it scares him in the way that life and dying scare him. Like there's a world within a world within a world, and you'll never quite know if you're in the innermost part where they keep what it is they keep even when they give you their body. It's like you're struggling to find it, to tear it open then clang it shut and put your hand, your seal on it, but there's no way, because women are a story. A mystery. The depths and the folds you break are paper thin like pastry or levels of infinity. The harder you make love, the more they disappear. That's why he feels like he's crying when he's making love—which he is doing now, to her and with her and without her—until his face is wet and he isn't sure if it's sweat or tears or blood or rain. When it's over, her face is like it was, like he knows it will always be—unblemished, foreign.

They throw on their jeans and walk back to the jail. They smoke in the parking lot and don't say a word. He thinks he's in love. Occasionally, he looks at the red and turquoise belt beads, her tiny hands. He is light-headed, the way you are when you've done it in a place where you shouldn't have done it with somebody you shouldn't have done it with—your legs wobbly like you've just left the scene of a crime. At exactly midnight, a side door opens and a group of people spew forth, handcuffed and moving in the awkward rhythm of prisoners who're being shepherded against their will. Behind them are Connor and Sugarfoot. Connor's wearing his herringbone hat and Sunday suit, and Benny wonders why the world can't see what a B movie history is in the end. Southern history, that is. Tomorrow they'll read about this move of Connor's in the newspaper, and they'll be reading it up in Michigan and to the uttermost parts of the earth. Benny takes it upon himself to walk over to Connor and shake his hand. Connor puts his fat chin up.

"And what in God's name are you doing here, boy?" he asks.

Benny nods over to Angel. "I brought her," he says. Connor's nose twitches as if gleaming a bad scent in the night air, as if he's literally sniffing this thing out.

Sugarfoot smiles at Benny.

Angel saunters over, hand still in back pocket. She embraces the handcuffed riders, one by one. Benny takes note of them, best he can in the dark. There's a white girl, a muscular colored guy, a colored girl, and two gray-haired men who look like professors.

"This is Jet," Angel says to Benny and takes the arm of the colored guy, who's built like a linebacker. Benny nods and backs up.

"Now, now," Connor says, brushing her away. "Don't touch the prisoners." Benny sees that Connor's having a fine time, and he wonders why Sugarfoot is here. All they need is for Dinah to show up with a platter of food.

"Where are you taking them?" Angel asks Connor.

Right as she asks, three state trooper cars arrive. The men quickly come forth from the idling cars, headlights piercing the dark, as if poised to make an arrest. They're wearing guns and smoking cigarets. Connor peers down at Angel. "I'm taking your friends to the state line, and I think you'd best come along, too."

Benny glances over at Sugarfoot for assurance that Connor's just making a suggestion, not ordering her. Sugarfoot's busy with his pencil, though, making notes and flipping paper.

The troopers take in the scene.

The guy named Jet is staring a hole in Benny. It makes his skin crawl. He thinks this must be Angel's freedom-riding boyfriend. He thinks of them under a blanket of a bus, making love. He thinks of Jet's dark hands toying with the rose tattoo.

"How's your mama?" Connor asks Benny.

"Fine," he replies.

"Sugarfoot, take note that I'm not going to order this fugitive from justice here to accompany her buddies to the state line. Take note that I'm letting her return to the hotel with this boy." Connor turns to one of the state troopers. "It's a fine family," he says. "A good family."

The trooper nods, as if this is serious business.

Benny scratches his head. He looks back at his father's Chevy—at how it's rusting from being underneath the fallout of the foundry's cupola all day, every day.

"You take her on home," Connor says to Benny.

"I'm not going back to the hotel," Angel announces. She is

167

right beside Connor, with her hands on her skinny hips.

"Well, aren't you a card," Connor says.

"I mean it. I'm riding up there, but you aren't dumping me."

Connor walks to his city car and gets a new cigar. He chews on it while he talks to the troopers. Sugarfoot puts his pencil behind his ear and walks over to Benny. "You want to go?" he asks under his breath.

Benny looks right at him to see if he's joking.

"Might be fun. Be something to tell your grandchildren," Sugarfoot adds and grins.

"I can't," Benny says.

He wants to go, though. The longer he stands here, and the more he begins to feel a part of this party, the more he wants to go. But in the end, he says no. He drives back to the hotel, letting the wind cool his face, taking in all the bad smells of Birmingham, the city he loves and hates, the one from which only a war, a real one, could and would and will tear him away.

8

Sugarfoot rides in the back of the car Connor drives. It's a police car, the kind with the glass partition. Angel is beside him, smoking cigarets and watching Alabama pass by in the night.

"Birmingham is one big industry, don't you think? I mean, everywhere you go, there's fire in the sky. It makes me think of Revelation and the Armageddon, of the seven seals and tribes, of the rider on the white horse and the thousand years," she says and crosses a leg.

Sugarfoot studies her profile, her hands. He's certain she's not into men. He is sure she's a woman's woman.

"Know what I mean?" she says and turns to him.

He says, "Not exactly."

In the front seat, Connor's hands grip the wheel. He's bent forward, mouthing things into the police radio, trying to appear official and serious. Sugarfoot wishes the world could be in this car so they could see what a fool he is.

"You know that place in Revelation where one of the seven angels comes to take the writer into a desert where he sees a scarlet beast?" Angel goes on, and Sugarfoot nods, though he has no idea what she's talking about.

"And there's this woman dressed in purple holding a golden cup, and there's a title on her forehead that says, *Mystery the Mother of Prostitutes*?" she asks.

He nods.

"See, I was thinking of the rumors, the rattlesnakes, the whorehouse, the way Dinah supposedly ran away with a preacher who claimed to be her father to some mountain up in north Alabama. She's a mystery, isn't she? She's not the mother of prostitutes as in Revelation, but the daughter of one. The woman is the great city. Maybe that's Birmingham," she concludes and smiles brightly.

"Maybe so," he says and flips over to his notes from the jail.

"So what do you think?" Angel pursues. "Do you think Birmingham is the great city in Revelation? Do you think this is the apocalypse?"

"Hardly," he says.

He glances back to the entourage of sheriff's cars. They're painted a pale aquamarine.

They drive on.

He turns to her just as they pass a sign that says *Nectar.* "So you think this is the end of the world?" he asks. He jots down a brief description of what he's seeing out the window. This is going to make a great on-the-road-journal kind of piece. *Connor Escorts Freedom Riders to State Line,* the headline will say.

"I think Dinah is the daughter of the prostitute, and I think there's a lot we don't know about her."

"Like what?" he asks and wonders for a moment if Connor has told her what he told him.

Angel shakes her pack of Kools and fingers the ends of the cigarets inside. "I don't know," she says. "I just get this feeling she's got secrets that probably no one knows."

"Like what?" Sugarfoot asks and watches to see if she's onto anything. But Angel just shrugs. He decides to drop it. He decides he's the only person in the world Connor's told about being Dinah's father.

Sugarfoot figures it's time to do surgery on her. "So what is it with you? What's in all this for you?" he asks, and she turns quickly to him and raises an eyebrow the way women do when you ask them something perversely personal. He lets her feign whatever it is she's wanting to feign—indignation over his invasion, perhaps—then she begins to talk. She tells him her mother is an anthropologist and is pushy and wanted her to get involved in the movement, that her father is a cop, and that they're divorced. She chain-smokes her cigarets, and when she's not smoking she's running her fingers over the black vinyl car seat. She tells him she likes the colored guy named Jet but that it's purely cerebral, "as most of my relationships with men are."

He asks if you can have a cerebral romance, and she stares at him for a long time before she says that it's the best kind when you're trying to get a grip on life. You can have all these wonderful adventures of the mind, she says, like reading poetry and doing something useful with your energy like fighting for equality or studying the classics. Sugarfoot nods and thinks what a blessing it was not to have gone to college. He thinks of all he didn't miss.

"Picture this," she says. "Think of yourself on an October morning in New England cutting class and in an open field of dancing leaves sharing a basket of grapes with a girl you love."

"A girl *I* love or a girl *you* love?" he asks.

"What do you think, Sugarfoot?"

He grins and leans over for a view of the small town they're going through. It's a poor place. Shacks line the road with broken-in porch swings, washtubs, and debris.

"I think a girl *you* love," he says.

She turns sideways, tucking a leg up.

"You think I like girls," she clarifies. He can literally feel the warm space where she is, in this city car, riding along this Alabama road, passing these sorry statements of poverty. He can feel her body as she shifts her legs. He doesn't say anything because he knows he doesn't have to. People love to say what they need to say. It's like they spend their days waiting for somebody, anybody, to ask them a direct question.

"Well, yes, Sugarfoot, I like girls and I like boys."

"That makes life full, doesn't it?" he asks and takes note of the tunnel of pines they're passing through on this highway to hell. He hates knowing how he won't sleep tonight, that he'll be writing this story when the birds wake up.

By the time they reach the Tennessee line, he's filled half a notebook with meaningless details of what he can make of north Alabama landscape in the dark. He's learned that Angel once believed she was in love with a girlfriend up in Michigan, and he thinks if he had to live in Michigan, he might fall in love with his own sex, too, if it was cold enough and miserable enough and if his mother was an anthropologist and the sky was blue. He's starting to feel all right about her. He's starting to feel like she's in his boat—an outsider witnessing a mud slide. By the time Connor gets out of the car and pokes his face in the window where they're sitting, then goes back to the sheriff's deputies' aqua cars and escorts the riders to a sign that says WELCOME TO TENNESSEE, THE VOLUNTEER STATE—by that time he's tired and hungry and lonely enough to say to her: "Connor says he could be her father."

At first she grins, then it fades quickly and she says, "Well, is he?" as if he, Sugarfoot, has the lie detector within himself.

Sugarfoot shakes his head. He knows he ought to be standing there with Connor, listening to whatever the hell he's saying to the freedom riders, but he just doesn't care anymore what Connor's saying to anybody. He's burned out on this story, and it's just started. "Who knows?" he says. "Who knows what that son of a bitch is up to?"

Angel is looking at him, her eyes wide.

"I don't know if it's true," he says, "but I can tell you one thing, you're going to think it every time you get near her."

"Maybe he's telling you that to cover some deeper truth about her," Angel says and tilts her head.

Her hand is on the door handle. It's silver as a bullet in her hand.

"Come on," she says abruptly, and they get out of the car.

Sugarfoot walks up to Connor and listens to the speech he's giving the riders. They're clustering over on the Tennessee side of the state line sign as if it's the boundary line that he can't cross. The truth of the matter is that they're stuck here, penniless, under the stars. Sugarfoot zips his jacket. It's cooler up here in the Appalachians. Lookout Mountain is to their right, and they're cradled in rolling hills and pockets of pine forest. The sky is dark and wide, and the colored guy named Jet is staring at Angel as if she's his. She jams her hands in her pockets and turns back toward Birmingham. Sugarfoot knows she isn't going with them. He knows she's staying on at the hotel because she wants something of what he wants, which is them—the family. The story might be the bus, the riders, and if he had any kind of journalistic drive, he'd stay here under the stars with them and trudge along on their pilgrimage, but he knows they'll be met within minutes by a new reporter from Chattanooga who will pick up where he left off, and they're only a piece of it all anyway, only one of many groups of riders who will streak the map this summer. Bull Connor is his story, or at least the one he's feeding to the newspaper. The other story—the Fraleys, baseball, the coloreds and the whites learning to drink the same water—that story is deeper than politics. It's the one that makes him want to get on home to Birmingham.

Sugarfoot slips two twenties into Jet's dark hands. Jet refuses them and nods toward Angel, as if to say, "Give it to her." Sugarfoot looks him in the eye.

He's a pimp, Sugarfoot thinks. He walks with Angel back to Connor's car and they ride in silence. After a while, Connor pulls the sliding window open so he can talk to them.

"Where's your notebook, Sugarfoot?" he asks and chews his cigar.

"You want to tell me something?" Sugarfoot replies and leans forward. His Weejuns and her boots are touching on the floorboard. It's like they're cuffed together.

"I think you ought to ask the questions, boy."

Sugarfoot runs his hands in his hair and inches forward so that his head is almost inside the sliding window. He waits for whatever it is Connor wants him to write in the newspaper. Connor whispers: "You think that Negro boy is her boyfriend?"

"Why don't you ask her that?"

"It's not my business," he says out of the corner of his mouth. "That's your department, Sugar—the news."

"Mr. Connor wants to know if that was your boyfriend," Sugarfoot says loudly to her, loud enough for Connor to hear.

"We've done it one hundred and forty-nine times," Angel says to Connor, leaning all the way over so that her lips almost brush his big earlobe.

She plops back and smiles at Sugarfoot.

Sugarfoot watches Connor's hands on the steering wheel as they grip, loosen, grip, like a batter on deck trying to stay calm but wanting to bat. Sugarfoot lets his head go back so that he can see the sky behind him, the way the stars disappear as they travel.

"Tired?" she asks him.

"Uh-hmm."

She drapes a leg over his. Her muscles are tight, like her jeans.

Sugarfoot tries to gauge if Connor can see.

She lets her leg dangle, swinging it back and forth. He isn't sure what she's up to. It's the kind of thing a girlfriend might do, after you've been together a year or so.

She yawns, rubs her eyes, stretches her neck.

He watches her.

"I'm tired, too," she says.

Then abruptly, she takes her leg from his and leans forward once again to Connor. "I lied," she says. "We've never done it, Eugene."

Connor lays his cigar in the car ashtray.

"You know, my wife calls me Eugene."

"Really, what's her name?"

"Beara."

"Cool," Angel says and leans back again. Sugarfoot waits to see if she's going to lay her leg back on his, but she doesn't. Connor's ready to talk now, though. She's got him in the mood. "So, what's your real name, Miss Angel Rider? What did your mama name you on that glorious day you graced the earth?"

"I can't say," she says. Sugarfoot looks at her belt with the turquoise and red beads. He'd like to touch her belt, the smooth leather. "She never told me the truth, never told me my name," Angel goes on. "That's why I don't know who I am, that's why I'm just riding on buses with Negroes, just *lookin* and *lookin* for the answers," she says in a fake Southern drawl and turns to grin at Sugarfoot.

Connor turns at a fork in the road. They're almost back to Birmingham. Sugarfoot can smell the mills, the foundries, the waste in the night breeze.

"Don't give me that bull," Connor says. "All women know

their names. They all know who they are and they know where they're going, just as you do, Miss Rider."

Sugarfoot turns to her. "His Achilles' heel," he whispers.

"What?"

"Women," he clarifies. "He's scared of them."

Angel leans forward again toward Connor. "You ever been with an African woman?" she asks.

Sugarfoot can almost see Connor's lips going. He can see the cigar vibrating. He can feel Connor's blood pressure rising with anger and interest.

Connor toys with the police radio, and Sugarfoot guesses he's turning it off. This isn't a conversation to be overheard by state troopers, though Sugarfoot bets it's a topic they've milked. "What did you say *African* for?" Connor asks her. "Is this the new thing, to say *African*? Do you riders say *African*? Do you mean *African* as in the Belgian Congo, as in people who still live there, or are you talking about the Negroes?"

Angel adjusts her body. Sugarfoot tries to not look at her backside, at the place where her turquoise-studded belt holds her jeans snug to her waist. He looks out the window.

"I mean, have you ever done it with a woman of color?" she says.

Connor slows down. The speedometer reads forty miles per hour, and they're heading over the viaduct for the hotel. Connor adjusts his rearview mirror and gets his sunglasses from their case, even though it's night.

"What's this *African* thing?" Connor keeps on. "Is this what you Yankees say now? You don't call me English, do you, or Sugarfoot German or yourself Mexicano."

"How did you know I'm German?" Sugarfoot asks him.

"You've got that Adolf Hitler quality to you," Connor replies.

"*I've* got a Hitler quality to *me*?" Sugarfoot says.

"Don't you think he does, Angelrider?"

Angel looks him over. "He looks German, if that's what you mean, but he isn't a murderer and he doesn't have a moustache or a power agenda like some people we know."

Connor slams on the brakes so hard Sugarfoot and Angel are pitched forward, and Sugarfoot hits his head on the glass partition. He feels his pulse rise. Connor's mad. Even though Sugarfoot's seen the man in all kinds of light, he's never really seen him mad, personally mad. Connor gets out of the car. He opens Angel's door and grabs her. Sugarfoot makes mental notes—the way Connor's stubby hands circle the girl's wrists, the street they're on, the avenue, the time.

The city is asleep. All the traffic lights flash yellow, and the sky is black as coal. Not a single department store bulb is on, and a whirlwind of debris—paper, leaves, globs of dust balls—skips and dances along the gutter. Sugarfoot thinks of how well he knows every particle of downtown, anywhere within a six-block radius of City Hall, of how he can almost smell the bus fumes before he sees them coming, bringing colored women back from the homes they tend, dumping them on the curb at Newberry's. He thinks he's got the city nailed down into a beat so tight and predictable he can almost write the story before it happens. It's got the kind of predictability that makes city reporters want to switch to the sports page, where at least upsets occasionally occur. But as Connor stands here gripping the wrists of this bisexual rebel-with-a-cause student, he feels something almost exhilarating growing inside himself, and he realizes it's panic. Panic—something he's not felt in years and something that makes his mouth dry and his face burn.

"Let's get something straight," Connor tells Angel, and Sugarfoot reaches for his notebook. Connor doesn't stop him, and he can't believe the man is going to let this—whatever it's going to be—happen in the presence of a reporter. "Let's get straight this power agenda you're speaking of, woman. I don't have a power agenda of my own. I'm an elected public servant, and it's my job, you hear, my *job* to enforce the law. I don't have the luxury of hopping on buses. I'm not some glorified hobo posing as a national hero. I work for a living. I know who you are, Miss Rider. I have my suspicions about you. I got the means to check you out, too. And let me tell you something else. You think that family you're staying with is sympathetic to you and your Negro inmates, but there are things you don't know about that family. There are things nobody knows but me." Connor turns to Sugarfoot. "I know things nobody knows about her and that hotel of hers, and if you people keep pushing me into a corner, innocent people are going to get hurt. A man can only be pushed so far."

Connor lets go of Angel.

He gets back in the black city car and slams the door. He screeches off, away from City Hall, going wherever he goes to sleep at night. It's hard to think of Bull Connor's home, of a living room and bedroom suite, a pantry full of mayonnaise and tuna fish and sweet pickles. It's hard to see a wife and a daughter, a piano replete with hymnals and sheet music. He and Angel turn and walk toward the hotel. The blue awning is flapping noisily in the midnight wind, and it's all they can hear. Sugarfoot doesn't ask her if her wrist hurts and he knows he isn't going to write for the newspaper what just happened to her, because it isn't even news. It's part of the other story, the family story, and he knows that it won't be long before, as Connor says, innocent people get hurt, and he knows it's going to be the children who live in the hotel. He knows Connor can and will hurt them, because you don't hurt a parent without hurting a kid. He takes his key from his pocket, and Angel gets her key from her pocket. They stand by the door with their keys, staring at their hands and at the sidewalk, a hundred things going in their minds, and Sugarfoot knows she's feeling what he is—that they're somehow body-guards or soldiers assigned by an unknown officer to patrol the hotel and try to keep the people inside from getting hurt. He knows they can't do this. He knows, in fact, that something about her is stirring them all up, like a shoe to an anthill. It makes it all the more poignant, then, when she looks up at him and says quietly, "I think Benny's falling in love with me."

9

Benny wakes to the sound of the alarm clock and remembers he's supposed to take his father to work this morning. He can't get Angel off his mind. He runs it over and over like a home movie, stopping at various junctures—the rose, her hips, the way her eyes caved in—and replays the best parts. Remembering making love to a girl is remembering a collage of it. You can't reenact the story, you just have to do it frame by frame.

The sky begins to light up. Benny opens the French doors to the balcony. The terminal's minarets are partly hidden by fog. He'll be leaving for somewhere in September, though he doesn't know where. He thinks of going to New York with Angel and getting into theater. He thinks of hopping a train to the West Coast like his daddy did during the war. He thinks sometimes of college, of how Pete has saved up two years' worth of college. He's been accepted at the university, but everything is different now that Angel's on board.

He throws on last night's clothes and sniffs the sleeves of his jacket for signs of her. He can't smell anything but cigarets, but then that's all there is to smell of her. For a moment, he wishes she had a smell like other girls—a particular perfume, a flavor.

After he's dressed, he walks down the stairs to the foyer. Through the café door he can see his father standing by the window, adjusting and readjusting his baseball cap. Benny gets a sweet roll from under the glass dome and tells Pete good morning. Pete looks at his watch and says they better be going. Benny licks sugar from his fingers, gets two more rolls, and takes his keys from his back pocket.

They don't talk much on the way. They cross the viaduct, go past the airport, and creep along Tenth Avenue in the direction of the foundry, passing clusters of Negroes at bus stops. Benny wonders if he's going to have to break up with Ginger Fortenberry before graduation. His mind is running away with him as he pictures himself going to the college Angel goes to—or went to. He thinks he might have to get involved in the race thing. He thinks of himself riding buses and eating from vending machines in Greyhound stations and caring about justice. It's hard to do, though, because he can't get past visions of his hands running up her legs under a blanket on the bus during the night. It's hard to think of causes when you're involved in them with a girl. He pulls into the foundry parking lot, where a group of colored men are standing with signs that read REMEMBER JACKIE ROBINSON, INTEGRATE COMPANY BALL. Pete says, "Just park here, son." He turns off the ignition, and they get out of the car. They stand with their hands on their hips, looking at the colored men as if they're a pack of animals who might attack. All the white men are keeping their distance. Their wives and children, who've deposited their men at work, are creeping out of the parking lot in their pastel Chevys, straining for one last look at the colored men in the rearview mirror.

Beyond the group, Benny can see Connor's big body. Connor is talking to somebody at the plant gate. Pete takes off his cap and runs a hand through his hair. After a few minutes, he turns to Benny and says, "You can go on home."

From where he's standing, Benny can see the house where they used to live. He suddenly feels sorry for Pete. He thinks of how they've never really discussed any of this, not race or politics or the way Connor is suddenly everywhere they go. It's as if he's eating with them, sleeping with them, living in their brains, drawing them up in his grip. It bothers him that Angel is part of it, and because he doesn't know what else to say, he says, "I think I'm in love with her, Dad," and lights a Marlboro.

Pete turns to him.

Benny's taller than his father now, and it makes him uncomfortable. It isn't natural. He can see the top of Pete's scalp—the dark curls flecked with gray.

"Say what?" Pete says.

Benny blows smoke to the sky. "I'm in love with Angel."

Pete acts like he hasn't heard. His eyes are fixed on Connor. He's no longer staring at the colored men with the signs. He is watching to see what Connor's going to do. When Connor does spot Pete, he quickly leaves the gate and makes his way over. Benny's never noticed how slew-footed Connor is, what a big duck he is.

"Pete," Connor says, "any of those men work under you?"

"Why are you here?" Pete asks him.

Connor chews his cigar and stares past the malleable unit to the baseball diamond. He takes note of Benny, chin up. "When did you start smoking, boy?" he asks.

Pete digs his work boots into the slag.

"That girl still sleeping over at your place?" Connor asks Pete.

"You know, you really shouldn't be here," Pete tells him.

Connor hooks a thumb in his suspenders. "Did you see that Negro's sign?" He chuckles. "They've spelled it *inter*grate."

Pete rolls up the sleeves of his green work shirt. His company watch—for twenty years of service—glistens in the morning sun. His eyes are hooded by his cap.

"That's why you don't want to have them teaching you," Connor says to Benny. "That's why we can't *inter*grate our schools or our churches or our baseball teams."

Pete takes off his blue cap and gets up in Connor's face. "I'd like to play baseball with them, myself," he says. "I'd really like to play ball with them, Connor."

Connor tucks his chin under and surveys Pete like a grandfather might good-naturedly do to a mischievous boy. "He don't mean that," Connor says to Benny. "Your daddy don't mean that."

"No, I *do* mean that," Pete says, and Connor's eyes draw up as if he's hurt. His cigar droops. His eyes are on the ground, staring at the place where Pete's boots have dug into slag.

Pete walks off.

Benny stands in the parking lot and watches his father move on past the colored men, through the gate and into the grey iron unit. Benny's been inside the plant. He knows the fire, the cupola, the deafening noise of the sand tumbling. He's heard his father speak of arbor makers and iron pourers and core makers, flanged Ls, Ts, and bull ladles. He knows that only Negroes can pour eight hundred pounds of liquid metal in a ladle so big it's called a bull ladle.

Connor turns to Benny. "The Negroes are all up in arms because the Saint Louis Cardinals *inter*grated their facilities in spring training. You read about that?"

Benny shakes his head.

"A Negro ballplayer decided he wanted to use the white bathroom and drink the white water and sleep in the white hotel, so now every Negro in the country thinks he's supposed to do the same thing. That's why they're carrying signs like those. It's like imprinting," Connor says and puts a hand on Benny's shoulder. "It's like what baby geese do. They'll follow anything that moves because they don't know any better."

Benny studies Connor's chin, the way it quivers like Jell-O when he speaks.

"I slept at City Hall last night," Connor says. Benny tries to tune him out. He tries to focus on the way the smoke is rising in puffs and then blowing its way to the baseball field. Connor is explaining that Beara is upset because he won't make peace with their Methodist preacher, who's sympathetic with the Negroes. The preacher's wife and Beara are trying to be civil with each other in hopes that their husbands will follow suit. "Blessed are the peacemakers," Connor says, "for they shall be called the children of God. Why doesn't your mama take y'all to church anymore?" he asks.

Benny smokes the last of his Marlboro and smushes the butt with the toe of his shoe. He keeps smushing it over and over until tidbits of mashed-up tobacco come out the end.

"The beatitudes are nice," Connor goes on, "when they're cross-stitched and hanging in somebody's hall right beside the bathroom door, know what I mean?"

Benny puts his hands in his pockets. The colored men with the sign are starting to disperse. Benny looks at the hands of Connor's watch. The whistle will blow in five minutes.

Connor watches the men walk in the gate. "That large Negro works for your daddy," Connor says. "Name's Nathan. He catches for the Negro team."

"How do you know that?" Benny asks incredulously.

Connor smiles at him and his cigar springs to life.

"You amaze me," Benny says, and he means it. He says it with a note of sarcasm, but he knows it doesn't matter. He knows Connor will take it as a compliment. The man has a blind spot the size of Texas.

"Yeah, we keep the cot at City Hall for snow days, when only necessary personnel report to work: doctors, nurses, preachers, and the commissioner of public safety, Bull Connor." Connor grins when he says his own name.

Benny looks at the sky.

Connor says he's got a plaid flannel blanket he puts over himself and that last night he kept thinking of "that Yankee freedom rider your mama's harboring."

Benny's heart starts pounding at the mention of her. Connor says he's got to make a call to Sugarfoot this morning to say how sorry he is for losing his temper at the freedom rider. Benny turns to the side. He's afraid Connor can see his shirt rise and fall with the thumping of his heart. He's afraid he's going to hyperventilate when Connor says he's going to go by the hotel and apologize to her face-to-face, in Dinah's presence. He says he hates the way he treated her every time he thinks of her pitiful Hispanic face and the way she was hanging on that colored pimp Jet and the way she was putting her leg over Sugarfoot's in the backseat of his car, how they didn't think he saw it. He thinks the girl is nothing more than a whore, a Mexican whore from somewhere near Galveston. Benny turns to walk to his car, and Connor puts a hand on his shoulder as if they're old buddies.

"I like Jackie Robinson," he says, as if baseball has been the subject at hand. "I like Willie Mays. I don't have nothing against Negroes playing baseball. I just know it's not good for any of us when we mix. You ask any Negro, he'll tell you that Jackie Robinson killed the Negro league when he came into the major leagues. This is the kind of thing I'm talking about. It is a practical matter, and don't ever let any Yankee liberal tell you there is justice in this," Connor says and opens Benny's car door for him.

Benny sits with his hands on the steering wheel.

"I know baseball," Connor yells as Benny spins off in the car.

Connor watches the kid drive off, then turns back to the foundry. This company is the epitome of Birmingham's industrial pride. It's got a reputation for hiring quality men like Pete Fraley. True, they're not above recruiting semipro baseball players as foundry men just for the sake of ensuring a winning season, but nonetheless Connor admires what they do here. Connor's seen the finished products, the butterfly valves, the threaded and union and bolted bonnets.

He tosses his cigar to the slag and wonders what to do.

It's clear that Pete Fraley is irritated with him, and he can't for the life of him figure out why. Pete's starting to be swayed by the pressure of the freedom riders, he thinks. He is going to have to ask the girl to leave the hotel. He can't stand the idea of Pete Fraley being cross with him. He walks over to the gate and asks the security guard for a pass. He takes his City Hall ID from his wallet and when the guard sees his name, he says, "Pleased to see you, Commissioner."

Connor likes this.

The guard gives him a pass, and Connor notes how blue the sky is. He thinks he sees a cardinal on the telephone wire. He reaches up and fingers the feather of his herringbone hat. He's certain that things with Pete can be negotiated.

He walks over to the grey iron unit and winces at the noise of the tumbling mills. The Negro men's faces are wet, and Connor marvels at how they can take the heat. He thinks what hard workers they make. He thinks of maids and janitors and butlers and field hands. He spots Pete with a clipboard speaking to the man who held the baseball sign. The man is pushing a ladle on the monorail, ignoring his boss.

"Pete," Connor calls above the shrill machinery.

Pete stares at him.

Connor yells, "You having any trouble from any of them?"

Pete's unit is a carousel of fire. Connor watches the molds moving past him. The ceilings are high, the noise is awful, and the place is dark and ugly and vibrating with production. Machines are everywhere, and if you don't watch where you step, you'll run right into something smoldering. Connor knows of a millwright who was butchered in this plant, a pourer who lost his sight for lack of safety glasses, another whose face was burned so bad the skin now sags like globs of candle wax.

Pete gets close to Connor's ear. "I don't think you need to be here," he says, and Connor feels the weight of his comment. "This is a private company. There's no trouble here, and this isn't a place where you ought to be." Pete has a pencil behind his ear, just like a reporter. It is disconcerting.

Connor sighs. Pete's still irate. He can't understand it.

"We're doing fine," Pete says.

"I love baseball," Connor tells Pete. "Those men of yours are misguided. You know integration hurt the dark players. You know what they'd do. A club would sign a Negro player from the Negro leagues and at the end of the season, no matter how well he did, they'd release the boy. He'd be drummed right out of baseball. You know this is so, Pete."

Pete turns to him. Connor sees he's mad as a hornet. "And what in God's name does this have to do with company ball?" Pete asks but doesn't wait for an answer. He paces his unit. He's sweating, clutching his clipboard, staring into the liquid fire that his colored pourer is pouring.

Connor thinks of Robinson and Campanella and Aaron and

Mays. He thinks of Satchel Paige leaning against the plane he bought so he could fly from game to game on his barnstorming circuit—Connor used to have a photograph of this in his scrapbook of baseball memorabilia. He thinks of Willie Mays and the Black Barons and how he used to go to Rickwood to the colored games and how nobody understands that he cares about baseball and the Negroes. He feels it in his throat as he watches Pete Fraley inch closer to the large Negro who was carrying the sign in the parking lot. He thinks of how Pete probably likes this large Negro more than he likes him, Connor. He thinks Pete has grown cold to their friendship, and he wonders how in the world they got into this predicament.

"Well, you holler if there's trouble, Pete," he calls and backs up. He bumps his ass on a dark green metal desk, which must be Pete's. He resists the urge to pick up the papers on Pete's desk to see what they say. He wonders what other men keep in their desks, if they have correspondence and whiskey bottles and traces of old affairs gone wrong. For a moment, he stands and takes in Pete's world. He knows the iron will get hard and the molds will travel to a shaking-out place, where the sand will be separated, then they'll clean and inspect them and send them to the tapping department for threading, and all this will happen in the hands of the Negroes under the eyes of the whites. What a great nation this was, Connor thinks as he lights a new cigar—when everybody knew their place. He thinks it all the way to his black city car, where the radio is blaring a report of a purse snatching over in north Birmingham.

He thinks of Yankees and how they can mix the races with no incidents. He thinks of how they live in apartments where the hallways are dark and how this type of lifestyle lends itself to association with the Negro. He thinks of how Northerners can drink lukewarm co-colas and be unaware of what's wrong. He thinks of how they're apt to scrimp on mayonnaise, ice, and manners. He thinks of Willie Mays leaving Rickwood Field, where good-natured white men like Eugene Connor came to watch him play ball. He thinks of all those dishonest Yankees pretending to understand Willie and making up stupid song lyrics like "Willie, Hey Willie," like he's some kind of teddy bear.

He picks up his car radio and asks the dispatcher, "Who wrote that song 'Hey, Willie'?"

The dispatcher says, "Do what, Mr. Connor?"

Connor tells him to forget it. He turns and looks back at the foundry sign that says *Valves and Fittings*. He thinks of Pete and how he's going to get him out of this Yankee mind-set he's in. It's the hotel, he thinks. The answer is crystal clear, he thinks, as he drives slowly past the home where the Fraleys used to live. Pete's living in a hotel, and hotels remind a person of Yankees—the unfamiliarity of a hotel, the antiques, dampness, dark hallways, keyholes, and rugs from the Orient. It all reeks of Northern ways. Pete's got to get his house built, quick. And in the meantime, Miss Angelrider's got to go. She's not the type you want to influence your daughter. Connor's almost out of the lot when something hits him. He backs up, parks by the personnel office, and gets out. He knows the director of personnel. He knows he can get the information he needs. He walks in, and the fellow—a Mr. L. T. McElroy, balder than Connor—says, "Well, look what the cat drug in," and in due time gets Connor the information he wants, which is the address of the large Negro who carried the sign. The man is one Nathan Stamps, and he lives over in the nicer projects, where they grow grass. Some believe he's a deaf mute, but there's also a rumor a white man beat him up once and he's only mute to whites. Connor tucks this bit of data away. He likes to know these kinds of details about people. It is always heartening to know other men have suffered.

Pete is watching Nathan pour, standing as close as he possibly can without endangering himself. He can't stand it any longer. He's felt this way in the past—when he left home, when he left the Pacific, when he made himself quit obsessing over Bo Harper's wife. He can't stand a single moment more of Connor. He's going to tell Dinah tonight. The plant is hot. It's like working in a barn that's on fire. The sign Nathan carried is propped against the wall.

"I hate the way his mind works," he screams into Nathan's ear. Nathan keeps moving.

"Do you hear me, Nathan? His brain is the size of a pea. He is everywhere I go!"

Nathan wipes his eyes with his sleeve.

The other colored men on Pete's unit glance up from whatever they're doing. He wonders what the hell they think of this insidious monologue he carries on.

"I'm going to get him out of our lives. My wife won't do it. I will."

Nathan's eyes meet Pete's. It's the first time he's ever looked Pete in the eye. Pete makes him stop working. He puts his hand over Nathan's and makes him stop pouring. "You hear me, don't you?"

He thinks he's going to break down, that they're going to have to carry him away on a stretcher just like they did when Bo Harper's ruptured lumbar disk finally sent him to his knees and they had to get an ambulance. He thinks of how it's going to be in a straightjacket, on tranquilizers, over at the V.A. insane unit.

"Bull Connor's got to end somewhere. Somebody's got to reel him in."

Nathan stands and stares at the cupola. He doesn't answer

Pete. Pete thinks maybe Nathan *is* deaf. He thinks of Helen Keller and how she learned to communicate by finger spelling into people's hands. He wonders if he can learn to do this.

"He was in love with my wife's mother. My wife's mother was a prostitute." As always, Pete watches Nathan's eyes for signs that the word *prostitute* has registered. He thinks surely this ought to quicken the man's curiosity. But Nathan's eyes are blank, fixed.

Pete takes the pencil from behind his ear and draws stars on the day's lineup. "You ever been with a prostitute, Nathan?"

Nathan says nothing. He's taking a short rest between pourings. The men are instructed to do this. Somebody, whoever was the foreman before Pete, taught Nathan to do this, which is proof that he's not deaf.

"I knew this Okinawan woman during the war," Pete begins, but he knows he's not going to finish the sentence. Nathan's moving toward the ladle.

"Listen," Pete says and follows after him. "I didn't ask Connor to come here today. I didn't know he was coming." Pete glances over at the sign Nathan was carrying in the parking lot. "I agree with you on that," he says. "I think we ought to be playing ball with you all." He waits. He watches the muscles in Nathan's arms.

"OK," Pete says. "OK."

He walks back over to his desk and tosses his clipboard aside. He opens the drawer and gets a Hershey bar. He breaks it up into pieces the way his daughter likes to do. He eats it square by square. When he's finished, he walks back over to Nathan.

He thinks of baseball. He thinks of all there is to talk about if they could ever get past all this, whatever it is.

"Ever heard of *béisbol paradiso?*" he asks Nathan when they take a formal break and Nathan sits on the floor and eats a red apple. "You remember how they all played in Latin America without a single incident? I think it was the Dominican Republic, where the sugarcane fields go all the way to the sea."

Pete looks away. He thinks of smoking a cigaret in Latin America, by the Caribbean. He thinks of the war, and he realizes he's never asked, "Did you fight, Nathan?" When he asks it, Pete knows there will be no reply, and there's not.

"I hear they made good money then," Pete rambles on. His unit has slowed, with only a skeletal crew to keep the fire moving while the others rest on the hot floor. They've got a big lineup today; the company is pressing hard on production. "Anywhere from five hundred dollars to four grand a month. Hard to believe, isn't it?"

Pete wonders what Havana looks like. He's heard the flowers grow up the sides of buildings and over the top and back along the other side. He thinks of blacks and whites playing in tropical places like that, where winter leagues flourished.

"Look," Pete says. "All I'm trying to say is that Connor's got to go. I know I can't get him out of public office, but I sure as hell can get him out of my life, out of my hotel. Bull Connor's got to go."

Nathan's lips part. Pete knows, he knows it's going to happen for an eternity before it does, way before his eyes are riveted to Nathan's lips, before the words tumble forth, before his ears hear it, before he feels himself go weak with surprise, before Nathan even takes a breath; Pete knows the man is going to speak to him, and he thinks he's going to come apart with relief when he hears Nathan say, "So what are you going to do about it?"

They sit there. The other colored men slow their pace, too, until eventually the entire unit—all twelve of Pete's crew—have heard it finally happen, and they gather. Pete stands up. Nathan stands up. And for the first time, Pete sees that whatever has been burning in him is the same thing that burns in them, too. It's the same kind of thing he used to feel in the holiness church and during the war and in prayer. They don't do anything in that moment but lose time and neglect work, sacrificing meeting the daily count for Ls and Ts. But something has happened to them, and Pete knows it. He feels it as Nathan crumples up the brown paper sack his apple came in. He feels it when he takes his men over to the cafeteria, and he goes through the white line while they go through the colored line. He eats his turnip greens, sweet potatoes, and fried corn, but his eyes are on his twelve men, who eat the same menu—only served up and devoured in a separate place. For the first time, he sees their hands and their eyes and the way they can't quit moving, as if they've got headphones on, and they're hearing a constant imperative to move, to act, to stop being passive. He only half listens to Bo Harper, who's laughing at the signs the colored men carried in the parking lot. He's got his men in the forefront of all his thoughts. When he takes them back to the unit and the conveyor begins moving and the ladles are hoisted, he stays close to Nathan. He doesn't try to get Nathan to talk now, because he doesn't have to. There is only one thing for them to talk about, and the ball is in Pete's court. Until he has an answer for Nathan, there's nothing to say. But when the whistle blows at four-thirty, Nathan stands beside Pete, and Pete's eyes travel up the tunnel of Nathan's nose.

"Baseball," Nathan tells him. "It's got to be baseball," he says.

Pete showers and gets in his car. He stops at all the yellow lights as if caution is suddenly the watchword of the day. He thinks of how he hasn't felt this much in control and alert since combat. His hands are steady on the wheel. No need to run lights, fight the flow of traffic, put himself in unnecessary peril. Connor's no longer a puddle of mercury. He is a bull's-eye, to be hit.

In the distance, the hotel café is lit up. It's a bright cube in a row of semidark storefronts. The hotel rises up over it, the color of wheat bread.

He parks in the back, and he walks through the private kitchen, the foyer, and into the café. Sugarfoot sits on a bar stool watching Dinah cook. Dinah is wearing a Gypsy skirt and making gumbo. "It's Cajun night," she says.

He puts his blue cap on the counter and gets a glass of ice water.

Sugarfoot, Angel, and the kids are playing cards, and Pete realizes they have only two guests now at the hotel, and only one is paying. The business isn't making any money; it's just a place to live this summer.

"He spoke to me," Pete tells Dinah.

She puts his wooden spoon on a trivet and stops everything she's doing. She knows he's talking about Nathan. "What did he say?"

Pete studies her. He's going to have to tell her it was concerning Connor. He's going to have to tell her what he decided. "It was about Connor," he says. "Connor was at the plant, causing trouble. Baby, Connor's got to go."

Dinah's eyes fall. She picks up her spoon and starts stirring the gumbo. The shrimp float like tiny babies in the brown roux, swimming in and out of okra and peppers. The smell is strong and spicy, and Pete thinks how you either love gumbo or you hate it. There's no in-between. He looks down at the long colorful skirt that brushes Dinah's ankles. She is ignoring him. She is growing icy.

"Well, it's one thing to keep him out of the plant. After all, it is a private, family-owned business," she begins.

"So is this hotel," Pete snaps.

Dinah glances over to see if the kids are listening in. They are. So are Sugarfoot and Angel. Pete walks over to the table, jerks a chair loose, and straddles it. "How is this done?" he asks Angel. "How is this race thing done?"

He looks at her plum lips and jungle eyes. She is pretty, and he distantly remembers his son saying this morning, "I'm in love with her."

"What do you mean, how is it done?" she asks Pete.

"I mean, how do you, we, go about, you know, mixing things up, making things happen, doing away with all this?" He stops short. He throws his head back. "Hell, I don't know what I mean."

Angel lights a Kool and puts a hand over Pete's. "You begin with what you've got," she tells him evenly. "Things happen when one person does one thing."

"Like what?"

"Well, say you work with a Negro. You ask him over for supper."

Pete looks at his family—Dinah, Benny, and Gracie. Their eyes nail him as if he's suddenly the head of the household, which he's never been, which men never are.

Pete shakes his head. "I can't do that. I can't just suddenly ask a colored man to come into this hotel and eat. 'Hey, want to come over for a bowl of gumbo? My wife makes gumbo.' I don't even know if they eat gumbo," Pete says and puts his cap on the table.

They laugh at him.

"Well, do you know?" he asks Sugarfoot. "Do you know if Negroes eat gumbo?"

Sugarfoot leans back in his chair and crosses his legs. His Weejuns have mud on them. Pete remembers they took the freedom riders to the state line last night. "How did it go last night?" he asks Sugarfoot. "Did Connor dump them in Ruby Falls?"

"It doesn't matter if Negroes eat gumbo or not," Angel interrupts. "Food isn't the issue. You're just trying to make a statement. I think it's incredible that you want to do something."

Pete looks over at Benny. His shirt is open at the neck where his lanyard hangs. He's got on that dark jacket he wears everywhere. Words like *beatnik* and *rebel* and *hoodlum* run through Pete's mind, but he can't control his son's destiny. Then he looks at Gracie. From under her dark bangs, she's studying the charms on her bracelet, or pretending to.

"But you do!" Angel says. "You wouldn't be having this conversation if you didn't want to do something." Pete looks over at Dinah. She's stopped stirring the gumbo. She comes from behind the counter, gets a chair, and sits beside him. It makes him feel better.

"I'm just tired," Pete says.

"No, you're not," Sugarfoot says to him. It's the first thing he's said all evening, and they all stare at him. He pushes his body forward and lays both hands open on the table. "You're not tired, Pete. You're not tired at all. You're fine."

Dinah puts a hand on his back and lightly runs her nails along his spine. If it weren't for Connor, they'd have integrated the hotel eons ago. Nobody's going to mention his name, though, Pete knows. Nobody's going to say it, though even at this very moment, Connor is here, prohibiting the flow of whatever it is he and his wife want to say to each other. Dinah gets up, takes six bowls from the cabinet, and begins ladling up the gumbo. Angel puts a soupspoon at everybody's plate, and Gracie gets the iced tea. Benny and Sugarfoot go over to the jukebox and select all the songs Connor hates. They eat the gumbo and talk about New Orleans and Negro saxophonists and who makes good bread pudding and what Sugarfoot's going to write about tonight. After dinner, they smoke and chat, and after a while, Benny and Angel wander out to the sidewalk, where they sit on the curb. The café door is open, and the music drifts out just as the sounds of city traffic drift in. The May night is perfectly calm, with no traces of thundershowers or other surprises of nature. The trains come and go. Gracie gets on the telephone, tucking her long legs up. Pete watches her grin as she whispers a conversation beyond his earshot, and he knows that even if he could hear it, he'd not understand it. She's changing by the moment, and he guesses she's got a boyfriend. Dinah makes coffee, and the three of them— Pete, Dinah, and Sugarfoot—take it up to the balcony, where they sit under a half-moon.

"Baseball, Pete," Sugarfoot says.

Pete turns abruptly, like he's heard a bugle call. He waits, and Sugarfoot repeats the word. Sugarfoot knows, Nathan knows, Pete knows, and—Pete suspects—Connor knows, too. The sign the men carried today wasn't a suggestion; it was a prediction, a premonition, a harbinger.

10

Nathan steps off the bus and walks down the sidewalk to the projects. On the porch stoop sits a mop and pail. Lydia must have cleaned the floors before going over to Mrs. Light's this morning. Lydia has to make three bus connections in order to get to and from Mrs. Light's. Mrs. Light lives over the mountain, where the trees hang over the streets like a canopy. Mrs. Light is a widow, and Lydia loves her. Lydia has described her home in some detail. Nathan can picture it. The kitchen has what white women call an accent color, Lydia says. In Mrs. Light's case, it's gold. The refrigerator is gold. The curtains are gold. The wallpaper is a series of dark yellow pineapples, and the cabinet handles are brass.

Mrs. Light is bent to the side a bit with arthritis, but her eyes are blue as the sky and she's got youthful skin. "Let's eat, Lydia," she says every day at exactly twelve noon and then bends to get a saucepan from the shelf under her sink. She opens a can of vegetable soup and slices a tomato for sandwiches. When they sit at the table, Mrs. Light puts the paper napkin in her lap and takes a bite of the tomato sandwich.

Nathan thinks of the civility of women, how they talk freely, even whites and coloreds. He thinks of how men don't do this, how they fumble for words and end up talking about things that don't matter. He thinks of Pete Fraley and how long it took him to say anything worth responding to. Nathan lets his body sink into the broken springs of the bed and stares through the slats in the blinds to the street, where a few girls in pigtails are chasing a cat.

He wakes to the sound of Lydia's voice calling *Nathan*.

He gets up, splashes water on his face, and goes to the living room, where Lydia's opening mail, wearing her starched maid's dress. He hugs her, inhaling Mrs. Light.

After she changes into a pair of light blue skeets from Mrs. Light's neighbor, they take their walk to the Silver Moon and order a beer. He likes the way Lydia's dark legs look against the pastel material. He thinks of Mrs. Light's neighbor, who keeps putting on weight and discarding her clothes. They sit at a table, drink their Colts and try to avoid drawing Mr. Hoots into conversation. Hoots is growing dimmer by the day, pushing his broom and jabbering. Word has it that Hoots chides his sunflowers for turning from God. Nathan lets Lydia banter on about all she has heard at Mrs. Light's house. Her son, who is scheduled to marry in June, has just started receiving calls from an old girlfriend, and he's torn apart. Lydia hears his phone conversations, and so does Mrs. Light.

Finally, Nathan says, "I spoke to him today."

Lydia's eyes narrow. "To Mr. Pete?"

"He was about to go off the deep end."

"Over your baseball poster?"

"No, over Bull Connor. He hates Bull Connor," he says and takes a long sip of beer.

Lydia takes a clasp from her hair. "Don't you know there's some awful things going on in white homes these days?"

"Like what?" Nathan asks.

"Differences of opinion over black folks. Mrs. Light and her son go at it all the time."

"In front of you?"

"Yes, in front of me."

Nathan pictures Lydia at Mrs. Light's ironing board, set up near the sunken den where Mrs. Light makes her telephone calls. She collects money for the associations that support the variety of diseases Mr. Light died of. In her den is a lime green parakeet named Skip. He thinks of Mrs. Light's son standing in the kitchen, arguing the merits of segregation while Lydia sprinkles water on his shirt to make the starched collar right. It makes him want to kill.

He gets another Colt from the cooler, not even bothering to ask Hoots for one.

"I felt sorry for him," he says. "I felt like he was worse off than me."

He drinks the Colt, feeling it all over his body, taking effect.

"So after I say something to Mr. Pete, we all just stand there like the big twelve waiting to see what the white Jesus is going to say to us."

"Which was?"

"Nothing. He didn't say a word. We just lost time and didn't make the cut for the day."

"So, are you glad?"

"Am I glad?" he repeats. He doesn't know the answer. Pete Fraley is a good pitcher, a fair boss. Nathan bets you could count on one hand the number of white men in Birmingham who'd go out on a limb, but he knows that Pete's got a wild side. He can feel it in his bones. The man bends his back like Sandy Koufax, he winds up like he's mad. Like he hates his catcher, like he'd rather have Nathan giving him signals. Nathan thinks these things as he and Lydia walk home at dusk. The May sky is red where the sun has left earth. The neighborhood has the smell of barbeque, fresh-baked bread, and bus fumes. Jump ropes, baseballs, and catcalls are flying in the streets. Women shell lady peas on the porch, and men in T-shirts tinker on the undersides of rusty cars. In the barbershop, old men sit in lather, immersed in magazines or idle gossip. By midsummer the dance halls and pool joints will carry the message of jazzman Erskine Hawkins to *come on down to Alabam, come on down to Birminham where people come to dance the night away*. He thinks of after-game beer and pool and the way a cigaret looks dangling from Lydia's lips. She smokes at pool halls only when she's got the long stick in her hand.

They go inside. He gets his glove from the closet and waits for Tyrell Jones, who plays left field, to pick him up for ball practice. All the way over to the foundry, Tyrell talks about the Giants. He talks about Bob Schmidt firing a pickoff throw last season and the wind taking the ball. On the return throw to the plate, Schmidt is barreled over and the run scores. He gets up and throws again, and the same thing happens again. "Three scores, man!" Tyrell says and slaps Nathan's knee. Nathan wishes he'd stop this story. It's not a good story for a catcher to hear.

When they get to the foundry's diamond, the white team is just finishing up. Nathan spots Pete, who hurries over to him, brushing grit from his arms. Pete's blue cap is on backwards, and he's got a few white men trailing after him. It's dark, and the spring night is breezy and starlit.

Pete holds his hand to Tyrell. "Pete Fraley," he says. "Grey iron."

"Tyrell Jones. Malleable, cleanup."

The other white men with Pete begin to shake Nathan's hands, and he thinks he's never seen so many white men be so cordial when nobody's died.

"Well," Pete says, running his hand in his hair and looking to the side, "we thought maybe we'd pitch a few with you guys tomorrow night."

Nathan looks at the white men's faces to see how many are in on this proposition. He feels like he's twelve years old and the white boys have come to ask a favor—they want a colored girl or an in to a shot house or somebody to cut the grass.

"Fine with me," Nathan says.

After Pete and his friends leave, the colored team practices. It's a good practice. It's like they're all pumped up on caffeine or sex or anticipation. The balls are quick and nobody's lackadaisical and nobody's exhausted and they're all just wanting to give all they've got. The manager stands with his long brown arms crossed and says nothing, because there's no coaching necessary. Nathan thinks of how crisp and mathematical and solid baseball is and how America integrated it because of sheer economics. The major owners knew black players would pull black crowds and help at the box office when the war decimated attendance. But how this all translates into company ball in Birmingham industry is beyond Nathan's grasp—until he sees Bull Connor's car pulling up into the parking lot.

Nathan and Tyrell walk toward Tyrell's car, and Nathan knows Connor is going to follow after him. He hears the city car's door open. Just as he starts to step into Tyrell's car, Connor calls his name. "Stamps," he says. "Nathan Stamps."

Tyrell's dark eyes widen.

Nathan turns to Connor. Connor's cigar is dangling, burnt.

"Nathan Stamps," Connor repeats, as if they're long-lost friends and Connor's just remembered Nathan's name from way back. Connor takes off his hat. "Just an old herringbone for me," he says. "For you boys, I guess it's hard hats by day, ball caps by night."

Nathan holds his mitt to his chest.

"Where'd you get that?" Connor asks.

Nathan stares at his mitt like it's a foreign object.

"First gloves men ever used were flesh colored," Connor says, and Nathan thinks of the color of white skin. "They put a piece of raw meat in the middle to cushion the numbing effect on the palm. Your chest protectors were made of sheepskin and stuffed with cotton, and catchers used to hide shin guards under their pants because they didn't want anyone to know how afraid they were of spike wounds," Connor tells him.

Nathan says, "Yes sir."

"Why is it y'all say that?" Connor asks him.

Nathan sees that Tyrell is in the car, spooked.

"Say what?" Nathan asks him.

"Why do you say *yes sir?*"

"Respect," Nathan tells him and makes himself look Connor in the eye. Connor's eyes are sky blue.

"Boy, that is the right answer," Connor says. Nathan looks down. Connor's shoes are shiny, black as coal. "But tell me," Connor goes on, "do you say it because you're afraid not to or because you think it's nice manners?"

Nathan shrugs.

"Well, these are important questions," Connor tells him, "because the South is being raped as we speak. Raped of manners and custom and law and order by outside extremists who hate both you and me."

Nathan thinks of Pete, of the inside track he—Nathan—has on Connor and the freedom riders and the inner workings of Connor's brain. It's like a shield at this moment, and Nathan knows that no matter what Connor says or does, he can't penetrate the armor of Nathan's knowledge of Connor, via Pete. As if reading his mind, Connor says, "Pete Fraley's your boss man."

"Yes sir."

"He's a good man," Connor says and juts his cigar up.

"Yes sir, he is."

"Your wife a domestic?"

"Yes sir."

"Where 'bouts?"

"Other side of Red Mountain," Nathan tells him.

Connor nods and says, "Rich folk."

Nathan says, "Yes sir."

Connor tosses his cigar toward the playing field and takes in the malleable unit, the grey iron, and what they call the Y, which holds the cafeteria and personnel offices. He puts his stubby hands on his wide hips and says to Nathan, "I'll tell you like it is, Stamps. I know you made that poster this morning. You misspelled *integrate,* by the way."

Nathan looks down.

Connor says, "But that's not my point. My point is that I know Pete Fraley. Know the family. Know the mother. Know the kids, knew the grandmother, know all the ghosts. Know more than they want me to know. Are you reading me, Stamps?"

Nathan looks up. He sees that one of Connor's blue eyes is made of glass.

"People make mistakes. Pete ought not to make a mistake, in this day and time. This is what we call a ganglion of history. Know what a ganglion is, Stamps?"

Nathan shakes his head. The parking lot is emptying. He knows his teammates are getting an eyeful of this encounter. He feels like he's been stopped for a moving violation he didn't make. "A ganglion," Connor says, "is a group of nerve cells."

Connor gestures to Tyrell, who's fingering his keys. "Just having a little lesson in anatomy," he says.

"Yes sir," Tyrell says.

Connor straightens back up, and Nathan's thinking to himself that Connor is shorter than he thought he was. "Now," Connor says and offers Nathan a cigar, which he declines, "a ganglion may be located outside the brain or the spinal cord, any site of power or activity or energy, so to speak. A ganglion of history means a time when there's lots going on, and a ganglion can then become a tumor. In a ganglion of history you'll see lots of heroes, lots of martyrs and missionaries and apostles. You a Christian, Stamps?"

"Yes sir."

"Then you can, I bet, think of a ganglion of history, can't you?"

"Yes sir."

"And when might that have been?" Connor asks him.

The parking lot is empty. The lights have been shut down. They are in the dark under the stars and there's a dim noise of traffic from over on Tenth Avenue. Otherwise all is quiet and eerie in the way it is when there are tornado warnings. "When might that have been?" Connor repeats.

"When Jesus died," Nathan says.

Connor nods and hikes his pants up with his red suspenders. He puts his hands in his pants pockets, making the huge pieces of gray material widen like a girl's skirt. "Correct," Connor says. "Now, Jesus isn't dying on any cross these days, of course, not in the *lit*ral sense of the term, but we are at a ganglion. You'll find ganglions during times of war and famine and pestilence and revolt. My point, Stamps, is that people get hurt during these times, and your Mr. Pete might be one of those martyrs who gets hurt. I-'m not saying *I'm* the one who'll hurt him,"—and the moment he says this, Nathan knows Connor can and wants to and will. He doesn't even hear much more of what Connor has to say in his biology and history lessons for the evening. Even when he gets home and begins to recount the event with Lydia, he can't for the life of him remember anything Connor said after this. He remembers Connor lighting a new cigar, shielding his good eye and his bad eye from the wind, and puffing smoke to the sky and drawing things to a conclusion and asking Tyrell's pardon for detaining them in this way, then Connor walking to his black city car and getting in and holding up the car radio in salute as he departed. He remembers Tyrell saying, "Need a beer?"

He tries to piece it all together as he lies next to Lydia, who rubs his back with her nimble hands and her fresh smells and her offers of hot chocolate and warm rolls, of leftover meatloaf and rice pilaf—whatever pilaf is—from Mrs. Light's house. They lie in the darkness and Lydia says to him, "Long as he don't hurt us," but Nathan's unable to think about himself alone anymore, apart from Pete or the other players, black and white. He knows Pete's got this burning idea inside him that they can all play ball and that this idea has become Pete's calling, if you will; that the Negro movement is—as Connor says—a ganglion and that Pete fancies himself one of the spokes of the wheel. He knows the hub isn't what Connor thinks it is. The hub isn't Yankee consciousness or outside agitators or freedom riders. He knows it's closer to home than that. It is a tumor of white Southern guilt that's about to spread, to grow into action. As much as he wants to be a full-class citizen, live like a white man lives—as much as any of that, Nathan wants men like Pete Fraley to get well. And he knows that a Northern invasion won't do it. Only a Southern colored man can cure a Southern white man's sin and guilt. He tells Lydia these things and she says this is the way the Holy Spirit works, that it works in tandem, preparing one man for another man's salvation. They lie perfectly still in their bedroom with the coral walls, watching the venetian blinds flutter and vibrate so hard they disappear like hummingbird wings.

But he can't sleep.

Most of the night he paces the bedroom, then the front porch, and then the street, where the moon illuminates the Negro grocery stores and dry cleaner's and barber shop and sidewalks. He thinks of what it is that Bull Connor wants to do to Pete Fraley. He knows there are things that men can do to other men without ever picking up a gun or a knife. He knows that white men's weapons are more sophisticated—the war of words and slander and lies and the bite of old wounds. He knows Bull Connor is going to hurt Pete Fraley, and there is nothing in the world he can do to stop it. He knows it's got something to do with his wife, but he doesn't know what it is.

Pete can't sleep, either. He feels like he's in the Pacific or on a honeymoon or awaiting the launch of Alan Shepard's rocket. He has a crisp, fresh sense of well-being, as if his muscles are toned and his mind alert. He puts a hand on Dinah's arm. She is sleeping so hard her lips are parted as if to speak. He thinks of the new home, of carpenters, painters, brick masons, Sheetrockers, and the blue-tile bathroom he's going to have.

When daylight breaks, he gets up and throws on his work clothes. He stops at a donut shop on Tenth Avenue. He goes inside and peers into the glass, where he surveys the situation: raspberry filled, chocolate coated, powdered sugar, and regular glazed. He gets three dozen glazed. He's never bought donuts for his unit, never in his life. It's not in keeping with the foundry way, but the world suddenly feels different. The dice are in midair.

He swings into the foundry parking lot. He knows his motives aren't pure. He knows it has more to do with conquering Connor than it does with social justice. He isn't sure why the others are willing to do it. He thinks of Bo Harper saying the word *nigra*. He thinks of Orland Gandy—he's probably Connor's age. He thinks of all the white foremen whose lives are so steeped in segregation they can't escape it even if they want to. Pete parks the car. He totes the bags of donuts and suddenly something happens. It's like his body belongs to a different magnetic field. A force tugs at his common sense. It's like he's sleepwalking as he makes his way to the colored gate. He grips the bar and hesitates, then moves alongside the colored men up to the guard's window. "Have you lost your damn mind, Fraley?" the guard asks and bolts from his chamber. He takes Pete by the shoulder and a few colored men scurry past, their eyes bright and puzzled. Pete stares at the guard as if he hasn't heard.

"Want a donut?" Pete asks.

The guard says, "You're going through the damn colored gate, Pete!"

Pete looks at the guard, at the scar drawn in his pasty cheek. He reads the guard's badge. It says *F. Scalisi*. Pete thinks of Italy, of immigrants from Europe. He frames an extemporaneous speech on the concept of segregation, but he can't quite articulate it. So he simply walks past F. Scalisi and reenters the correct gate, the white one, as if he's made a mistake and he's sorry.

When he gets to his unit, he puts the donuts on his green metal desk and looks at the day's lineup. There are the usual number of Ls and Ts. His men are already in place for the most part, and when they see Pete their eyes dodge and divert they way they always do. Pete wants to shake them and say, "Look me in the eye." Instead he walks around the carousel of molds, past the cupola, with the donuts in his hands, and makes all twelve of them take one. Nathan is wordless again, but he takes what Pete offers and Pete reminds him the players are going to practice together this evening if that's all right with the colored manager.

Nathan nods.

At break, Pete walks over to Bo Harper's unit. He has another dozen donuts with him, and he offers them around to Bo and his men. Bo says, "We're only going to do this nigra ball game once, right?" Bo gets a handkerchief from his pocket and wipes his brow. The sight of the handkerchief makes Pete think of Bo's wife. He can't look at Bo without thinking of his wife.

"I'm on my way to ask the colored manager," Pete says.

"I think you've lost your marbles," Bo says and stuffs his handkerchief back in his pocket. He flips a penny up. "But I'm game," he says, and Pete knows why. Bo likes danger.

"Heard you tried to get through the colored gate this morning," he says, grinning at the copper coin as it tumbles to his palm.

Pete says, "Yeah."

Bo won't look at Pete. "So, you're into this race thing, huh?"

Pete isn't sure what to say. He thinks of the civility of foundry men, how they swallow their prejudices to be convivial. Bo's a good third baseman; nobody's ever stolen third when Pete's pitched and Bo's been at third, and that's the crux of what they know of each other and admire in each other.

Pete goes over to the tapping department, where the colored manager, Elbert Polk, works. He is a short, squashed-looking man who wears boots up to his knees, causing his work pants to bloom like knickers at the kneecap. Elbert Polk is a hard worker, and he knows baseball better than anyone in the company. Pete shakes his hand and Elbert says, "You pulled that last baby out, didn't you, Mr. Pete?"—meaning the last game. He gives Pete a gold-tooth smile. Pete tells him why he's there, and Elbert says, "Yes sir. I reckon so," when Pete asks him if they can practice together. On the way back to his unit, Pete starts to feel bad. It has something to do with the way Elbert said the words *reckon* and *sir*. It was like Pete had asked him to wash his car or mow his lawn or shine his shoes. Pete thinks they must all see this as some kind of comical chore they have to do because white management wants to, like dunking the superintendent of foundries in a barrel of water during the fall carnival.

Back in his unit, Pete pulls Nathan aside.

"You think I'm crazy?"

Nathan's forehead is dripping with sweat. Summer heat is emerging. Nathan wipes his face with his shirtsleeve, and Pete looks at his eyes—the dark iris, the jaundiced white part. He knows Nathan is going to speak, and he waits. It takes an eternity for him to reply.

"No, you're not crazy," Nathan says and stares, glares, pierces Pete with his eyes. It's like he wonders if Pete knows the seriousness of what he's up to, and Pete says, "I asked your manager, and he said, 'Fine.' No, he actually said, 'Yes sir,' and, 'I reckon so,' and that made me think maybe—that made me wonder if you people feel like you *have* to do this because some boss man says so."

Nathan half smiles. Pete looks at the flecks of grey along his temple. He thinks of how you can't tell how old Negro men are. He wonders how old Nathan is.

"Well?" Pete presses.

The eleven other workers are starting to draw near, just as they did the other day. None of the others play on the colored team, but they're wanting to hear all the same. Nathan gestures to them. "They're waiting. They're waiting for your orders."

"I don't want to order anything," Pete says to Nathan. "Nothing outside of work," he says.

Nathan holds his hand up, and Pete pictures his brown mitt on the brown fingers. Nathan says, "We don't know what to do. You can make posters, you can go to the church meetings, you can ride buses if you don't have to work for a living, but other than that, what can you do?" He gestures to the other men. "I'm asking you, huh? What can they do? What can I do? I'm serious, what is there for a man to do?"

Pete walks back over to his desk and looks at the lineup, scratching his head, not even seeing the numbers and the orders and the signature of the superintendent. He looks at the third bag of donuts he's stuffed under his desk, and he can't think of anything to say. Nathan has gone back to work. Pete watches his arms, his biceps, the way he maneuvers the gigantic bull ladle of pulsating fire-iron. The other men go back to their jobs, and the carousel turns and turns, and they keep working until the whistle blows. At day's end, he makes every one of them take a donut again, and they do it. They do it because he's white and they're not and he's the foreman. They're probably hungry, but even if they weren't they'd take it. They'd eat it and force it down their throats no matter what it was or how they felt, and Pete hates this knowledge. He hates it more than he hates Connor.

11

Birmingham's smoke, red iron ore, and outlying industrial towns pass by, disappear quickly. Dinah rolls down her window and lets the breeze take her. But it doesn't help any. She is scared, and she can't say why. Something awful is in the air. She fears something is going to happen to her children. She passes tin roofs, junk-yards, and fenced sinner's pens, where people repent during camp revivals. All you must travel through in order to get home, she thinks. Today, the mimosa trees throw pink spiderwebs along the land. Cows graze, baby goats nurse, all the world is new, and it makes her want to do something awful.

On the mountain, acres of farmland spread on either side of the Chevy. She's near the Tennessee Valley, where Nickajack Cave swallows you in Tennessee and spits you out in Alabama or Georgia. She drives by the old holiness church and on toward Tyler's place. She passes by barnyards full of goats, a farm wife hanging long johns on her clothesline. It's Marla Vines, who's lived here forever. Dinah crawls up the far side of the ravine, where frost collects on winter mornings. Today, the ledge is on the brink of summer.

She pulls into the yard and parks beside the pin oak.

The house is wood frame, painted white. A big screen porch wraps it up. This was where Dinah sat in starlight, remembering her mother's hotel. Tyler comes to the door, smelling of Old

Spice. He is wearing a faded work shirt and overalls. His gray curls are wet. He's been hauling bags of sawdust. Dinah knows by the smell. "Daddy," she says and gathers him up. He's growing thinner in the inevitable way men get skinny when they don't have a wife. She takes one look into the yard and empty henhouse and sees that the hens are gone for slaughter. It's part of the cycle, like the moon or a woman's body. It's part of her life. The hens are gone for slaughter, leaving miles of droppings, sawdust, and mice. Dinah used to come home every nine weeks to help her father clean up. These days, it's hit-and-miss. She's hit this trip.

Dinah takes her father's shoulders in her hands and surveys him as you would a child. "You getting sleep?" she asks him, staring at his sunken eyes. For a moment she thinks she hears the hens fly up to the rafters in unison. But it's just the flapping of clothesline sheets in a gust of wind.

They go inside. For a moment she forgets Connor and Pete and the children and the hotel. She's thinking of Tyler's vegetables. There's nothing like her daddy's vegetables. The big black pot is full of stew. The carrots and potatoes are mushy, just the way Tyler likes things. He's fried some catfish, too, and left it to drain on a piece of newspaper—yesterday's *Birmingham News*.

"A lot's been happening," she tells him, eyeing the editorial that reads, "Thugs Must Not Take Over Our City."

The red clock over the gas stove shows it is ten-thirty. She puts the skillet of corn bread on a trivet, butter in a saucer. The salt and pepper shakers are painted with sailboats.

"Too early to eat," he says, "but get us some buttermilk, baby."

They sit down at the table, Tyler leans forward, his eyes fixed as if ready to preach. His suspender buckle glistens.

"The kids saw the fight at the bus station." She studies his eyes to see if this registers, to ascertain if he's read the paper carefully.

He nods, gets up, and retrieves Monday's paper from a brown sack by the sleeping porch. "I read it," he says and begins thumbing through the paper.

After a bit, he folds the newspaper. "Tell Mr. Connor I'm available," he says to her. He takes a red bandana from his jeans suspenders. "To show him Jesus," he explains, wiping his brow. He gets up from the table and picks up the cat's yellow bowl.

"I've been thinking of Mama," Dinah says. The moment the words are out of her mouth, she realizes the weight of them. She knows just how badly she's been wanting to tell him this.

Tyler turns to her.

"I feel like I'm going to start remembering everything."

Tyler's blue eyes search her.

He looks away, his face falling apart. She hates it when he does this, when he feels like she is unhappy and it's his fault. "Remembering won't hurt you," he says. "Nobody can hurt the children of God."

She hates it when he talks like this. She hates the idiocy of it. Everybody knows the children of God are the first to be hurt. It's part of the package. It's why she can't go to church anymore.

"Connor's up to something. I can feel it," she tells Tyler.

"He needs help, sugar."

"The city has gone mad. You have no idea," she says, pushing her glass of buttermilk to the side and staring out the window to the tree swing, garden, and pots of geranium.

"How's Benny?" he says.

"Fine. In love. Fine," she says and drums her fingernails on the table. She takes off her set of rainbow bracelets and puts them on the tabletop.

"In *love?*" he says in his Appalachian drawl, as if love is a new and quaint idea.

"Yes, in love," she says.

"With a church girl?" he asks and brings the corn bread to the table. He sits down and breaks it into crumbs and sprinkles them into the dregs of his buttermilk.

"With a freedom rider," she tells him.

"A what, sugar?" he says.

"An out-of-towner, a guest at the hotel. Somebody he's met."

"And Gracie?" he asks.

Dinah throws her hands up. "Who knows? She's a mystery."

"She's going to be a missionary," he says.

"OK," she says. "OK, a missionary. That's nice."

She feels impatient with him. She doesn't know what she wants from him. She feels the ends of her fingers tingling, in the way they did when she wanted to handle a snake. She thinks of how that felt, the looming apprehension that you shouldn't have let yourself fall in with people who do such things. It's how she's always felt.

"The girl Benny's in love with," she says and moves her knife and spoon up a bit, away from her. "I'm worried that he's going to get hurt." She looks away, out the window. "She's like me."

She waits for Tyler to ask her, "In what way?"

But he's silent.

She puts her hands in her lap. "I think she's suffered."

"Jesus suffered, too."

Dinah feels like she's going to come out of her skin. She pushes away from the table. "Let's go clean up," she says.

The chicken house is a wreck.

Honey light comes in the cracks, striping Tyler's shirt like a convict's. Dinah sits on a bin. She isn't eager to clean up the mess. There are so many things nobody knows but the two of them. How chickens pile up when startled by a coyote or skunk, how they'll bake to death in summer heat if you don't stir them up.

Feathers are all over the sawdust where the men grabbed the girls in the dark. Dinah glances at her moccasins to see if they've picked up any droppings. Tyler eyes the rafters. He doesn't flinch at the odors. An empty chicken house is like a church on Monday morning. Quiet, meaningless.

"There are many forms of cannibalism among chickens," Tyler says. He's told her this endless times. He takes off his cap, scratches his head. "They'll pick each other's toes, eat each other's eggs and feathers, peck each other's eyes."

She nods. She knows he's avoiding talking about the things she wants to talk about. She tries to relax, but her body won't let her.

"Only one cause: crowded quarters," Tyler says, then chuckles. "Just a bit of education." Dinah looks at Tyler's hands. They're gnarled with arthritis.

"I just wish you'd raise them to lay," Dinah says to him. "You get some lights, those birds will lay like crazy," she says, taking a shovel and tossing sawdust into the wheelbarrow. When it's full, Tyler carts it to the compost and returns for more. Dinah cleans the feed trays and prepares new broiler mash: cornmeal, wheat shorts, bran, oats, and alfalfa leaf. They'll be getting a new brood of white leghorns because the pinfeathers of dark ones look bad on the dressed carcass.

Now Tyler bends to mix new broiler mash. The henhouse is cool. By July, it will be baking. "Don't you ever get tired of raising birds in order for some men to come here in the middle of the night every nine weeks and haul them off to kill, Daddy?"

He stirs the mash. His overalls are caked with crud, the soles of his feet in droppings. "Mr. Connor needs to follow after Jesus." Tyler turns to her, preaching with his stirring stick. "Jesus didn't give us any long-winded instructions, baby. All he said was, 'Follow me.' "

Dinah looks at her hands.

"Fishermen put down their nets just like that. They didn't ask where. They didn't ask how. They just followed. Mr. Connor needs to do this, too."

She eyes the broiler mash and listens to a rooster in the distance, choosing her words so as to not hurt his feelings. "There's a part of me," she begins, and hates what she's about to say, "there's a part of me that loves him," she says and looks up at Tyler. It's a confession, and she feels the weight of it. It feels like a sin. Saying the words *I love Bull Connor* feels like an awful, ugly, and unpardonable sin.

"Love is a frightful thing," he says to her.

She mixes up castor and motor oil, then adds kerosene. With a paintbrush, she applies the mixture to the roost to kill mites. The flies will breed in spring and summer.

"I don't understand why I love something ugly," she says and lets the paintbrush rest in the can.

"Mr. Connor's not ugly," Tyler tells her.

She squats, letting her moccasins get buried in the nasty hay. "I'm afraid he has a dark side," she says, and she knows the brevity of this understatement would make Pete's head spin.

"He can't hurt you," Tyler says.

"But he can!" she says and gets up and whirls to him. She knocks the castor oil and kerosene over and stares at the stain it makes in the floor of the pen. She stands and takes him in—the man he is, a skinny chicken farmer, whose sandy curls have turned lead gray; a whorehouse preacher.

"Pete hates him."

"Pete oughtn't hate," Tyler says and gets a bandana from the back pocket of his overalls.

"You don't understand," she tells him. Dinah can almost see her reflection in Tyler's eyes. She's wearing work clothes—men's overalls, a jacket.

"I may not have a education," he begins, but she cuts him short.

"Don't say that," she says. "Don't start discounting yourself."

"Ye shall know the truth," he begins, but she stops the words in midair. "Please," she says. "Don't quote me a verse."

Light comes in the slats, making her hands warm. She stares at her paintbrush and wishes she hadn't been so short with him. The Bible is all he knows. It's how he talks to people. It's how he sees the world. There's no way she could ever explain to him what Birmingham is like, what marriage is like, what it's like to carry lust and sin and children and outsiders on your back day after day.

"I've told you," she reminds him, "that there are things I can't remember."

"God won't give you more than you can bear," he says.

"I'm not saying I can't bear it, I'm saying I can't remember it."

"Remember what, baby?" he says and draws closer to her—so close she can smell the Old Spice, manure, and vegetables. When she was living here, she couldn't put her head on his pillow during afternoon naps because she hated the scent a farmer's scalp left.

"I can't remember anything," she says, running her moccasin over the hay. "I can't remember being little. I can't remember going to sleep at night or waking. All I can see is men—their faces, the way they smoked into newspapers."

"You remember Jasmine?" he asks and wipes his brow.

"I remember Jasmine."

"Remember the girls?"

Dinah looks down at her hands, at her thin wrists and olive skin. She wonders if any of the girls are alive. She can conjure up pictures of them bathing in big tubs in the backyard. She remembers them like big sisters who threw themselves across beds and complained and put on makeup and cried at the bureau.

"You remember Pansy?"

"Who?" she laughs.

"Pansy. One of your mama's girls."

"No, who was she?"

"A whore," he says flatly, with not a trace of wit. "Looked like a Mexican."

The minute he says it, she remembers. She knows, then, who Angel reminds her of.

His hazel eyes widen as if he's watching something grow bigger and bigger. She turns to the right side, the left, and then up to the rafters. She begins to wonder if he is seeing the Holy Ghost.

"What?" she asks him.

"I'm listening to you," he says.

"What are you looking at?" she asks him.

Tyler puts a hand on her head, as if he's going to anoint her, like he used to do in church. "And when the day of Pentecost was fully come, they were all with one accord in one place. And suddenly there came a sound from heaven as of a rushing mighty wind, and it filled all the house where they were sitting."

She thinks of roofs coming off buildings and glass breaking. She has no idea what Pentecost has to do with Connor or Birmingham or what she's just told him, but all the same it makes her mad—his preoccupation with Acts at this particular moment. She turns, squats, and starts painting the walls again with the bad-smelling kerosene mixture.

"Why don't you go to church anymore, baby?" he says, his hand still on her. She is kneeling, painting the walls, her back to him.

"Because city preachers aren't a mystery," she tells him.

"And do we need a mystery, sugar?"

"Well you do, don't you?" she snaps. "Isn't Jesus a mystery? Wasn't Mother one?"

She turns to see what his eyes are going to do. They stay steady.

She thinks of him, of her. She tries to make her mother's red hair and his farm-bred arms go hand in hand. She tries to make them translate into her, Dinah. It won't work. It's as if she burst into being like a star.

She turns back to her can of mite-killer mixture and wonders what to do. She knows Tyler knows she isn't finished confessing. She thinks of all her sins, but they're all rolled up into a big, dark trough where Bull Connor drinks.

"I just know that if he gets mad at us, he will say something to hurt the children."

"What will he say?" Tyler asks, takes his hand from her, and leans against his shovel.

Dinah sits in the hay, holding her paintbrush. The heels of her moccasins are crushed. She can't tell him that she's been remembering how close Connor stood to her when she was a little girl, how he pinned her up against the cupboard when he talked to her.

She mixes up more castor and motor oil, splashes in a bit of kerosene and starts painting again. She doesn't know what this memory has to do with her children. She can't name the thing she fears. She stays at Tyler's until past noon. They have lunch, and she tells him he ought to start raising laying hens, that June Cargo has told her they'll bring in $30 a month profit. Even the Rhode Island Reds or Barred Rocks do good, she tells him. When morning lights are used, one forty-watt bulb should be placed where it will light the floor on the henhouse, according to June Cargo. Tyler takes all his buttermilk in one gulp, his Adam's apple bobbing. Right before she leaves, he says to her, "Tell Mr. Connor I'm here for him." She drives off. "And read John 16:12 when you get home," he hollers after her, chasing her car and waving his thin arm in the air, like a man hailing a city cab.

On the drive back to Birmingham, she puts her hand in the

wind and lets it push against her and she pushes back, like the wind is a wall she can't move.

In the café, Pete is behind the counter, wearing his baseball uniform and frying pork chops. Gracie slices lemons. Benny and Angel are standing in the doorway, watching traffic.

Sugarfoot is at a table, smoking.

Pete hugs Dinah when she walks in.

"Do I smell like chicken shit?" she asks him.

Sugarfoot looks over and smiles. Gracie says, "Mom, please," and Dinah apologizes. Suddenly, everybody is staring at her. "What?" she asks. "What is it?"

"We're practicing with the colored team tonight," Pete tells her.

They all draw close, like it's a press conference. They're wanting her reaction to this news.

"And so what does this have to do with me?" she asks.

She sees that Sugarfoot is staring at her clothes. She unzips her jacket and tugs at her pants. "I wear this when I know I'm going to be shoveling shit," she says and apologizes again, to Gracie.

"I shovel shit all day," Sugarfoot replies.

Angel leans over the counter. "You're going to give Bull Connor cardiac arrest," she says, grinning. She puts a hand in her back pocket. *Pansy,* Dinah thinks.

Pete's eyes are out the window. He stops turning the pork chops. "There he is," he says.

Connor's car is slowing in front of the café.

"He'll be there tonight," Angel says.

Dinah watches the black car stalling at the yellow curb. He tips his hat at all of them gathered at the counter, then he drives on.

"What a guy," Sugarfoot says flatly.

"He's a fool," Angel says.

"He may be a fool, but he's our fool, right, Mom?" Benny asks.

Dinah looks at him. She looks across the counter to his eyes, which are her eyes, and his dark skin, which is her skin. The comment makes her uncomfortable.

Sugarfoot and Angel turn away, as houseguests do when there's a family undercurrent going on and they don't want to hear it.

After dinner, Pete turns on the ceiling fan, throws open the café door, and lets the spring night circulate. Sugarfoot leaves for the newspaper office. Dinah goes to the parlor and gets her mother's New Testament from the shelf. She finds the verse Tyler called to her in John. *I have many things to say to you, but you cannot bear them now.* She thinks it all the way to the ballpark. A new moon is up. She feels something hovering, something nearby, something frightful, something at hand.

12

It's dark. From his window, Connor can see a light is on in the county courthouse across the park. Connor thinks maybe the judge is in his chambers having orange juice. The judge is diabetic. The judge is a crook. But nobody bandies his name about in the national media bank, Connor thinks. No, they want old Eugene "Bull" Connor to kick around.

He picks through the memos on his desk. There's a note from the fire chief, who says that while fighting a blaze in the *Birmingham News* building yesterday, fifteen firefighters were exposed to carbon tetrachloride gas. All had symptoms of gas poisoning, some more than others. The memo says there was a similar occurrence at the *News* building a while back and they'd promised to convert the extinguishers from tetrachloride to water. It was a gentlemen's agreement that the newspaper didn't follow up on, and the fire chief is mad. Connor puffs his cigar and picks up the phone. He figures Sugarfoot is on the city desk, trying to make up a story for tomorrow.

When Sugarfoot answers, Connor says, "Connor here."

Sugarfoot's voice is breathy, "Evening, Commissioner."

"Got a memo here, Sugar," Connor tells him. "Says you all had a fire over there yesterday."

"I hear we did," Sugarfoot says.

"And did you witness it?"

"No, I was out."

Connor thinks of Sugarfoot wasting time in the hotel, standing by a bureau brushing his thick blond Raggedy Andy hair and choosing which socks not to wear. He thinks of Sugarfoot's wardrobe, all tan, camel, and suede.

He waits for whatever Sugarfoot wants to say.

"So, what's up?" Sugarfoot asks him. "Why're you working so late?"

Connor shuffles more papers on his desk. He finds his weekly interoffice memo from the police chief, detailing the most recent Negro church meeting. He says to Sugarfoot, "I think you might be interested to know that I have a report here stating that The Reverend—you know which one I mean—told his church that the attorney general of the United States has called him three times since the bus incident. The Reverend refers to the attorney general as Bob."

Connor chuckles. "Bob," he repeats. "Not Mr. Kennedy, not Robert, but Bob. What do you think of that, Sugar?"

Sugarfoot is quiet. Connor thinks of the drive up to the state line.

"Sugarfoot," he says, "I owe you and Miss Angelrider an apology for my behavior the other night."

"I think you better apologize to her, not me," Sugarfoot says.

Connor says, "Uh-hmm," and opens a letter from the director of personnel at Pete's foundry, which says the white team and the colored team will be practicing ball with one another on May 28. He looks at his calendar. That's tonight. He puts his cigar in an ashtray.

"Got to go," Sugarfoot says.

Connor leans forward. "No, wait, Sugar. I need to talk some things over with you. I need some personal advice. It's baseball related."

224

Sugarfoot says he's going to come over.

Connor gets his file on Nathan Stamps from a cabinet marked *Private*. He reviews the information. Nathan Stamps married to a Lydia Clarke, no children. Nathan's worked for Harcort six years. No criminal record. Connor's obtained from the director of personnel a brief bio on all the men on the colored baseball team. There's somebody named Burly, who molds in the malleable unit; a Myree, who ran shakeout before he went to inspection; Arthur, who worked the charging crane as long as it was in operation; Spencer, who rolls fittings from the cleaning shed to blank stock and who had also sorted iron and been a grinder; Curry, who assembles flange unions; Washington, who rolls in the tapping room; and so forth.

Sugarfoot knocks on his door ten minutes later. He's wearing his camel jacket and new cap. "You call that a tam, don't you?" Connor asks him, thinking how it makes him look like a French artist queer.

Sugarfoot takes a chair. Connor checks to make sure he's not wearing socks.

"So," Connor says and sits down. He gets to the point. "I'm going over to this ball practice tonight. Bet you already knew about it, didn't you?" Connor looks at Sugarfoot's flaxen hair. "Maybe you're Scandinavian," Connor notes. "You know, Sweden, Denmark, one of those countries where they have free love."

Sugarfoot runs a Weejun over the tile floor.

"Now, for the record, I'm not calling in the police. Nobody's said there's going to be trouble over at Harcort at this *inter*grated ball game, and I think the presence of the commissioner of public safety ought to ward off any disputes that might arise, right, Sugar?"

On the way to the foundry, Sugarfoot won't talk. Connor tries to interest him in a diatribe against the attorney general's office, inside information as to what's going on at the colored church meetings, but Sugarfoot's pencil won't budge. Sugar's got something on his mind. As they get close to Pete's industry, Connor starts thinking it might be Dinah. He thinks of Sugar's bedroom at the hotel, of what color the bedspread might be—some kind of fruity shade like lime or grape or lemon—and this makes him think of Sugar lying on his back staring at the ceiling with Dinah on his mind. It makes Connor mad, not that Sugarfoot would have a thing for her, but that he wouldn't discuss it with Connor. He's never met a man in all his years who'd have an honest conversation with him about women. They always hide their lusty ways, just like women do. They stuff it in their back pockets and won't bring it out, not even for a rainy day of conversation in the office of Eugene Connor, who needs, more than anything in the world, to have a man to talk to. He needs to tell somebody he married Beara because he knew she'd grow up to be his mother, watering her plants and sewing burial gowns for little dead colored babies.

"Dinah's mother," Connor begins.

Sugarfoot's head spins like a top. Yes, Connor thinks, that's what he wants to hear. This is the boy's story, here's the scoop. "Her mother did the deflowering. The most convincing virgin act since Mary."

Sugarfoot's Iowa farm boy eyes are wide. "What do you mean?" he asks.

Connor stalls at the entrance to the foundry. He can't decide what it is that Sugarfoot wants to hear. Maybe he's into whores. Maybe he's never had one, Connor thinks.

"What do you want to know?" Connor asks him and lights a cigar.

Sugarfoot won't ask.

"The deflowering was performed for Yankees," Connor tells him.

Sugarfoot says, "Oh yeah?" and laughs.

"Yeah," Connor says and parks his car under the oak tree. His blood starts racing when he looks at the ball field. Pete Fraley on the field with a bunch of Negroes.

Connor makes a mental note of where everybody is in the bleachers. Dinah is sitting beside a colored woman. Angelrider is in between the Fraley kids, wearing a black cap that looks for all the world like Sugarfoot's tam. Hats, Connor thinks and reaches for his own herringbone; hats have gone to hell.

They get out of the car and stand under the tree.

"So why was the deflowering for Yankees?" Sugarfoot asks him.

"News travels fast in Birmingham," Connor says, chewing on his cigar and staring at Dinah and the colored woman. Dinah is wearing a man's clothes, it looks like—baggy pants and a big jacket.

"What's that supposed to mean?" Sugarfoot asks, and he looks at the bleachers, too. But Connor knows he isn't on to this *inter-*grated ball practice story, he's on to whores.

"Locals might talk, catch on, get the idea that Candy wasn't a virgin after all," Connor tells him, "so she just did it for Yankees," Connor says and starts walking toward the bleachers.

Sugarfoot is carrying his windbreaker over his shoulder, the way men do in the movies. Connor looks at the Negro players on the field, all mixed up with the white ones. He feels like he's high on helium. He tries to act calm, to spin a story for Sugarfoot. He forces a chuckle. "Yeah, those were the days when Birmingham was becoming the Pittsburgh of the South. Men were coming in a stream from up North. Roosevelt was in office. Hard times were easing somewhat. Men were talking about how the Frisco, Saint

227

Louis, and San Francisco railroad ordered twenty thousand tons of steel rails from the plant in Birmingham." All the while he's talking, Connor's growing more and more light-headed, the way he bets officers feel when they're going to make an arrest, when they're standing at a bolted door in a Negro project. Connor feels the coins in his pockets. They're smooth and perfectly distinguishable—three quarters, a nickel, four pennies. He runs his fingers over them, thinking of George Washington's face, of Mr. Lincoln and Thomas Jefferson. He thinks of how nickels used to be, with the Indian head and the buffalo.

"The world's gone to hell," he says to Sugarfoot.

Sugarfoot eyes him, gets his notebook out. Their pace quickens as they approach the bleachers. Sugarfoot is already taking notes, and though Connor isn't reading what he's scribbling, he knows it is a description of this ugly ball field with its muddy outfield, old-fashioned scoreboard, and concession stand. Sugarfoot is writing the preamble to his article, which will include quotes from the coloreds and whites alike, quotes that will paint a picture of industrial life in Birmingham. Connor hates the naivete of it all. To think that playing ball will not lead to other things like eating in the same cafés and occupying hospital rooms side by side and dating and marrying. Connor no longer feels inflated with helium; he feels weights forming in his wrists and jawbones and kneecaps and hip joints, all the places where things must work together to make a man maneuver his body. Dinah is staring a hole in him. It's the gaze of her mother—a bossy, mean-streaked, strong look that cuts her beauty in two. Only a daughter can look at a father in this daring way.

"I got a daughter in Washington, D.C.," he says to Sugarfoot.

"Huh?" Sugar's pencil stops moving.

It's not worth repeating. "Forget it," Connor says and swats his fingers at Sugarfoot the way you do an insect.

Connor can't decide how to do what must be done.

Angelrider and Benny and Gracie are up in the bleachers, their legs brushing one another's. They're smiling big, but it's the smile of anarchists. It's the fake glee of those who think it's fun to tear up a culture. It makes him want to throttle the girl. It's all her fault. If she hadn't moved in with the Fraleys, things wouldn't be progressing like this. He thinks she's probably the one who put this harebrained idea in Pete's head. He thinks of how Pete won't hardly speak to him anymore. The colored people in the bleachers aren't even watching Connor, it's only the whites. Negroes, he thinks, don't even know who he is since they don't know how to read and are too poor to have TV sets, except stolen ones. He looks up at Dinah once again, and she's still staring at him like he's an old lover who did her wrong. Her green dagger eyes penetrate and defy his authority. Untamed, Connor thinks. Like a cheetah or a wildebeest, one of those African animals that runs over the landscape so hard and fast they never stop to think of what danger is.

He can't bear it. Keeping his eyes fixed on her, he turns to the bleachers as if they're a choir and he's the choirmaster. He can sense the baseball in Pete's hand, he can feel Pete's face staring at the dirt. "I've told you people once," he calls and looks up at the checkerboard of dark and light skin. The sight of it makes him certain he's right. Gracie's eyes are downcast, and her bangs are in her eyes; Benny's looking to the right in the direction of the grey iron unit where his daddy works; Angel's big agitator smile has vanished; the colored people are stiff as scarecrows. "You people of Birmingham have been hoodwinked, robbed, taken to the cleaners by a handful of misguided Northern college students. It's enough to break a man's heart," he says, as he tries to look people in the eye the way you do when you're making a speech. He can't find eyes to look into, though, other than

Dinah's. She is furious. She is coming to her feet. She is standing up in the crowd like a sore thumb, like a person who's on the wrong side of the stands, a fan from the other team who's standing up to cheer the opponent.

"Get out of here," she yells at him.

"I hate having to do this," Connor says, finally.

"Do what?" a colored lady calls.

As if set afire, Connor snaps: "I hate to tell you all that I'm saying to you, as commissioner of public safety, to separate. Now, you white boys under there," he calls under the bleachers. "You all shoo. Go on over to those trees. You colored boys stay near your mamas."

The wind is blowing. The big oaks sway. Anticipation is all over the baseball diamond, like they're listening for the opening of the National Anthem. Connor turns back to the field. Nathan Stamps, the Negro catcher, is holding his catcher's mask and staring up, defying him. Nobody is going anywhere.

Dinah scampers from the bleachers and walks clear onto the field. Connor's never seen a woman on a baseball field, and the sight of it makes him sick. The world has gone to hell, he thinks once again, and looks for Sugarfoot, who is trying to get quotes from Negroes, dancing and prancing like an elf the way journalists do when they're interviewing reluctant bystanders who keep trying to walk past the press. Connor isn't sure where to go now or what to do. Nobody's obeying him and it's clear there will be an incident, that they're going to play ball—once they get the women off the field. What the hell, he thinks. What are the women doing on the field?

"Jesus," Sugarfoot says, writing in his notebook.

"Jesus, what?" Connor wants to know. "Jesus, what? Why did you say that? Why did you say *Jesus?* What are those women doing on the field?" he demands.

He snatches Sugar's tam and snaps it up. Sugar's blond, thick hair goes every which way.

"They're showing their support," Sugarfoot says of the women. Sugar's eyes are glazed the way ideologues' eyes tend to do when they're witnessing a bunch of bullshit they think has meaning. It makes Connor want to kick him, but there's nothing he can do but stand here and watch Dinah's hand on Pete's shoulder. They're on the field. They're walking in the direction of Nathan Stamps and a colored lady who is, Connor assumes, Stamps's wife. Here you have, on the field, Connor thinks, the end-all of life as we know it in America.

Baseball's gone, he thinks, as he slaps his herringbone hat against his knee. Hats are gone. Decency is gone, and it's all—he stares up at Angel, who is all over Benny Fraley—it's all because of the likes of her.

He walks over to the city car and calls the north precinct. He tells the dispatcher to be on standby, that there might be trouble at Harcort. He sits under the oak tree, where a few new green leaves brush against his car. Pete is on the mound and Stamps walks toward home plate. Pete Fraley is going to do it. He is going to throw a ball into the mitt of a colored laborer. Connor feels naked. He jumps from the car and grabs Sugarfoot's elbow so hard his pencil leaps up and lands beside the foot of a large Negro. Sugarfoot says, "What?" to him, irritated and puzzled. Connor tells him he's got to help stop this thing.

Nathan throws on his mask, chest protector, and shin guards. Tyrell stands awkwardly near the plate until Pete yells, "Hit a few." Pete's white buddies disperse themselves haphazardly, a shortstop leaning a bit to third, a first baseman idling midway to second as if trying to steal, a lone outfielder under a bright star. Nathan and Pete mumble their way through some rough, simple

signals and Nathan lets Pete throw the kinds of balls he knows
Pete likes to throw. He knows Pete better than he knows the colored pitcher, he's watched him so many times. He signals and
watches Pete's body. They're in sync. Nathan thinks of how long
he's wanted to do this. He knows Pete's arm, his mind, his ruth-
lessness, his lack of consistency. If he could catch for him just one
game, he's always known, he'd change Pete's way of looking at
home. He isn't aware of Bull Connor. He isn't aware of the stands
or the crowd or the foundry or the sky or the night. His eyes are
on Pete.

Pete winds up. His body is muscled and, for a brief instant, on
the brink of ecstasy. Nathan is there, suspended with him. He
knows what this release means for Pete. He knows that this ball is
more than cork and yarn and rubber cement and alum-tanned
leather. He knows that this ball is worth a thousand times its
weight in gold when it's thrown by a white man to a colored man
in Birmingham, Alabama, in 1961 and the man throwing it is the
boss man and the man catching it is the one who handles fire. He
knows if he could put a stop action on Pete's face, you'd be able to
see the wince and the joy and the pent-up guilt begging to come.
Nathan knows it takes a Negro to catch that kind of ball—for a
white man.

He catches it.

White and colored players stand with their hands up against
the chain-link fence and nobody says a word. Nathan has no sign
what the verdict is. He has a fleeting fear that he's going to hear a
gun any moment. He glances around at the white families and at
the handful of Pete's friends manning the field as if they're mixed
up or drunk. But then one makes a friendly quip to Pete, and the
others laugh, and there are jokes and insults, and somebody yells
to Nathan, "It's gone take a long time to teach that white boy to
pitch." Nathan breathes in. He knows it's all right. He knows it's

just a matter of time now. Nathan's heard a superstition that a given bat holds only a certain number of hits, and a batter must discard it when it reaches its quota. He knows that a given man holds a certain number of risks he's willing to take, and he knows that Pete Fraley hasn't used his up yet.

Nathan's glove is beside him, separating his body from Lydia's. Pete's car smells like upholstery, leather, and shellac. It's reminiscent of a shoe repair shop, indigo ink, the way Lydia smells when she's been polishing Mrs. Light's sterling silver.

"Where we going, Mr. Pete?" he asks.

"Home," Pete says.

"To the hotel," Dinah clarifies.

Nathan's fingers, splayed on the car seat, seem remote as if they belong to another man, somebody with sense. He feels queasy, like at the end of Thanksgiving or the morning after a drunk or the way it feels to inhale ether upon entering a hospital ward. He thinks he and Lydia ought to be home or at the bar, drinking a Colt and watching Hoots sweep. Lydia's talking to Pete's wife. They're making nervous small talk—fabrics and grocery lists and working for Mrs. Light and running a hotel, sheets and bedspreads and the peculiar ways of some men.

This wasn't part of the plan. But Pete invited them right in Bull Connor's face, so what could Nathan say?

He stares at the back of Pete's head—at the black curls that form corkscrews at the base of his neck, like Pete's a Negro, too.

"Don't worry," Pete says to Nathan in the rearview mirror.

"Worry about what?" Pete's wife asks him. Her long hair is blowing in a thousand directions.

"Connor," Pete says to his wife.

Dinah turns to Nathan and Lydia and waves it away. "He's a fool," she says, "a friend of ours from way back. He'd never do anything to hurt us or you, not really," she says.

Nathan turns away to the dark night out his window. He thinks Pete's wife is wrong, he knows she's wrong. He knows Connor will do everything to hurt them. He knows Connor's trailing them, and he doesn't want to look back. He doesn't want to do anything to ignite Connor.

"He's got some power," Lydia notes.

Pete's wife turns to her. "Just at City Hall."

Nobody says anything. Nathan can feel all that's between himself and Pete—all Pete's told him about Connor, the history he's privy to, all of Pete's passions and resentments and cowardice, all of his rage pinned to this May night ride.

Nathan takes Lydia's hand. Her maid's dress is stark white in the dark car. Her brown eyes sparkle, reflecting the light from street lamps. This is it, he thinks. This is what she wanted—to be involved.

"I'm sorry you lost a baby," Pete's wife says to Lydia, but even as she says it, her eyes are in the side mirror, watching Connor's car. Nathan can't see the car, won't turn to look, but he knows it is there. The ghost of it shines in Dinah's eyes.

"We'll try again," Lydia says, in her fake, talking-to-whites voice. "Yes, we'll keep on trying for a baby," she says.

"It'll happen," Dinah says, and Nathan watches her eyes. They're cat's eyes. They're green and piercing, and he wonders if she has certain powers, like maybe she can predict the future. She's turned back to face them. She looks at Lydia and then at him in the way whites generally won't look at you unless they're mad at you for a job poorly done. "It'll happen," she affirms and keeps on penetrating Lydia with her eyes, as if she's capable of impregnating her with the power of a gaze. "God's in this," she says, and Nathan wonders if she's talking about a baby or about what they're doing.

Nathan can't stand it any longer. He turns quickly for a view of Connor's black city car.

Connor's face is crystal clear. It has layers of skin, like a rhinoceros or an elephant.

Pete, as if sensing Nathan's alarm, says, "He won't call the police. He'll want to handle this himself."

Handle this. Nathan wonders what that means. He thinks of handcuffs and pistols and saloons. He wishes he hadn't come. It was enough to catch for him. He thinks of the murky ways of white people, how they brood and hide what they feel and throw underhanded at one another, how they'd rather play bridge than shoot pool, how they sit like statues in church and don't move when they feel the Spirit moving them, how they don't dance when they're drunk; they just sit at tables and have slurred conversations. He thinks of how they fasten their cuff links and adjust and readjust their neckties and how they're never satisfied with how they look or smell or feel, how they suck their Luden's wild cherry cough drops, how they get preoccupied with scrubbing their whitewall tires, how they let things build up inside. He thinks of Pete buying this Chevrolet, how he must have paced the car lot wondering if it was the right or the wrong color, if he'd get a good payback when he traded it in. They're always looking ahead, Nathan thinks, always wanting the present moment to breed a future event. So they get bogged down with savings bonds and life insurance and education and elections. Their salvation is only the assurance of eternal life—not cause for immediate joy. Doctors quell pain. Lawyers settle fights. Companies rule.

Dinah keeps an eye on the mirror outside her window. She sees Connor's face. She's going to have words with him. She's going to straighten him out. She's going to make him sit and have blackberry pie with these Negroes. She thinks of his fat hands folded on the tabletop as he listens to Negroes talk, but she knows the Negroes won't talk. She knows they're scared to death of him.

She thinks of Lydia Stamps in the backseat—her big eyes and dark skin. She thinks of the tip of Africa, of how a hooker once told her Eve in the Bible was colored. She conjures up cavemen, tribal dances, painted faces. She thinks of big fat colored women in artist's drawings of cotton fields, mammies, and how ignorant she is of Negroes. She thinks of Jasmine. "Is this strange to you?" she asks Lydia Stamps suddenly.

"No," Lydia says.

Her hands are in her lap.

"She wanted to," Nathan says, staring out the window.

"Wanted to?"

"To do something like this," Nathan says. "She wanted to get involved," he says to Dinah, but he's staring at the factories they're passing.

Involved, Dinah thinks, turning back to the road. Involved. Birmingham is cracking. An earthquake is occurring, a long protracted tremor from deep within. But for her, the world has always had a schism. The hotel, Connor, her mother, keyholes, Tyler, snakes, the Holy Ghost. Nothing has ever been logical. Odd things take on the shape of order when you live like she has. Any anchor will suffice when you have none. When it's all you've got, she thinks, but she can't complete this thought. She watches Connor in the rearview mirror. She looks at his herringbone hat, and she feels guilty. She is afraid he will drive off a cliff or wreck the city car.

Dinah glances over at Pete. His eyes are on the road. She can see his jaw working, the veins along the side of his temple pulsing—a candidate, she thinks, for a stroke.

She remembers Connor was there the night her mother was

murdered. He came crashing in the front door like a big gray ghost with scurrying men at his heels. He called an ambulance, then he scooped Dinah up like she was a package to be mailed and took her to the sidewalk, where he handed her a $5 bill and a Hershey bar. It was all he had on him, she knew. She ate the Hershey bar. Jesus, she thinks, running her hands in her hair and staring at herself in the side window. I ate the damn Hershey bar. She tosses her hair back and slides down a bit in the seat.

"Worried?" Pete asks her.

Worry, Dinah sees, is up to Pete's fingers, which grip and regrip the wheel like men grip golf clubs. "No," she lies to him, smiling. "I'm not worried."

She turns to Nathan. "You're a great catcher," she says.

His dark eyes go to her. "Yes'm," he says.

She wishes he wouldn't say *yes'm* to her, but she knows this won't change. He'll say *yes'm* and *no'm* and call Pete *Mr. Pete* till hell freezes over.

"What do you do when you're not at work?" she asks Lydia, glancing back to Connor's car. A light from the street lamp cuts over his windshield, making his face hard to see.

"I plant flowers," Lydia says.

Dinah adjusts her body sideways as to have a better view of her. She's a fashionable-looking maid. She's got on earrings. Dinah wonders if Negroes say *high yellow* or if that's a white phrase.

"I guess you know we have a freedom rider living with us," Dinah says to her.

Lydia Stamps's lips part.

"She's from up North."

Lydia's hands are in her lap.

"She's staying on with us," Dinah says. She wants Lydia Stamps to think they're involved in the Negro situation. She wants her to think they have a conscience.

"It's to aggravate Bull Connor," Pete quips. "That's why she's staying on with us."

Dinah turns to Nathan and Lydia. "It is not," she argues. "You'll meet her tonight. She's in the car with my son and daughter."

It's peculiar and exciting—the physical proximity. It'd be different if they were her maid and yardman. They aren't. They're going to break a law with her. "Breaking the law," she says, to no one in particular. "Breaking it." She watches Pete's hands grip the steering wheel. "I mean, when you think of breaking something, do you think of holding a stick and jerking it in two with your knee? Is breaking the law a mean and deliberate thing?"

"No, baby," Lydia says softly. "It's like snapping beans."

Dinah looks at her.

"It's so easy," she says.

Dinah pictures herself with Lydia Stamps snapping beans in the hotel café.

"She wanted to get involved," Nathan reminds Dinah.

"This wasn't exactly what I had in mind," Lydia says to Dinah, smiling. Nathan must weigh twice what his wife weighs, Dinah thinks. She's so small she might pass for a daughter.

"So, what did you picture yourself doing?" Dinah asks her. "Riding a bus?"

Lydia stares out the window. "I reckon so," she says.

"Things never turn out how you thought they would," Dinah says.

"That's right," Lydia agrees.

"You have to take these things one step at a time," Dinah says to her, though she has no idea what she means. She's no more an integrationist than the man in the moon. She hates politics.

Pete keeps his eyes fixed on the road.

What's she thinking? What on earth is she thinking? he wonders as he takes her strong hand in his and holds it tight. She's not like other women, who hide the innermost compartment from you. She keeps her wild, green eyes wide open, even when she's making love. Yet he can't make her tell him of the past. Who she is—right now—is evident. It's the past he can't know. It's Connor. It's her mother. It's the whores and the rooms of the hotel and Connor. There are no photographs of her when she was a child, no documents, nothing to give him a picture of her going in and out of doorways. "I played in the alley," she has told him. "It was a mess of honeysuckle vines, and I hid and watched the girls bathe in the washtubs during summer, and I was happy." But to this day when he parks his car in the alley behind the hotel he can't *see* this.

He looks back at Connor's black city car following his. He's heard other men discuss the midlife breaking point, that moment when you take your life in your hands; he's heard the term *modern man*. He wonders if Connor has a gun. He's sure he does. He bets it's a .38 chief's special snubnose or maybe a .45-caliber Colt automatic. He wonders if it's in the glove compartment or on Connor's person. It's on him, Pete thinks as he lets his hands relax a bit on the wheel. The car smells like Nathan—a foundry smell, sand, iron, fire, and brass.

"He's not dangerous," Pete says to Nathan.

Nathan says nothing.

Pete's glove is on the floorboard, amidst the mud and debris and candy wrappers that litter a family car. He thinks of family situations on TV, how they're never riding in a car. They're in homes, homes that have a stairway and carpets and a wife wearing a snug dress.

"Do you like ice cream?" Dinah is asking Lydia Stamps.

"Yes'm."

Pete wonders what Dinah has in mind for dessert. He wonders

what they're going to do at the hotel. A game of bingo? Dancing? Shop talk? What if they have to go to the bathroom?

He panics. The bathroom. Which bathroom will they use? He hasn't thought this thing out. There is a bathroom in the back kitchen; maybe that's the right one.

He hopes Nathan won't have to go. It won't be so bad if it's his wife. He thinks of the foundry gates, of the cafeteria lines, lockers, showers, and water fountains. It is insurmountable. It is, Pete thinks, tedious. It'd be like trying to take apart a model airplane without breaking the parts. He thinks of airplane glue. He thinks of the color silver, and this makes him think of Alan Shepard and astronauts and what a powerful diversion space rockets are for the modern man. He looks up at the moon and thinks the recurring thought he's been thinking as he gets near forty—that life is far from right.

We're wandering off course, he'd like to say to Nathan, but he doesn't know if Nathan thinks these things. Maybe Negroes don't see the sky the same way; maybe they steer away from dark thoughts since they are, themselves, dark.

Connor holds the car radio in hand as if it's a safety device, as if at any moment he might need to signal for help. He feels in terrific distress, like a family member is in a medical emergency, like the way he felt when his daughter cut her leg open and had to be rushed to the hospital. It's as if life now rides on how he controls his car, like he's got to both be somewhere in the nick of time and yet be paced to perfection in order to avoid arriving too quickly. He knows—somewhere in the back of his mind—that nobody's in danger. Yet he can't let the car escape his eye. It would mean losing control of the situation, and the situation is so far out of control he is frantic. He's got to track Pete's footsteps because it is clear that Pete Fraley has lost his mind. He is like the man over at the V.A. who stepped out of a twelfth-floor window and stood on the precipice threatening to jump. Pete has stepped over the edge and he's taking his whole family with him. Connor must prevent this family suicide pact, and it's as if his whole life has led him to this juncture. Dinah needs him as she never has before. "Damn," he says into the car radio.

"What is it, Mr. Connor?" the dispatcher says.

"Nothing," Connor replies.

He adjusts his rearview mirror, and he catches sight of Benny's car with Angel in the front seat and Sugarfoot and Gracie in the back. Well, isn't this the Easter parade? he thinks. He keeps his hand on the mirror, fiddling with it to make his view of them deliberate. He wants Benny and Angelrider to know he's watching them, that he's got an eye on their antics. Pete's car turns to the viaduct and Connor begins to get the picture: Pete is taking the Negroes to the hotel. He calls up the dispatcher and says, "No need to send any cars, but just want to say I'm on my way to the Crescent Hotel by the terminal. Not expecting any trouble. Don't," he says, "I repeat, don't send any cars."

The fins of Pete's Chevy sail over the viaduct. Connor glances over at the Sloss furnaces and remembers what an aerial view of Harcort is like, with its acres of dark warehouses and foundries and incinerators, the way the baseball field spreads northward and every bit of the property is bathed in debris from the cupola. The soot, the stench, the murky slag. He thinks of Sugarfoot's Weejuns caked in it. He looks back at Benny's car.

Angelrider's cap is perched sideways. She probably fancies herself on a stagecoach, stirring up dust and forging westward. What's she saying? *This is a statement, an act of courage. People will go to jail, people will have crosses burned in their yards, people will be injured, all for a holy purpose. Aren't you proud to be a part of history?* They'll nod their heads and watch her with their starstruck eyes that have no perception of history. They just want to be a part of her. He thinks of how love is manufactured in the same way Pete's valves and pipe fittings are—as cheaply as possible.

The fins of Pete's Chevy travel to the end of the viaduct, where a red light stops them. When he was a boy, Connor believed the viaduct's arc was a rainbow and the blast furnace fire was where Satan lived. If you weren't good, the bus driver might toss you over into a stream of orange flames and there you'd roast like a pig—hence the term *pig iron*. To this day he can see himself a charred slab of pork turning on a rotisserie for all the world to see, and indeed that's how he felt when he was caught with Chris. He feels his pulse quicken. He thinks of his friends who put nitroglycerine tablets under their tongue at a time like this, of one Billy Gloglotten—a sheriff's deputy who had a heart attack on Lake Martin catching an oversized bass. He thinks of fish and dolphins and whales and sharks and Charles Darwin. He thinks of Nathan Stamps's wife riding in Pete Fraley's car and wonders if the car smells like starch and Dentyne. He wonders if Sugarfoot has ever had a fantasy for a Negro. He glances in the rearview mirror to see Angelhooker planting a kiss on Benny Fraley's lifeguard face—*For my benefit,* Connor thinks.

It's all mixed up in his mind—Benny, Angelrider, Sugarfoot, Dinah, Pete, Nathan, Lydia. He can't sort through it anymore; it's all just a hodgepodge of sin and lust and greed, and the only thing that's for certain is that he, Connor, isn't included. He's the guy standing by the carousel that Pete operates, where all the pretty horses go up and down, up and down on their painted hooves.

Pete's Chevy slows near the hotel and comes to a stop under the blue awning. Dinah hops in her farm clothes from the passenger's side and opens the door for the Negroes. Nathan still has his mitt in his hand as if they're going to play ball in the street. His wife is striking, thin, and light skinned.

Connor grips his walkie-talkie, but there is nothing to say, nobody to talk to. He's never felt so lonely in all his life. Benny has pulled up now, and the others tumble forth to the sidewalk, chipper and electrified as if they're kids trying to act like they're not scared by the presence of a rabid dog.

Connor hops from the car.

"It's not me," he calls to them. "I'm not the mad dog. It's yourself, it's you, it's that dark side of you, Benny, that you inherited from your mama and daddy, that's what you're scared of, even if you don't know it," Connor says, breathing hard. Saying this takes the edge off. It's the way he feels when he backs up from a woman he's just kissed, allowing himself a moment.

But Angel approaches him. "Don't do this, Eugene. You'll hate yourself." She's under the street lamp, and her spritelike body makes him want to spank her.

"You don't know anything," he tells her.

Her eyes widen.

"I know this family," he tells her.

"What are you, their father?" she says, and he grabs her arm.

"Come on," he tells her, leading her like she's a convict, struggling with the temptation to pinch the fire out of her. You can do that to children, according to the experts who preceded Dr. Spock. You can pinch a nerve at the base of a kid's neck and it's perfectly in order. "Come on," he repeats, stalking past Sugarfoot and the Fraley kids on the sidewalk near the yellow curb, "we're going inside."

He leads her in. The café is so yellow it makes his eyes hurt. The Negroes are at a table. "Put them to work," he says to Dinah, who is scurrying to make desserts. "Put them to frying some chicken," he says to Pete. "Slice a tad of watermelon. Hey," he says to Nathan Stamps's wife, "this used to be a brothel." He's still clutching Angel's arm like she's a hostage. "We make our beds, then we lie in them, right, Miss Angelrider?"

Pete throws his blue cap on a table, his face ghostly.

"Now, now," Connor chides. "Not to worry, not to worry. This is a family gathering, Pete. I'm not going to cause a scene." He chuckles.

"You already have," Angel says, and Connor squeezes her elbow like it's a lemon wedge. He looks at her eyes, and it's almost erotic, the sight of her trying not to wince. It makes him want to take her to the city car and escort her somewhere special.

No need to hurry, he thinks. No need to panic. No need to break this party up so quickly. Relax, Eugene, he says to himself. Let this thing work itself out. Negroes, he knows, hate white places in the end. They'd never *choose* a white church or school or mate. In a while, Nathan Stamps will be dying to get home to his own bar, his own home, to get the hell out of this honky nightmare Pete Fraley is having.

Connor releases Angel's arm but she stays at his side.

Things have taken a turn. "So," he says and pulls a chair up beside Nathan. "You a pourer, huh?"

Nathan's eyes are on his wife. He keeps looking at her, even when he says, "Yes sir."

Connor puts a hand on her shoulder. "And what might your name be?"

"Lydia Stamps," she says.

Connor looks at her downcast eyes. God, they're pretty when they're demure like this—all ebony and sweet. "Hey," he says, tugging at his trouser legs, "it's good you two are married. I know some Negroes aren't."

244

Dinah's voice is shrill as a peacock. "That is a racist remark. Go home."

Connor knows she doesn't mean it; he can tell by the tone of it. It's something you say to a stray dog you know hasn't quite had the scraps it needs.

"You work over the mountain?" he says to Nathan's wife.

"Yes sir," she says. She's fingering a lavender hanky.

Dinah whirls her tall body away. She isn't built a thing like her mother.

Gracie and Benny bring the hot fudge sundaes to the table. Gracie puts one in front of Connor and he says, "Thank you, honey." To Lydia Stamps, he says, "What a kid."

There's no sign of Pete. "Where's your husband?" he asks Dinah, who doesn't respond. "Come on, Sugarfoot," he says. "Come get your dessert."

Sugarfoot is standing by the jukebox as if the right music is the issue at hand. "Don't put on that song about the lion in the jungle," Connor says.

He gets up, walks over the jukebox, and puts a hand on Sugarfoot's shoulder, surveying his tam. "This is a reporter," he says to Nathan. "This is Mr. Beau Sleigh, otherwise known as Sugarfoot."

Gracie is at a table with Angel, eating ice cream. Connor thinks of how it'd be if Angelrider's foot brushed his under a table. He turns to her and locks his thumbs in his suspenders. "Did anybody ever tell you that you look like Peter Pan?"

She ignores him. She gets up and goes over behind the counter, where Benny is spraying whipped cream. She leans in to him. She's so like a boy, Connor thinks to himself, they look like a couple of queers—a big one, a little one.

Nathan and Lydia Stamps keep their spoons busy, making

dents in the mountain of vanilla ice cream until the nuts slide into the melted part and the fudge mixes in so that what you have, he thinks, is a portrait of ugly miscegenation.

Connor goes over to Dinah, who is leaning against the wall. He gestures to Benny and Angel, who are holding hands. "Don't you think you ought to say something to those kids about doing this in public?"

"This isn't public," she snaps.

"Now, that's debatable," Connor tells her. Just as he says the word *debatable*, Pete reappears from the back kitchen.

"Feeling better?" he asks Pete.

Pete motions for Connor to step inside the back kitchen, the private kitchen, where Connor loves to drink coffee with Dinah and talk of the old days. Pete closes the door behind him. He is shaking like a leaf. Connor's never seen a man shake like this. Pete's entire body is shivering, and his lips are bluish and his eyes are twitching so hard the brown iris is a living being. "Listen," he says, "you got to leave here. Dinah's not going to do it; never in a hundred years would she ask you to leave, no matter what you did. Do you understand me?"

Connor thinks of his herringbone hat. He can't remember where he left it.

"Are you hearing me, Connor?"

"Pete," Connor says and looks at the floor. It's a tile floor, and it was laid in 1929, right before the stock market crashed. Connor knows who laid it, a fellow by the name of Fig Marley.

Pete won't speak now. He's just staring at the floor, shaking, and Connor is afraid he's going to cry. He can almost see Pete's shoulders bending in, the way men do when they cry. He's only seen three men cry in his life, and they were all Negroes.

"Pete," Connor says again, "did you bring those Negroes here because you wanted to make a point for me?"

Pete looks up at him. His eyes are brown and wild and boylike.
"Go to hell," Pete says.

"I can't do that, Pete. I'm not dead yet."

"Get out of here," Pete says and shoves him back against the wall. Pete's jaw is working overtime. He's got a fist ready to hit Connor, all reared back.

"I'll call the law if you hit me," Connor says to him.

"You're a sorry bastard," Pete says. "You and that circus you operate at City Hall. You're the laughingstock of America. When you're dead and rotting in hell, people will still be talking about you."

Connor's blood is going. He wants to kick Pete between the legs. Pete Fraley, he thinks, is acting like a Negro.

Connor turns to go. But the moment he is back in the café, he can't leave. Dinah is sitting beside Lydia Stamps, eating a hot fudge sundae, so close the leg of Dinah's farm pants brushes Lydia's uniform. The sight of it makes him turn to steel.

He walks over to Sugarfoot, who is at a table by himself, scribbling in his notebook. "I can't take this," Connor says. He can feel his face shaking, like the skin's going to shed.

Sugarfoot studies him like he's from another planet, his face blank as an empty page, like he's doesn't know who Connor is. His pencil is moving across the notebook, though, as if he's drawing what he sees. Connor jerks the pencil from his hand, and it flies up in the air. "I hate that habit of yours," Connor says. "The way you people keep writing even when you're talking to a person. It's bad manners. I hate you people," he says.

He goes over to Dinah's table and leans over Nathan and Lydia. "You people are going to pay for all this trouble," he says. He starts to tip his hat but remembers he's not wearing it and doesn't know where he left it. "Lost my hat," he yells in Dinah's face. "Lost my goddamn hat." She stares at him in the way Sugarfoot did, like she's never met him before in her life. Hurt and furious, he inches closer to the door and stops beside Gracie, who has just popped a cherry in her mouth. She bites into it, watching him like he's a bear. "You scared of me?" he asks her.

"No," she says.

"Well," he says. "Just wondering." Right before he turns to go, Dinah throws her head back in laughter. They're laughing at me, he thinks. It makes him panic again.

He walks to the city car, slides in, gets the .38 special from the glove compartment, and puts it in his belt. He stares at the logo on the café door—COME ON IN, IT'S KOOL INSIDE. He feels himself coming apart, like a bag of groceries breaking in two, tumbling to the street, and the more you try to pick them up, the more you drop.

He storms back in.

"OK," he yells at Pete. "OK, Pete. I understand. I've been booted. I get it. Gone. Tossed. Garbage. Buried. Sure," he clips, unable to get out more than a word at a time, his pulse is so fast. "But," he says and tries to catch his breath. He bends over, hands on thighs. "But let me say, let me warn." He sits at a table, thinking he's about to have an aneurism or a myocardial infarction, as they say in the firehouse. But does Dinah Fraley give a damn?

She is picking her painted orange nails.

"Look at me!" he calls to her.

She won't.

"Goddamn," he says and gets up. Pete stops him. Sugarfoot stands in the way of Pete's fist, clinched, ready. "Sit down," Sugarfoot orders Pete. Pete shoves Sugarfoot aside. He comes after Connor, but Connor walks over to Nathan and Lydia Stamps, and he peers into the whites of their eyes. "How come it's yellow?" he asks Stamps, surveying him like an optometrist. "The white part," he clarifies, truly curious. "Is is a physical by-product of Africa? Is it jaundice? Is it cowardice?"

He backs up.

Pete grabs his arm and pushes him toward the door. Connor slaps his hands away and looks over at Dinah, who brushes lint from her pants legs. "You been up to see your preacher daddy?" he asks her. "You been crawling in chicken shit, baby? You been picking up rattlesnakes?" he asks then turns sharply to Nathan. "Boo!" he says. "Boo! Snakes. You scared of them?"

Connor wipes his brow with a handkerchief.

"Get out of here," Pete says.

Connor takes the gun from his belt and lets Pete see it, then he moves behind the counter. Pete doesn't stop him. No siree. Pete's not going to fight City Hall, not when City Hall's carrying a gun. Pete's family is clustered at a table. The girl, Gracie, inches to-ward the door. Connor calls to her, "Gracie!" and with the gun gestures to the table where he wants her to sit. He's going to have to talk fast in order to let everybody get this story straight. Angel is up against the jukebox, smoking a Kool. "You just stay right there, Angelrider," he says.

He spots Dinah's hand over Lydia Stamps's.

"Stop it," he says to her, looking at the hands overlapping. "Stop holding her hand." He checks to see where Sugarfoot is. He's over by Angel at the jukebox, smoking one of her Kools. "Toss me one of those menthol cigarets," he says to Angel, "and take off that Paris cap you're wearing."

She walks over, lights a Kool, and sticks it between Connor's lips.

Straddling a stool like a boy, she grins her impish grin and gives him a languid, dreamy-eyed look. "Trying to distract me from business," he whispers and bends close in.

"If you'll leave this place," she whispers back, "I'll come see you."

He backs up, bumping his backside against the grill. He can see what she's up to; he's not to be tricked. "Go sit over by Mama," he instructs her, but her compact ass stays on the bar stool.

"Leave this place," she says to him.

The way she says it, with that yankee *leeeve*, makes him burn. He looks her right in the eye. "You understand, Miss Rider, that you've been living in a whorehouse." He glances over to Nathan Stamps. "You people call whores *whores* or do you have another name for it?" He turns back to Angel, whose arms are folded on the countertop like a frustrated customer. "Maybe you know, since you fancy yourself a Negro. Do they call a whore a whore?"

"This is a family," she says.

"Oh," Connor says and holds his hands up. "Oh, a family. Angel Freedom Rider thinks this is a family. Who's the family, Angel-rider? Is it the mother, the father, the sister, the brother? Or are *you* part of it, too? Maybe you're the kissing cousin? And Sugarfoot, here, is he part of the *family?* What's he? The mother's boyfriend? And these Negroes, are they part of the *family?* Oh, not the maids or the butlers or the yardmen, but the in-laws. So we have this family, in this café, with this mean old grandfather," he says, and cups his mouth to speak sideways to Gracie, "That's me, sugar. That's Eugene Connor."

Angel walks to the jukebox and he follows after her. He rolls up the sleeves of his white work shirt and gets near her, dodging her cigaret. He puts the .38 in her belly button.

"You want to know about this family? I'll tell you about this family."

Pete is walking toward him. Connor can feel the heat of it,

moving closer. Pete's face isn't red, it's pasty. Ah, yes, Connor thinks, he's scared. He's not mad, he's scared.

Sugarfoot leads Connor back behind the soda fountain. "Don't do this," Sugar says. "You'll regret it," he says.

"Don't need you, buddy," Connor says.

Sugarfoot says, "Come on, let's go get a drink somewhere. A whiskey. Let's find some women," he says and raises an eyebrow.

"I'm just doing my job, Sugar. Do yours. Go," he says, shooing Sugar with his hands, "go get your notebook."

Sugar runs his hands in his thick blond hair, scratching his scalp hard like he's got lice. Sugar's frustrated, Connor thinks. Sugar's worried. Sugar's off duty and can't be objective.

He takes in the napkin holders and pewter dessert mugs and Formica countertop, the stools, and the chalkboard menu erased of lunch specials. He thinks of macaroni and cheese, of Dinah's pale green order pad and the way the place is at noon, the city abustle and the train whistles blowing and the blast furnaces on fire. "Birmingham," he says and looks into the dark eyes of Nathan and Lydia Stamps. "You people," he says and looks at them one by one—Dinah, Pete, Benny, Gracie—"you people, I see, have changed."

His anger is being converted; he can taste it. It's a metal, a hard metal burning his tongue, gums, throat. He thinks of molten pig iron being tapped from the furnace, how slag floats to the top. "By-products," he says, staring at them all. "By-products of the Kennedys." He walks over to the door and stares at the street, where his black car sits by the yellow curb. "Family," he says and turns back to Angel. "This *family*," he says and chuckles. "You've chosen a bad family, Miss Rider, for the revolution." Connor puts his thumbs in his suspenders and tugs at his gray pants. He looks down at the black-and-white tile floor, then walks back behind the counter. He fingers the plates with the green band and the milk shake machine and the little silver boxes holding cherries, hot fudge, caramel, nuts, limes, and jelly. He lifts up the scoops one by one, as if it's the last time he'll ever peek in. He thinks of the private kitchen in the back where he and Dinah talk under the gas-jet lights. He thinks of how she'd run in and out of the swinging door as a kid, saying, "Mama, Mr. Peterson is here," or, "Mr. Raston," or, "Mr. Lawler." All the men who visited the brothel, bearing cash and trinkets.

Connor leans over the counter and says to Angel, "You want to know about this family. I'll tell you about this family. Let's start with the grandmother. This was called the red light district," Connor says and the moment he says it, Dinah is up from her chair, coming toward him in her farm clothes with that wild mess of hair flying behind her like a Gypsy.

"Red light district, nineteen thirty-four," he says and reaches for a cigar.

She's in his face. He can feel the heat of her, the beauty, the green swampy eyes. She's moist like the Everglades and the Tamiama Trail and the corridor of tropical backroads you drive through before you get to the very tip of Florida. She's nothing like her mother.

"There was the Rabbit Foot saloon on Morris, remember?" he says to her, and though she's mad as a hornet, he knows she loves to hear him say it. "Old horse stable they'd converted to a wine-room, hauled in a piano."

Her eyes are torrid. "Go home," she says.

"Jennie Bell's brothel, Scratch Ankle, over on Second, a house of black prostitutes. Jennie was a mulatto," he says and leans over the counter, toward Angel's bar stool, "like you."

Angel's smoking her Kool like there's no tomorrow. She's getting anxious. He can smell it on her; he can see it in the way she flicks her cigaret over and over into a jar lid.

"Hey, Stamps," he calls to Nathan, "you know any mulattoes?"

Nathan Stamps stares at the floor.

Connor chuckles.

Dinah almost comes over the counter, knocking over a plastic mustard dispenser. "Leave, right this minute," she tells him, and he knows he's got to talk fast. Her eyes are moist and she is breathing hard, so hard her chest rises and falls under the farm shirt, but Pete restrains her, watching the gun.

"Now, this place here was called the White House, and the girls had names like Ruby, Pansy, and Candy—things to eat or wear or smell. Sugarfoot, you'd of loved them."

Dinah leans so far over the counter that her breasts touch the Formica. Her work shirt is open at the neck, and Connor looks at her Mediterranean skin and her eyes. "Mama grew up by the coast, didn't she, baby?" he asks her.

Dinah puts a hand over his mouth. He smells her; it's the smell of dinner, Ajax, Windex, and water. It's the smell of the new home they're building: wood and carpenters and men. He thinks of her in a subdivision, trying to act right.

"But Mama moved inland at fifteen when *her* mother died, leaving her in charge of a baby sister, isn't that right, baby?" Connor's never told her all this; he's been saving it for the right moment, and, man, is this it. Dinah's eyes are hungry for it, hungry for every sorry detail of her family tree. She is at his mercy. "Oh, Sugarfoot," he says without taking his eyes from Dinah, "how they love to dig in the dirt for the ancestral bones."

"Go," she yells at him. "Go." Connor sees that Nathan Stamps is coming up from his chair. I'm going to kill a Negro, he thinks.

He can taste it in his mouth again. It's the taste of iron ore and blood and salt, but he knows they call it adrenaline.

"An older man took them all in, gave Mama and her baby sister a farm cottage and garden for growing vegetables. He wanted sex in return, though," Connor says and turns to Sugar. "Don't they all, Sugar? Don't they always want it?"

Sugarfoot is positioning himself, Connor can see peripherally. He's left the jukebox, and he's walking toward the pay phone. "Don't try to call the law, Sugar," Connor says. "I am the law." He can see Sugarfoot's hand go to his right ear, for the pencil.

To Dinah, he says, "So the old man wanted sex for giving Mama a cottage and garden, so Mama gave it."

Pete and Nathan Stamps and Sugarfoot are closing in—from the left, right, and center. Connor's mouth is going dry, and he knows his cheeks are bright as Christmas lights.

"After yellow fever took her sister, Mama went to Birmingham, didn't she, baby? She worked as hired help, doing chores, cooking, scrubbing for a wealthy family. Went to church with this family, and there she'd studied the habits of the rich," he says.

Dinah's eyes are on her hands. She's turning her wedding band round and round.

Connor bends over so only she can hear. "Mama copied their speech and affectations and moved easily in the homes. One day she was strolling a baby in the park and met Birmingham's best madam, who hired her and trained her to do the deflowering. A fresh petal," he says and puts a finger under Dinah's chin. "It was Mama's special gift. Baby blue cardigans, oxfords, schoolgirl bows."

Angel slams her pack of Kools on the counter. "You're sick!" she yells at him.

He slams his fist by her hands. "I ought to arrest you!"

254

Pete's moved back in from the left side. He's inching down the counter, past the grill and the plates and the cups and saucers, past the cupboard, the ice machine, and the sign that says *Coca-Cola*. Pete is moving closer, but Connor knows he'll sic the nigger on him. He knows Pete is a coward. Connor turns to Angel: "You better keep those sweet lips zipped up," he says. "I got the goods on you. I know who you are because some little somebody in this room snooped and got your real name. I checked you out good, Miss Maria Juarez. You keep quiet, though, baby, because this don't have one thing to do with you. This isn't your life or your home or your family. This is *my* family."

"We're not your family," Dinah says to him, and by this time, they're all clustering nearby—Gracie, Benny, Pete, Sugar, Dinah, Angel, Stamps, and even Stamps's wife. He stares at them, all eight of them. It's like a horrible thing building in him, like what he bets labor pains are like, like his brain is going haywire, like he has a tic in his eye that's caused by sudden faulty wiring and if he doesn't say what needs to be said, he *will* have a stroke or a heart attack or the roof will cave in. He looks at Dinah one last time, as if it's the last time he'll know her, like he's standing over an injured horse—a stunning, dark thoroughbred who's run for the roses—he's standing by this horse with a rifle watching its flanks and wondering what it'll do for a final breath. He remembers Chris and how her face drew in like a raisin at the height of passion.

He thinks of how Dinah's hands smelled on his mouth. It's the closest she's been to him since she was little. It's as if she knew, has always known, that to get any closer would be to commit incest, and the moment he thinks this, he knows it is the last moment. He takes one quick look at the café and stares upward to the last hotel for women, then he gets in Dinah's face. "Child whore," he says. "Don't think I don't know why you're protecting Miss Angelrider. She got arrested for solicitation when she was fifteen."

"Get out of here!" Dinah shouts.

He turns to Gracie. "Want to know why Mother loves Angel so much? Want to know why Mother wants to protect her? Because Mother was a little whore herself. About your age. I had her," he says.

Connor can't bear to look at Pete after he's said it. From the corner of his eye, he catches Pete's blue-and-white baseball uniform moving inward, but he doesn't have time to think of anything else because the blow to his face is sudden and jarring as a car wreck, and for a moment he isn't sure who hit him. But his vision gradually comes back and he knows he was hit with the cigar still in his mouth and that whoever hit him didn't care if her hand got burned or if Connor's face caught fire or where the wallop was intended to land. He puts his hand to his nose and understands that he's bleeding, that a ring has cut his lips, and he knows who is wearing that ring.

Dinah is pale as a ghost, and he sees that she's come halfway over the counter to deliver the blow. He comes from behind the counter, and he thinks he's going to cry. He walks past the men and past Benny and Gracie and Lydia Stamps, who is clutching the neck of her starched maid's dress, her eyes big as saucers.

"You can't come back here," Dinah says to him.

He looks at his hands. He still doesn't know where he left his herringbone hat. "I lost my hat," he says. He doesn't know what to do with his hands. He balls them up and thinks how fat they are, how babylike and chapped, so puffy. His cuticles are where he's bitten them, and the veins of his hands are blue and thicker than they ought to be. He can't get his mind off himself, can't bring himself to set foot on the sidewalk.

He takes one last look at the freedom rider. Her boots rest on the bar stool's metal footrest. Her tam is crooked. "One last thing," he says to Dinah and puts his hand on the door. "I take it you're letting her stay on. Do you want your daughter to grow up to be like her? Do you want that? Do you want Gracie to be like *her?*"

He walks over to Gracie and sees that she's sweating up under the brown bangs. "You be like Mama and Grandmama," he says. "You be good to the men."

Then he walks to his car and sees that he left his hat there.

13

Connor cranks up the black city car and whips it to the street. He can't believe he did it. He doesn't know why he did it. He picks up the radio and phones the city PD. A man named Romaine Ledbetter answers.

"Just wanted you to know I'm leaving the Crescent Hotel, where two Negroes are eating with six whites. No need to send anybody over, just wanted somebody to know, Romaine. Hear me, Romaine? You know the place. The old whorehouse. They've taken in a freedom rider. They've turned it into no good."

Romaine is having dinner. Connor thinks he's eating barbeque or a hamburger, something that requires huge bites—because Romaine is short on words, long on *mmm*s and *uh-hmm*s.

He drives by City Hall, but he doesn't even slow down. He is having chest pains. He thinks he's going to die tonight. For the first time in his life, he's desperate to get home. He crosses over the viaduct, past the airport, to the corner where the Rexall, the hardware store, and the Methodist church come together, to the Sinclair where Benny Fraley works.

His car bumps over the railroad tracks and ascends the hills, past the track people, the semi-new homes where insurance salesmen and plumbers and foundry men live, then the sprawling ranch-style bricks.

He turns into his driveway. The floodlight plays on the yard.

Connor's lawn is zoysia grass, pruned to perfection. He's got a yardman, Mercer Standridge, and he's proud to have a Negro with such a dignified-sounding name. He's bragged to the police force that Mercer can spell his name right and signs his own checks. Mercer has a bank account, and Connor enjoys paying him for this reason. He wishes he could talk to Mercer now. He'd like to try out the speech he's working on, where he says he wants the black race to prosper, side by side with the whites—but not *inter*grated, as Nathan Stamps might say.

Connor parks the city car in his garage. He runs his fingers over the tools Mercer uses for the lawn—mower, mattock, spade, rake, fertilizer, posthole digger. He feels like he's in a hardware store, handling merchandise. It's like he doesn't live here. "Mercer," he whispers, and he starts to whimper. "Mercer, buddy, oh Mercer." He wonders if other men feel they want to cry when they pull into their driveways and go to their garages and open their jalousied side door.

The kitchen is sparkling under the stove's light.

It's got the smell of Beara in it, and he can't bear the sight of his supper under the tinfoil atop the stove. He knows how the carrots will look, the coagulated gravy, the broccoli limp and discolored. The pot roast will be in shreds, as if it has come apart bit by bit, like it's sad he didn't come eat it on time, like it's got a life of its own in the way a wife has a life.

Beara's a wife. She plants things. She cleans things. She has recipes for this and that. She shops at the A&P. She hooks her bra straps after she lets her big breasts jiggle in. She holds the telephone up with her left shoulder and chin while she opens a can of chicken à la king and puts it in the saucepan. She sleeps in nylon pajamas that he runs his hands over once in a blue moon.

Connor slips his plate of supper into the icebox. He thinks of Dinah, like you think of a woman who's broken you in two.

He picks up the kitchen phone and dials the newspaper. He asks for Sugarfoot. Sugar is eating something, too. "You having supper?" Connor asks, pulls up a stool, and takes off his shoes. His feet smell like shrimp. "What you eating?" he asks Sugarfoot.

Sugarfoot's voice is flat. "A sandwich," he says.

"You writing a story?"

"Yeah," Sugar says.

"You writing about me?"

"Yeah."

Connor looks at his socks. They're argyle, burgundy, gray, and black. They're nice socks, the kind you'd wear if you knew you were going to do it with a woman you didn't know very well that day. "What you writing about?" Connor asks. He unfastens his suspenders and the red straps fall to his lap. The kitchen is quiet. The fluorescent light over the stove makes the countertops a ghostly silver blue.

"Don't know yet," Sugarfoot tells him.

"You doing the baseball game or the café?" Connor asks, trying to sound casual.

"Where you calling me from?" Sugar asks him.

"Home."

"What is it you want?"

Connor thinks this is a cruel question. Can't he see what has happened? Sugarfoot's getting to be a hard-nosed reporter, this is clear. He wonders what went wrong between the two of them, why it didn't pan out. He would have liked to have had the kind of relationship where they both benefited, he tells Sugar.

"You want to tell me something?" Sugar presses.

"No," Connor says. "I don't have a thing to say."

"Well, then, I'll be going," Sugar says.

"Sugar," Connor begins, but he doesn't know how to phrase it.

He can't decide how to ask it. "Did you believe what I said in there tonight?"

"Jesus," Sugar says, disgusted.

"You want to know if it's true or not, don't you?" Connor asks him.

"It's not news," Sugarfoot says.

Connor thinks this is unnecessarily stern. He thinks Sugar ought to remember they have a friendship, that they drank whiskey side by side in his office. He wonders if he ought to remind Sugar that politicians and reporters in Alabama once shared a camaraderie that included more than *the news.*

Connor takes off his socks. His toes are hot, moist, pale—which makes the tiny black hairs stand in start contrast. He wriggles them and touches them to the cold floor. "You sick of me?"

"You got it," Sugarfoot says and Connor hears him taking a sip of something. He bets it's a beer, a long-neck Miller, all gold and frothy.

"I guess it's on to Mississippi, huh?" Connor asks him.

"I'm working on it," Sugarfoot says, and Connor's sure he hears his lips pop off the mouth of the bottle.

"Having a cold one?" Connor asks.

"I'm going now, Connor," Sugarfoot says.

"You taking Angelrider with you?"

Sugar doesn't respond. Connor waits. He remembers one thing he hasn't told him yet. "Sugar, her name was Molly," he says.

"What are you talking about?"

"My mama."

Sugar doesn't say anything.

"She was from Plantersville, like Beara."

"I'm covering City Hall," Sugarfoot tells him.

261

"Bullshit," Connor says.

He can hear a match strike. Sugarfoot's got his Weejuns on the desk, staring at the copy and smoking a cigaret, running a hand over his Raggedy Andy curls.

"You're like me," Connor tells him.

Sugar is quiet. Connor can hear voices in the newsroom, suggesting a locker-room, championship-season kind of ambience that makes him jealous.

"You love Dinah Fraley. You love her because you can't have her," Connor says. "You want to rescue her, Sugarfoot, from me and this filthy city, but you can't, boy."

Sugarfoot hangs up on him. No manners, Connor thinks, not like *Alabama* farm boys.

He walks into the living room. It's a men's room, with a hi-fi and an upright and a wet bar and a recliner. He pours himself a finger of Jack Daniel's green label. He's buying the stepped-down liquors because it's better politics. He sits back and tries to let the bourbon do its job, but he can't relax.

It's like he's never seen this place in his life—his very own living room. He picks up a *Reader's Digest*. Condensed reading, condensed milk, condensed life. That's me, he thinks, and he gets up and goes back over to the wet bar. He takes a swig of the green Jack. Out the window, a cocker spaniel is peeing against a tulip poplar. He can see the blue hydrangea and gardenia bushes that Mercer prunes.

Mercer, he thinks.

Mercer Standridge. He says the name aloud. He goes to his desk and gets a fountain pen and writes it on a piece of stationery that's got *E. "Bull" Connor* engraved in gold letters. He tries to find Mercer's number in the phone book, but he's unlisted. After a time, he gets up and makes his way down the hallway to his bedroom.

A night-light burns in the bathroom.

The bedroom of Eugene Bull Connor is painted pink. They'd love to get a view of it, he thinks. They'd call it a sissy's room. They'd fondle the fuzzy balls that dangle from the draperies Beara made on her Singer sewing machine. They'd want to make news of the fact he likes shoehorns to stay lodged in his dress shoes.

He lets his pants fall to the carpet. He takes off his white shirt and throws it over the quilt stand. He stands in his boxers in the middle of his bedroom and puts a palm on his gut. The skin is stretched taut as a tent. In the moonlight, Beara's face is broad, ivory, maternal. "Mama," he whispers as he gets in with her. Her body is big as his, and it turns over like ocean tide. The mattress sinks in the center from their combined weight. They lie in the crater they've made.

He drank too much Jack Daniel's. He can feel it in his brain, cold and dark as ink. He's got central air conditioning, and he thinks he'll turn it on later. He'll take a Bayer. "I'm going to take a Bayer," he says and puts his face on his wife's breasts. She is all he's got. She has forgiven him of Chris, the secretary. She took Valium—yellow ones and blue ones—in order to get over it. She knows nothing of Dinah Fraley or the hotel. He will not tell her, not now and not ever. Dinah has, after all, booted him from her life—just like their daughter did.

This new generation of women, he thinks, will be running all the hotels. He pictures a drove of Dinahs, tall, dark, in a hurry, workingwomen with bills to pay and trains to catch and briefcases flung like purses over their broad shoulders.

He's at their mercy, and they're changing so fast he can't keep up with it. They're coming out of the woodwork, spinning from the city's gold revolving doors. They don't trip anymore. They don't make mistakes. They're in the rooms, on the elevators, in the lobbies, behind the desk, checking you in and out. Jesus Christ, he thinks, the hotel will never be the same.

It's the last hotel for women left in Birmingham, and Bull Connor can't get in.

14

Gracie sits up in bed, sorry she has on her yellow kidlike pajamas with the feet built in. She puts her hands to her bangs and brushes them to the side. The violet walls are muted to mauve in the dark of night.

Angel kicks her boots in a corner as if it's her room, too. Gracie watches as she tosses the jacket, tam, cigarets, and socks to the rattan chair.

Gracie puts her fingers up to make a rabbit shadow on the wall. She makes a dragon, a snake, and a bird.

"I suppose you won't have to worry about Mr. Connor anymore," Angel says finally and pulls the covers back so that she can slide in beside Gracie. Gracie looks over at Angel and, for the first time, sees the rose on Angel's chest, growing up from her left breast.

"It's a tattoo," Angel says.

Gracie stares out the window. Her bed is up against the wall, and the glass pane is all that separates her from a leap to the street below, where the sidewalk is cracked and Bull Connor parks his car.

She's sorry she's twelve and not seventeen like Benny, sorry she isn't a boy, sorry, most of all, that she gave Connor Angel's real name. She doesn't know why she did it.

She can't let herself think about it. She thinks instead of constellations Pete taught her, of how Paris is the capital of France, the Sahara is the largest desert on earth, the deepest lake in the world is in Russia. She tries to imagine how deep is deepest. She knows there's a place called the Land of the Midnight Sun, where winters are long and cold and summers are short and cool. This is where she needs to live, she thinks—a place where it's dark and summers are just a fleeting idea. "Twilight," she says and stares into the city night.

"What, sweetheart?" Angel wants to know. Her voice is quiet and tender.

"Twilight," Gracie says, her hand still on the pane. "It means half-light, and I learned that in geography. Lapland has twilight instead of day or night. I never think to look for twilight here until it's over. I always miss it. I can't tell you what it even looks like, what color it is."

Angel puts a hand on the sleeve of Gracie's yellow pajamas.

"Are you all right?"

"I've had these pajamas since I was nine," she tells Angel but still doesn't turn to see her. She doesn't want to look at Angel. She doesn't want to talk about her mother. She wants to think of fjords and nomads and caribou, things that don't concern her, things you can't find in Birmingham.

"Ever seen a wolf?" Angel asks.

Gray, red, she can't conjure up what a wolf looks like, whether it resembles a fox or a dog or a coyote or a bear. She opens her nightstand drawer and gets her flashlight. She shines it down to the street to the place that marks the absence of Connor's black car on the yellow curb. Is he gone forever, like Angel will be?

"Your mother is one," Angel says.

"One what?" Gracie asks.

266

"A wolf. *My* mother is the world's best imposter wolf," Angel says to her. "She thinks that just because you're into good causes you're free in the forest and that isn't true."

Gracie turns the flashlight to the wall. She makes the orb of light travel to her bookshelf, desk, then back to Angel. She doesn't want to pursue this. She's heard her mother called a lot of different things in her life. She doesn't want to know what a wolf means or what an imposter wolf means. She thinks Angel is talking about what Mr. Connor said, only in disguised language. She's afraid wolf has something to do with whores.

"I grew up in the woodlands," Angel is saying as she turns to her side. Her left hip is up, under her T-shirt. Her dark thin legs are on top of the cover. "Farmlands, apple orchards. There was a stream near the place where I was born, and there was a she-wolf who sometimes visited and drank from it," Angel says.

All fours, Gracie thinks, watching Angel's lips. She wonders if Angel's dentist is in love with her. She wonders if Angel has a dentist. She knows Angel isn't from Michigan, she's from California. She doubts that her mother is an anthropologist. It doesn't matter.

"It's not me you think you love," Angel says to her, and Gracie flips off the flashlight. She feels her cheeks light up like red berries. She can't believe Angel has said this. "It's just the way I'm different that you love," Angel says.

Gracie turns the flashlight back on and then off again.

"The thing you're attracted to in me isn't sex or sin, it's freedom. It's freedom from men like Bull Connor."

The flame at the end of Angel's cigaret burns down, further and further, until there's hardly a thing left in her hand, just an inch-long brown filter that she cups in her palm.

Gracie gets up and walks over to her bookshelf. There are the biographies of women. You make a flag, Gracie thinks, or fly aircraft, discover a cure, write lyrics, or be a nurse—and suddenly your life is bound up in an orange hardback book for girls to read. She thinks of how none of the women in the biographies ever lived in Birmingham.

She gets her glow-in-the-dark night sky book. It's inscribed *To Gracie, from Daddy, Christmas 1987.* She opens it to the section marked "Late Spring." It shows her where she is right now. May bleeding into June means she can see Polaris, the dippers, the Cat, Bear, Herdsman, Snake, and Virgin. She's never been able to identify the Snake in the sky. It's too long and curvy and elusive. Her eye won't let her follow it to where it ends. Once she believed she saw the head of it, where the fangs would be. Now she glances at the pictures in the book. One page shows the stars. The opposite page is a colorful portrait of the Herdsman and the Cat and the Bear all staring at the Virgin. The Virgin's got long hair just like Dinah, and she's holding to her breast a crystal ball, a leaf. Her face is bereft, as if she has just missed the train.

Gracie turns to Angel. "Why would an artist paint a sad virgin? If you don't know what you're missing, how can you miss it?"

"Good question," Angel says.

Gracie stands by the window. "You can't see any stars downtown. There are too many lights."

She turns the dial of her transistor radio to WSGN. They're playing "A Summer Place." She listens for trains, but it's not time yet. She sits up in bed, props all of her pillows behind her, and studies the minarets of the terminal.

"I'm going to have to leave Birmingham," Angel says.

"When?" Gracie asks.

"Soon," Angel says. "Maybe tomorrow or the next day. The people who are in jail now are going to be released. We've got to go on to Mississippi," she says.

"Why?"

"It's a movement," Angel replies. Gracie looks down at the street again and thinks of the way the colored and white players looked on the baseball field, how curious a sight it was, like an eclipse of the moon. You're staring at this thing that's been predicted and is a natural part of life that people in other parts of the world have seen before, but when it happens in your own backyard, it's eerie.

"Do you love Benny?" Gracie asks her.

Angel smiles and runs her fingers on the sheet, pillowcase, and quilt. She is smiling downward, the way people do when they're embarrassed or caught off guard, when they're going to tell a lie.

She glances up at Gracie. "I don't think so, sweetheart."

"I thought you did," Gracie tells her.

"Why did you think that?"

Gracie shrugs. She is suddenly aware of her skin, her hands.

Angel tilts her head to the side. "I guess you have a lot of people come and go, running a hotel like this."

"Mostly men," Gracie says. She lets the flashlight travel up Angel's legs. The skin is like the bark of crepe myrtle. Tiny blondish hairs congregate on the kneecaps. Angel's eyes make Gracie think of geysers and canyons and falls. Her mouth is—Gracie searches for the right word—an *invitation*. She sends the light all over Angel's body, up and down, from one end to the other and back, as if Angel's a body she's found at night in the woods. She makes the flashlight scan Angel's ears. The lobes are thin and translucent, like mice's or cats'. Gracie takes it all in, everything she's wanted to take in—the thimble nose, the chiseled hands, the breasts. She wonders what it-'d be like to touch them, if they'd be like clay, if they'd give under her hands. She wonders what Angel smells like, if she smells of rainwater or lime juice or leather. The light moves all over Angel's body from head to toe, from beginning to end, and even though Gracie can't touch it or smell it, she's gotten to look at it. When Angel leaves, Gracie isn't going to feel abandoned or cheated or sad. She's had hold of the light. She's made it go everywhere.

Angel gets up, throws on her jeans, and puts her boots back on. She pulls her green knapsack from the corner. Gracie thinks of the song, *I love to go a-wandering along the mountain track, and as I go I love to sing, my knapsack on my back.* She liked those words when she was seven or eight. She felt like she knew what they meant then. Now it's hard to remember. She feels trapped in city streets. She keeps looking down where Connor's car is supposed to be. She has a sudden, bizarre desire to talk things over with him, though he's never seemed to listen to her. His chin is always up; he's always looking slightly over her head, as if a bear is looming behind her and he's got to keep an eye on it.

"I will write to you," Angel says and puts her hands on Gracie's shoulders. Gracie is still on the bed. Angel stands before her. She pulls Gracie's head up to her chest.

Gracie's glad she isn't prone to cry. She'd hate to cry into Angel's T-shirt. Angel jerks the shoulder strap up and the green material bumps against her back as she walks away.

Gracie turns out the lamp. She doesn't think anything. She just lies still in the dark and waits for Dinah to come check on her. When she hears the knock, Gracie says, "Come in, Mom." Dinah sits on the edge of Gracie's bed. Gracie surveys her mother's face, and it looks like it's always looked—serene, like nothing in the world is wrong. "Why did Mr. Connor say that?" Gracie asks.

"Because he's deranged," Dinah says.

Gracie looks at her quickly for signs of lying or joking or sadness, but there isn't any of that. It's a flat, effortless statement. Gracie snuggles up to her mother. It's almost the end of May

270

1961, and she's going to turn thirteen during the summer. She's heard it's different after you cross on over past twelve. Twelve's a special number. All you have to do is look at a clock and you know that twelve means something. After twelve, you get to start over. You start back with one and you get to begin the cycle again; your hand gets to retrace its path past two and three and four, and soon you're past the midmark and you're returning again.

You can ask questions during the next twelve, Gracie thinks. You don't have to know everything the first time around.

There are degrees of things, Benny thinks as he watches everybody fumbling in the debris. Wars, hurricanes, floods, accidents, murders—they're all the same thing, they just vary in severity.

His mother was wearing a red scarf before she went upstairs to check on Gracie. If he slid it down her hair until it fell into his hands, he'd thought, it would have been like removing a bandage. He thinks of how she came over that counter like an outlaw and how she'd walked over to the jukebox where Sugarfoot was standing. "Nice story," she'd said dryly. "File it."

He opens the café door.

Nathan Stamps is smoking a cigaret. Sugarfoot asks him what his job is at the foundry and how long he's worked for Pete. He asks him what the point was in playing the white team this evening, and he asks Pete the same question. He jots down their answers. Pete asks Nathan for a cigaret. Benny has never seen his father smoke, but now he smokes like he's wanted this particular cigaret all his life. Occasionally he holds it to his eye and rolls it in his fingers, surveying it like it's a jewel.

When it's smoked, Pete tosses the butt to the sewer.

Benny studies the way his father's blue baseball cap hoods his eyes. It's like Pete's lost somebody, like they're at a funeral home, where the men shuffle to and fro on the sidewalk, not knowing the right thing to say. Benny feels like it's their mother they've lost.

"Want me to drive?" Benny asks Pete.

Pete looks up at him as if he's a kind stranger. "Sure," he says. Lydia and Nathan Stamps get in the backseat. Pete gets in the passenger's side. Benny drives. When he starts to pull away from the curb, he looks up at the hotel's blue awning. He wonders if Angel is in her room. He's afraid she's going to be gone when he gets back.

Pete tells Benny where to turn. They wind their way toward Legion Field, through streets and alleys foreign to Benny.

Before a brick apartment project, Pete says, "Slow down, son," and Benny puts on the brakes. Nathan and Lydia slide from the backseat saying, "Bye, Mr. Pete."

On the way back, Benny takes the long way, making detours to the ballpark, the airport, their old home. They don't talk, but Benny knows Pete doesn't want to go back to the hotel either. Benny wants to smoke and think. He thinks of how, by the time you're graduating from high school, home is prison. It's like being in a pressure cooker, steaming and dying to pop the lid, blow the cover.

When they cross the viaduct, Benny sees that they're tapping the furnace at Sloss. He pulls over to the side of the road, and they get out of the car. They stand by the viaduct railing. Pete's taken off his baseball cap, and his dark curls blow in the wind. The night sky is bright with the fiery light from the stream of electric orange iron. Benny stares at the sequence of tall, cylindrical stoves heating the air that's pumped into the furnaces. Pete's told him everything—how the turboblowers are driven by steam turbines, how the skip hoist and the ladle car and the pig casters work. He knows the inside of the stoves are lined with heat-resistant brick, that the ore and limestone and coke come in by railway to the trestle, how the slag accumulates along with the molten iron. He watches it now, coming forth from the furnace like volcano lava. It's strong and powerful, running along the curved trough into the pig molds. It is ugly and beautiful, and he is, as always, filled with pride and shame at the sight of it. He thinks of how he didn't bring Angel over to watch it because it seemed such a horrid landmark. He could have taken her to Vulcan, the big statue up on Red Mountain, but when you're up there you're just looking back down to Sloss. All you're seeing is fire, no matter where you go or how you try to view things. Stoves, pipes, tools, pots, pans, machines—the world is made of metal, and Benny wants out. But as he stands here with Pete, he thinks of how the world—albeit metal—has, as its core, his father.

He wonders how you leave your father.

If Benny were younger, Pete would say, *Now look into the fire for the ghost.* He'd retell him the legend of the Sloss ghost, which is simply the story of a man named Jowers who fell into the blast furnace. A piece of sheet iron was attached to a length of gas pipe, and they fished his heart out with it, according to the story. Benny wonders if he's going to repeat the story to his own son— if he ever has one. He thinks of Ginger Fortenberry, of how he can conjure up a mental picture of a son they might have together. He can't do this with Angel. He can only visualize them making love in dark places and riding trains in Europe.

"You think I ought to call Ginger?" he asks Pete.

Pete turns to him, his face aglow with the burning iron.

"Sure," he says. "You still love her, don't you?"

Benny looks down at the slag pit between the cast shed and the

273

viaduct. He thinks of Connor saying "By-products of the Kennedys," and he starts to laugh.

"What?" Pete asks, his eyes bright with the fire's light.

"Connor," Benny says.

"Old fool," Pete replies.

They lean against the rail. For a moment, Benny is aware of the lines in his father's face, of a scar that runs up his jawbone where he had a birthmark removed during the war. "They did it on the ship," Pete's told him. Benny sees the graying temples. It dawns on him that Pete is growing older every minute of every day, that the foundry and the colored situation and Connor have taken their toll. He knows men used to die in their forties—in the mines, of diseases, of things like gangrene and black lung. He wonders if he'll live longer if he studies art.

"I guess she's had enough of us," he says to Pete.

Pete turns. "What's that?"

"Angel. I bet she's going to leave."

"You'll get over her," Pete says.

They watch the men scurrying in the orange light of the fire. They don't say anything for a long time, and when Pete finally speaks he says, "I don't know what to think of it." Benny asks him, *what,* but he knows what Pete's thinking, he knows what he's going to say. When he says, "Connor," Benny turns back to Sloss. "He's a liar," Pete says. "A damn liar."

They get back in the car.

When they get to the hotel, Benny parks on the yellow line, in Bull Connor's parking place. He goes upstairs and knocks on Angel's door. She doesn't answer. He knocks on Sugarfoot's door, and he doesn't answer either.

Pete is in the hallway, standing on the Oriental rug, about to enter his own bedroom. Benny scratches his head, thinking of calling Ginger Fortenberry, but instead he walks over to his father. Pete's hand turns the brass doorknob. Once more, Benny has the feeling they're at a funeral home. Pete is standing by the mortuary door, and they're going to view the body—the body of his mother. He inches closer to Pete and stands back, behind him, under a painting of a girl holding a watering can. It is, he knows, a Renoir print, but when he was a boy he used to think it was his mother as a child. She's wearing a navy-blue dress with white lace, a red scarf in her hair and there are flowers all over the place.

Pete opens the door and when he does, Benny sees his mother—not dead, but smiling and bundled up in a big quilt with his sister. He watches Pete go on in and kiss them both on the forehead, like he does when he comes home from work. He tosses his blue baseball cap to Gracie, and she puts it on. Benny stands there, in the hallway of the hotel, under the girl with the watering can and stares at his family. He thinks of how he's going to miss them when he leaves for college. Things aren't going to be the same after the summer's over. It's not like he's going to die, but he knows the family—as they know it, right now—will die.

He thinks of how quickly dates change, of how you have to get used to a new year when you mark 1956, or 1957, or worse yet, 1961 on paper. He wonders if he'll live to the year 2000. Of course he will, he thinks. He wonders if his parents will. They'll be old by then if they do. He wonders what he'll do with his life, who he'll marry, what will become of the hotel. He wonders if the Negroes will start mixing with the whites and if they will marry one another. He wonders if Angel will remember him when she's old, and if he'll remember her. He wonders if the Sloss furnace will keep making orange fire and if he'll ever know the truth about his family. He wonders if John F. Kennedy will be president for more than one term and if he'll have a lot of kids who look Kennedylike. He wonders if Bull Connor is gone for good or if he'll be like the man named Jowers who died in the blast furnace but keeps reappearing to the people of Birmingham.

Benny stands against the doorjamb and raises a hand to greet his mother, his sister.

"You OK?" he asks them.

They smile. They're glad he's back, glad Pete's back, glad Connor's gone, glad the Negroes are gone, glad they're in bed under a quilt in the hotel. Very soon they will not be all together like this. He knows he will remember what it was like when they were.

15

The newsroom is thinning now. Wads of paper, cigaret butts, and spilt 7UP dirty the floor. Sugarfoot looks over at the sportswriter's desk.

Angel has called and said she wants to talk to him.

He looks down at the street and sees her leaning against a lamppost, smoking. His story is written and filed. He grabs his things and heads for the stairs. He passes the mezzanine and winds down to the lobby, where the security guard nods and lets him pass.

He opens the door.

It's the kind of tepid night that often brings tornadoes up from Tuscaloosa.

Angel turns and swings a half circle around the lamppost.

"File your story?" she asks.

He nods and looks down at her. She's under five feet tall, he thinks. She wouldn't qualify for certain jobs, like a cop or stewardess or astronaut. "Where to?" he asks her.

"Let's walk."

They head down Fourth Avenue, past the department stores. She walks fast and smokes, like there's a story breaking and the TV people are already there. "I like this part of the city," she says as they pass a mercantile store. A cowboy lassoing a horse is painted on the tan brick, and in the window are Western belt buckles and saddles and fringed shirts, bins of corn, squash, and bean seeds, and a display of guitars and ukeleles. "Crazy-ass town," she says. "I'm leaving."

There is no traffic. The city's dead.

"You need to get out of this place, too," she tells him. "It may seem like the end of the line, but it's not. Jackson's the end. Think of a map," she says and draws one in the air. "Think of a line from Washington to Richmond, Petersburg, Lynchburg, and on to Greensboro, Charlotte, to Columbia, Atlanta, Birmingham, Jackson. Jackson is where we're headed, Sugarfoot. Birmingham is not the end of the world; Jackson is," she says and lights another Kool.

She crumples up the empty aqua pack and puts it in her back jeans pocket. She nudges him with her elbow. "Got it?" she asks.

"You tell Dinah you're leaving?" he asks.

She turns away, to the street. "No," she says and then turns back to him.

They don't say anything. They pass another seed store. Finally, she says, "I can't stay there anymore. I feel like I'm living in somebody else's skin." She takes a drag of her cigaret. "Like I'm making a bad situation worse."

Sugarfoot waits for her to say more. The sky is overcast, a bruised color. There's not a trace of wind.

"There's something I need to tell you," she says and stops him by grabbing his wrist. She leans up against a parking meter. She zips up her jacket and jams her hands in her pockets. He wonders if she calms down in bed. "It's something I haven't told anybody here. It's embarrassing," she concludes and puts her chin up.

He waits.

"I missed the bus that morning in Nashville," she says and jams her hands farther down so that the waist of her jeans falls low. "I overslept. They left at dawn. I had to overtake them, by car, fifty miles down Highway 31, in Pulaski, Tennessee."

Sugarfoot smiles at her.

"It's not funny," she says.

He holds his palms up. "Am I laughing?"

"I mean, it made me think what a show this is. I didn't make curtain call."

Sugarfoot looks at how her hands keep going farther and farther into her pockets, making her thin shoulders roll inward and her skinny forearms hyperextend. "That's it," she says. "That's what I needed to confess."

"I'm asking to go to Jackson," he tells her.

"That's great, Sugarfoot. That's great."

"Just for a few days," he adds and looks over to City Hall to see if the light is on in Connor's office. It's not. He can't conceive of Connor at home. He wonders what his wife is like, if they have a cat or a dog, an ice-cream maker. He tries to picture Connor in a lawn chair, making the big silver handle go round and round.

When they get to the hotel, they sit on the curb. It's like they're waiting for a bus or a train or a carpool to pick them up and take them somewhere. They don't talk, they just watch the traffic light blink yellow. He knows she's tired like he is, and if she's catching a bus to Jackson in the morning and has a tendency to miss early-morning connections, she surely ought to be asleep. She picks a leaf from the gutter and twirls it in between her fingertips. Her nails are squared off, blunt, like a boy's.

"I've never seen anything quite like it," she says finally and holds the leaf so close to her nose that her eyes cross. "For him to say something like that in front of her kids."

279

She turns to him. Her lips are parted, and he gets a view of the chipped tooth. He wonders who kicked her.

"You know, don't you, that Connor is doing more for you guys than Robert Kennedy? Just by being who is he and saying what he says to the press? When it's all said and done, he's going to have done more for your movement than anybody. You almost owe him a thank-you note once you get home."

She throws the leaf back in the gutter.

"Yeah," she says, "like, 'Thank you, Mr. Connor, for letting my buddies get beat up at your bus station, and thank you for almost breaking my arm, and thank you for your insightful comments about my character, and thank you for protecting me so valiantly during my stay in Birmingham.' "

Sugarfoot looks at her. She's young, he thinks as he studies her profile—the crisp ins and outs of her bone structure. She is jaded, but she has no irony.

"Back up," he tells her.

She looks at him.

"Your life is in your face," he tells her.

Her eyes take in the street, the traffic light, the dark sky.

"You say Birmingham isn't the end of the line, but neither is Jackson. This is just a piece of your life, and when you look back at it, you're going to remember the strangest things," he tells her, but he knows it isn't sinking in. Her eyes are flat as buttons.

"I feel so sorry for these people," she says. "They're stuck here in Birmingham with all this metal and fire and dirty sky, and they can't see beyond those ugly blast furnaces and that ugly man."

A car is coming. Is it black? Sugarfoot wonders. Does it have a city government tag, a tinted windshield, and a .38 special in the glove compartment?

Suddenly they hear something coming from the balcony overhead. Sugarfoot glances up beyond the blue awning, and he sees that somebody's thrown open the French doors. He hears laughter. It is all of them, the whole family, and they are laughing.

"Jesus," Angel says and looks up to the balcony. "What's wrong with them? Their lives are coming apart, and they're up there laughing."

It is a kind of laughter Sugarfoot recognizes, though he's lived in the South only a few years. He's heard it at funerals and weddings. It's a dark, bloody, mad laughter. One of his friends married a girl from Savannah. The wedding was high society and the bridesmaids talked about pickle forks and tomato forks and shrimp forks and lobster forks and grapefruit spoons and dessert spoons and olive spoons. And during the ceremony itself, right when the preacher, wearing a tux and holding a King James— right when he asked the bride to say "I do"—she went into this dark laughter. She couldn't stop, and the harder she laughed the worse it got, and it wasn't until much later, after he'd moved South, that Sugarfoot heard this same kind of laughing. It was during a funeral for a lady in Montgomery. The preacher started reading, *Who can find a virtuous woman?* from Proverbs, and the daughters of the woman who had died started laughing and couldn't stop.

He decides not to try to explain this to Angel. He decides it's not worth the effort and that it would be better to just take her hand and help her up from the curb.

They walk inside.

They go to the foyer, then up the winding stairway to the second floor, where guests stay. He has the distinct feeling that they will be the last guests to register at this hotel, that very soon Dinah will close it or sell it or make it into something different, like a clothing outlet or an antique store. He wonders how she's stayed in business as long as she has and how much money they're losing. Maybe she can keep the café, he thinks, and rent out the upstairs. When they get to the middle of the hallway, he pulls Angel toward him and he hugs her. She is young and carnal and not his. "Mississippi," he says to her, and her eyes travel to her door. There is a note taped to it, and he watches her go to the door and tear it down. She stands in the hallway and reads it over and over though it's clearly just one sentence. "My father called," she tells him. "He thinks I'm in jail. He wants to come get me."

"Let him," Sugarfoot says to her.

He puts the key in his door. He turns once more to see her standing by her door reading the note. In his room, the bed is made. The dust ruffle is blue like the drapes. He can't get between the sheets without thinking of Dinah's hands busily tucking here and there. He walks to the bureau and empties his pockets of pennies, Chap Stick, and scraps of paper. He looks in the mirror and runs his hands through his blond curls. He needs a haircut. He kicks his Weejuns off and strips to his T-shirt and briefs. In the corner is a stack of newspapers. KENNEDY AWAITS REPORT ON RIDERS, it says. He tries to picture Kennedy in a swivel chair, his hands behind his head, a cryptic smile crossing his handsome face. Next to the article on Kennedy is an ad for Smirnoff vodka. In the ad, a man sits at a table drinking and staring at a birdcage. *Distilled from grain,* it says.

He thinks of Iowa.

VIOLENCE LEAVES NINE INJURED, the paper says. Night riders strip and flog Sylacaugans. Freedom riders mobbed, beaten. Lucky newsman tells of bloody incident. Thugs mustn't take over our city. Trouble blamed on out-of-towners. "I have said for the last twenty years that these out-of-town meddlers were going to cause bloodshed if they kept meddling in the South's business,"

Connor says under Sugarfoot's byline. *The South's business.* Sugarfoot lies on the bed, thinking how he should have asked Connor what the South's business is.

Sugarfoot gets up and walks to the closet. He gets his Connor file and thumbs through the clippings from the secretary scandal. In a photo, Chris is wearing a triple strand of pearls and a wounding smile. CHURCHWOMEN ASK FOR RESIGNATION, another column says. Yet in a courtroom photo they're all there clutching their black patent-leather purses in their laps and taking in every moment. They love it, he thinks. Southerners love a story, even when it wounds them and ruins their reputation, wrecks their economy and sets fire to things. "Y'all come by afterwards," they holler to friends at the cemetery as they're burying the dead. They'll get together when it's over and laugh that dark laugh and eat deviled eggs. They make their own misery, he thinks. They're addicted to it. They can't live unless their backs are to the wall. They want to fight. *Someone's in the kitchen with Dinah, someone's in the kitchen, I know, oh, oh, oh. Someone's in the kitchen with Dinahhhh, strumming on the old banjo.* Damn, he thinks and walks to the window. He wonders how she's going to live without Connor. Who is she going to fight with in the back kitchen under the lights?

He can hear them overhead, the family. Maybe they're celebrating, he thinks. They've killed the beast.

He gets in bed, under the sheets, and he can hear them long into the night. Their voices ebb and flow. They grow quiet, so quiet he can hear the walls creak, then they're at it again. He can't distinguish who's who; they're all in it together. It makes him want to move somewhere else, to get married and have kids who will come to you in the night; who will ride in the car and see it all and hear it all and not run away; who will, in time, want to ask you the very things you want to give answers to; who will watch you come across the bar to deliver the blow or catch the ball or save the day; who will bear all things and believe all things and hope all things and endure all things—for you, for themselves, for the sake of the place, the past, the family.

Halfway through his shower, Nathan stops and stares at the hot and cold faucet knobs that say *Kohler* on them. He's always wondered where the Kohler plant is and what the molds look like.

The spray mists up his eyelashes. Water droplets ricochet from the tile to his face. He rinses the soap from his arms. He turns, and the suds run down his thighs and ankles in the direction of the drain. He steps out and takes the rough towel from the rack. Back first, then chest, arms, legs, face, and hair. "Don't put nothing in it," Lydia will say of his hair. She doesn't like wax or colognes or aftershave or talcum powder. She likes bodies to be bodies, she says.

He brushes his teeth with baking soda and gargles hydrogen peroxide to make his gums quit hurting. Back in the bedroom, he pulls the drop cord, and the light comes on, making the waxed floors glisten. He's painted the walls yellow, the woodwork white. It's like a sunny-side-up egg.

He sits on the edge of the bed, finishes towel-drying his hair, and falls back. He looks up at the ceiling and puts his hand on his chest. Whites are, he thinks, like Jacob in the Old Testament, wrestling with the big angel, struggling and defiant yet all the while demanding a blessing. *Redeem me, brother.*

Lydia sits in the straight-back chair beside the chest of drawers. She's in a slip. The strap falls from her dark shoulder. The windows are open, the blinds up. He wonders if anybody is looking in at her.

"Did you see how she bloodied his nose? Have you ever seen a woman do that to a man, stone sober?" she asks, and the other strap falls to her arm, too.

A car passes, throwing light into the cramped bedroom. The bed, chest, and chair take up all the space, so that there's hardly room to walk. A cracked mirror hangs on the wall. "Come here," Nathan says to her.

She gets up and takes the three steps to the bed. He pulls her down close. He likes the way her slip feels. It's like running your hands over the surface of water. Nathan faces her on the ivory bedspread. Cars pass by, and a breeze is blowing summer in bit by bit. He thinks of how she lives with whites, day in and day out; every waking moment she is caught up in the rhythm of their arguments and their ironing and their beds. She picks up their salt-shakers, umbrellas, towels, and babies. She's the fly on the wall, the hidden camera, the Peeping Tom. She knows why, where, how they live.

"I can't get her off my mind," she tells him.

She goes to the chest of drawers and gets her pajamas. He takes a T-shirt and boxers from his side, and they get under the covers. The pillow is damp from his hair. She turns to him. "I think their children won't suffer," she says.

He closes his eyes. He can see the ballpark, the way Pete winds up on the mound. He can see the ball leaving his hand and sailing in the dark night, perfect and white with a life of its own. He can feel it coming to him, landing in his mitt, safe and crisp—caught.

She flips off the lamp, and they lie in the dark. Occasionally they can hear, from the sidewalk below, the conversation of passersby. Right as Nathan begins to drift to sleep, Lydia puts her lips to his ear. "I can't not tell you this," she whispers. "I'm late." He turns to her, making out the silhouette of her face in the dark.

He turns his head to the side. "Yes," she says. "Late."

He takes her hand. It's too much to hope for. It's too good to be true. He's not going to think it or encourage it or believe it. But he squeezes her hand under the sheets and draws her hand up to his lips, where he leaves it. Something begins crawling up his legs to his belly. It is something he's felt many times. It's called blessed assurance, and he smiles in the dark. When he falls asleep, he dreams the same dream. Pete is handing him a baby boy. They're going in and out of airports and train stations and bus stations, travelers.

16

Connor can't sleep. He gets up from the bed and takes a clean white shirt from the closet and the shoehorns from his shoes. He rummages for his socks. He gets his suspenders, hat, and wallet.

He steps outside. The night is cooler.

He opens the garage door and gets in the car. He sails down the neighborhood streets, neglecting to stop for the signs. He barrels over the railroad tracks and passes the Sinclair station, then backtracks a bit and maneuvers past the power yard that separates Pete Fraley's new home from Negro quarters. He slows the car and lights a cigar, staring up to where the foundation has been laid. He thinks of Pete carrying Dinah over the threshold like Clark Gable scooping up Vivien Leigh. Dinah's prettier than Vivien Leigh, he thinks. At the corner is a mailbox. "I'm gonna sit right down and write myself a letter," he sings to himself. He thinks of "Love Letters in the Sand" and Perry Como and Dave Garroway and Ralph Edwards. This is your life, he thinks. He's often pictured himself on the show. He thinks he is foolish to have thought it, now that his life is over.

He heads for the foundry. He wants to see how Pete will drive to work once he's moved to the new place. He will pass a chiropractor's office and a florist, a beauty salon, the airport highway, a cookie factory named Greg's. Greg who?

Once he's on Tenth, it's all municipal buildings—police, fire, sanitation, and whatnot. It's the kind of street where a man feels protected under the umbrella of modern life. Connor pulls into the foundry parking lot and gets out. He's got the weight of the world on his shoulders, he thinks. He's a man without a country. His face is still sore where she hit him. He couldn't believe the force of her hand, and he can't figure out if it was her palm or her knuckles or what. You only get angry at those you love the most, he's read in *Reader's Digest*. Children lash out at their parents when they know they're loved, he's read. Maybe Dr. Spock can give him some insight into his relationship with Dinah. He stops by a sign at the foundry gate and reads the message. It says:

WE EMPLOY COLORED LABOR AS MOLDERS AND OPERATORS ON OUR TAPPING AND FINISHING MACHINES, ALSO AS INSPECTORS AND SHIPPERS. THE SELF-RESPECTING, HONEST, DEPENDABLE, AND AMBITIOUS COLORED MAN HAS AN OPPORTUNITY IN OUR PLANT TO ADVANCE HIMSELF MENTALLY, PHYSICALLY, AND SPIRITUALLY SO THAT HE MAY THEREBY BECOME A BETTER CITIZEN AND DERIVE A GREATER REAL HAPPINESS FROM LIFE.

Well, damn the torpedoes, he thinks. More power to them. He spits in the dirt. He chews his cigar way down till he's to the hot part. For a moment, he thinks of what it was like to cry when he was a boy—how you got a runny nose if you tried to fight the tears, how your eyes felt chlorinated. He looks back across the street, past the baseball field at the Fraleys' old home and then back to the foundry, to the galvanizing building, pattern shop, tapping room, annealing oven headquarters, and the big sawtooth roof that holds it all. He wonders what the lockers are like, if they've got squeaky metal doors or if everybody puts their belongings in big wire baskets near the showers. He wonders what kind of soap other men use, if they like Dial or Ivory or that new green kind that's supposed to make you feel you're surfing off the island of Waikiki.

He wonders if Pete Fraley has another woman he thinks of when he takes a shower at work. But it's too late now, he thinks. Pete's never going to tell him. Pete's a thing of the past. He can't stomach it. It makes him want to kill himself.

He gets back in the car and drives into the city. *The Absent-Minded Professor* is showing at the Strand with Fred MacMurray, and Connor wonders how this could possibly have a new twist, in that all professors are absentminded, they all got bad wiring. *Posse from Hell* is at the Melba, *The Young Savages* at the Empire, with Burt Lancaster, and *Friendly Persuasion* at the Ritz. Gary Cooper, Dorothy McGuire, and Anthony Perkins, what a trio. It's the kind of movie you'd take a woman to, he thinks. This makes a part of him ache, and he thinks of how he never could figure out which part of him it is that aches over women. Persuasion. He thinks of a field of grass and how if he could just lie down in it with somebody quiet and experience this thing called *persuasion* it wouldn't matter if he was persuading or persuaded, just so it was friendly. But, no, they won't have it. They just stand there and control you with their eyes. It drips off them like sap.

He drives by all the hotels. The Thomas Jefferson over on Sixteenth and Second with terra-cotta, Italian-looking arched windows that decorate the part of the terrace not enclosed by the ballroom. He's never liked the Thomas Jefferson, too blue-bloodish. It makes him aware of how he can't dance. He drives by the Redmont and the Tutwiler, which he likes better, but the Tutwiler's got too many colored men wearing fancy uniforms like they ought to be working at Buckingham Palace, like they think they're a color guard rather than a *colored* guard. They stand beside thick velvety ropes snaking from one gold post to another in the lobby. The Redmont, however, just goes straight up the way a hotel ought to, so that you check in, grab your bag, take the elevator up, and never know what hit you. You're just there, in your room, with or without a woman. Take your pick, he thinks. You have your choices. You ruin your life or you don't.

He lights a new cigar and drives toward the projects. He passes the Greyhound Bus Lines repair garage. He passes Southern Dairy. Milk and transportation, he thinks. That's what makes the world go round. He passes Negro churches, wondering why they call themselves tabernacles. There's the Morning Star Tabernacle and the Zion Hope Tabernacle and the Reaching Heights Tabernacle. He isn't sure which building is Nathan's. He slows down, hoping a stray Negro will see the city car and act real nice, the way they do when they see the law. But nobody is out at three in the morning.

He isn't sure where to go next. There are foundries and factories on every corner, where they make farm implements and air compressors and hoistings and school supplies, floor coverings, plate glass, cement, gaskets, mattresses, meat packaging, undertakers, dry cleaners, ball bearings, gypsum, saw works, iron works, aluminum, feed and grain, cemeteries, landing sheds, salvage yards, junk storage, boiler rooms, incinerators, and waxed paper.

Waxed paper. How do these men feel, making something that will hold a kid's peanut-butter-and-jelly sandwich in a Sky King lunch box? Do they feel a sense of pride or do they hang their heads when somebody asks, "Where do you work?"

He passes the Salvation Army, Paradise Motel, Browns-Ridout mortuary, and the Ambrosia Cake Bakeries. Ambrosia cake? Ambrosia isn't supposed to be made into a cake, is it? But what does he know? What does he know about women's things?

He's got to talk to her. He can't stand this any longer. He's going to park in front of the hotel and wait until morning. When the sun comes up, she's going to come down the stairway and throw back her long hair, looping it in and out of a rubber band.

He parks on the yellow curb. It's his place, and once he's parked the car he feels secure. She hasn't yet come down to the café, hasn't glanced out to his car, hasn't motioned to him, "Oh, come on in, for Christ's sake," but he has a ray of hope. He sits and watches the windows. If astronauts can go through isolation units where they sit quiet for a day, he can surely sit in this spot until dawn. He leans his head back and dozes off. Occasionally, his head jerks and he sits up and checks his watch and the sky. It's like the night, years ago, when his other daughter had her tonsils out and he stayed there all night watching her go in and out of the ether.

At five, he sits upright. He thinks if he doesn't have a cup of coffee, he's going to get a migraine. He considers his options. He wants her to see him sitting here when she comes down the stairs. He wants her to know he's been here all night. He wants it to be perfect. He wants a friendly persuasion.

The sky is pinkening up, ever so slightly. It's the color of baby blankets. He thinks of the places that're open nearby, and he knows the terminal lobby will have fresh coffee. He doesn't want to go in there, though. He's afraid somebody will recognize him, and he'll get into conversation. He's going to tough it out. He dozes once more, then wakes at quarter of. He knows Pete leaves for work at six-thirty. He glances up. Sure enough, there are lights on in their bedroom. He thinks of her standing by the bureau brushing her long hair, just like she did when she was a youngster in her mother's brothel. He thinks of her doing the wash in the backyard for the whores. Panties, garters, and lacy underpinnings in a wash pot, Dinah stirring them with a broom handle. At one point Candy had converted the master bedroom into a dance floor. She installed a parquet floor of Honduran mahogany and mirrors and walnut facings and a rotating silver ball that threw prisms of light. Every Wednesday afternoon, she opened the brothel to high school boys, who came to dance with the girls. Dinah greeted them at the door, taking their jackets and baseball caps like she did the men's overcoats and hats. She'd turn on the Victrola, and she'd sit in a leopard-skin chair donated by a Texas banker while the boys took turns dancing with the whores. They were young boys, Connor thinks. Young boys.

He waits until his watch says six o'clock. He watches the light from her bedroom, and he knows if he keeps watching, he's going to see what he wants to see, and he does. The drapes part, and she peeks down to the street. He knew she would do this. She had to know if he was there, and he was. He thinks of how his legs hurt from being cramped in the car but how pain is worth it when you've done your job. His job is to protect, and he does. He can feel his heart beating. He can see the light coming from the upstairs hallway onto the stairs. Any minute she is going to come galloping down the stairs. She's going to want to get to him before Pete does because she knows Pete will make him leave. She doesn't want him to leave, he is certain.

Life holds truths. We hold these truths to be self-evident, he thinks as he sees her coming down the stairway, wearing a man's jacket and a long skirt, tossing her hair back just like he knew she'd do. It's a nightgown, he thinks. She's wearing a nightgown under Pete's jacket. She hasn't taken time to get dressed, it's so urgent she get to him first. "I'm sorry," she's going to say. "I didn't mean it." He can feel his heart in his chest. She is halfway down the flight of stairs, and she is flying. She passes through the foyer and into the café. She's seen him, he knows it, but she hasn't come out to him like he thought she would.

He takes off his herringbone. He lays it beside him, on the vinyl seat of the city car.

Dinah stands on her tiptoes to reach the skillet. She's going to fry bacon, fix coffee, stir grits. He can almost smell it. But why isn't she coming to the car? She's pretending he isn't there. He gets out of the car and walks to the café door. She looks up. She looks right through him as if he's a ghost. "Open up," he mouths, but she keeps staring into thin air.

Her nightgown sleeves stick out from under Pete's jacket. They have lace, ivory lace.

"Open up," he repeats and puts a palm to the glass.

She's busy, in the way they're always busy. Women love to be mad in the kitchen; they love to slam the box of grits to the wooden chopping board and reach for the sugar on their tiptoes so you can see their backside.

He taps on the glass.

Her nightgown must be made of flannel. He's felt this kind of material. The hem of it brushes the floor, and it's like she's on water. The blue nightgown trails after her like a sail.

"Open up," he says again, and this time he bangs on the glass door with the base of his hand. She looks up, and her eyes take him in this time. She's not looking at a ghost; she is defying him.

Gorgeous, he thinks.

He puts his palms up, as if making a point. He shapes something in the air with his hands. He shapes, for her, his regret and his need and her mistake in cutting him to bits and pieces. "Mama," he finally says, and he makes his mouth say it slowly, like she's a deaf mute who has to see the word. It is the final word, the last straw. She is messing with sweet-roll dough. It's in a red bowl. She's doing it while she stares a hole in Connor.

She gets a big green bowl. It's a different batch of dough. It's already risen. It must have been rising all night. It's bloated, like he is. She pricks it, and the thin outer edge collapses. She puts it on a board, and she starts to knead it. He can't stand to look at her fingers working. They gouge, penetrate, bring the stuff to the middle. Her hands are moving faster and faster. "Mama," he says again, and her hands keep working as her eyes keep nailing him, driving him farther and farther away. He's afraid Pete's going to come break it up.

"Mama's never coming back," he hollers to her. People have come from the terminal building, strangers who don't know he's the commissioner of public safety. They're dodging him, eyes to the sidewalk. They think he's a mental patient. He could be arrested for public intoxication or disturbing the peace.

He thinks her eyes are giving in. He believes the pupil is growing, making the forest green iris recede. This, he thinks, is the friendly persuasion. They might as well be in that field of grass. "Mama," he whispers, "let's talk about Mama," and he watches her hands slow to a methodical rhythm.

He puts his legs apart. He stands weighted like a big anchor. In the glass, he can see his reflection—the way his gray pants balloon in the morning wind. He puts his face closer to the pane. His breath frosts the penguin logo. He puts both of his hands to the glass, thinking he has the power to make her hands come up, too. He knows the word, *levitation*. He wants to pry her fingers from the baking dough but they're stuck firm. She is still as a ceramic girl, standing in her mother's kitchen.

"Mama," he says to the glass.

There's a part of her like her mama, a speck of something askew, a crookedness that she can't fix, a hat that keeps wanting to blow off.

He watches how her hands start to come apart from the dough, how she pulls the fingers loose one by one. He thinks of what's up under her nails, of how she's going to walk over—now—to the sink and let lukewarm water work on the shortening that's made her hands slick. She's going to stand there and let the aqua detergent and tap water clean her up. They like to clean up, he thinks. It makes them feel better. She's standing with her back to him. The water falls on her hands. He adjusts his weight, first to the right then to the left. He wasn't in the army, but he knows this is how soldiers must feel on red alert.

She wipes her hands on a café towel, one of the thin kind waitresses use to mop up a table. She wipes them carefully, taking time to blot her wrists. Her face is serene, and she's not thinking. He knows this about women: he knows how, once they surrender, they put themselves in a trance. They neither think nor want nor regret. They simply move; they sleepwalk in and out of it.

His hands are moist on the glass. He knows if he takes them away, there will be wet handprints. He can feel her coming toward him. She walks from back behind the counter. If she were wearing an apron, she'd take it off now, the way they do when they're no longer in the kitchen business mind-set. She walks past the jukebox. The nightgown is a shade of blue they're apt to put a baby boy in. Once she's right by the door, her body grows perfectly still and she's so close he can see the insignia on Pete's jacket.

He watches her right hand. He waits for it to unlock the door, but it doesn't. She stands by the glass, on the other side of the penguin, studying the palms of his hands that're pressed hard

295

against the pane. She cups her hands in front of her, fingers inter-locked as if she is a choir girl preparing to sing a song. She is eye level with him. Her eyes are soft, yielding. But she doesn't move for the lock. "Open," he says to her, but she is frozen in place. She's wearing the broken-beauty look they have right before they let you start, but she won't unlock it. "Open," he says again, but it's almost a question now. She stands on the other side of the glass. "Why not, open?" he asks her, growing impatient. It's an empty and desperate thing inside him. He wants to be inside the café with her. He wants her to rush past him, scurrying to make sunny-side-up eggs for newspaper reporters. He wants her to chide him and fuss at him and act indignant, all the while hoping he's got a new story, something he's never told her. "Mama," he tries again. He says it louder. "Mama," he calls to her. The sky is opening up with morning now. The train terminal is emptying it-self of night passengers. Pigeons are flying from the rafters. "I've got something to tell you about Mama," he screams.

Her lips part.

She isn't going to let him in. He can feel this knowledge travel-ing from his brain to his hands, and he pounds the glass. Her eyes are resolute. Her pupils are receding as if the light has taken over and they have no choice in the matter. Women's pupils, he's heard, grow big as they get close to ecstasy. He's never known a woman who'd keep her eyes open. They want you to miss it. It be-longs to them. Unlike men, they unleash backwards, back into themselves.

Her eyes are wide open now. They're yielding, and he realizes she is smiling at him. She is smiling because she has shut him out. She puts her hands up to the glass as if to signify her will. She isn't going to open up. "Please," he calls to her, and he sees Pete coming down the steps. Pete stops dead on the stairway as if Connor had a gun. But Connor's on his knees, unarmed. "Pete," he says, as if Pete might help. Pete turns to the wall, like he's caught Connor pissing on the sidewalk or something and he isn't going to humiliate him by staring. Dinah puts her hand to her lips and then puts her fingers to the air, like she is blowing him a kiss. "Mama," he says again. People are milling about, they are coming toward him, they think he's hurt. "Mama," he tries once more, but she isn't going to answer him. She isn't going to save him. She's just going to stand there in her blue nightgown and watch him on his knees. She sits down on the floor of the café so she can be near him, eye level, where he is. He's on the sidewalk, and the door separates them. He can see her but she isn't going to let him be with her.

He picks up his hat, which has fallen to the sidewalk. He brushes it off, and he brushes the wet from his pasty cheeks. He hasn't cried since he was eight. He hoists himself up, walks to the city car, and starts it. He gets a handkerchief from his pocket and blows his nose. It makes an awful sound, like brakes screeching. When he turns back to the hotel, he sees her still on the café floor with her hands in her lap watching him drive away. Pete is going on down the stairway, and up on the balcony Sugarfoot leans over the railing. Sugarfoot waves to him, and Connor tips his hat.

He drives for a half hour then stops at a waffle shop and orders scrambled eggs and coffee. He puts a lot of cream in it. Nobody knows who he is up this way. He buys a newspaper and reads the headline, KENNEDY TO EMPHASIZE FREEDOM IN TALKS WITH KHRUSHCHEV. He reads an article prefaced by the statement "Printed so readers may know how Southern racial stories are being reported in other areas of the country." "The state of Mississippi glowed with self-adulation," it says, "after proving through its handling of freedom riders that the tactical application of non-violence can cut both ways. Cosmetically sealed into Trailway buses as they went hurtling across the countryside like precious treasures, they were feted later at the jail with ice cream and excruciatingly cordial Southern police."

He gets back on the road and drives past junkyards and barns and deer crossings. Tunnels of pine draw him in like he's on a train. The mountain isn't really a mountain; it's more of a slow and unremarkable incline that leaves you wondering how and when you got there. But once he's on the mountain, he remembers where he's going. It's a plateau of farmland. His heart is in his throat. He's lost her. He can't drive right. It's like his car's got a life of its own, like it wants to veer to the side. He's in foreign territory, and he knows it. He's a city boy.

He hasn't been up here since he delivered her to the preacher after her mother died. The preacher was, he recalls, one of those hilly kind of fellows with the sun-baked skin and strong farming arms. He winds along the dirt road, and he checks the mailboxes. He's got the RR and box number. A few double-wides are set up on slabs of concrete, but otherwise these are nice country farm places. He remembers how the preacher stood in the doorway and gathered Dinah up in his arms. He finds the right mailbox, and he pulls off the side of the road into the yard. He parks near a henhouse. He can smell it. He can hear it. The sky is overcast. The clouds curdle and blow listlessly.

His coal black shoes scrunch down past the weeds into the moist, sandy earth. He has no idea what they grow here, other than chickens. His heart is going.

He can't believe he's here. It's the same feeling he had when he entered the chambers of the Catholic priest after he'd been caught with his secretary.

On the porch is a rusty swing, farm implements, a bag of sawdust. The place smells like peat moss and buttermilk. He feels for his wallet. For a moment, he considers taking his ID card from it. He thinks of sticking it in the preacher's face. "Eugene Connor, city of Birmingham," he'd say. But he doesn't have a chance to think about it further because the door is opening. The preacher is standing there, and the years fall away like they always do when you see somebody from your youth. The preacher is skinny, his eyes bright.

They don't say a word. Connor tries to think of the appropriate salutation, but he can't find the right thing. The preacher opens the door farther. "She kicked me out," Connor says. The preacher smells like turnip greens and candied yams, bed linens and fresh mint. He smells aftershave and leather and he looks long and hard into the preacher's eyes. They're fierce like hers are. "Where did she get her height?" he asks. The preacher's face is blank. He surveys Tyler's arms and the shape of his nose—it's hers.

"I been waiting for you," the preacher says.

Connor takes off his hat. He runs his hand over his bald spot. The preacher's got a headful of sand gray hair. The preacher stands in the doorway and starts talking to Connor. He says he's heard they got problems down in Birmingham. He tells Connor that Jesus is going to come over Red Mountain riding a donkey and that down in the valley there'll be a big party with all the blacks and the whites dancing in the streets. He's a madman, Connor thinks. But Connor's starting to inch his feet in the door, and he knows he has to go in. There's a way out of this for you, the man tells him. Connor lights a cigar. It's an ordinary room. There is a gray sofa, a table, a lantern. The floor is pine. He isn't sure where he'd sit if he did walk in. The man would probably offer him nothing—no coffee, no footstool, no ashtray. Some men are stubborn, the preacher is saying as Connor puts one foot in the doorway. Some men got a thorn in the flesh, he says. Some are born to err, to stumble and blunder and walk right into traps. Some die and start to fall backwards. They panic, and they think they're in quicksand or bad water or hell itself, but don't let anybody fool you, the old man is telling him. We're always being reached for.